THE WHISPER OF LEGENDS

BARBARA FRADKIN

THE WHISPER OF LEGENDS

AN INSPECTOR GREEN MYSTERY

DUNDURN
TORONTO

Editor: Cheryl Hawley
Design: Jennifer Scott
Printer: Webcom

Library and Archives Canada Cataloguing in Publication

Fradkin, Barbara Fraser, 1947-
The whisper of legends / by Barbara Fradkin.

(An Inspector Green mystery)
Also issued in electronic format.
ISBN 978-1-4597-0567-8

I. Title. II. Series: Fradkin, Barbara Fraser, 1947- Inspector Green mystery

1 2 3 4 5 17 16 15 14 13

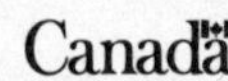

We acknowledge the support of the **Canada Council for the Arts** and the **Ontario Arts Council** for our publishing program. We also acknowledge the financial support of the **Government of Canada** through the **Canada Book Fund** and **Livres Canada Books**, and the **Government of Ontario** through the **Ontario Book Publishing Tax Credit** and the **Ontario Media Development Corporation**.

Printed and bound in Canada.

Visit us at
Dundurn.com | Definingcanada.ca | @dundurnpress | Facebook.com/dundurnpress

Dundurn
3 Church Street, Suite 500
Toronto, Ontario, Canada
M5E 1M2

Gazelle Book Services Limited
White Cross Mills
High Town, Lancaster, England
LA1 4XS

Dundurn
2250 Military Road
Tonawanda, NY
U.S.A. 14150

CHAPTER ONE

Nahanni, July 4

The river was barely a whisper as it licked past Hannah's toes. Its surface shone like burnished bronze in the late evening sun. She drew a deep, grateful breath and looked across to the opposite shore, where black spruce rose up in jagged silhouette against the distant peaks of the Mackenzie Mountains.

So peaceful now!

Hannah pressed her palms against the rock beneath her, not quite believing it wouldn't move. In her mind's eye, the river continued to pitch and roll, and rocks reared up out of the foamy mist in a never-ending rush. Her head throbbed. Every muscle in her body shook with fatigue.

For three solid days they'd been battling the white-water of the upper South Nahanni River. Stunning wilderness and thrilling rapids, Scott had promised her when he'd sold her on the trip. Sixty kilometres of class II to IV rapids. He knew she loved a good adrenaline rush, the more remote and wild the better, but this was beyond wild. This was suicidal.

It had been three long days of scouting and arguing, of trying to read the river and plan a route through the rocks and holes. Scott was getting on her nerves. He seemed distracted and hurried, as if he had somewhere to go and no time to enjoy the trip. Surrounded by incredible glacial peaks and black spruce wilderness, this was a river to be savoured. Each bend should be analyzed to plan the safest paddling course, and each eddy should be a resting spot to admire the pink wildflowers along the shore and to search the mountain ridges for sheep. They were Dall's Sheep, he'd told her, as if the rare, reclusive creatures sat on the right side of God. Not that she believed in God, but up here, cradled by soaring peaks and sky a blue you never saw in the city, even she could hear the faint, haunting whisper of something divine.

So what was Scott's hurry? Ever since the Twin Otter had dropped them and their gear at the Nahanni headwaters, he'd been in a mad rush to get down the river. Instead of enjoying the thrill of each successful run and eddying out at the end to relax and celebrate, he'd herded them through the shallow, boulder-strewn current of the infamous Rock Gardens at breakneck speed. For three days she had sideslipped and backferried and fought each wave that rose up before them. The constant, churning surprises of the river had exhausted and hypnotized her.

At noon on the third day, their canoe had rebelled. Hit a rock in the middle of Hollywood Rapids, flipped over, and dumped Scott and her into the racing foam. She remembered plunging into the frigid darkness, struggling to position herself as she'd been taught, facing downstream on her back with her feet up, watching for trouble.

She'd surfed down the rapids, deafened by the roar of water. A smooth, shiny rock rose up ahead. Too late she'd scooped her arms to the right. Her head glanced off the rock, helmet cracking and body jolting. Pain shot through her. She floundered to regain her position but felt herself swirling, sucked under, lungs bursting, head exploding.

Until the rushing water spat her out into an eddy and she drifted to shore.

Scott had been waiting for her, their rescued canoe in tow. He had barely waited for her to regain her breath, let alone check out her scrapes and bruises. As soon as they'd bailed out the water and secured their spray skirts, he'd urged her back down the river toward the next set of rapids. She could barely paddle. Her head ached and the world heaved.

Finally they'd arrived at the end of the run and paddled ashore to wait for Daniel and Pete. Exhausted and shivering, she'd crawled up on a flat rock in the sun.

Now Scott was glancing uneasily at the sky. Overhead it was a deep, crisp blue, but grey clouds were massing behind the mountain range to the west. "That's the last of the rapids," he said. "Now it's an easy drift down to the Little Nahanni, where there's a great place to set up camp."

"Easy drift," she muttered. "What's wrong with right here?"

"There's still lots of daylight left. And we should take advantage of this good weather." Squatting by the canoe, he fished the GPS out of his sodden life jacket. His dark hair fell in wet curls over his eyes, and when he looked up at her he tossed it back impatiently. There was no hint of concern in his eyes, even though she knew the cut on her forehead was bleeding. Anger flashed through her. What's with the jerk?

He must have caught her glare because he flashed his killer smile. "This thing is on the fritz. Battery or circuitry got wet in that swim. No big deal, I've got all the maps. We'll stay put tomorrow to dry out our stuff and try to repair this. Maybe take a hike."

One minute you're breaking speed records and the next you're planning hikes, she thought but hadn't the strength to argue. He had that faraway look in his eyes that she'd come to know too well. Once they were on the water again, he barely spoke to her. Instead he let her steer while he scanned the mountains ahead through his binoculars. Beneath the canoe, the river hissed as it swept them along in the fast, smooth current.

He removed a topographical map from its plastic casing and spread it out in front of him. This isn't rocket science, she thought. The river's only going in one direction and we'll get there eventually. Her head throbbed and her hands were blistered. What the hell use was a boyfriend if he couldn't show a little heart every now and then?

It was past ten in the evening when they rounded yet another bend and found a creek with wide gravel beaches at its mouth. She glanced at Scott questioningly, but his binoculars were trained on the huge ragged mountains in the distance. The golden light of evening polished them copper and black.

Not waiting for him to object, she steered the canoe toward the widest part of the gravel bar. It was a perfect spot for the tents and she was damned if she was going one foot further than she had to.

Scott lowered his binoculars in surprise when the canoe ground up on the beach, but he didn't protest. Behind them, she heard Pete and Daniel cheer as they too rounded the bend and spotted the beach. Together they pulled the boats far up on the gravel and fanned out to patrol the beach, looking for danger signs. Recent grizzly scat or wolf tracks.

Hannah could barely walk. The ground seemed to tilt as waves of dizziness washed over her. She took off her helmet and probed her head gingerly. Her right temple felt swollen and tight, and the light stabbed her eyes. She doused herself in more bug spray and sat down on a large log, hoping to give her body a rest. Pete and Scott seemed oblivious, but Daniel was watching her through narrowed eyes. He drifted over to join her.

"You feeling nauseous?"

She nodded, wincing at the movement. She forced a small laugh. "All that up and down in the rapids made me seasick."

He stared into her eyes. First-year med students make the worst friends. They're always diagnosing you with fatal illnesses.

"I'll be all right. The helmet took most of the hit."

"Even so, you should rest. We'll set up camp without you." He smiled. He reminded her of a rabbit, small and jumpy, but he had a nice smile. Gentle and even a little wistful. Why had she never noticed that before? She knew why. Because next to wild, dangerous, incredibly sexy Scott, he was as fussy and boring as a little old lady. Right now she was grateful for boring.

"I'll call you when dinner's ready," he said.

Scott had disappeared into the bush, probably scouting a place for the latrine. Daniel and Pete grumbled as they set about putting up the tents and collecting driftwood by themselves. Hannah watched from her log, feeling guilty but afraid she wouldn't be able to stand up without falling on her face. They had the fire blazing and the preparations for dinner well underway before they began to wonder where Scott was. At first it was just a low mutter between the two of them, barely audible above the hiss of the river, but finally Daniel came over to her. Worry pinched his thin face.

"We have to go look for him,"

She felt irrationally irritated. "He's probably just gone to scout out tomorrow's hike. You know Scott, always planning the next adventure."

"He knows better than to go alone."

Hannah tried to think through the throbbing in her head. Their voices were like gunshots to her ears. "Did he take his bear spray? And the banger?"

Pete strolled over. He was Scott's friend from university, and Hannah wasn't sure she liked him. No sense of humour and a shell even pricklier than hers. From the beginning she'd sensed that he wasn't happy to have her on the trip.

"If anyone knows the bush, it's Scott," Pete said. "He'll be back. He's hoping we can climb that mountain tomorrow." He pointed to the nearest mountain thrusting its bare flank out of the forest. It looked impossibly steep and high. Hannah's stomach lurched at the thought, and Daniel shot her a worried look.

A flicker of movement partway up the slope caught her eye, but by the time she got her mini-binoculars out of her day pack, it was gone. She focused her binoculars and drew them slowly over the slope. Nothing. Had she seen something, or were her eyes playing tricks? Mesmerized by hours of dancing water?

She could swear it had been a flash of brown. A grizzly, a moose? Or a human? But before she could voice her thoughts or ask the men to take a second look, Scott burst out of the trees and crossed the gravel bar toward them at a half-run. Gone was his look of irritation and impatience. His eyes danced. He paused to give her a big hug.

"That's going to be an awesome hike! I found a game trail through the woods and once we get on that slope, it's an easy day's climb to the top." He pointed high up toward a barren peak. "We'll be able to see all the way to the Yukon!"

She thought of her throbbing head and wobbly legs, of the mysterious brown shape halfway up the mountainside. "Did you see anything, Scott? Or hear anything?"

He swung around to stare at her. "What are you talking about?"

"While you were scouting. Other hikers?"

He hesitated. Concern flashed across his face but before he could answer, Pete broke in.

"Of course not! No one hikes that mountain. It's not in the guidebooks. But look at it! Scott's right. What a challenge!"

Ottawa, July 5

For the tenth time in ten minutes, Ottawa Police Inspector Michael Green abandoned the dreary operations report and sneaked a peek at his BlackBerry. The time was inching toward noon. What time was that in the Yukon? Nine a.m.? The start of their business day? Of course, he had no idea what time the owner of Nahanni River Adventures actually came to the office, nor even whether he had an office in the normal sense of the word. But Green figured nine a.m. was a respectable time to phone. It would sound like a reasonable request for an update, which it was, rather than a panicked call for reassurance.

Which it also was.

Hannah had told him very firmly that there were no cellphone towers or Internet signals in the Nahanni National Park Reserve. It was thirty thousand square kilometres of mountains, glaciers, canyons, and waterfalls along a wilderness river so spectacular that it had been named a UNESCO World Heritage Site. There was no communication, period. Cut off from the outside world. That's the point, Dad.

The police officer in him was horrified. What if you get hurt or lost, or crash your canoe?

Once a Jewish parent, always a Jewish parent, he'd thought wryly, but he couldn't help himself. He'd grown up on the inner-city streets of Ottawa, more at home with shadowy back alleys and roving gangs than with trees and rock. At first Hannah hadn't even dignified that with an answer, but she finally admitted that the tour guide would have a battery-powered satellite phone strictly for emergencies.

It was almost a week now since she'd begun her odyssey. A week of silence. He toyed briefly with the idea of phoning his ex-wife. Knowing Hannah's hysteria-prone mother, if anyone could manage to track down news on their daughter, it would be Ashley. But that would mean admitting to Ashley that he was worried, after he, anxious to stay on Hannah's good side, had unwisely supported her claim that hurtling down a river in the middle of bear country was a perfect summer vacation.

He'd never hear the end of it.

No, the sensible thing would be to call the tour company and speak to the man in charge of things. Man to man. According to his website, the man had thirty years' experience piloting groups down northern rivers, and he would know exactly how Hannah's group was faring.

Ian Elliott sounded confident and reassuring over the phone, as if he fielded such calls all the time. "What's your daughter's name?"

"Hannah Green. Or possibly Hannah Pollock. She uses both names." Depending on which parent she's more mad at, he thought gloomily.

There was a long pause, and when Elliott spoke again, his voice was less confident. "Nahanni, you said?"

When Green agreed, there was another long pause. He could hear the man muttering to himself. "I've checked all our lists. She's not with us. I didn't think I recognized the name."

"She must be. She's been up there almost a week. Last we heard, she was catching a float plane with your outfit out of Fort Simpson." Even that thought had been scary, but Green had resisted the urge to phone South Nahanni Airways to make sure the plane had landed safely.

"Maybe she went with another tour company. There are a couple of others who guide on the Nahanni." He supplied names and phone numbers. "They are both excellent companies with experienced guides. I'm sure your daughter is fine," he added in a patient tone that suggested he said those words often.

But neither company had any record of Hannah. Pollock or Green. After he made the second call, Green stared at the phone in disbelief. There had to be another explanation. Another company. Maybe a private tour out of Vancouver, where Ashley lived.

He had no choice but to phone her now. She didn't answer until the fifth ring and her voice sounded foggy. It was eight-thirty in the morning in Vancouver. He pictured her hovering slit-eyed over her first cup of coffee, trying to summon a welcome for the new day. Wisely, Fred would have left for work before she was even up. Ashley was still a beautiful woman, but at forty, that beauty took more and more coaxing. Right now she would be a tangle of over-bleached hair and smudged mascara.

"You did what?" she asked.

He explained again about his calls to Whitehorse. This time there was a pause.

"Oh."

"What do you mean, oh?"

"I guess she didn't tell you."

"Tell me what?"

"Don't get mad at me, Mike."

"Tell me *what*?"

"She didn't go with a tour."

Green stiffened. "Who did she go with?"

"Scott and a few other friends."

"A few friends? A few friends just packed up, flew two thousand kilometres into the north, and figured they'd go camping?"

"I thought she told you."

"No, she didn't tell me! She told me she was going with Nahanni River Adventures. How could you just let her go on her own?"

Her voice gathered force. "Since when could I stop her? Since when could you?"

"You could have refused to pay —"

"She's nineteen years old, Mike. She's been doing what she wanted since she was two!"

He took a deep breath. Shouting at Ashley would accomplish nothing; this wasn't her fault. But he hated feeling so powerless. Hannah had been back in Vancouver with her mother for over six months now. She had intended to stay only for the Christmas holidays, but a wild New Year's Eve party had changed all that. That's where she had met a University of British Columbia geology graduate student with a devilish charm and a craving for adventure. For Hannah, that was a magnetic combination in a man. Ashley said that until the attraction had run its course, nothing was going to budge Hannah from Vancouver. Before Green knew it, Hannah had applied to and been accepted into UBC for the fall. It was Green's worst fear.

Until now. He knew very little about Scott. Hannah had emailed a single photo of the two of them. Scott had the kind of rangy, effortless athleticism Green had always envied. Hannah barely reached his chest as she tilted her adoring pixie face up at him. Green had disliked him instantly.

He reined himself in. Petty jealousy had no place here. "What do you know about Scott and his friends? Do they know what they're doing?"

"Scott spent his college summers up in northern B.C. and he's done river trips a few times. He's gone wilderness camping since he was a kid. His friends too."

"That's a far cry from —"

"I think they wanted the challenge, Mike. They didn't want to be part of a group being led by the nose."

"But Hannah is a city girl. Summer camp doesn't count."

"She's in good hands. Scott is a good kid, and she's no pushover herself."

He glanced at the calendar on the desk beside him, where he had blocked off the dates of her trip. He forced himself to be calm. "Okay. She's due back in Fort Simpson on Monday anyway. Let's hope she calls when she gets there. The minute you hear, call me."

"Oh," Ashley said. Another ominous *oh*.

"Now what?"

"She's not due out for more than two weeks."

"She said the tour was ten days. I know she's not on a tour, but that's how long the river trip takes."

"She ..." Ashley's voice faded. "She went up to the headwaters, Mike. They started at the top of the river."

"But that's —" He broke off, his fear rising again. When he'd read up on Hannah's expedition, he'd paid scant attention to the upper parts of the river, concentrating instead on Virginia Falls and the canyons he thought she'd be travelling through. But he had a vague recollection of extreme whitewater that only expert paddlers should attempt.

"She told me ..." He sank back in his chair. "Damn it, she didn't tell me."

Ashley grunted something dismissive, but when she spoke, her voice had mellowed. "They have a satellite phone and if they run into trouble, they'll call for help. That's what I keep telling myself, Mike."

After he hung up, he pulled up the trip descriptions on the tour website and read about the upper river. He'd been born and raised in the inner city, and the wilderness was an alien world full of threat and ambush. He felt a prick of shame that Ashley was being the more sensible one. She seemed to have sensed what was beneath his anger and his outrage. Not only fear for his daughter's safety, but also hurt. That she had lied to him.

As if he, a homicide cop of nearly fifteen years, needed to be shielded from the dangers she had chosen.

CHAPTER TWO

Nahanni, July 5

By eight a.m., when they set off up the mountain, the sun was already high in the sky, sparkling on the river below and burnishing the pinks and greens along the shore. Hannah knew the view was awesome, but despite her sunglasses and her hat pulled down low over her eyes the brightness drilled right into her head. Spots floated in her vision and her head pounded. She stumbled as the rocky trail wound relentlessly uphill around boulders and through prickly spruce. At each jolt her stomach lurched.

It will pass, she kept telling herself. It's just because I didn't eat breakfast. She'd pushed the oatmeal around in her bowl, hoping Daniel wouldn't notice. He'd been giving her the eagle eye and there was no way she was getting left behind at the camp while the rest of them hiked. Even if there weren't the possibility of bears, there was no way she was letting Scott down. He was so excited he'd hardly slept last night, and this morning he'd herded them onto the trail as soon as their dishes were washed and their backpacks stuffed. He'd insisted they pack in most of their gear, in case the climb took more than one day. Anyway, leaving it behind was an invitation to bears.

An invitation she could do without.

She supposed they were following a game trail, although only Scott seemed to know where it was. He raced up ahead and stopped at lookouts to peer at the topographical map and scan the mountains ahead through binoculars. It didn't seem to be the easiest route, but what did she know? Orienteering at summer camp didn't quite compare to this.

Eventually the trees thinned and they emerged onto a steep, rocky slope. A flat rock, slick with lichen, slipped beneath her foot and she fell hard. Pain shot through her hip and she shrieked "Fuck!" so loud that even Scott, way ahead, turned around.

Daniel was at her side before the world stopped spinning. He pulled off her sunglasses and peered into her eyes. When she looked away, he took her hands in his. "Squeeze my hands as hard as you can."

She pulled away. "Daniel, leave it! It was that stupid rock. I just need to catch my breath."

He dug into the side pocket of his bag for a power bar. "I want you to drink and eat. Now."

Her stomach flipped, but she knew Mr. Worrywart was watching. "I'll take some water."

From far above, Scott asked what was wrong. His impatient shout seemed to echo forever across the valley. Or is it just my banged-up brain? she wondered, wincing as the echoes drilled into her.

Daniel pretended he didn't hear Scott as he got her water bottle for her. She brought it clumsily to her lips, spilling some down her shirt. *Fuck, keep it together!*

"Scott!" Daniel shouted. "I'm taking her back. You two can go on, I'll stay with her."

She pushed herself to her feet. "Don't I get a say in this?"

"Hannah, you can't —"

"I can!" She started ahead, trying to walk straight. All those years of trying to act sober when she was wasted should be good for something. Feet, don't mess up again.

Scott came back down, half slithering on the loose rock. He peered at her, and a little concern flickered through his impatience. He pointed up at a dip between two peaks. "We should make that level spot in a couple of hours. It's a good place to rest and have lunch."

Daniel peered up the slope. "There's no way —"

"We're not splitting up," Scott said. "That's a cardinal rule of wilderness trekking."

"Then we should all go back. We can try again tomorrow."

"Tomorrow it may be raining," Scott countered.

Hannah squinted at the sky. It was a deep blue without a single cloud. The first perfect day on their whole trip. But weather, she'd learned, could turn on a dime up here. Far below them, pale slivers of river wove in and out between the trees. Up above, the mountaintop still seemed impossibly far away. But to go back now was a terrible waste of all that effort.

"Trust me, if we pace ourselves, she'll be fine," Scott said. "I've seen much worse."

Hannah watched the two stare each other down. Daniel was the one with the medical training, but Scott had more experience in the wilderness. He'd been tramping over mountains and running rivers since he was a kid. If she had to choose sides, she would throw her lot with Scott even if he wasn't her boyfriend. He might not be the warmest guy in the world right now, but he did love her. If he wasn't worried about her, then there must be nothing to worry about.

She pushed past both men and clambered over a boulder in the path. She could make it to lunch. A bit of food in this butterfly stomach, a little rest, and she'd be fine.

The slope was steeper now. They seemed to be following a creek bed and she had to clamber over boulders on all fours, steadying her balance with her hands. Each footstep caused a mini landslide of loose gravel. Spots clouded her vision and she had to stop frequently to catch her breath. Blood pounded in her ears. Scott had been after her to train for this trip and she'd taken up running with him some mornings, more to get time with him than to get fit. But obviously her idea of fitness was way off. He was far ahead now, out of sight beyond the rocks. The rest were straggling along in a line, finding their footing and making their own speed. Mindful of bears, Pete ran through his entire repertoire of Hawksley Workman songs, but she and Daniel just panted their way up the hill. Daniel lagged behind her and she knew it was on purpose. He kept up an endless babble.

Look at that pretty coloured stone. Wow, all these different colours! Do you think there's gold in these mountains?

"I'm still alive, Daniel. I'm walking, okay?"

"I know you are. But Scott's a moron and if he had half a heart, he'd be here himself."

She stopped so suddenly he bumped into her. He jumped back as if she'd burned him. "Scott's getting us there. That's his job right now. So put a cork in it, Daniel."

He shut up then for at least half an hour, while she dragged herself up over boulders and along rocky ledges. The only sounds were the ragged rhythm of their breathing and Pete's off-key singing. Wildflowers peeked out of the cracks, delicate bursts of purple and white. It should have been pretty, but Hannah could only think of getting to that level spot. One inch at a time.

"I also think," Daniel said, so softly she wondered if he was talking to himself, "that this is really beautiful and I don't understand why he's rushing to the top. He's a geologist. He should be in total awe of this landscape. Look at these layers! I bet there are hidden secrets of the earth in every single one."

Hannah didn't know one rock from another. She'd seen nothing but rocks since they began this expedition, and they all looked alike. Okay, they were different sizes and colours but they were all in her way. Now she took the little jagged black rock Daniel held out to her. It had a ribbon of white crystal running through it, and flecks of silver on the surface.

"There must have been a landslide," he said. "I'm not an expert like Scott, but I do remember my environmental sciences course. This is quartz formed by huge pressure inside the mountain. I bet it's on the surface now because of a landslide. It's not eroded enough to be on the surface very long."

She looked at the other rocks in the creek bed. Some were smooth and rounded, but a swath of jagged rocks ran down the edge. The landslide was only a metre wide, but she shivered as she looked at the boulder up ahead. If it decided to roll, it would crush them both.

"Let's catch up. I'm hungry." It was a lie but she surged ahead with new energy. After awhile the trail levelled out and she paused to steady herself. They had reached the plateau. Thank God, she thought, hiding her exhaustion from Daniel.

All around her mountain peaks rippled like a carelessly tossed cloak toward the misty horizon, and far below, a blue ribbon of river meandered into the canyons. The sky was still clear overhead, but dark clouds had begun massing behind the mountains to the west. She caught sight of Pete just ahead, sitting on a rock in a meadow of wild grasses. He was wolfing down a pita sandwich.

Scott, however, was exploring the rocky meadow, map in hand and eyes on the ground. Every now and then, he nudged some rocks with his toe. He didn't even wave to her as she and Daniel appeared over the rise. Annoyed, she marched up to him.

"What are you up to now?"

He looked up, puzzled, as if returning from some place far away. Then he smiled. "How's the head?"

"Still attached."

His grin widened. He took a deep breath and drew her to him. "Isn't this awesome? Look at those mountain peaks. Billions of years old."

They strolled arm in arm. She nestled against him, revelling in his moment of tenderness. "Daniel says there is lots of interesting geology around here. Landslides, minerals ..."

She felt him tense. "Daniel said that? What does he know about geology?"

She shrugged. "Maybe we'll discover gold, like in the Klondike!"

He stopped dead. At first she thought it was the idea of gold, but he was staring at the ground. In front of him, almost hidden under a rocky overhang, was a strange-looking pile of stones. Old from the looks of it, blackened and covered in lichen, but too tall and symmetrical to be arranged by the forces of nature alone. An animal lair? Scott squatted beside it and reached for the top stone. His hand shook slightly.

"What is it?" She felt a frisson of fear that an animal might leap out.

He didn't answer. He removed the top stone, revealing more underneath. He took them off one by one.

"Scott? What is it?"

"A cairn." His hand hovered over a stone the size of a football.

Her scalp pricked. "A cairn? You mean a grave?"

"I don't know. Explorers used to bury things up here. Sometimes bodies, sometimes mementoes."

"Bodies?" she squeaked. But as soon as the word was out, she knew it was wrong. The pile was too small to hide a body. Even so, she held her breath as he lifted the last rock.

Underneath was a glass jar. Miraculously intact.

Inside she could see a folded square of paper. "Ohmigod!" she whispered. "Someone left a note!"

His hands were shaking so hard now that he had trouble unscrewing the lid. Weather and rust had sealed the threads. He picked up a small rock and smashed it against the jar, cracking it into pieces. Oblivious to the sharp glass, he reached inside to pull the folded paper out. It looked as crisp and white as the day it was placed inside.

She forgot her headache, her dizziness, and her exhaustion. She leaned over his shoulder as he carefully unfolded the paper to reveal a sketch of a landscape. Mountains, valleys, distances, and a little arrow in the corner marked *N*.

Nahanni, July 7

Constable Christian Tymko eased up on the throttle and dropped down two hundred feet. Billows of dark cloud buffeted the little plane but Chris wasn't concerned. The storm had blown over earlier in the morning and now sun was streaming through ragged holes in the clouds.

He was still well above the blunt tops of the Nahanni Range, but the braided strands of the South Nahanni River valley were visible on his left. They shimmered silver and misty green in the fresh sunlight, but looks could be deceiving. He knew the river was swollen and angry as it raged over gravel bars and swept through canyons. He dropped down still further to take a closer look. Last night's storm had rampaged across the mountains, dumping almost ninety millimetres of rain, which ran off the mountains into the creeks and rivers, causing potential flash floods.

The Nahanni was legendary for its sudden storms. There were always campers and canoeists who ignored the advisories and found themselves stranded on gravel bars or fighting dangerous currents. Chris was on a weekend's leave from the RCMP detachment at Fort Simpson, and he was flying up to join some buddies at a fishing camp on O'Grady Lake. But like most bush pilots, he was always on the lookout for trouble. Floating debris, stranded campers, or dangerous water levels.

Today the turbulent river worried him. On any given day during July and August there might be up to a hundred visitors in the park. Although some were only on day trips to Virginia Falls and others were backpacking in the mountains, the vast majority came to the Nahanni for the spectacular wilderness river trip. Chris knew the tour company guides were skilled at reading the river and the skies, and would keep their charges safe. It was the self-guided adventurers and thrill-seekers who worried him, especially the Europeans and Japanese who had no idea of the vastness, isolation, and sheer savagery of the land.

He stayed low over the river and followed its wandering course between the mountain ranges on either side. He wished he'd invited a friend along on the trip to provide another pair of eyes on the ground. The sun was gradually heating up the valley and burning off the mist as he flew northwest above the stunning canyons carved eons ago through the limestone rock. He slowed over the eddies at the end of rapids, scanning the shore for dumped or damaged canoes.

Even from five hundred feet, Hell's Gate looked scary. A red canoe was bucking down the middle of the channel, its solo paddler frantically trying to keep it on course and away from the canyon wall. Chris watched until he reached the end of the stretch and paddled gratefully for shore.

Chris passed one other group, but no signs of distress as he flew past Virginia Falls toward the park warden's cabin at Sunblood Mountain just above. Mists from the swollen falls plumed high into the air, blurring his view of the river. He spotted a massive spruce tree swirling in the Sluice Box Rapids just above the falls, and farther inland a thin column of smoke rose up from the forest floor. On impulse, he radioed the park warden. Reggie Fontaine would have reported any major difficulties to the Fort Simpson RCMP, but what the hell. Chris was here.

"Just coming up on you now, Reggie. There's a small fire about one kilometre inland below you, looks like it's just starting up. Everything all right? Need some backup?"

Reggie's familiar voice came through the airwaves, gravelly from forty years of cigars and bad whisky. "Yeah, we're watching it. Lightning strike in last night's storm, probably. Blew that big old tree right out of her boots. I've got a couple of kids keeping an eye on the wind, just in case it spreads this way, but it looks okay so far."

"Anyone in trouble? Any 'failures to report?'"

"So far no one's phoned in. But I'm guessing a couple of groups will be late, waiting out the high water."

Chris could just see the warden's cabin through the trees as he flew overhead. He raised his hand in a salute that he knew Reggie couldn't see. "Okay, I'm off fishing. I'll keep you posted if I see anything."

"Okay, have a good one." Reggie said cheerfully. The man had been a warden for over twenty years and Chris had never seen him in bad humour. Scared once or twice, when a storm or a rogue animal threatened the park, but never out of sorts.

"Maybe I'll drop off a couple of sunfish for you on my way back Sunday," he said.

Reggie snorted. "Make that two bull trout, you stingy bastard."

Chris signed off with that promise and continued upriver toward Rabbitkettle Lake. On this stretch the river lazed along a slow, meandering course. Mud and debris from the storm cluttered the shore and tree branches drifted in the slow current. They would wash ashore on the next gravel bar and eventually bleach to the greyish white of perfect firewood. Nature recycled.

The midday sun beat down on the white river stones, forcing him to squint. Up past Rabbitkettle Lake he spotted an odd shape drifting downstream. Ragged and red against the muddy grey of the water. He dropped down farther to peer at it as he flew overhead. It looked like a tarp or a tent. Some camper will be unhappy tonight, he thought. He continued on, searching the banks more carefully now. Up ahead was a sharp bend in the river and as he rounded it he saw a bright turquoise canoe washed up in the shallows. It lay deep in the reeds as if tossed up on shore by a mighty force. As indeed it had.

How long had it been there? Its shiny colour suggested it was fairly new, not yet weathered by sun or sandpapered by the silt in the river.

A tent and a canoe, but no people signalling from the riverbank. Not a good sign.

He reached for his radio to let Reggie know.

Reggie was his typical unflappable self, but suggested Chris double back to check the Rabbitkettle campground and warden's cabin there.

"That's where they'll likely go if they're stranded," he said. "But Lord knows how long that canoe's been there. The storm could have taken it from anywheres and thrown it up there."

Chris banked the Cessna low as he circled back. "Still no reports?"

"Well, to lose a canoe on that stretch, they might be coming from up above the park. There's four guided parties coming down from Moose Ponds and one from the Broken Skull River. The next group's expected in Rabbitkettle tomorrow. Could be them."

"Most likely. Any unguided parties?"

"Not on my books, but you can check with your buddies in Fort Simpson. Of course, that don't mean squat."

Reggie didn't need to explain. Visitors entering the park itself were required to get a permit and register with the park office. Those who started at the Nahanni headwaters outside the park boundaries were advised to register their planned itinerary with the Fort Simpson RCMP, but it was not mandatory. The official airways flying visitors in and out of the Nahanni kept careful records and encouraged reporting, but there were always enterprising bush pilots eager to make a buck or two without asking too many questions.

Chris said goodbye as he spotted Rabbitkettle Lake spread out before him, rippling gently in the afternoon breeze. There was no sign of people, but a cow moose and her calf were down at the water's edge, nibbling the tender reeds. As he circled to line up the landing, they looked up and bolted for the trees. A pair of Mallards took flight. A Prairie farm boy from southern Manitoba, he'd been raised on wide open skies and endless fields of golden wheat. When he'd first been posted to the north five years ago, he'd found the trees and mountains claustrophobic, but then his partner invited him to climb Mount Wilson. Changed his life. With a view of mountains peaks and glaciers that stretched for miles, he'd felt if he reached up, he could touch heaven. There wasn't much for a young single guy to do in Fort Simpson, and certainly few enough women to choose from, but he dreaded the day he'd be posted away.

He splashed down and taxied toward the dock and warden's cabin at the end of the lake. The small wooden cabin was unmanned these days but served as a base and emergency way station for park staff and visitors alike. It was stocked with emergency supplies and equipment, including satellite radio and personal locator beacons. Chris patrolled the perimeter but saw no signs of occupation. The door was locked, the windows intact, and the emergency key covered in dust. He peered through the windows. Porcupines were making some headway chewing their way inside, but otherwise the cabin looked untouched. Chris made a mental note to warn Reggie about the prickly invaders.

Chris hiked the path through the woods to the river to check the camping spots on the shore. He was pleased to see not a single residue of human habitation, not even a pop-can tab. People came and went like whispers in the wind, leaving no trace of their stay. He unlatched the information kiosk and took out the logbook, where all visitors were encouraged to record their passing. Besides the park staff, who had checked out the site that spring, the only entry was a group from Moose Ponds, which had come through three days earlier.

The damaged canoe was becoming something of a mystery to him. The RCMP and the park office had no record of any other parties, and none of the guided trips coming down from the headwaters had radioed in to report a party in distress. Yet some group was without at least one of their canoes and quite possibly the gear and food that went with it.

The next float plane landing site was at Island Lake, nearly a hundred kilometres farther upriver to the west. It was extremely unlikely that the canoeists would have dumped that far up. The meandering stretch of water between Island Lake and Rabbitkettle was the most likely place. The river was peaceful but full of islands and twists. Chris was betting on Elbow Rapids, the only substantial bit of whitewater on the stretch. Its sharp bend and series of tiny islands took many an unwary boater by surprise.

Back in the air he flew low over the abandoned outfitter's cabin at the mouth of Broken Skull River, about twenty kilometres downstream from the rapids. He examined the gravel shore carefully. Anyone who dumped at Elbow Rapids might very well regroup here, but there were no beacons, fires, or SOS signals in the sand. No piles of bright-coloured gear. He circled and did another pass, with the same result. A little farther up he spotted a canoeing party paddling lazily down the river, likely one of the guided trips from Moose Ponds. The leader waved cheerfully but made no signal to suggest he was concerned about stranded boaters farther upstream. With increasing puzzlement, Chris flew on, reaching the cabins and hot springs of the Island Lakes at two o'clock.

On his first pass he saw a group lounging in the hot springs by the creek and more sunning on the river's edge. Colourful gear was spread out on the upturned canoes to dry. Must have got a soaking in the storm, Chris figured. The sunbathers shielded their eyes and waved. This crowd has no worries either. Even so, he banked north to land on the largest lake and hiked across to the river. For a moment he felt a schoolboy flush as he recognized one of the tour leaders, Olivia Manning, walking toward him. In shorts and tank top she glided with the fluid elegance of a long-limbed colt. Her skin was a riot of freckles and her hair was bleached almost white from the sun.

She pushed it out of her eyes as she smiled up at him. "Hello, fly boy."

He returned the grin. "Still the river rat, I see. Couldn't resist the bugs and the bears?"

She gave him a teasing nudge. "Or the other local

wildlife. I had a job at the university, but at the last minute Ian Elliott called. How could I say no? I dread the day I finish grad school and have to get a real job. Want a drink? A Kool-Aid special?"

He shook his head. Much as he would have loved to spend time with Olivia, the mystery of the canoe, not to mention his fishing buddies, took priority. "Your group get wet in the storm?"

She laughed. "Did we ever! Blew one tent right over and soaked everything inside. Plus four went swimming in the Sequel yesterday. We're taking today off to hike until the water drops." She touched his arm and led him farther out of earshot. "We've got some inexperienced paddlers this time. A history prof and his wife, and some mining tycoon from Utah. They shouldn't have booked Moose Ponds. We had to repair two canoes yesterday."

"Any get away from you?"

She looked surprised. "No, why?"

"There's a turquoise one on the rocks just above Broken Skull River. Did you see anyone? Here or farther up?"

"Does a grizzly count?" She gave a light laugh. "We haven't seen a soul since we started. Usually we don't, this far up. Yesterday we had to stop early just above the Little Nahanni, because of the storm. We just got here." Her blue eyes narrowed. "Are you worried, Chris? Is there a group missing?"

He liked the way she looked at him, as if she too knew the implications of the damaged canoe. "Well, you know," he said, "there's no one unaccounted for, but it's a long swim down the river without a canoe. I'm just checking things out. Unofficially."

"Okay. If I see anything or hear any news, I'll call it in to Reggie Fontaine."

"Thanks, Olivia." He paused. "Maybe … Well …"

"Well what?"

"Drop by to say hi next time you're in town."

She grinned, that gorgeous, toothy grin that had first tied his tongue in knots the summer before. "I'll even buy you a proper drink," she said

Back in the sky, he made one more pass and dipped his wing at her before shoving the throttle forward and banking hard into a climb. His heart was racing. He knew she would likely not have given him the time of day back in Ontario, surrounded by her university friends, but up here under the magical spell of a Nahanni summer, anything was possible.

He lost his concentration briefly, his thoughts on Olivia instead of the stranded canoeists on the river. Shaking his head, he forced himself back on track and dropped back low over the endless swaths of spruce.

Olivia called him by satellite phone the next evening, just as he and his friends were stoking the campfire to fry some trout.

"I've already notified the park warden, but I thought you'd want to know," she said in her clipped eastern accent. She was a native of Northern Ontario, from bush country almost as remote and wild as the territories, but years of schooling in Southern Ontario had gentrified her speech. "We found your turquoise canoe. I had a good look at it. The storm really battered it around so it's hard to tell what happened. But it was beyond repairing, so maybe they just ditched it. We didn't find anything else, like gear, or …" Her voice trailed off.

Drowned bodies, he thought. "Could you get the serial number?"

"Yup, and I passed it on to Reggie. He checked it against their registration list, but no go."

"No canoe with that serial number?"

"Not only that, but no group listing a turquoise canoe even registered for the park. No reservation at Virginia Falls either."

He pondered this. Both park registration and reservation of a camp site at Virginia Falls were mandatory. "So we have a rogue."

"Looks like it. Who knows, maybe it was some guy paddling solo, or someone who never intended to go into the park at all."

In which case, Chris thought, this is a hell of a big place to get lost in.

CHAPTER THREE

Ottawa, July 10

Green's cellphone vibrated on his belt while he was in the middle of a meeting with the deputy chief and the head of human resources. The meeting concerned the reassignment of Staff Sergeant Brian Sullivan, who was back from sick leave, and Green was determined to have him back in Major Crimes. Human resources was of the view that no one was indispensable, but where Major Crimes was concerned, she was wrong. Green ignored his phone but when it vibrated for the third time in less than five minutes, he peeked at the call display.

ASHLEY CALLING

Hastily he excused himself and rushed out into the hall.

"She's missing!" Ashley wailed.

"What?"

"She's gone! No trace of them! The canoe's wrecked and she's … oh God, Mike!"

Green cut through the wails. "What happened?"

"They found the canoe abandoned —"

"Who?"

"What? I don't know! They found it on the rocks."

"Who called you?"

"I don't know, I said! Some cop. They won't tell me anything! Just questions. Where was she going? Who was she with? What was she up to? Like she'd done something wrong!"

Green wrestled his own fear under control. "Ashley, hang up and look at your call display. Write down the number and phone me back."

"I don't have call display! Not on our home line."

"Jesus." He bit back his frustration. "Hang up, dial star-six-nine, and phone me back."

"Mike, please!"

Belatedly his own cop's mind kicked into gear. "Okay, Ashley, I'll find out. Sit tight and I'll get back to you."

The words were barely out of his mouth before he hung up and opened the meeting room door to make his apologies and his escape. Back in his office, it took him less than five minutes to track down the police detachment with jurisdiction in Nahanni National Park. The park lay in the southwestern corner of the Northwest Territories, which meant the RCMP were in charge. Careful to identify his rank, he asked to speak to the officer who had called about Hannah Pollock.

"Oh, that would be Constable Tymko." The woman on the phone sounded impossibly young. "He's out on a call but ..."

"Then please patch me through."

There was a pause, during which Green wondered whether such basic communication technology was beyond them up in the north. But just then the woman spoke again, in a muffled tone as if she were covering the phone.

"Oh, Chris! There's an Inspector Green from the police in Ottawa on the phone, calling about that canoe."

The man answered in less than two seconds, his voice crisp and well-rehearsed. "Constable Tymko here. How can I help you, sir?"

Green forced himself to be equally professional. "I understand you found an abandoned canoe on the Nahanni. I believe you traced it to my daughter Hannah. What's happened?"

"Yes, Inspector, I phoned her emergency contact —"

"I know, and she phoned me. Tell me what's happened."

"That's what we're trying to determine. We're not sure anything has happened, we just haven't been able to locate them."

Green listened as the man described his sighting of the canoe and the subsequent tracing of the canoe's serial number. "The park office has no record of this serial number —"

"And should they?"

"Park regulations require visitors to provide details of their gear; colours, makes, and any serial numbers; to assist in identification and rescue." Before Green could interrupt, the man plowed methodically on. "The canoe was found just inside the park, so technically they may not have been in breach of park regulations. Technically we don't even know if they're missing. But it's a big wilderness out there, Inspector, and the well-being of everyone in it is our responsibility. I'm not too happy to ignore a wrecked canoe and the fact there's no sign of its owners. I understand your daughter was canoeing the Nahanni from Moose Ponds?"

Reason found a toehold in Green's fear. "Yes, but what makes you think it's my daughter's canoe?"

"I traced the serial number to an outfitter in Whitehorse. It was purchased in June by a Scott Lasalle."

Scott. All hope that it was someone else's canoe vanished.

"Do you know Mr. Lasalle?" Tymko was asking.

Reluctantly Green admitted that he did.

"I checked airways and independent operators until I found the plane he hired. A bush pilot who does private runs. The flight manifest lists four in the party. Is that correct?"

"I don't —" Green stopped himself from admitting how little he really knew. "I believe so."

"The pilot says he dropped them off at Moose Ponds with two canoes. That sound right?"

With sinking heart, Green agreed.

"Four people can't travel in one canoe, if that's all that remains. What was their planned itinerary?"

I haven't a fucking clue, Green wanted to say. Because my daughter lied to me. "I believe they were travelling all the way to the end, to Nahanni Butte."

"They weren't registered to enter the park," Tymko said. "Do you know if they were carrying emergency communications equipment, like a satellite phone or GPS?"

"Yes, they were. At least that's what my ex-wife was told."

Tymko paused for a beat. "Who was leading the group?"

"Scott Lasalle."

"Is he an experienced outdoorsman?"

"I don't know him, but my ex-wife says he is." Green grimaced at how ineffectual he sounded. How had he let this happen?

"What about the others in the party?"

Green had to admit he didn't know them either. "My daughter has some canoeing and camping experience from summer camp in British Columbia, but nothing that would prepare her for this." He forced his fear back. "What are you planning to do?"

"Officially, nothing yet, sir. We have received no distress signals or calls for help, and no one has spotted any signs of injury or —"

"Except their canoe! You yourself said four people can't get down the river in a single canoe. That's what? Over five hundred kilometres?"

"Yes, but it's early days yet. And sometimes there are other canoes cached up there for emergencies. Technically, they're not yet missing and no one has reported them missing."

"I'm reporting them missing!"

"But you don't know that. According to this bush pilot, their take-out from Lindsberg Landing is July 23, and until they miss that —"

"That's nearly two weeks away! Two weeks wandering the bush. Maybe lost, maybe hurt —"

"That's why I said *officially*," Tymko began, but Green barely heard him through the roar of blood in his ears.

"Goddamn it, I'm coming up there!"

"Of course you have to go," Sharon said.

Green was surprised. He had been expecting a thousand objections, and who could blame her? Even now, as the words were out of her mouth, she lay back on the couch and propped her swollen feet on the coffee table, wincing at the pummelling the baby was inflicting. This baby was proving more difficult than Tony. At six months' gestation, it was already shoving its feet under her rib cage, making her nauseous and short of breath. She laid her hand on her belly and caressed it. She'd had all the genetic testing done and knew the baby was a girl. She'd even chosen her name, Aviva, which meant springtime. A new beginning.

Green had accepted the name without hesitation, feeling guilty enough that everyone treated him like an equal partner in this venture. All the suffering and indignity had been hers. At forty-one years old and five-foot-two-inches tall, those were numerous. She'd waved aside the doctor's mutterings about "geriatric" and "high-risk" pregnancy with an impatient snort. For eons, good Catholic women dropped out fifteen to twenty babies between farm chores, so why should a healthy, modern Jewish woman not manage two?

But this pregnancy was wreaking havoc with her body. High blood pressure, weight gain, water retention, and dizziness had laid her flat on her back a few times, and she'd finally heeded the doctor's advice to take a leave of absence from her nursing job. To help her cope, she had even organized day camps and carpools for Tony so that she could nap in the afternoon.

As a husband and father, Green knew he wasn't much help. Between his erratic, demanding job and his general domestic ineptitude, Sharon had often been left carrying the responsibility. And now he was proposing to leave her all by herself in charge of the household and their five-year-old son, who was a full-time job in himself.

She was entitled to be a diva, pampered with breakfast in bed and back rubs after dinner. Instead, he was deserting her.

"If there was any other way ..." he said, feeling even guiltier.

"There is no other way. I'd go with you if I could."

He slipped his arm under her shoulder and massaged her neck. She purred. At their feet as always, their oversized dog sprawled the length of the couch, snoring softly. It was a rare moment of quiet in the house. Green had come home from the station in the middle of the afternoon, before Tony's arrival from day camp.

He chuckled. "What a pair we'd be. Me, who's never been in a canoe in my life, let alone a tent. And you ..."

"The princess from Toronto?"

"Worse than Toronto — Mississauga."

She laughed. She'd been living down her over-protected, suburban Toronto roots since she was sixteen and first felt the stirrings of her global social conscience. And her need to rebel. "But the local RCMP and Parks Canada staff will know what they're doing, Mike. That's their turf."

Hardly a comforting thought. Green was used to being in charge and he hated to feel at a disadvantage. "But they'll have their own procedures and priorities. I know. I'm a cop. I don't want to be twiddling my thumbs in some one-room RCMP shack in the boonies listening to them debate procedure." He pulled his arms free and stood up, too restless to relax. In truth, the prospect of going up into the hinterland, where he didn't understand the land and couldn't read the danger signs, terrified him. Only Hannah's disappearance terrified him more.

Outside a car door thudded and then the front door banged open. Tony spilled into the hallway, stopping short at the sight of his father. A big, gap-toothed grin split his face. He dropped his camp bag on the floor and bounced into the room.

"Daddy, you're home!"

Green swept the little boy up in his arms and tossed him overhead, barely catching him on the way down. Either he was getting too old or his son too big.

"Is it a special treat, Daddy? Can we go to the beach?"

Westboro Beach was one of the many delights of their neighbourhood, a quiet enclave of aging houses, overgrown trees, and narrow streets located mere minutes from the shops of Westboro and the parks of the Ottawa River. At Sharon's insistence, Tony had been taking swimming lessons since he was six months old. Unlike Green, who could barely manage a dog paddle, he had developed a passion for the water.

"Not today, buddy. I have to go away on a trip for a few days."

"In an airplane?"

Planes were another of Tony's passions. Where are my genes? Green sometimes wondered ruefully. But he knew that despite having the curly dark hair, the chocolate brown eyes, and the adventurous spirit of his mother, his character was all Green. Impatient, obsessive, impetuous, and dogged as a mule.

"Yes, in an airplane."

"What kind? A Boeing 737, an Airbus 330, a ..."

I'll be lucky if it has wings, Green thought, but before he could formulate a reply, Sharon interrupted. "Daddy is flying up north to Yellowknife. Remember? Where Hannah went."

Tony looked incredulous. "You're going to go with her in a canoe?"

Green had to laugh. "Probably not. I just have to meet with some people up there."

Sharon interrupted again. She was propped up on pillows now, looking very serious. "Hannah might be lost, honey. Daddy is going to help find her."

Green shot her a silencing look, which she pretended not to see. Tony's expression changed from excitement to alarm as he tried to figure out the news. "Lost? You mean in the woods?"

Sharon nodded.

"With all those bears?"

"Who told you there were bears?" Green asked.

"Hannah did. She said there were six hundred grizzlies in the park she was going to."

So much for sheltering the kid, Green thought. "Well, not all in one place. It's a big park."

Tony's excitement was back. "Will you see a grizzly bear, Daddy?"

"I certainly hope not, but if I do, the police officers I'll be with will know what to do. And you, my little man —" He hugged the boy close, "you be a help to your mother back here. Remember she's got little Aviva in there to look after, and she needs all the rest she can get."

Sharon smiled. "You take care of us, and Daddy will take care of Hannah."

"And the bears," Tony replied.

The doorbell rang. Modo, roused to reluctant guard duty, lumbered into the hall, barking. To Green's astonishment, Brian Sullivan was standing on the doorstep, dressed in jeans, T-shirt, and sandals. Green was so completely thrown off guard that he could only gape.

Before he could find words, Sullivan spoke. "I heard your daughter's giving you a few more grey hairs."

Green grabbed Modo's collar. "Where did you —?"

"I hear everything, remember? I also heard you're planning on heading out after her."

"Well, I can't just sit around waiting." He wrestled the dog back. She was a hundred-pound Lab-Rottweiler mix, and immoveable if she so chose.

Sullivan ruffled her ears. "I figured that. And I figured you might need some company."

Green stared at him. "Seriously?"

"Absolutely. It might take two of us to tackle those Mounties, and anyway, Mike, what do you know about the bush?"

Green laughed to cover the rush of gratitude that welled up. "But your —"

He left the word hanging unspoken between them, but Sullivan brushed it off. "I'm in better shape now than I've been in years. I've been running again, and my boys and I just came back from a week hiking the Appalachian Trail. It's not like they got me doing any important work over in recruitment, Mike, and you know it." He gestured inside. "So come on, let's get you geared up and ready to go!"

Green led the way, speaking over his shoulder. "I've been trying to find a flight that would get me into Fort Simpson tonight, but it's a rinky-dink airport that seems to have only one flight a day."

"Forget that. We can't rush into this thing blind, Mike. We have to plan. Get maps, equipment, survival gear —"

"Meanwhile Hannah could be trapped or hurt."

"And you want to join her, do you? And make it two more people the SAR guys have to rescue?" He stopped at the entrance archway to the living room and grinned at Sharon reclining on the sofa. "I don't suppose this man of yours even owns a pair of hiking boots, does he?"

Sharon laughed, but Green's temper flared. "I'm not a complete idiot, Brian. I've printed off an equipment list from this outfitting guide online. The one Hannah was supposed to be going with."

Sullivan snatched the paper from him and his eyebrows shot up. "We'd better get cracking if we're going to get all this stuff by tomorrow morning."

CHAPTER FOUR

Fort Simpson, July 11

Despite what felt like an interminable day, the sun was still high in the western sky when the small turboprop plane banked over the sprawling river plain and swept in low for a landing. The shadows were stark and the sun glared off the little cluster of roads and buildings below. Green peered out the window with interest.

During their long travel day, most of it seemingly spent waiting in airports for connecting flights, Green had managed to learn quite a lot about the village of Fort Simpson and its local law enforcement. Fort Simpson, population twelve hundred, occupied an island at the confluence of two massive northern rivers, the Liard and the Mackenzie, which at 2,635 miles long was the longest river in North America. The village had once been a bustling fort of the Hudson's Bay Company during the height of the fur trade, but now served mainly as a base camp for adventurers and ecotourists bound for the Nahanni.

In the summer months it did a booming business in hospitality, outfitting, and Native arts and crafts. Float planes, wheeled aircraft, and barges ferried the tourists to and from the surrounding wilderness, and a highway connected the village to civilization farther south across what was euphemistically called an ice bridge. Meaning you drove across the frozen river and if the river was thawed, you took a ferry.

Adventure tourism flourished three months of the year, while during the other nine months the village seemed to return to its traditional life, albeit connected to the larger world by satellite TV and Internet. Fort Simpson was the metropolis for the surrounding area, boasting community centres, a high school, an RCMP detachment, a fully operational airport, and even a golf course. But it was still a simple northern village, Green observed as the plane descended. The so-called airport was a single runway carved into a meadow, and when the plane taxied to a halt he and Sullivan clambered out into the middle of a field. The other passengers on the plane were all tourists bound for the wilderness, and they talked excitedly among themselves about their upcoming adventures. They discussed bug sprays, wilderness toilet facilities, and the latest in paddling gear.

Assorted vans and pickups were waiting at the edge of the runway and quickly loaded their charges and gear aboard. Green was standing in the surprising warmth of the mid-afternoon sun, wondering where one got a taxi, when the co-pilot walked over.

"Where you two staying?"

"Wherever we can find a room."

The co-pilot arched his eyebrow. "This time of year? Without a reservation?" He squinted across at the ring of trees and roads in the distance. "I've got a minute while they refuel and load me up, so I'll make some calls for you. I'll try Andy's place first. Not fancy, but they can usually squeeze a couple of strays in."

Andy, as it turned out, was a tiny bird of a woman with a steel grey braid down her back and skin like parched leather. What she lacked in size, she made up for in strength. She hefted their packs — Green's with the price tag still attached — into the back of her truck for the trek into town. The hand-carved sign outside her little bungalow announced it as Andy's Crossroads. Painted statues of a moose and grizzly graced the lawn, and a few geraniums struggled to grow in window boxes out front.

"You can bunk down here for tonight —" She gestured to the painted plywood floor in the main room. "And in the morning maybe we can find you a proper bed. I've got two checking out."

"You're a saint, Andy," Sullivan said with his easy grin. She grinned back like a dewy-eyed school girl.

"You want some food?" Without waiting for an answer she disappeared through a door in the back.

Green eyed the bare floor dubiously. Sullivan had already tossed his Therm-a-Rest and sleeping bag into the corner, and he laughed. "Get used to it. At least this is flat."

Green was still trying to make sense of his sleeping-bag zippers when Andy reappeared with two steaming bowls of stew. After a day of pretzels and miniature sandwich buns, they smelled heavenly.

Andy looked at his tangled sleeping bag and smiled. "Cops, eh? First time in the north?"

Green nodded and explained about Hannah. "We're hoping to see Constable Tymko today. You know him?"

"Chris is a good man. But he's away in Fort Liard. I'll call him in the morning for you."

"But I want to get started as soon as possible. Is there anyone else?"

She shrugged. "Better to wait for Chris. Everything is closed for the day."

Green glanced at his watch in surprise. It read 10:00, still on Ottawa time, but he realized it was already eight at night. Andy shrugged again. "Daylight tricks the mind. You should eat and get some rest. Morning comes early."

Morning arrived around 4:00 a.m. when the sun, barely having gone to bed, peeked back out from the other side of the Mackenzie River and washed the living room in lemon yellow light. Birdsong filled the air. Green gave up trying to sleep. He'd spent four hours tossing and turning on the ridiculously thin Therm-a-Rest, trying to ignore Sullivan's snoring, the pale grey of the northern night, and the fear worming within him. He'd felt a temporarily relief when they'd landed in Fort Simpson, for the weather was warm, the river placid, and the village civilized. Hardly the deadly wilderness of his imagination. But fear crept back in the solitude of the night.

At five o'clock he gave up the effort, slipped on some clothes, and tiptoed outside. It was far too early for the police station to be open, but maybe they had a man on duty.

Despite the sun, the air was frigid. Dew glistened on the grass and pink mist rose from the water. The sky was a ragged patchwork of clouds rolling in from the west.

The village was still asleep and only dogs roamed the streets, ignoring Green as he walked toward the village office. It was a handsome, modern two-storey building that doubled as a visitor's centre and housed most of the municipal offices, including the police. It was locked up tight, however.

Green turned back, disappointed but not surprised. The detachment had a total of six officers, hardly enough to provide twenty-four-hour coverage. Probably the officers took turns being on call. When he returned to the B&B Andy was awake and the smell of fresh coffee greeted him. She smiled and offered him a cup as he squeezed into her tiny kitchen. He cradled it gratefully to warm his hands.

"You get used to it," she said. He wasn't sure what she was referring to, but she said no more. Just sipped her coffee.

"What's it like on the Nahanni? Colder than this?"

"Sometimes." She sipped again. "Your daughter is healthy?"

He nodded.

"Smart?"

He hesitated. She smiled. "Yes, she's smart. But she doesn't know this kind of wilderness."

"It is wild, but there are many people on the Nahanni River. If she's in trouble, they will help her." She began in her gentle, unhurried way to gather the fixings for breakfast.

"What time does the police detachment open up?"

She dumped flour into a bowl. "Chris will come. When we're finished breakfast."

He quelled his impatience and went out to rouse Sullivan. When this Chris guy did show up, Green intended to be ready for action.

Just as they were draining their second cups of coffee, a dusty Jeep pulled up outside and an RCMP officer climbed out. He tossed his cap on the seat and adjusted his sunglasses against the morning glare.

Andy glanced out the window and a slight frown puckered her placid face. She flicked Green a look. "I guess I was wrong."

The Mountie knocked on the doorframe and, without waiting for an answer, pushed open the door. Like Green, he was about five-foot-ten and one hundred and seventy pounds, but there the similarity ended. This man worked out, obsessively from the look of it. Muscles rippled across his shoulders and chest, and he moved with the bounce of a coiled spring. As if to reinforce the effect, he wore his grizzled grey hair in a marine-style buzz cut and mirrored aviator sunglasses, which he now propped on his head. He nodded a perfunctory greeting at Andy before turning to Green.

"Inspector Green? Sergeant Nihls." He thrust out his hand to grip Green's in a vice. Green managed not to wince. Ah, he thought. Detachment Commander Travis Nihls. Was this a show of respect, or power? He decided to sidestep the potential power struggle.

"Thanks for coming. Travis, right? And I'm Mike." He introduced Sullivan. Nihls's manner changed subtly as the two men sized each other up. Sullivan had at least six inches on him and even in his new, trimmer shape, fifty pounds. Whereas Green could be dismissed as a mere suit, obeyed only because his rank required it, Sullivan commanded respect effortlessly. An alpha male among alpha males, Sharon always said. But Nihls did not look impressed.

"What can I do for you gentlemen?"

"We're not here in any official capacity," Green said. "My daughter has gone missing on a canoe trip and we're here to lend a hand with the search."

"Missing." Sergeant Nihls pulled a chair back and joined them at the table. Andy had been very quiet, and now she pulled back from the table. "I understand your concern, Inspector, but it may be premature. Constable Tymko apprised me of the situation, and it seems to me you daughter does not yet meet the criteria for missing. No distress signals or reports have been received, nor have they missed their take-out."

"But their canoe was found —"

"When canoes get damaged beyond repair, as in this case, the party simply doubles up and carries on. Your daughter's party will turn up." He paused and seemed to realize a greater show of sympathy was required. "I've seen this before, Inspector. Plenty of times."

"What have you done so far?"

"Done? About what?"

"About verifying their status."

"Nothing. As I said, we have no reason to think they're missing."

"I know, but have you interviewed other travellers or searched the area for distress signals?"

"Searched the area?" Nihls's face tightened. "With all due respect, Inspector, we're talking about five hundred kilometres of river, surrounded by hundreds more of mountains and forests."

"Even a simple aerial trip —"

"Do you have any idea of the cost of a simple pass up the river? And where am I going to get a plane? Civilian pilot? Armed forces? Who's going to authorize that expenditure?"

"I understand Constable Tymko has a float plane."

"Constable Tymko has other duties. He has done a preliminary pass on his own initiative and on his own time, but beyond that he has no authority to investigate further."

"Who does have the authority to order a search and authorize the expenditure?"

Nihls's eyes narrowed. "I do, sir. If I deem human life is at risk. Until such time —"

"Sergeant, please give me some credit. I've been a homicide investigator for nearly twenty years and I know all about danger to human life. I know all about chain of command. If you have to authority to say yes, do it!"

Nihls sat perfectly still but the muscles in his neck twitched. Andy leaned across the table, and even Green found himself holding his breath. He knew he'd crossed the line. "Please."

"Sir," Nihls said quietly, "I cannot authorize that. I have limited human and financial resources at my disposal, and with those I have to provide police services to this entire district, including the Nahanni Park. My responsibility is to all the citizens, and the rules of police engagement are there to help me make an informed decision. If I committed my officers to the search, hundreds of kilometres up in the bush, then I would be ill-prepared to handle a real emergency down here, or even elsewhere in the Nahanni."

"But can't you use civilian search-and-rescue personnel?"

"I do, but the same concerns apply."

The man was maddeningly right, and Green took a deep breath. All his career he had butted heads with the likes of Sergeant Nihls. Men who never took a step without checking the procedure manual, who said no if there was no box to check *yes*. By contrast, Green followed instinct that often led him into territory for which there were no procedures. The only thing that saved him from the wrath of the senior brass was the fact he was usually right.

Frustrated by his own impotence, Green considered threatening to go over the man's head to his superiors, but he knew Nihls had already done that. Procedure, and the protection of his own ass, would have dictated that.

Now the man made his exit on that high note, tipping his head to Andy on his way out. She said nothing, but poured them all a fresh cup of coffee.

"That went well," Sullivan said.

"Don't." Green paced restlessly to look out the window, where a sheen of dust from the Jeep still hung in the air. "I need to talk to that Constable Tymko."

"You'll get him in trouble."

Green shot him a defiant look. "Only if Nihls finds out."

"In this tiny town, he'll find out."

Andy stirred. "I have a cousin."

Both men looked at her expectantly. She smiled. "He teaches at the high school, but in the summer he runs a youth camp. He can ask Chris to come over for some advice."

Green nodded. "Thanks."

Andy's cousin Jethro was a clone of her, a tiny stick man with leather skin and the same quiet smile. His black hair was drawn into a neat ponytail that almost reached his waist. He was sitting on the riverbank with a bicycle propped beside him and a collection of willow strips and a half-woven basket at his feet. A tall, lanky man in an RCMP uniform and windbreaker was sitting on a log beside him. He was all limbs and angles, like an adolescent still growing into his body, and if not for the uniform Green would have taken him for one of the campers. But then he unfolded himself to his full six-and-a-half feet and stepped forward. He hesitated between Green and Sullivan before extending his hand toward Sullivan.

"Inspector Green? Chris Tymko."

Sullivan laughed but Green suppressed a flash of annoyance. With his footballer frame and his unflinching gaze, Sullivan looked like a cop, whereas Green blended into the shadows. Smaller, slighter, and deceptively young-looking. It was an old problem, one that Green usually accepted with good humour. Being underestimated, indeed often invisible, had proved useful in the past.

Tymko blushed a deep crimson when he realized his mistake. Choosing his words carefully so as not to put the young man on the spot, Green explained his meeting with Nihls.

"The sergeant is correct, sir, as I informed you on the phone. There have been no developments in the case since we spoke two days ago."

Chris had avoided his eyes, pretending to study the sand at his feet as he spoke. Green sighed and sat down on the log, motioning to Tymko to join him. “Chris, I’m here as a father, not a police officer. I need to know what to do to find my daughter. I don’t care how it’s done, whether it’s official or not. I just want to look for her, and I need your help.”

Chris chewed his lip. He had a friendly face that invited trust. Still too inexperienced to stonewall with conviction, Green thought.

“The Parks Office has been informed, sir, and they’re keeping an eye out. Asking boaters as they come down the river. And the pilots flying upriver know to keep an eye out too. She’ll show up.”

The muddy river swished past Green’s feet, carrying small bits of debris. A family of ducklings played in an eddy along the shore. He gazed out across the wide, flat valley that seemed to stretch to infinity. The place was so damned huge. He felt like an insignificant little speck in the cosmos. Somewhere out there, Hannah was in trouble.

“I can’t just do nothing,” he said. “You have a float plane. Could you —?”

Chris shifted his long limbs awkwardly. A dull flush spread up his neck. “The sergeant would have my ass in a sling, sir.”

Andy’s cousin, who until now had been quiet, looked up. “You could rent a plane. There’s always some for hire to fly people into the park and pick them up. You could hire one to fly you up the river valley.”

Green and Sullivan exchanged looks. At that moment, as if on cue, an engine roared and a moment later a float plane came into view from the direction of the town. It was lumbering through the water, laden down with huge pontoons. Green's heart rose in his throat as it ran out of water and almost clipped some trees in its struggle to get airborne.

He nodded. "A plane like that?"

"Oh, likely smaller than that."

CHAPTER FIVE

"Sooner or later, you know, we're going to have to fly in one of those things," Sullivan said.

Green had been peering through the truck window at the village. It had the prosperous look of a place lavished with government money as befitted the gateway to a world heritage site. It had a new arena, a visitor information centre, a library, and a couple of modern schools. It seemed a very civilized place from which to conduct a search.

Now he shot Sullivan a reproachful look. "Not before I try to light a fire under the park superintendent. I can understand the RCMP dragging its feet. They've got enough on their plate with this whole area and the whole gamut of crimes, emergencies, and crises to respond to. But everything that happens in the park is the responsibility of the park super, and a bungled rescue operation is not the sort of PR he'd want. I bet if he says 'jump,' the RCMP will."

The Parks Canada office turned out to be a simple bungalow on the outskirts of the town, and except for the familiar bilingual Government of Canada sign on the lawn, it might have been the home of some moderately successful entrepreneur. A cluster of SUVs and pickups sat in the gravel parking lot out front, and when Green and Sullivan walked in they found several people browsing the pamphlets in the main room. It was an eclectic mix that included two young, bearded outdoor enthusiasts and an aging hippie couple. A young woman with spiked purple hair and a dozen piercings sat at a computer. She reminded Green of Hannah.

Introducing himself this time simply as Michael Green from Ottawa, he asked to speak to the superintendent.

"I don't know," she said without moving. "Can I tell him what it's about?"

"My daughter is in a party of four who seem to have gone missing up in the park."

"Oh!" She seemed about to say more but stopped herself. Instead she stuck her head inside one of the offices, and he heard a muffled exchange before she reappeared. "Come on in here, guys. Your lucky day, you get two for one today."

About as deferential as Hannah too, Green thought as he and Sullivan made their way to the office. Inside were two men, both middle-aged and casually dressed in plaid shirts and jeans. The white man had a shiny bald dome, stooped shoulders, and a gut that spoke of too many hours chained to a desk. The Native was half his size but powerfully built with sun-creased skin and deep-set brown eyes. Despite the prominent no-smoking signs the smell of cigars hung in the air, and both men were grinning, perhaps enjoying the girl's spunk.

"Pearce Bugden," said the white man, extending his hand. "I'm the super here, and this is Reg Fontaine, chief park warden."

Green picked up a trace of Newfoundland in Bugden's speech. He introduced himself and Sullivan, but before he could even launch his opening strike, Bugden pre-empted him.

"We were just talking about your girl. Reg is up at our main Virginia Falls station, and he's been asking every party that's come through if they've spotted anything. Nothing. Your wife says —"

Green started. When had Sharon called? But an instant later he made the connection. "Ex wife."

"Oh. Well, she says they have communications equipment, But they haven't used it, at least to call for help. We've asked all pilots to keep an eye out — we have flights up there almost every day, at least to the lower river. We're asking new visitors to report any signs. So far, nothing."

"What else can you do?"

"At this point? Nothing."

"But four young people have gone missing!"

"In all honesty, Mike, I don't think they're in trouble. It's just not reasonable that an entire party and all their gear would be swallowed up without a trace. We'd find someone waving from the riverbank, or a backpack caught up in the brush. There haven't even been reports of four people crammed into one canoe either."

"But isn't that significant in itself? Can four people just disappear into thin air?"

"They didn't file an itinerary, so we don't know where they were headed. Maybe they're on a hike. We can't search the whole backcountry. There's thirty thousand square kilometres of park and that doesn't count the section above the park where they started. They could be anywhere."

"So you're going to do nothing."

Bugden's expression hardened. "We're not doing nothing. We have numerous search procedures in place. But until we find further evidence of distress or they miss their take-out rendezvous, more intensive procedures are not warranted."

Green fought back his impatience. He needed the man's help, and bullying him would not gain him that. He softened his tone. "I know my daughter. I know she would try to get word to me if she thought I was worried. She would know that a lost canoe would scare the hell out of me."

Green saw Sullivan glance at him, and he prayed the big man would have the sense to keep quiet. In truth, Hannah thrived on scaring the hell out of her parents. In her younger, angrier days, she thought nothing of disappearing into the street culture for days at a time. In the past year he thought she'd made some headway on growing up, but maybe six months back with Ashley had reversed all that.

"And maybe she will call, Mike. Let's give it a couple more days at least," Bugden said, his temper back in check. He stood up, signalling the end of the interview.

"I'd like to go up there myself," Green said. "At least fly over, to get an idea what we're dealing with. Can you recommend a good pilot I can hire?"

The superintendent pursed his lips in thought. "Sure

thing. Good idea. It'll run you about three grand, but Ben of Wolverine Air —"

Green sucked in his breath at the cost.

"I'm flying back up in a couple of hours," Reg said in a singsong gravel drawl. "I just came down for this meeting."

"Who are you flying with?" Bugden asked.

"Ian Elliott. He wants to check out the storm damage up the river and plan some alternatives for his groups. But he'll be coming back down here first thing in the morning. He might be willing to take you along."

"Ian Elliott?" Green masked his surprise. "The head of Nahanni River Adventures?"

"Yup. He's much more than a suit. He's a legend, been guiding on the Nahanni for over thirty years. He personally vets every trip he sets up. You can't get a more knowledgeable river man than him."

"What kind of plane does he use?" A Learjet hopefully, Green thought.

"He's got a little Cessna 185. Can't get a better bush plane than that up here. Hundreds of kilometres of bush with mountains rising out of nowhere, and you never know what kind of postage-stamp lake you'll have to land on at the end of it."

By now Green had revised his image of Elliott from a jet-setting businessman to a shaggy-haired bushman, so the sheer ordinariness of the man came as a surprise. First his sunny blue eyes and broad smile, then his battered Tilley hat perched atop pure white hair. He had plain, practical clothes and a slight frame that looked neither muscular nor strong. In short, an everyman like Green, easy to underestimate.

He also required no explanation or cajoling to agree to their request. They met down at the dock where Elliott's little plane was docked. As soon as the handshakes were over, he gestured to Green and Sullivan's light windbreakers.

"First, let's get you some warmer gear. We'll stay overnight somewhere up there, and the temperature can really drop. You two have sleeping bags and a tent, right?"

Green manage a nod, still transfixed by the tiny cigar tube he was about to board. This whole day was rapidly spinning out of control.

"Our gear is all at Andy's," Sullivan said.

An hour later Green was clinging to the roof strap as the little plane bounced over the water and accelerated down the river. The noise was deafening. Elliott had equipped them all with earphones and headset, and as the plane miraculously angled up into the sky, he smiled. "How are you doing? First time?"

It was not actually Green's first time. Years ago, as part of a drug raid in rural Quebec, he'd flown in on an RCMP helicopter and vowed never again. He croaked a "Fine."

"You're in for a treat. Usually we don't fly directly over the river, so as not to disturb the wilderness experience for those down below, but today we'll follow it up. You'll see some astonishing topography. Once we reach the juncture with the Nahanni itself, I'm going to fly as low as I can, but sometimes the winds make it hard to get over the mountains. I don't want to crash into a mountaintop." He flashed a teasing grin.

As if in response, the little plane bounced around as it climbed toward the clouds, and Green felt his stomach lurch. Shreds of white mist whipped past his window. Elliott flew over the Liard River as it meandered west in fat, lazy loops through a wide green valley. Gentle rolling hills rose up the sides, forested in rich, dark green. Beautiful, Green thought. Almost tame.

After almost an hour of endless water and trees, Green's optimism began to fade. The winds picked up and the plane swayed and pitched. White clouds grew thicker around them, obscuring the ground. Elliott slowed and dropped down below the clouds just as a small cluster of buildings appeared on the riverbank.

"Nahanni Butte," Elliott said. "Used to be a fur trading post, now it's a Dene village. This is where the South Nahanni comes in. All the canoe trips pass through here."

"I checked with them," Reg said. "But your daughter's party won't be this far down yet. Not for at least another week."

"Even so," Elliott said, "we'll keep an eye out from here on. If you're being swept along by the current ..." His voice trailed off but Green's imagination finished the thought. If the person was not in control, if they were unconscious or dead, their body might continue far downstream.

"But that's a thousand to one shot," Elliott added hastily. "The river is full of twists and shallows. Much more likely they'd run aground. Watch the elbows and the islands especially — one of you river right and the other river left."

Sitting in the front, Reg reached into a forward compartment and extracted two pairs of binoculars, which he handed back to the detectives. Soon the river spread out into an intricate pattern of narrow channels and gravel islands that looked from the air like a loosely woven braid. Irrepressible, as if programmed by years of guiding, Elliott kept up a running patter about the land below. About the legends of dead trappers and prospectors, about the local First Nations bands and the unique topography. Sinkholes, tufa mounds, hot springs, sand blowouts.

After the first mention of Deadman's Valley and Headless Creek, Green could barely listen. He alternated between peering through binoculars and staring out over the whole. The land was huge. The canyons — the deepest river canyons in Canada, Elliott announced proudly — soared up three thousand feet of sheer cliff in spots, and the river raged through them in a churn of white. On either side, flat-topped mountains thrust up through the blanket of trees. Miles and miles of barren, unforgiving rock.

How was he ever going to find her?

"Awesome," he heard Sullivan mutter. Sullivan had given up on the binoculars and was staring ahead in fascination. Up ahead, out of the mist, rose Virginia Falls, twin tongues of foam split around a tall thrust of rock.

"Twice the height of Niagara," Elliott was saying. "Can you believe they were going to build a hydroelectric dam on it? Can you imagine! All this obliterated by power stations and generating plants and huge corridors of hydro towers?"

He flew on, banking over the falls and coming back for another pass. From the air even Green could see the rugged beauty of the falls plunging down between rock cliffs and spewing white foam high into the air. A cluster of hikers stood on top of the cliff, dwarfed by the sheer size of nature.

They flew on to the park warden's station, where they stopped to drop off Reg Fontaine, talk to the summer staff, and check the visitors' log. No word. After another stomach-lurching takeoff, Elliott pointed the Cessna west along the river again and they flew on over the endless ribbon of river. They spotted a bear along the shore but not a trace of humans. Around them, mountains rippled out beneath the leaden sky.

"God, they could be anywhere!" Green said.

"For what it's worth, I don't think they're in real trouble," Elliott said. "Thousands of people have gone down the Nahanni but the list of casualties is very, very small. I know one of their canoes has dumped, but I suspect it's a matter of pride for them to finish the trip. Paddlers are a stubborn lot. If they were in real trouble, they'd be on the riverbank waving for help or trying to get to the next park station to use the radio. They'd leave their gear where it could be easily spotted from the air or the river. They're not doing any of the basic things a wilderness paddler would do to get help." Elliott put on dark glasses as the afternoon sun slipped below the clouds, and he tilted his head to the side, searching the ground.

"They could be injured or trapped!" Green said. "One wrong step or one loose patch of gravel could pitch you off a cliff."

"Again, it's possible, but what are the chances all four of them are so badly incapacitated that no one can go for help?"

"They could be lost! Going in the wrong direction. How do you tell where you are in this endless ..." Green gestured to the expanse, lost for words.

"Anyone with a basic compass or knowledge of the sun would eventually find the Nahanni. There are dozens of creeks slicing through these mountain ranges and they all flow into the Nahanni. All you'd have to do is follow one of them. Or climb up above the treeline to get a view. Most boy scouts could do it."

"Maybe Yukon boy scouts, but these are city kids. If their leader, Scott, were injured, I don't know if any of the others would know what to do."

Elliott shot him a glance. Behind his dark glasses his face was inscrutable, but he'd stopped smiling. "We're a long way from doomsday," he said. "For one thing, if they've lost both their canoes, they'd still be a lot further upriver. We'll go up as far as the Island Lakes and see if we can spot anything. Besides the riverbanks, try searching the nearby creek beds and the alpine slopes. If they're on foot, they will try to stay out in the open. The walking is easier and they'll want to be visible."

They continued to work their way up the river, skimming the razor peaks. Elliott flew as low as he dared. After another hour of staring, Green's eyes blurred. He sank into a trance. Mountains, valleys, tumbling creeks. Rocky meadows and dark forests. He began to doubt his eyes and his mind. Would he even spot them in all this vastness? Even if they were standing on a mountain peak, waving a dozen red flags?

Just when he thought they'd left civilization for good,

they spotted a group of campers on the shore. Nearby the land bubbled and mounded like moon craters.

"Tufa mounds, one of Nahanni's natural wonders," Elliott said. "This is one of my groups. We'll land on the lake and ask them."

Elliott set the little plane down expertly and taxied to the dock. A short hike took them to the riverbank, where a group was gathering driftwood and pitching their tents. A tall, tanned blonde waved as she walked toward them. She gave Elliott an enthusiastic hug.

"This is a surprise. You staying with us?"

Elliott shook his head and introduced her to Green and Sullivan. "Olivia Manning, another of Nahanni's treasures. Mike is looking for his daughter. Her party lost a canoe and we're not sure where they are."

"The turquoise canoe? Right. We saw it up above Broken Skull River a few days ago."

Broken Skull River, Green thought, hiding a shudder. Headless Range, Deadman's Valley, and now Broken Skull River. Good God, what circle of hell had Hannah blundered into?

"Any sign of them along the way?" Elliott asked.

She shook her head. "Not even an SOS marking on the shore. I've been on the lookout. If they're between Island Lakes and here, they're not making any effort to be seen."

As a precaution Elliott searched the area and checked the logbook but Green knew Hannah wasn't there. Olivia was right. If Hannah and her friends were somewhere on the river, they weren't trying to be found.

Almost as if …

Green pushed that thought away, and once they were airborne again he renewed his search with vigour. Elliott wanted to cover the hundred miles to Island Lake before dinner while the light was still good and before the thickening clouds shrouded the surrounding mountains in fog. The river was peaceful here, drifting down the green valley like a twisting silver ribbon. In the distance to the south, the massive peaks of snow-capped mountains loomed up. Creeks carved erratic paths through the valleys between.

Soon the river took a sudden, angry turn, churning whitewater as it poured around a rock face. Terrifying spires of sheer black rock stabbed up into the sky, marring the landscape like a surreal city of skyscrapers in an alien planet.

"Vampire Peaks," Elliott said.

"They look impenetrable."

Elliott grinned. "For some, that's the challenge."

They flew over more creeks and gullies. Finally Elliott banked and descended toward a cluster of small lakes that gleamed black beneath the gunmetal sky. He skimmed the surface of the largest lake, rose, and came back around to land. All three men clambered from the plane onto the pontoon, stiff from hours in the air. Mosquitoes swarmed them instantly. Green swatted at them ineffectually as he massaged his aching neck. Sullivan dug out the bug spray.

Elliott seemed oblivious as he stood on the pebble shore, studying the clouds. They had eclipsed the sun and looked restless. "We may get a storm tonight. You two pitch the tent and I'll get supper."

Green had never pitched a tent in his life, nor had he ever felt the inclination. His mood was black as he followed Sullivan's directions. He was exhausted from hours of fruitless searching and terrified at the sheer size of the wilderness in which Hannah was lost. At the core of his despair and fear, against his will and his better judgement, a small kernel of anger was beginning to form.

Elliott himself put words to it as they shared a can of beer and the steaks he had grilled. "It's odd that we've found no trace of them. No distress signals, no gear abandoned to lighten the load. It's almost as if they didn't come this way." He paused and took a long, thoughtful swig of beer. "They never registered with the park, never left a trip plan with the RCMP. As if they didn't want anyone to know what they were up to. If you're stranded and want to be found, there are a half dozen ways you can signal for help. But if you don't want to be found, well then, in this forty thousand square kilometres of wilderness, all you'd have to do is hide. Could that be it?" He looked at Green in the fading twilight.

"Instead of trying to be found, could they be trying to hide?"

Green slept fitfully, disturbed not so much by the tandem snoring of the other two men nor by the eerie grey of the northern night, but by fragments of dreams lurking at the borders of his consciousness. Images of roiling rapids, plunging waterfalls, sheer cliffs, and endless, desolate mountains. Was Hannah wandering around at the mercy of Scott, an unwitting pawn in some scheme of his? Or had she been party to the devious plot from the start? Lying to her parents about her destination and her purpose? He didn't know which possibility upset him more. That she was a hapless captive or a witting liar.

How well did Green know her anymore? She'd arrived on his doorstep an angry, untrusting teenager consumed with the need to punish him for his years of neglect. She'd lived a reckless life on the edge. Drugs, men, deception — she'd embraced them all in her quest for love, meaning, or just pure oblivion. Father and daughter had won each other over step by timid step, but all too soon she had slipped from his grasp again, back into that toxic swamp of guilt, narcissism, and manipulation that was her mother's life. Scott had become her next great fascination, her next great answer to the meaning of it all.

In her eagerness to please Scott, what had she done to herself?

The faint baying of a wolf travelled on the night wind. The sound stirred the hairs on Green's neck. He shivered and pulled his sleeping bag over his head, as much to block out sound as light. Heard a crunch of gravel outside the tent. He lay rigid, barely breathing as he sifted the night sounds. More crunching, sniffing. A bear? A wolverine? Or an inquisitive racoon in search of leftovers?

The other two snored on, oblivious, but long after the snuffling had faded away Green lay awake, new fears competing with the old ones in his mind. He was helpless in this environment, but investigation was what he did best. As soon as he got back to the civilized, manmade world, he would start looking for answers.

The next afternoon, after another fruitless search without a sighting, Elliott piloted the little Cessna back down to the landing dock at Fort Simpson and dropped them off. No sooner was Green back in Andy's B&B, this time in his own proper guest room with a bed, sheets, and a hot shower, than he was on the phone to Ashley.

"Don't blame me, Mike!" she whined as soon as he explained his concerns. She always contrived to act as if she was the innocent dupe in everything. "I hardly know anything about Scott!"

"I'm not blaming you. I just need answers. What is Scott's background? What's his family like?"

"I never met them. Honestly, Mike, you know Hannah. She lives for herself. Doesn't share a lot."

"But she's been living with you for the past six months."

"With me? Come on, Mike! Since March she's practically lived at his place. But he's a Ph.D. student, Mike. I mean, compared to what she used to bring home …"

Ashley had a point. Where men were concerned, Hannah had the taste of a tomcat and the attention span of a gnat. Six months with any guy, let alone a Ph.D. student, was a minor miracle. "Okay," he said. "But do you know anything about his background?"

"He's an only child, grew up in Vancouver with his father. Oh, wait —" Ashley forgot to whine, "he died last winter. The father, I mean. Cancer. He went quicker than expected, and Scott was pretty shaken up. Hannah asked if I could store a bunch of old furniture and boxes from his dad's place in our basement, just till Scott got his own place."

"So Scott lived with his father?"

"Yeah. He sold the house, rambling old place in Richmond. He got a nice pile of money for it, that's why he splurged on this trip. The Nahanni was a dream of a lifetime, Hannah said."

"What did the father do?"

"I don't know, Mike." The whine was back. Green heard some conversation in the background, presumably with Fred. "A prof at UBC, retired last year, Fred says. History. But he was born in the north."

Green grew alert. "Where in the north?"

Her voice was muffled. "Fred, did Scott say where in the north? ... Whitehorse?"

Green pondered the relevance. Whitehorse was in a different territory much farther west. "Any relatives up there? Brothers and sisters?"

"Scott was an only child."

"What about his mother?"

"Never mentioned her. Estranged, I think, living on the east coast somewhere." More input from Fred. "Fred says she remarried. I don't see what all this has to do with what's happened, Mike."

"I'm covering bases, that's all. Trying to figure out if Scott was up to more than he let on."

"He's a lone wolf, I know that. That's what attracted Hannah. And I think this trip was a kind of tracing his roots thing. I got the impression he and his father were close but his father lived for the past. Well, I guess he would, being a history professor. The house was full of papers. Stacks and stacks of mouldy old notes, student exams, whatever the father had accumulated his whole life. Even stuff from his grandmother. He was supposedly writing his memoirs. Fred tried to help Scott clean some stuff out one day with a truck and it was so bad he came down with an asthma attack. Scott wouldn't let him set foot in the place after that." Ashley paused. "That's what makes me think he's a good guy, Mike. He cares about Hannah. I think outside his studies, she's the only thing he cares about now."

Green had seen plenty of damage caused by men who cared too much, but there was no point arguing with Ashley. The woman had always painted the world in bubblegum pink. He shifted gears.

"You said last week he was a geology student at UBC?"

"Geo-something. To do with rocks, anyway."

"Do you know who he's studying with?"

"No, Mike, why would I know that?"

"I just thought maybe he mentioned it."

"He hardly ever talked about himself. Shy that way. When he talked about himself, it was always about his summers up north. He had summer jobs researching rocks for his professor. I don't see the appeal, myself, but he could get quite excited talking about how a little rock on a mountainside can tell us a whole story of how the mountain was formed."

Something stirred in Green's intuition. Rocks. Mountains. Was that Scott's passion? Was that the real reason for his adventure on the Nahanni? Not a white-water thrill but some sort of field exploration to further his own research?

He signed off, tracked down the number, and put in a call to the University of British Columbia geology department. He glanced at his watch as he listened to the ringing at the other end of the line. It was past five o'clock, and in July, what were the chances of reaching a professor in his office anyway? Green was mentally rehearsing a voicemail message when the phone was snatched up by a woman, breathless and very young.

"They're all gone for the day," she said when he asked to speak to the department secretary. "No one's here but me, and I'm only here because I couldn't get the spectrograph. Well, you don't want to know that. You can call back, maybe tomorrow, but I don't know because a lot of us are on holiday or out in the field or ... and anyway, the real secretary is on mat leave. So that's not much help."

"Well, maybe you can help me. I'm trying to get in touch with Scott Lasalle's supervisor, but I don't know his name."

For once the woman was at a loss for words. "Scott?" she said finally.

"Yes, do you know him?"

"Yes, I do. I mean did. Well, I guess I still do. But he's not here anymore."

"No, I know he's on holidays up north."

"That's not what I mean. I mean he's not in the department anymore."

Green waited, hoping she'd continue. "He quit. Had a big fight with his supervisor and up and left."

"Who was his supervisor?"

"Professor Valencia. Not somebody you usually walk away from, not if you want a future in the field."

"Do you know what the fight was about?"

"Nope. Big mystery. Scott just said it wasn't for him anymore."

"When was this? Recently?"

"Oh no! Months ago. Sometime in February, maybe? We all wondered if it had to do with his father. Dying and all. Some sort of delayed nervous breakdown."

CHAPTER SIX

Whitehorse, September 20, 1943

My Darling Guy,
Parting is such sweet sorrow! Even though I know it's not forever and it's in a good cause, I wish there was an easier way. I know you are worried about me, but I'm in the best of hands. We women of the north stick together out of sheer necessity. Everyone is busy knitting booties and bonnets and bunting bags. Goodness, so many Bs!

You and Gaetan are the talk of the town. I know he will have success in Edmonton. With all this excitement, investors will be lining up, and you will prove all those horrid naysayers wrong. With the papers so full of dreadful war news, what warms the heart more than beautiful jewellery? There will be plenty of buyers, even here in town. Whitehorse is overrun with Americans since they joined the war. They have quite taken over the place. Building new highways, airport, oil pipeline, and refinery. And soldiers everywhere! There are so many new buildings that you will scarcely recognize the place when you return. An eventuality which is all too far away!

As always, I remain,
Your loving wife, Lydia

Prince Edward Island, July 14

A cellphone trilled deep in the jumble of clothes and towels beside them. Detective Bob Gibbs sat up and began rummaging in pockets. Detective Sue Peters rolled over and shielded her eyes from the broiling sun.

"Seriously, Gibbsie! You brought it to the beach?"

"Well, I …" He gave a sheepish grin. "A hard habit to break."

"This is our honeymoon. We're incommunicado, remember? July, Prince Edward Island, red sandy beach?"

He was still rummaging, first in his pants pockets and then in his shoes. The phone continued to ring. "I know, but it might be an emergency. People know not to call us."

"Let voicemail pick up. You can check it when we get back to the cottage."

He plunged his hand into their day bag. It emerged triumphantly clutching his phone, silent now.

"Who was it?" she asked, sitting up and brushing sand from her bare stomach. The pink and yellow bikini had been a wedding present from her sister, a message that she had nothing to be ashamed of. That she was alive and whole and in love, the scars more badges of honour than disfigurements.

It had taken her nearly a week to work up the courage to wear it to a beach, with its clamourous parade of perfect bodies and glistening copper skin. There were no stares, no pitying smiles, no averted eyes. Bob — wonderful, shy, bumbling Bob — had been right.

Now he was sitting beside her on their beach towel, a thick, fluffy number featuring a garish collage of seashells and suns that had been another gift from her sister. He was staring at his phone display. Nothing shy and bumbling about his expression; he had snapped to attention.

"It's the inspector."

"What inspector?"

"Inspector Green."

Sitting here on the beach with the volleyball players and gaily coloured umbrellas, she felt so far removed from the Ottawa Police Major Crimes squad room that at first the name made no sense to her. "What's he doing calling you here?"

"He has all our cell numbers. It must be important, it's his private cell. Probably a question about a case due in court." He started to clamber to his feet. "I should call him back."

"Gibbsie! Listen to his message at least. Maybe it can wait."

He looked down at her with a rueful smile. They both knew he would call right away. When it came to the job, Bob Gibbs could never say no. Particularly to Inspector Michael Green.

"I'll only be a minute." He leaned over to plant a kiss on her lips. She slid her hand up his inner thigh, trying to tempt him, but he merely grinned and slipped away.

He was gone longer than a minute, and when she saw him coming back toward her along the wide beach his stride was purposeful and his expression worried. She struggled to her feet, trying to hide the stiffness of her damaged body.

"What's wrong? What's the emergency?"

"Not an emergency. At least, not like you'd think. He has something he wants us to d-do. Off the record, not a case, and he said we c-could refuse but I-I …" His stutter betrayed his confusion even more than his bobbing Adam's apple.

"Bob! What! What's going on?"

"His daughter has gone missing up north, and he and Staff Sergeant Sullivan have gone up there to look for her."

"Oh, no! How? Where?"

Gibbs told her about the Nahanni canoe trip and the broken canoe.

"But we're in Prince Edward Island," she said, puzzled. "The other end of the country. How can we help?"

Flustered, he explained about Hannah's boyfriend and the possibility he had lied about his plans.

"He may be unbalanced. There's a mother out east here somewhere —"

"Out east is a big place. Where?"

"He doesn't know. He wants us to try to locate her

and find out if she knows anything about what her son is up to."

"Try to locate her. Hmm. Do we have a name, at least?"

"No, but we have her son's name, and we know she used to live in Vancouver —"

"Ah." She smiled wryly. "He wants you to work your Internet magic to find out her name, address, and whole life story."

He sat down beside her and ran his hand across her back. For a moment he didn't say anything. Together they listened to the rush and hiss of the surf.

"He sounds really worried, Sue."

She sighed. It had been on the tip of her tongue to protest. This was their honeymoon. A hard-fought, hard-won reward for the struggle that had brought them to the altar, when two years ago she'd thought she would never walk again.

The inspector had no right to intrude on this. He ran every moment of their lives the rest of the year. His whim was their command. Yet even as the protest formed on her lips, Sue knew they would not turn him down. For all his demands and his impossible hours, he had always been there for them. The first to champion her efforts to return to work, the first to see the unique talents in rookie Bob Gibbs when he'd been too timid to interview his own shadow.

She laid her head on Bob's shoulder and gave a rueful laugh. "Well, we've had one week of sun and sand. Not bad. And our cottage has wireless Internet, so we should be able to get a lot done without even leaving the privacy of our bedroom."

He kissed the top of her curly head. She'd cut her unruly hair short for her wedding and dyed it the same carrot red it had been before the attack.

"You," he murmured.

Fort Simpson, July 14

"You did *what*?"

"I asked Gibbs to track down Scott Lasalle's mother."

Sullivan continued to stare. His fried eggs sat forgotten and his coffee cup was suspended halfway to his lips. Slowly he lowered it. "I don't fucking believe you."

"He's on the east coast. So's the mother."

"He's on his honeymoon!"

"I know. He could have said no."

"But he didn't, did he? Jesus, Mike, we may not know what the hell's going on here, but this is not a full-scale, no-holds-barred police investigation."

Green shoved away his own plate of fried eggs. "And I'm not sitting around here waiting for Nihls and Bugden to decide it is! There's not a lot I can do up here, Brian. I don't know a riffle from a raffle, but I do know how to conduct an investigation. I'm going to find out everything I can about this bastard who's seduced my daughter. I'm going to get inside his mind until I understand his every move. Where he's gone and why."

Finally Sullivan raised his cup to his lips and took a long, deliberate sip. He set the cup down. "All right. I understand. If it was Lizzie —"

"But it's not Lizzie. Your daughter grew up in a nice,

stable home. She's got brains and a father who's been there for her all her life, so she doesn't do crazy things. She doesn't go running after guys who will give her nothing but grief."

Sullivan eyed him searchingly, then thrust back his chair and stood up from the table. Andy, who'd been hovering near the kitchen archway, gave him a stern look. "You guys have to eat. Before the hunt, a warrior has to eat. Old wives' tale."

Sullivan laughed. "I'm not letting those outstanding eggs go to waste, don't worry. But right now, can you get us a couple of notebooks? Old cop's habit."

She grinned and disappeared. Alone in the room, Green sensed Sullivan's eyes upon him. He knew he'd gone too far, opened up the wound too deep, but he'd felt powerless in the face of his fear. He'd had to lance the wound.

Andy was back within a minute. Sensibly, Sullivan said nothing as he returned to the table with two notepads emblazoned with ANDY'S CROSSROADS and featuring her trademark moose and grizzly on the front. He gave one to Green, opened his, and took out a pen. "Okay, what do we need to know?"

"Scott's state of mind. His intentions. Not what he told the bush pilot, but what he really planned to do. Why the hell he went to the Nahanni. Why he insisted on starting at the very top, at Moose Ponds."

"We don't know he insisted. Your ex-wife said they wanted the challenge. It's all remote whitewater up there, the road less travelled. Adventurers like that."

Green had been jotting some notes and he slashed a line through his page impatiently. "But it all boils down to his state of mind. I've got Gibbs and Peters working on what the mother knows, but we need other sources. His graduate supervisor, what he was working on, why he quit, his fellow students, other friends." Green glanced at his watch. He had woken late after a fitful night. The sun was already high in the sky and the village was enjoying the weekend. Andy had made them breakfast at nine o'clock but it was still early to call anyone in Vancouver.

"There are also the two other guys on the trip. We can talk to their families."

"Right." Green shook his head to clear the cobwebs. That line of inquiry should have been obvious to him. "Their names should be on the bush pilot's manifest. That Constable Tymko should have it."

When they arrived at the RCMP detachment, however, they ran into the stonewall of Sergeant Nihls, who informed them that Constable Tymko was responding to a call in Jean Marie River and might be gone all day. Green explained that they simply needed some information from Tymko's file.

"Those files are confidential, as you well know."

"I do know that. And I also know I could call up Eagle Air to request the information, but I'm trying to be of some help here, Sergeant. You said you were thin on the ground up here, and I respect that. Staff Sergeant Sullivan and I are investigators. We can't do wilderness search and rescue, but we can gather background and provide leads that would help you focus your search."

"Trust me," Sullivan injected with an affable grin, "you'd rather have him busy than not."

Green knew it was part of a game, but when Sergeant Nihls returned the smile, he bristled. That simple non-verbal exchange spoke volumes about the folly of the senior brass and the brotherhood of NCOs. Without a word the sergeant turned to his computer, which looked several years more modern than Green's, and accessed the file. He shielded the screen subtly as he clicked through links.

"Constable Tymko doesn't have a lot of detail on this case. He tracked down the canoe, spoke to the pilot, recorded the passengers and the dates of entry and exit. Here we are. Four passengers: Scott Lasalle, Daniel Rothman, Peter Carlyle, and Hannah Pollock." He looked up with a sharp frown. "Pollock?"

"That's her mother's name," Green said, forcing the twinge of hurt away. It had taken Hannah almost two years with him before she added *Green* to her name. "What are the addresses and emergency contacts of Rothman and Carlyle?"

Nihls scrolled through the file, his frown deepening. "There aren't any. There are phone numbers with a Vancouver area code." He read them out and Sullivan jotted them down.

"Okay," Green said, "we'll follow up on Carlyle and Rothman —"

"And I assume you will pass on any information relevant to the case?"

Green was itching to get his hands on the computer, to run a simple CPC search on the two names to find out if they had a police record. But he knew Nihls would be a tight-ass, because there were strict regulations against accessing police databases for personal reasons.

He was searching for a way around the roadblock when Sullivan snapped his notebook shut and stood up.

"Absolutely," Sullivan said.

"And should you acquire any information that changes the status of this case ...?"

"We'll be back on your doorstep in a flash," Green said without a trace of a smile.

Not surprisingly, there were no car rental agencies in Fort Simpson since there were not many places to go, but rather than having them tie up the single taxi, Andy had lent Green and Sullivan her aging truck for the day. As Sullivan backed out of the detachment parking lot, which was little more than a thin dusting of gravel outside the front door, he looked across at Green.

"We need a command post," he said. "Or at least a base of operations where we can make and receive phone calls and use the Internet."

They drove in silence for a block. "Has to be Andy's," Green said finally. "Poor woman's going to wish she never took us in."

Sullivan shook his head. "Not up here. It's like the country everywhere; something happens, everyone pulls together."

Sure enough, Andy set them up at her dining table with a spare phone, a printer and fax machine, and a Northwest Territories business directory. She even volunteered to take messages. She shrugged when Sullivan thanked her. "I have three daughters. They're down south now, but they never leave your heart."

Green's first call was to Rothman's Vancouver number, his second to Carlyle's. Both netted him an answering machine with a young male asking him to leave a message. Of course they weren't home, they were lost in the wilderness!

His third call was to Eagle Air, which seemed to be nothing but a voicemail box somewhere in cyberspace. Frustrated, he left a message for the pilot to call him and slammed the phone down. "Voicemail is going to be the end of us. God knows when they'll pick up those messages." He turned his attention to the Internet. A simple Google search of Daniel Rothman turned up a Facebook page, a few articles in the University of British Columbia's medical students' newsletter, and a comment on someone's wilderness adventure blog about the treatment of hypothermia. Scanning the articles, he concluded Daniel Rothman was a medical student. His hopes lifted. Hardly a sinister portrait; in fact a useful addition to a stranded wilderness party.

Next came a search for contact information. Neither Daniel nor Peter had filled in the emergency contact portion of their Eagle Air ticket — indeed, Eagle Air seemed to be quite casual about such things — but since Daniel Rothman was a medical student, there was no guarantee that his family lived in Vancouver. Or even in Canada.

According to Canada 411, there were eighty-eight Rothmans with listed landlines spread across the country. Far too many to begin cold calls. But of those, eleven lived in British Columbia and almost half of those in Vancouver. If Daniel Rothman was Jewish, as Green suspected, someone would know him. Most Jewish families kept close ties.

Half an hour later, he hung up in discouragement. Of those he'd been able to reach, none had ever heard of Daniel the med student, even when they combed their memories for distant cousins. Over half the calls had gone to voicemail, however, forcing Green to leave a vague, rather cryptic message about trying to locate a friend of his daughter's who might be in trouble.

After the last such message, he stared at the phone grimly. "No one's going to answer that. Even I wouldn't. I'd think it was a crank. Why are people too goddamn busy to answer their phone these days?"

"Too busy, or too suspicious," Sullivan replied. He'd had slightly better luck with the Carlyles, locating one woman in Whistler who said Peter was her brother, although she only saw him twice a year and had no idea what he was up to. Studying mountains, she thought. Pete wasn't big on family ties, but none of them were. Their parents were off on a round-the-world sailing trip and would know even less about Pete than she did.

"Did she seem worried that Pete was missing?" Green asked.

"No, she said he'll show up when he's ready. He's used to doing his own thing and not thinking about anyone else. We're both boarding school brats, she said, and Peter's not the most lovey guy in the world. But she said he's pretty experienced in the wilds. Grew up mountain climbing and kayaking on the B.C. coast."

"Terrific," Green said glumly. "Someone else who thinks he's immortal."

Sullivan tipped his chair back. It was hand-carved and it creaked beneath his footballer's frame. "On the plus side, Hannah's in good company. One has medical training, the other wilderness experience. Good people to have when you're lost."

Green shook off his foreboding with an effort. He knew Sullivan was right. He needed to think like a cop and turn a rational eye to the next step of the investigation. Glancing at his watch, he saw that it was almost noon. Eleven a.m. in Vancouver. He wanted to follow up at the university but first he had to phone Ashley. Steeling himself, he dialed.

For the first two minutes she did nothing but rant. She'd been sitting by the phone all day and she was half dead with worry she hadn't eaten she'd called every single one of Hannah's friends and why the hell hadn't he bothered to call her she was only the mother after all.

When she drew breath, Green plunged in. "Ashley, I need your help. We haven't found her, but we don't really know where to look."

"She's in the park!" Ashley screeched.

"It's a fucking big park."

That shut her up. Two octaves lower, she said, "Oh."

"I need information on the other two friends."

"I don't know much, Mike. Hannah didn't tell me."

"And you didn't ask?"

"They were both friends of Scott. What difference would it make who they are?"

Green gritted his teeth in search of patience. He always thought like an investigator, trying to fill in the gaps and follow the leads to get the whole picture. It was a habit that had not been well received by Hannah over the years. Hannah lived by the motto "The less he knows the better."

A motto Green himself often followed in his relations with his superiors. The irony did not amuse him.

"Maybe Scott or Hannah mentioned something about them," he said. "Daniel Rothman is a med student and Peter Carlyle is also a student of some kind. Any other details, however unrelated?"

"Mike, I don't —"

"Try to remember, Ashley!"

There was silence and he hoped she was searching her memory. But when she spoke, her voice was low and thin. "I'm not a moron, Mike. Don't you think I've tried to remember? I never heard of Daniel Rothman. There was a Pete I met a few months ago, maybe that was him."

"What can you remember?"

"Nothing! I think he was in school with Scott. Fred didn't like him much, thought he only hung around Scott because he had money. Scott and him were grumbling about some professor who had a fancy condo on Granville Island. They'd been invited there for a Christmas party."

"Did you know Scott quit university?"

"What? Who told you that?"

"He had a falling out with his professor. He hasn't been there in months."

She was silent a moment. "I don't think Hannah knew that. She said he was really excited about his research and planned to do some rock collecting on their trip."

He perked up. "Where on their trip?"

"I don't know. The mountains up there. It meant nothing to me."

"What kind of rocks?"

"Little rocks. I don't think he was planning to bring boulders home on the plane."

He could almost see her pout. Patience, he told himself. "What kind of rocks was he studying?"

"Those hard, brown bits of ground? How anyone can find that exciting is beyond me."

Sensing he'd pressed her imperfect memory and her even more imperfect understanding as far as he could, he switched gears. "Ashley, how did he seem in the past few months? Any changes in his mood or behaviour?"

"What are you getting at, Mike?"

"Just exploring. You said his father died last winter and now we know he quit university. I'm just wondering if he seemed depressed."

"He had been, I think. Hannah had a couple of rough months with him, they got into a lot of arguments. He was very close to his father, and clearing out the house was really hard on him. Being stuck with all those memories. He didn't have anybody left, just some cousin he'd never even met, and he was feeling pretty alone. But he took some time away last winter, and that helped. When he came back, he'd kind of found a new purpose. He was really excited about this trip to his father's roots. Planning every detail, spending a lot of money as well — he got a lot of money from his father's house. No, I'd say far from being depressed, by the time they left he was just the opposite."

CHAPTER SEVEN

Prince Edward Island, July 14

"Cops, eh?" Veronica Taylor raised one black, pencilled eyebrow as she looked them up and down. "You don't look like cops."

Sue Peters bristled. To help out the inspector she had ditched the bikini and flip-flops for sensible flats, navy slacks, and a white-and-navy-striped jacket. When she'd bought clothes for her seaside honeymoon she'd gone overboard on the nautical theme, an impulse she now regretted. Gibbsie at least was wearing what he always did: khaki pants and polyester golf shirt with a dinky collar.

He seemed oblivious to the veiled insult. "This is not an official inquiry, Mrs. Taylor," he said. "We're helping out a colleague on a personal matter."

"It's not Taylor anymore." The woman flicked a dismissive hand as if to bat the name away. "I ditched him last year."

"My apologies. That was the information I had."

"I haven't bothered to make it official yet, but I've

gone back to Pratt, my maiden name. Not the prettiest name, but after five husbands the whole business was getting to be a nuisance. I spend winters in Florida, and since they've made all these ridiculous passport requirements, I end up in silly arguments all the time."

Sue had already guessed there was a sun destination involved. According to the records, Veronica whatever-her-name-was-right-now was fifty-six years old, but despite the maroon hair, the trowels of makeup, and the inexpertly applied red lipstick, she had skin the texture of a parched desert. Sue's own grasp of fashion was dubious but even she could see that the clingy, see-through tank top and the denim miniskirt were a bad idea. Links of stuffed sausages came to mind.

Gibbsie had worked some major miracles on the Internet to track her down. She had come a long way from her humble logging-town roots in northern British Columbia, passing through Vancouver long enough to meet and marry Scott's father before hopping across Canada to land, ultimately, on the southeastern shore of Prince Edward Island. She was comfortably ensconced in a chaise longue overlooking her pool. A half-smoked cigarette sat in the ashtray on the chair arm. Narrowing her eyes to take in Bob's reed-thin body, she didn't invite them to sit. Without a word, Sue yanked a patio chair back from the table and plunked herself down. Bob, ever the gentleman, remained standing.

"But I'm sure you're not interested in my travels." Veronica chuckled. "I hope. What's this about?"

"Scott Lasalle."

A look of blank incomprehension passed over her face. She reached for the cigarette and took a long drag. It seemed to take her a full five seconds to remember. "My son? Good grief."

"When was the last time you had contact with him?"

"Last year sometime?" She looked more wary than concerned. "What about him?"

"Are you aware he took a canoe trip up north to the Nahanni?"

Surprise flickered in her eyes. More than surprise. Interest. "The Nahanni? Huh!"

Even Bob picked up the clue. "Is that significant?"

"I don't know. That's where his grandfather lived."

"Are they close?"

She chuckled and drew another puff. "I hope not. He's dead. Way before Scott was born. In fact, his father was just a baby."

"What was he doing up there?"

"I have no idea! We're talking sixty years and four husbands ago! I think he was one of those bushmen chasing gold or something. One winter he just ..." She snapped her fingers. "Vanished."

"Are there any relatives still up there that Scott could be in touch with?"

"Never heard of any. Look, I don't know what he's up to. I haven't known what he was up to since he was six years old."

"You've had no contact with him?"

She thrust her lower lip out in a gesture more combative than rueful. "Some. But like I said, that was four husbands ago. Lot of water under the bridge."

Bob looked flummoxed. Even after eight years on the job, he still clung to a rosy view of motherly love. Wasn't it innate? Universal?

Sue could see he was about to say something stupid, so she leaned forward. "What happened?"

"Life. Men." Veronica blew out a stream of smoke. "Too many adventures, too little time."

Sue waited.

"Look, it's not like I miss him. I hardly know him. He hasn't been a part of my life in nearly a quarter century."

Still Sue held herself in check. The old Sue would have barged in, demanding to know details of the custody agreement and the reason for the estrangement, but she'd learned a thing or two about patience while lying in pieces in a hospital bed and struggling to put one foot in front of the other in rehab. This woman had a story to tell, but only if she chose to.

"So what's the deal?" Veronica said finally. "What's he done up on the Nahanni?"

"Scott is leading a group of friends on a wilderness canoe trip, and they seem to have disappeared."

"What do you mean by disappeared?"

Sue explained about the broken canoe and the lack of sightings. Veronica looked unperturbed. "He'll show up. Once he ran away from home when he was three years old. Wanted to go somewhere he wasn't allowed, and threw one hell of a tantrum. He was gone six hours, the cops were looking all over town, but then he walks through the front door cool as a cucumber. He'd been down where he wasn't allowed. The gravel pit on the far side of town, collecting rocks. Miles away."

Bob was frowning. "You think he's doing this to punish someone?"

"No, no. It's just when he got an idea into his head, he'd go full steam ahead on it. Didn't think about anyone else, but smart enough to get himself out of anything."

"Was he close to his father?"

"Oh yeah. Because his father gave him everything. Said he was a genius and we had to encourage that. William was a two-bit lecturer making peanuts and taking a dog's life to finish his degree. The younger guys were all passing him by. He was never going to go places." She stubbed the cigarette out with sharp, angry jabs. "I blame his mother for that. She was a bitter old hag stuck in the past, never could get over losing her husband. Blamed everyone but the fool himself. The Indians were lying, the RCMP were incompetent. It was all one big cover-up. She taught her son to complain about what could have been instead of grabbing what could be. That's why I had to get out."

Sue saw a thread of a lead. When Bob didn't pick it up, she leaned in. "Was Scott interested in these stories about the Nahanni and his grandfather?"

Veronica reached for the cigarette pack. Twiddled a cigarette longingly, but didn't light it. She shrugged. "Could be. Scott asked me once, when he was a kid, if his grandfather had been murdered. That was my mother-in-law's pet theory. His body was never found so she figured someone had deliberately got rid of it. Wacky stuff. Nobody paid any attention to her, including the cops, I heard."

Sue saw Bob jot something in his notebook. "What did the cops think?" she asked.

"Beats me. I turned a deaf ear when she started up. So did William. Been doing that all his life, I think. He'd never have passed it on to Scott." She finally stuck the cigarette in the corner of her mouth. "William used to say that Scott got all his brains, but my energy and my character. Properly harnessed, he said, Scott could go places we could only dream of." She paused and her painted lips parted in a mischievous smile. "I was a bit of a wild thing, truth be told. Those tantrums? They were mine. And the spirit, the stubbornness. I could see it all in Scott, and I think that's what scared William more than anything. That if I stuck around, all that would rub off on him. The extremes, the passion, the blackness. The hunger for more." She shrugged. "He was probably right. I had no patience for runny noses and soccer games and all those fucking questions, 'Why?' The kid was better off without me, even if it pissed me right off to hear the judge agree with him."

Bob was looking thoughtful and Sue could see he was working up to something. She gave him an encouraging look.

"This is an awkward question," he said. "We're trying to gather as much information as we can about Scott's motives and his state of mind. You mentioned his tantrums and extremes. Do you think there could be any instability — I mean, is there any history of mental illness on either his grandmother's or father's side, or...?"

She flushed. "Mental illness. Mental illness. Fuck, that's a condescending term. Like it's something to whisper behind curtains. Wacko. Nuts. Those are nice, clear words. William is as sane and boring as anyone I've ever known. If Scott is wacko, he got it from Lydia or me. But look at me." She spread her arms to encompass her luxury bungalow, her pool, and the Northumberland Strait lapping the shore just beyond. "I've done all right for myself. Just don't bore me. Or cross me."

"Not sure all that's very helpful to the inspector," Bob said as they tucked into a huge bucket of mussels. Fresh homemade bread sat at their elbow, ready to soak up the tomato garlic sauce, and two glasses of crisp Pinot Gris glowed in the setting sun. Beyond the patio, the ocean licked over the rocks and seaweed of low tide, and gulls wheeled overhead. The rich smells of salt, seaweed, and garlic mingled in the air.

Sue savoured a mussel. "The grandfather's death is a lead he can follow up on up there," she said.

"The man is worried sick about his daughter. There's got to be more we can do down here."

She reached for his hand, turned it over, and stroked his palm. "Can we talk about this later? First things first. Food, wine, and then … maybe …"

He laughed then, and his fingers tightened around hers. She managed to keep his attention focused on her, and on the spectacular food, until their dessert arrived. Homemade cinnamon apple pie with ice cream oozing down its sides, a dessert straight out of her own small-town Ontario childhood. But after three bites, he thrust it away and pulled out his cellphone.

"After I make this report, the evening will be all yours."

Sue's twinge of irritation vanished when she heard Inspector Green's hello on the line. If Bob had had to leave a message, God knows when he'd call back and what he'd be interrupting.

Bob flipped open his makeshift notebook, all business. "Any news, sir? Oh … w-well, it's early.… No, we didn't have much luck at this end either. I mean, yes, we found the mother but she doesn't know much. She hasn't lived with her son since he was six.… No, she didn't seem worried." Bob passed on the mother's story about Scott's stubborn streak and her apparent total lack of interest in her son. "She didn't ask a single question about him, and I got the impression she wouldn't lose a wink of sleep over his disappearance."

"Don't forget the grandfather," Sue whispered.

"What? N-no, sir, that was Sue, reminding me. The one thing the mother showed any interest in was the fact Scott was going to the Nahanni. His grandfather disappeared up there, but that was years ago. Scott never knew him." Bob extended his fork and carved off a mouthful of pie. "No, sir, no relatives, but I did find out some background on Scott's parents. I don't know if it's relevant, but do you want…? Y-yes, sir." He flipped back a few pages in his notebook.

"The father was born in Whitehorse in 1944, but moved to Vancouver early on and went to school there. I guess that was after the grandfather died. He met Scott's mother, Veronica, there, but she's from Prince George.… I don't know, sir. She's ten years younger than him. They got married in Vancouver, June 3rd, 1979, and Scott was born October 24th, 1980. William Lasalle

— that's Scott's father — got his B.A. from Simon Fraser University in 1970, his M.A. in 1979, and Ph.D. in 1988, both from the University of British Columbia."

Listening to Bob's succinct summary, Sue did the math in her head. William Lasalle had been a late bloomer, both in marriage and in educational achievement, and there was a peculiar, nine year gap between his B.A. and M.A. that seemed long even for the poorest or most lackadaisical student. The pregnancy had come hard on the heels of the marriage but not within nine months. Veronica had been ten years younger than him, and her speech and current lifestyle suggested a woman far less interested in education and ideas that he was.

Sue could understand Veronica's interest in him. For one thing, where men were concerned, she seemed pretty indiscriminate. If it walked upright, it was a candidate. For another, Veronica was from a rough logging town in the middle of nowhere. Her choice had probably been between mill workers and fishermen. An older man with not just one university degree but two must have seemed like the perfect catch.

On the other hand, what had William seen in her? Her zest and passion? Her sex appeal? Sue tried to imagine Veronica before the assault of advancing years. Without the leathery skin, the over-bleached hair, and garish makeup. Without the ripples of fat where once there had been curves.

The marriage had lasted a mere eight years. A mismatch that had probably been a disappointment for both of them. Sue dismissed the small niggle of doubt that crept into her own thoughts as she looked at her own brand new husband, so stiff, formal, and unsure of himself on the phone. When he was with her, he never stammered, yet he could barely manage a single report to the inspector without tripping over his words. Gibbsie and she were as different as earth and wind, and yet they shared the same passions: solving crimes, catching bad guys, helping victims to find justice. Drummed into them by that man on the other end of the phone.

She thought about how they had both reacted to the inspector's request. With only the barest flicker of hesitation, they had interrupted their holiday to lend him a hand.

Even now, as she listened to Gibbsie's fumbling answers over the phone, she knew it was not over. There were more questions to answer, more background to unearth, if they were to get to the core of Scott Lasalle. Veronica had revealed a lot about the influences that had shaped his early years, but her insights stopped at age six. Sue could almost hear the inspector's voice inside her head. Find out more about the grandfather. The grandmother. Other relatives.

If anyone knew what Scott was up to and why, she and Bob would be trying to find them. That was the message behind Green's questions. She smiled ruefully as she watched the coral ocean slowly fade to grey on this working honeymoon day. There was more work to be done.

Fort Simpson, July 14

When Chris Tymko finally arrived back at Fort Simpson it was 8:00 p.m. The sky was still bright but his shift was long over and an ice-cold beer on his deck was calling to him. He planned to stop off at the detachment office only long enough to file a brief report on the Jean Marie River call — a toddler gone missing but fortunately found unharmed and fast asleep in a neighbour's shed.

However, he was surprised to see a familiar Jeep parked next to a cruiser in the gravel parking lot, and when he pulled up next to it, the driver's door opened. Out stepped Hunter Kerry, the Eagle Air pilot he'd spoken to about the Lasalle/Pollock case. He knew Hunt casually through local fishing derbies and charity air shows, but the man remained an enigma to him. Ex-military, Hunt was generous with his time for a good cause but he kept to himself. He was rumoured to cultivate his personal supply of marijuana in his bungalow outside of town, but no one had ever been invited inside. He seemed happiest when he was in the air, but he hunkered down in the cockpit of his Otter as if he was still in enemy territory. Chris suspected he clung to his own rule of law and survival. Don't trust anyone.

Hunt opened the cruiser door and slipped in beside him. In his hand he held a small black canvas satchel.

"They told me inside you were due in around eight, so I figured I'd catch you before."

With Hunt, it was wise to know all the subtext. In the evening light, he studied the man. Pupils normal, speech clear. No smell of booze or pot. He grinned. "Avoiding the sarge, are you?"

Hunt flushed. "I didn't want this too official if it didn't have to be."

"What?"

"I got a voicemail this morning on the company line from some Ottawa cop, name of Inspector Green?"

Chris nodded, volunteering nothing.

"He wanted info on that missing party of canoeists I flew into Moose Ponds."

Still Chris volunteered nothing.

"I figured I'd rather talk to you about it than some brass from national headquarters. I mean, it's your case. So I figured you should be in on it. What's Ottawa's interest anyway?"

"That cop is not on the job. He's a city cop, not RCMP. Hannah Pollock is his daughter."

"Oh." Hunt fingered the black satchel, pulling the zipper open and closed. "Well, anyways, I already told you everything I know."

Chris knew Hunt had not lain in wait for him that evening just to relay that message. He thought he saw a flash of relief on Hunt's face when he'd heard there was no national-level investigation. He nodded at the bag. "What's this? You mug an old lady?"

The man glanced at the bag in his lap. "There's not much in it. It's a waterproof pouch, the kind boaters carry everyday stuff they need to keep dry. Medical first aid, spare batteries, repair kit ..."

"Typical old lady stuff. Does it belong to one of the canoeists?"

"Oh, I didn't take it! No, no! Don't get that idea. I found it under the seat, when I cleaned out the plane back at my dock."

"Under the seat? Imagine." He sensed Hunt had one foot out the door. Hunt was a skilled and focused pilot who knew the southwestern territories like his own backyard, but the rest of his mind had been pretty much fried on a so-called peacekeeping tour with the Canadian Airborne Regiment in Somalia twenty years earlier. Conversation was like pulling teeth. Even Chris's best teasing was not softening him up. Chris reached out to take the bag, but Hunt tightened his grip.

"What's in the bag, Hunt? Any essentials they're going to miss?"

"Nothing much. Well, maybe the phone battery."

Chris snapped to attention. "So they have no phone?"

"Well, most people bring a backup battery. In case one gets wet, like."

"Most people but not all. Weight and space are always at a premium. What else is in the bag?"

"Just some first aid and canoe repair stuff, matches, documents ..."

"What kind of documents?"

"Not maps. Just some legal looking papers about some dead guy. They looked pretty old and I couldn't make heads or tails of them."

"Heads and tails are my specialty." Chris tugged on the bag and this time Hunt relinquished it. Chris opened it and spread the contents on his lap. It was as Hunt had described; a basic wilderness first-aid kit, but luckily not the main one the group would have brought along. If they had half a head on their shoulders, that one would contain thermal blankets, antibiotics, splints, and many kinds of bandages. This was a small one for treating small cuts and blisters on the fly during the day's travel.

The phone battery was a late model Iridium, suggesting that it had been purchased just before the trip, and the knife was a standard sheathed blade, sharp enough to cut straps free in a river emergency but not much defence against a wolf or bear.

Crumpled in the bottom of the fanny pack was an invoice from a wilderness outfitting company in Whitehorse, the same one Scott had bought the turquoise canoe from in June. This invoice was from the same transaction. It listed the purchase of waterproof barrels, dry bags, sleeping bags, tents, and a dozen other pieces of equipment that travellers usually rented for a fraction of the cost. The total was $3,781, paid in cash by Scott Lasalle.

Out of habit, Chris jotted down the list. If he decided to follow up on Lasalle's intentions the outfitter might be a good place to start.

Tucked into a side pocket of the bag, encased in two plastic sheaths, was the legal document Hunt had mentioned. The paper was clean and white, as if it were new. But it looked like a photocopy of a much older document. The lettering was faded and fuzzy, like a copy made with carbon paper rather than a photocopier. It bore the crest of a Whitehorse law firm, and from what Chris could determine it was the last will and testament of one Guy H. Lasalle, dated August 10, 1944.

Chris glanced through it. It was a very short will, leaving all his worldly goods to his wife, Lydia, including an insurance policy, a prospecting kit, some mining shares, and the rights to any claims still active at the time of his death. Written by hand in the margin was a number, a date, and a scribbled note.

60 to Dawson, 20 miles to Nahanni, 128 days 30 miles to Watson

It seemed like directions of some kind. Chris scrutinized the page in the light. The added writing was photocopied but not fuzzy like the original carbon copy, suggesting that someone had written the numbers into the margin of the carbon copy itself, and then photocopied the whole. Scott perhaps? Did it mean anything to the current investigation? Why else would Scott have it with him, carefully encased in double waterproof sheaths?

Hunt was shifting in his seat, anxious to bolt. Maybe being confined to a police cruiser brought back bad memories.

"So do you need all that stuff?" Hunt's fingers inched toward the paper. "I mean, if you don't ..."

"What do you want with this, Hunt? It belongs to the kids and should be returned to them."

"Oh, yeah! Oh, sure. No problem. I just thought, it doesn't look very important."

Like hell, Chris thought, tightening his grip on the will. "Did you show this document to anyone else besides me? To help you understand it, maybe?" He used the term loosely. Understand its worth, is what he meant.

"Well. I …" Hunt hung his head and wagged it back and forth. "I did show it to Olivia. You know, that river guide?"

"Olivia Manning?" Chris frowned. Olivia was still on the river. To have talked to her, Hunt would have had to fly into Virginia Falls and intercept her. Hardly a chance or spur of the moment meeting. "Why would you show it to her?"

"Well, she's in university. Graduate school. Engineering, I think, right? I figured she'd know what it all meant."

"And did she?"

He shook his head. "Just said it was an old will. Probably not worth a thing anymore. Nobody can even get up in some of them mountains, unless you're a mountain goat."

Chris grew alert. "That's what she said this was? These directions pointed to some land in the mountains?"

Too late, Hunt seemed to see his mistake. He scrunched up his face, trying to look confused. "I-I don't remember. She just tossed the idea off, that it might refer to land. Wilderness, mountains, barrens … I can't remember."

CHAPTER EIGHT

Edmonton, November 3, 1943

Salut mon frère,
I hope you are not disappointed. I am not going to spend Christmas in Whitehorse with you and Lydia. The Edmonton backers seem interested, but they are waiting for more results. We need to save money until we are more sure of them. I think we should trap again this winter. I have made friends with a nice Indian family in Nahanni Butte and will spend Christmas with them. The Indians are starting to trust me and I hope this will stop the disputes over the traplines. There is a lot of beaver and marten in the upper Nahanni for everybody.

With Lydia's condition and your small house, you do not need me in the way. But I wish you a most joyous Noël.

Your devoted brother, Gaetan

The next morning Chris radioed the park warden's station at Virginia Falls. When Reggie's soft drawl came over the airways, he wondered what excuse he could possibly give for his inquiry. He pretended to be calling for an update about the missing canoeists.

"You know I'll tell you the minute I get any word on them," the warden said.

"Did Hunter Kerry fly in there yesterday to drop off some people?"

"Yeah, he brought a party of Japanese hikers in to do Sunblood Mountain. Dropped them off and hung around all day for them. Getting in my hair, the crazy warrior."

"They must have some big money to tie him up like that."

Reggie chuckled. "I don't think he minded. He could have done an extra run, but I think it was all an excuse to check out a certain woman."

"You mean Olivia Manning of Nahanni River Adventures?"

"You noticed. Yup. They went off for a nice little pow-wow while her group was setting up camp. Not that the crazy old warrior is going to get to first base with that one."

"Hunt's not one to let reality stand in his way. Do you know what they talked about?"

"No idea. But I can ask her. She'll be dropping in here later to say hi. Her group is hiking the mountain today and they'll be dead asleep by nine tonight."

Chris had a vision of Olivia striding up the ridge across open alpine meadows, her long tanned legs fluid and her blond ponytail flying in the wind. He felt a jolt of arousal. Nine o'clock that night. Theoretically he was off shift at four, although on call throughout the evening. He could fly up there in plenty of time, provided no fools got too drunk or argumentative here in town tonight.

"Thanks, Reg. Tell her to stay put and I'll fly up. I'll need to borrow her for a half hour or so. Official business."

Reggie chuckled again. "Official. Sure thing, Chris. You guys get all the perks."

It was not at all official, in truth, and Chris knew he was going against both the rules and his sergeant's express orders, but in the north more than anywhere else, officers had to follow their own instincts. There was often no backup, just a lone constable responding to a situation and making the best judgment call he could.

Chris persuaded himself that since he was doing this on his own time, the sergeant's rules and orders did not apply. He packed an overnight bag and a couple of bottles of Mission Hill Sauvignon Blanc from British Columbia. He knew almost nothing about wine, but it was expensive. It had better be good. Less than thirty minutes after he signed off duty, he was airborne, sweeping west over the river and up toward Virginia Falls. The sky was cloudless and the evening sun burnished the canyon cliffs in stunning red. The stress of his job slipped away, and by the time he circled around and touched down on the upper river he felt as light and free as an eagle.

When he spotted Olivia walking toward the dock his joy reached even greater heights. With the westerly wind whipping her hair and no trace of makeup, she was gorgeous. And she was smiling at him.

He waved the wine bottles aloft as he leaped nimbly from the pontoon to the dock. Her smile widened.

"Well, well, flyboy. Is this work or play?"

He returned her grin. "Some work, all play."

"Just like my job." She gestured to a driftwood log on the beach a little upstream, out of sight of the warden's cabin. "Reg said you wanted to know what Hunter Kerry talked to me about."

He nodded. "Hunt's the one who flew those canoeists in, but he's a crafty bugger. Doesn't like cops."

"Law enforcement in general. RCMP bureaucrats specifically. My guess is he doesn't want anyone turning a magnifying glass on his own activities, in the air or on the ground." She sat down on the log, kicked off her sturdy sandals, and wriggled her bare feet in the sand. Her toenails were painted bright pink.

Chris resisted the urge to ask why. In the main, Hunt was a good pilot, experienced in a crisis and the first to jump in and lend a hand in search-and-rescue missions. If he grew a couple of plants in his attic or occasionally bent the rules in his business records, that was not Chris's concern. Let the bureaucrats and bean-counters do their own investigating.

He began as open-ended as he could. Let her lead. "So what did he want?"

"First things first." She waggled her fingers toward the wine that he had propped against the log. "We wouldn't want that to get warm."

Although the evening sun still washed the mountains across the way, deep purple shadows stretched along the river and a chill had settled in. A brisk breeze kept the blackflies and mosquitoes at bay. Not much chance of the wine getting warm, but he wasn't going to argue. He unscrewed it and filled two clear plastic glasses almost to the brim. Closing her eyes to concentrate on the flavour, she took an appreciative sip.

"Ah-h. So much better than the plonk we bring on the trip."

As they traded banter about bad wine, he almost forgot his pretext for seeing her. Almost lost himself in the warm closeness of her body and the soft gaiety of her voice. He forced himself to steer the conversation back to business.

"What Hunt asked me about didn't really have anything to do with the missing canoeists," she replied. "I mean, it doesn't shed any light on what's happened to them."

He chuckled. "Light never was his strong suit. But what was it?"

Instead of answering, she ducked the question. "Has he spoken to you?"

"Yes." He frowned, debating. "He brought me the fanny pack they left in the plane."

"Oh, good. I told him to, but I wasn't sure he would."

"Why did he bring it to you?"

"I … I …" She looked nonplussed. "Is this an interrogation, Chris?"

"No! No."

"Because I don't like it. I feel like you're fishing when you already know the answer. Trying to trip me up."

He reached for the bottle and topped up both their glasses. Ostensibly as a peace offering but also to buy himself time to regroup. "I'm sorry. Thumbscrews put away, I promise." When she didn't even smile, he blundered on. "It's an occupational hazard, Olivia. Don't give away information, just ask for it. Verify and verify."

She studied her wine through narrowed eyes. "So do you know the answer?"

"I know what he told me. That he wanted your interpretation of a document."

"Did you see the document?"

More questions. He felt the interview slipping through his fingers. He nodded.

"And what did you make of it?"

"The will? The notes looked like a date and some directions. Maybe to a piece of land."

"Agreed. It was hard to read, but that's what I thought. That's what I told him."

"But why did he want to know? What difference would it make to him what it was? It belonged to Scott Lasalle. Not even to him, to some distant ancestor."

She didn't answer for a moment. Instead she watched a hawk sweep across the mountainside opposite and hover almost motionless before plunging out of sight. She shivered and pulled her jacket more tightly over her shoulders. He longed to put his arm around her but he didn't dare. "I think he just wanted to satisfy his curiosity," she said. "He didn't like not knowing."

"It wasn't because he figured it might be relevant to what they were doing up here, and there might be some angle he could work?"

"What the hell does that mean?"

"Oh, come on, why else would he ask about it, if he didn't think there might be something in it for him?"

"You're a suspicious bastard, aren't you?"

He felt a flush crawl up his neck. "Another occupational hazard. It keeps us alive sometimes. Olivia, what did you tell him?"

"I'm not sure I feel like telling you."

"Olivia, four young people are missing. I need to know if Hunt is withholding relevant information."

"I told him exactly what you just said. That it could be a piece of land, maybe an old land grant, but that it was probably way too old to have any meaning today. The will is a copy and it's not even a notarized one, so it has very little legal value. The directions seemed like gibberish — Dawson, Nahanni, and Watson Lake are hardly near each other. Unless you triangulate or something. And chances are good it's park or Dene land now anyway."

He sipped his wine, feeling the tension between them. He tried to salvage the evening. "I don't want Hunt going off half-cocked, that's all. As much to keep him out of trouble as to not make things worse for the missing party."

She said nothing.

"Truce?"

She nodded. Very slowly. "Hunt is a nice enough guy, but flying is all he knows. He can hang out in his own flying cocoon, he can land and take off just about anywhere, he can read clouds and wind like a Native. But he has trouble with all the forms and regulations and red tape. He wouldn't survive a week down south in one of the more commercial airports with advanced instrumentation. He doesn't like to admit it, but I think he's afraid someday they'll take his licence away. So he comes to me sometimes for help with forms or new regulations. He knows I won't laugh at him and I won't turn him in. We need him up here."

He sneaked a glance at her profile, which was soft and affectionate in the fading light — at her downcast eyes and her slightly rueful smile. He hated to break the spell.

"I know … I know this puts you on the spot, but could you keep an eye on him? If he seems to be getting himself into something he shouldn't — concerning those missing canoeists, I mean — or if he tells you any more, could you …" His voice died in his throat at the look in her eyes. Dark, stormy, and full of reproach.

Fort Simpson, July 16

Green checked Andy's answering machine for the third time in an hour. It was Monday morning. They had been in the north since Wednesday, but he felt no closer to finding Hannah.

"We would have heard the phone," Andy said, pouring him more coffee. He'd already had more than enough that morning, but he didn't object. "And I would have answered it."

"I know." He forced a tight smile. "But I can't stand just sitting around waiting for answers. Why don't people call back? Where the hell is that pilot? I left him four messages!"

Sullivan sipped his own coffee wordlessly. How well he knows me, Green thought. Words were a waste of effort until he wound down.

"Weekends are slow," Andy said. She was still trying for rationality. "A few people called back. That Daniel Rothman's mother."

"And all I succeeded in doing was freaking the poor woman out. It looks like he didn't tell his mother anything either!"

Now even Sullivan joined in. "But now we know Daniel has wilderness first-aid training and was a last-minute addition to the group. Not a close friend of Scott's, so maybe not in on the planning."

Green nodded glumly, recalling his conversation with Mrs. Rothman. Her son — Danny, she called him, as if he were six years old — had met Scott on a weekend canoe trip on the Fraser River earlier that spring, where they were both practising their whitewater skills. Scott's interest had been piqued by Danny's paddling skills — that he gets from his father, Mrs. Rothman said with heavy disbelief — and even more by his medical training. "You're the answer to my prayers, he'd said, and he even offered to pay half the cost of Danny's trip. I thought that was suspicious, but you know, you mention a wilderness river to my son and there's no way he's not going. Sure didn't get that from me, but his father's been taking him and his sister camping since they were little. Me? Bugs, snakes, bears? Not on your life. But who listens to me?"

Who indeed? Green thought when he finally extricated himself. He felt a rueful twinge when he realized that Daniel had probably kept quiet for the same reason Hannah had. To avoid the panicked parental rants.

If Daniel Rothman had been included in the party because of his medical skills, an idea that set Green's fear racing, Pete Carlyle appeared to be the only true friend of Scott's going on the expedition besides Hannah. The two men had been studying under the same professor in graduate school. The professor Scott had disagreed with so strongly that he'd quit the department and walked away from his graduate degree. Professor Valencia was off doing field research in Colombia and had not yet returned Green's phone calls.

Green picked up the phone again, flipped through his notebook, and dialed Pete's sister again. Luckily she was home.

"I told you everything I know on Saturday," she said.

"I know. But I'm looking further into what they were studying. I understand Pete and Scott were both studying geology. Do you know exactly what?"

"Geology, right. Something to do with what happens inside mountains when the ground thaws. I know Pete spent a few months researching in the mountains up near the Alaskan border last summer."

"Do you know what he was working on?"

"No. Like I said, I just tune him out when he gets talking." Her voice rose. "But I do remember him saying Scott was upset after he quit the program. Maybe even obsessed? Like he was throwing everything else aside for this one new project. He was even paying Pete's way, and they weren't even that close."

"No?"

"Not before this. But Pete never was one to turn down an offer of free money, not since our father turned off the tap."

Through Andy's living-room window, Green saw a

dusty black Jeep pull into the drive. An unfamiliar man climbed out, small, wiry, and wrinkled from the sun. He took off his baseball cap to scratch his bald head, then reached into his cab for a little black bag.

Andy glanced out. "Here's your pilot now."

Hastily Green thanked Pete's sister and hung up just as Hunter Kerry pushed through the front door. He favoured one leg, which gave him a rolling gait. He and Andy nodded to each other cordially but Green sensed no warmth between them. Kerry tossed the bag onto the dining table amid the clutter of notebooks, pens, and laptops, then swung his stiff leg around a chair to sit down.

"I was passing by and decided to save us both a phone call."

"Thank you for taking the time, Mr. Kerry," Green said. Despite his best behaviour, a touch of sarcasm crept into his voice.

"I'm out in the bush a lot," Kerry said as if to explain the delay. "And I got no reason to think anything's gone wrong with that party. They're not due for pickup for another week. But I'm glad to get rid of this meantime." He tapped the bag.

Green pulled it closer and opened it. "What's this?"

"One of their day packs. Left it on the aircraft. Usually you wear it around your waist so it's nearby if you dump."

Green rummaged through the contents, which appeared to be mostly emergency supplies. "Does this mean one of them is without their emergency supplies?"

"Yes, sir, but the others will have them. Not a big problem. The phone battery is another story."

Green picked up the battery and his chest tightened. “This means they have no way to call for help.”

“No new-fangled way, but there’s still lots of ways. Ways we’ve been using for decades, before all this satellite shit. Flares, beacons, bright-coloured flags, even old-fashioned smoke signals. Any experienced wilderness trekker knows to go out into the open on the riverbank and wait. And those guys are experienced.”

“How do you know?”

“Just listening to them talk as we flew up. They knew every mountain range and landmark. They could tell alpine and boreal and moraines and kettles, and all the different rock patterns like solifluction lobes and frost polygons. They can read the land, and if you’re going to get lost that’s a good thing.”

“What else did they say? Anything to hint where they might go besides the river?”

“No, sir. Mind you, I wasn’t listening the whole time. I’m kinda deaf and so it’s hard work over the engine noise. They did get pretty excited by the Ragged Range, but then it’s a pretty awesome sight. Serious rock climbers practically cream themselves.” He shot a sheepish glance at Andy, who didn’t react.

“Why didn’t you give this bag to the police?”

Hunt shrugged. “Why would I? I was gonna give it back to the party when I picked them up. But then you called, and I figured …”

“But you must have known there’s concern about them. Did you at least tell the RCMP about it?”

Hunt shoved his chair back and stood up. “Like I said, sir, I been in the bush. But I did tell Tymko, off the record. Anyways, I got a run to make, and that's about all I can tell you. I still have their take-out in my book, so if they show up earlier or you hear any different, let me know." He headed toward the door.

Green didn't move. "Just a couple more questions, Mr. Kerry. The young woman, Hannah, how did she seem?"

He scrunched up his face. "Fine, I'd say. What do you mean?"

"I mean was she excited, scared, unhappy to be there?"

"Oh, no, definitely excited. If she'd leaned any farther to see out the window, she'd have fallen out. And she was all over that Scott guy too."

"How did he seem?"

"I wondered about that. He was super excited but uptight, like the whole trip was his responsibility. He was the one did all the talking. On and on about the mountains, the creeks, and the water flow. Stuff that was Greek to her. Still, in all, they were a good bunch of kids. I'm betting they're just off adventuring, the way kids do."

After he'd gone, Green examined the contents of the bag more closely. It was then that he found the small plastic packet with the piece of paper folded inside. Once he had it spread out in front of him, his heart began to race. He'd seen enough crucial clues as a detective to recognize a possible breakthrough.

It was an old will dated 1944 in the name of Guy H. Lasalle, presumably a relative of Scott. The grandfather, perhaps? The will mentioned mining shares and mining claims, but it was the handwritten notations that caught his interest. A date, some directions, and a string of numbers that meant nothing to Green, although he sensed they were important. Why had Scott brought this? Why take such care to pack it up and transport it into the wilderness if it was irrelevant to their journey?

He refolded the paper carefully and stood up. "I'm going to pay another visit to Sergeant Nihls at the RCMP. See if he knows what these notations refer to. I have no idea, but I'm willing to bet Scott does."

CHAPTER NINE

Sergeant Nihls mouthed the numbers silently as if it would help him understand them. His eyes drifted down the flimsy piece of paper. He turned it over to look at the blank back, and then he squinted at his computer screen, clicking through links. For several minutes he ignored the two detectives seated opposite him.

Green resisted the urge to drum his fingers. He and Sullivan had waylaid the RCMP commander on his way into the detachment at 10 a.m. Nihls strode in, harried and impatient like a man who'd already done a day's work on the battlefield and had another awaiting him inside. Since Green needed the man's co-operation, he forced himself to behave.

"You say Hunter Kerry just gave this to you?"

Green nodded. This had already been mentioned several times, but he bit his tongue.

"There's no mention of it in Constable Tymko's report."

"Mr. Kerry didn't report it."

The sergeant raised an eyebrow then, the first hint of reaction on his deadpan face. "He didn't, eh?"

Green leaned forward, as if willing the sergeant to

share his urgency. “This changes things. It gives us two new pieces of information. First of all, the kids don’t have a functioning emergency phone —”

“May not have.”

“That’s close enough. So if they’re in trouble, they may not be able to call for help. And second, this wasn’t a simple pleasure trip down the Nahanni. Scott Lasalle is after something, and whatever it is, those numbers are a clue. Do you know what they are?”

The Mountie pursed his lips. “They wouldn’t tell him a thing by themselves.”

“But what do they refer to? A piece of property? A file or case number?”

“If I had to guess …”

“Guess.”

A shadow of a smile flitted across the man’s rigid face. “It’s probably a mining claim number.”

Green stared at him. “You mean this Guy Lasalle owned a mine?”

“Not owned, no. No one owns mines in this country, Inspector. People can own the surface land but, with rare exceptions, everything under the surface is still owned by the Crown.”

Green knew that. It was one of those obscure quirks of law that sometimes found its way into trouble. Mainly when some poor unsuspecting farmer or cottager suddenly found his property being dug up by a mining speculator who’d decided there might be nickel, uranium, or some other valuable metal under his fields. All the speculator needed was a permit from the Crown, and the drills and back hoes could move in.

He rephrased his question. “He had a claim to a mine?”

“Looks like it could be,” the officer said. “The first number, that is. But it's all irrelevant today. That claim is almost seventy years old. I don't know what the law was back then, but now a claim is only good for two years unless you do some work on it, and even then it's only good for ten. After that you have to piss or get off the pot.” He waved the paper dismissively. “This is nothing but a historical curiosity.”

“But Scott might not know that. And if he's gone looking for a mine ...” Green looked at the huge map of the southwestern district of the Northwest Territories that hung on the commander's wall. Apart from a few small villages clustered along the rivers, the land was empty. He went for a closer look. “If he went looking and ran into trouble, without a satellite phone —”

“There are other ways to signal for help. We have found nothing.”

“But you've been searching only along the river. These directions say it's twenty miles to Nahanni. What if they ventured inland and ran into trouble?”

Sergeant Nihls looked grim. “The South Nahanni River is over five hundred kilometres long. And there's also the North Nahanni and the Little Nahanni. That is millions of acres. Without more details, impossible to search.”

“But we have reference points: Watson and Dawson. Where are they?”

“Those directions make no sense. Dawson's up near Alaska, way off the map. Watson Lake is nowhere near here either.”

Green studied the map. Nihls was right. Even using the locations as triangulation points, the result was nowhere near Nahanni National Park. He considered the notations again. "What about this mining claim number? Somewhere there will be a record of the claim. Where?"

"That's outside my expertise. It's so long ago that it is probably stored in some archive somewhere. Yellowknife is my guess."

"Can you make some inquiries?"

The sergeant cut him off with a look. "And I have nothing better to do than run all over the territory to track down a seventy-year-old document, on the off chance some Vancouver city kids with too much time and money on their hands decided to go chasing after a family legend?" He slapped his hand on a stack of papers. "These are incident reports and witness statements from the past week, and I have to go through every one, because if we miss something a wife could die, or a kid could be beaten, or an argument in a bar could mean a knife in the back the next time the two meet."

Green fought back his frustration with a deep breath. "I understand that, believe me. I'm in charge of major cases in Ottawa, and I've been knee deep in blood and rage for over twenty years. But these are not just spoiled city kids —" He felt his voice snagging and fought for control.

To his surprise, Sullivan reached for the piece of paper and stood up. "This is already a big help, Travis. We can take it from here, and if we get any useful leads we'll let you know."

The sergeant met his gaze, and once again Green felt a silent understanding pass between the two NCOs.

He barely managed a civil thank you before heading out of the office into the bracing morning air. Clouds lay low over the town, draping the streets in a chilly grey shroud. Rain threatened. Rain and cold. And four kids were wandering in the mountains somewhere, in search of some mythical pot of gold.

Gravel crunched as Sullivan came up behind him. "You know nothing about being a northern detachment commander, Mike."

"That's not the issue. He doesn't think beyond his rules."

"You don't know that. How would you react if he barged into your office and started giving orders?"

"I'd like to think I would —"

"You wouldn't."

Reluctantly Green laughed. He felt the tension thaw as they headed back to the truck. They heard the drone only seconds before a float plane broke through the cloud cover and began its descent toward the river. As the plane approached, Green made out the trademark canoe painted on its side.

"Isn't that Ian Elliott's plane?" Sullivan asked.

"Yes, it is," Green said, setting off at a run toward the landing dock. "Elliott knows everything there is to know about the Nahanni. Maybe he'll be more help than that tight-ass horseman."

By the time they reached the dock, Green was gasping for breath. Sullivan, he noticed, had barely broken a sweat. All that cardiac conditioning was obviously paying off. Elliott taxied his plane to a mooring spot, jumped down, and secured it before turning his attention to the two detectives on the shore.

"Any news on your girl?"

Green shook his head. "But we're making some progress on what they might be up to. I want to ask you about mining claims."

Elliott didn't mask his surprise. "Up here in the Nahanni? There is no mining allowed in the park. That was one of the major reasons for establishing the park in the first place and for pushing for the recent expansion."

"Well, it's an old claim, predates the park."

Elliott unloaded some packs from the plane. "Then it's useless."

"So Sergeant Nihls told us. But I'd still like to pick your brains. Can I buy you an early lunch somewhere?"

Elliott glanced at his watch. "I have a tour group flying in from Yellowknife in a couple of hours and I have to get this gear to the inn, but yeah, I could use some lunch. We can grab a bite at the inn."

Elliott seemed to know every patron in the restaurant, and he stopped to chat with each one. Green envied him his effortless charm. There was not a hint of boredom or pretence in his smile as he asked about their families or latest ventures. Green wrestled his impatience back and waited until they were all settled over burgers, fries, and coffee before pulling out a copy of the will. He pointed to the number.

"Does this mean anything to you?"

Elliott smiled. "Nineteen-forty-four. Wow, the heyday of prospecting! Every Tom, Dick, and Harry was out in the mountains, laying down stakes and filing claims. You know, in the Klondike gold rush thousands of guys who knew nothing about the north and even less about gold came pouring over the Chilkoot Pass. Almost none of them struck it rich, but the dreams and the hopes kept them coming."

"But the Klondike was much earlier and farther west. Was there a similar gold rush here too?"

"Oh yeah! Back in the early twentieth century." Elliott piled his burger high with pickles, onions, and coleslaw and licked his fingers with alacrity. "There's the story of the McLeod brothers, who claimed they found gold in one of the creeks up the Nahanni, but they died in mysterious circumstances. Lots of people died in the wilderness in those days. Starved, frozen, drowned, beheaded ..." His devilish grin faded as if he realized too late the implications of his words. He rushed on. "Anyway, that news spawned a flood of adventurers and prospectors trying to find the creek. Every time a reporter ran the story a new bunch would show up."

He stretched his mouth wide enough to take a huge bite of his towering burger, and for a moment he was reduced to shaking his head. "Sorry," he mumbled, mustard dribbling down his chin, "there is no other way to eat Lilian's burgers than to go for it. So! Back to gold. There's no verified record of gold ever being found in the Nahanni watershed, but there are plenty of other valuable minerals. The mountains, especially in the upper Nahanni from the Ragged Range on up to Moose Ponds, are perfect for that. Earthquakes, glacial scouring, fluvial deposits, frost heave, and of course the eruption of the mountains themselves make them a diverse place for rare earth metals, which are all the rage right now, but also for gemstones."

"What kind of gemstones?"

"All kinds." He chuckled and his sunny blue eyes lit up. "Back in the early days, when this place was mostly fur trappers and speculators, the mining companies used to hand out prospecting kits with samples of the different stones and send the adventurers out into the wilds with a pick, a trowel, some sacks for samples, and a mineral identification kit to see what they could find. These weren't geologists, they were bushmen, trappers, and assorted dreamers seduced by the get-rich-quick scheme."

Elliott looked as if he were settling back to regale them with colourful tales of the wild, wild north. It was clear he loved his land, but Green had other priorities.

"So this mining claim could be one of many?"

"Oh, absolutely. The motto back then was stake a claim first and then send the real prospectors in to find out if there's anything worthwhile. The point is, you can't do any work in an area until you've registered your claim with the Mining Recorder's Office. They record where the claim is, who staked it, and when, and that gives that person exclusive right to work the area for a set period. That's to prevent a whole bunch of prospectors claiming they found gold on the same land. The guy who registers it first has the legal right."

"So how do you actually stake it? Literally with a stake in the ground?"

Elliott laughed. "Yup. You mark the borders of your claim using wooden stakes stamped with your company name and the date, you draw a rough location map, and then you take that information to the Mining Recorder's Office."

"So it's a kind of race to get there first and prevent others from beating you to it?"

Elliott nodded gleefully. "And there were plenty of dirty tricks, believe me. Lies, misdirection, secrecy... When diamond deposits were found in the barrens up north, speculators went crazy. Staked half the wilderness."

Sounds like a recipe for paranoia, Green thought as he studied the cryptic notes on the will. "Whenever there's big money to be made ..."

"Well, most of the time there's nothing valuable in the land. Or it's valuable but far too expensive or too small a deposit to justify developing it. But mining companies and speculators still stake claims willy-nilly in the hope that one in a thousand will pan out."

Green thought about the miles and miles of mountainous wilderness they had flown over. All impenetrable and unreadable. "But how do they even know where to look? I mean, you could walk your whole life and never cover the whole area!"

"That's why they hired the trappers, who were there anyway. Sometimes it's a chance sighting, for example a trapper stumbles upon an interesting rock on the trail. But prospectors also look for favourable geological conditions. As I mentioned, places where the glacier had dug deep into a hillside or a landslide had brought mineral deposits up to the surface. Prospectors also waited for the Canadian Geological Surveys being done in a particular area. The moment the scientists released their findings, the prospectors were ready to pounce. They've been known to fly over the promising areas in a helicopter and drop their stakes out the door."

He chuckled as he finished off his burger and licked his fingers. "Takes half the fun out of it, but that's progress."

"But back in 1944 ...?"

"Back then it would have been old-fashioned staking. Guys would tromp over the ground, studying soil composition, glacial deposits, geological reports, rock layering on mountainsides, and they'd take soil samples in promising areas to look for indicator minerals. Back then they wouldn't have been looking for rare earth metals, which are all the rage today for use in modern electronics and technology. Back then it would have been the old standbys: gold, silver, copper, zinc." Elliott glanced at his watch and exclaimed in dismay. They were now the only people in the restaurant.

"One more thing," Green asked hastily. "You said this mining claim number is recorded somewhere? Where? And would that tell me where the claim was staked?"

"Absolutely. To register a claim you have to provide a map. Back then it might be hand drawn and pretty iffy, but it should at least have the coordinates and the major landmarks."

For the first time Green felt a swell of hope. Here was a concrete direction, a place to start the search. "And where would this record be?"

"That old? Probably archived in Yellowknife. But one of my former guides, Kim Swift, works at the Mining Recorder's Office there. She's a sweetheart, she always kept a soft spot for the Nahanni. And I bet she can track it down." Elliott was standing now, pulling some money out of his wallet. "I'll give you her number and tell her to expect your call."

Nahanni Butte, January 2, 1944

My Darling Lydia,

Leaving you yesterday was the hardest day of my life. But this is not forever. We are not giving up. I don't trust the sample report. Once we get more money, we will expand the claim ourselves. Gaetan will leave soon to earn good pay on the CANOL pipeline, and I will continue the traplines near the claim. The Indians are angry about all the white trappers using poison to bait their traps. They say it is wrong and the land is punishing us all. The beaver and marten stop coming to our traps. Bizarre ideas these people have.

But the marten are still very plentiful farther up the Nahanni. I made a good bargain with the post here. When I will come home in May, my wallet will be full. I wish I could be there to hold you, but my bad English writing is all I can offer. But with all the books you gave me, Dickens, Shelley, and your favourite Shakespeare, I will get better. What is the news of your health? Gaetan tells me he will be a father soon too. Nicolette, a daughter in the family he is lodging with.

I remain,

Your lonely but loving husband, Guy

When the two detectives got back to Andy's B&B, Green put in an immediate call to Kim Swift, but was connected to her voicemail. Frustrated, he left a message and then began to toss some clothes into his backpack.

"What are you doing?" Sullivan asked.

"I'm getting ready. We have to go up there again."

Sullivan watched in silence for a moment. "We'll need a whole lot more than a couple of sleeping bags and backpacks."

"Then we'll rent the gear," Green said. "There must be some place to rent in town."

Andy, in her usual quiet way, had come to stand in the doorway of the bedroom. "My cousin can get you what you need," she said. "He used to do private guiding when he was younger."

Andy's cousin Jethro arrived in less than half an hour. Sitting at her dining room table, he was as serene as always, and didn't blink an eye when Green explained their request. He spread a checklist out before him. "How many in the party?" he asked.

Green glanced at Sullivan. "Just the two of us."

"And a guide," Sullivan cut in. "We'll need a guide. Do you know someone?"

"Maybe. Four people is better. Three canoes. Can you paddle whitewater?"

"I can," Sullivan said. Green's denial stuck in his throat.

Jethro kept words to a bare minimum as he worked his way through his list, checking off items. "First-aid training?"

"Some. We're cops," Sullivan said without looking at Green. Green had passed his medical course by the barest of margins, and despite — or perhaps because of — attending dozens of crime scenes and post-mortems, the sight of blood still made him queasy.

"How many days?"

"We don't know. Probably a week."

"Until we find her," Green said.

Jethro pushed back from the table and went into Andy's front room, which she had decorated in a cozy frontier style with a wood stove, a mismatched jumble of well-worn couches, and a woven Native rug on the floor. Tacked on the wall beside a huge pair of moose antlers and assorted stuffed fish was a large map of the Nahanni watershed. Jethro stood in front of it, motionless. "The Naha Dene is a big place."

Green joined him and traced his finger up the river until he found Broken Skull River. "Their canoe was found around here, so they may have capsized somewhere before that, up here."

"That's still a lot of —"

The phone rang and Green snatched it up. A woman with a high-pitched, impossibly young voice asked for him, and then introduced herself. Kim Swift.

"Ian Elliott told me about the situation. Sorry it took so long, but I had to hunt for the original files. Those ledger books don't seem to be on microfilm here yet, for some reason. The paper is yellowed and hard to read, sometimes the quality isn't the best, and the entries were handwritten, so I can't be exact."

"Anything would help."

"It was registered by two brothers from Whitehorse, Gaetan and Guy Lasalle. Two adjacent claims actually, forming a swath of the Selwyn Mountains on the south side of the South Nahanni River, just below its confluence with the Little Nahanni River."

A thrill ran through Green. That was not far above where the canoe had been found. Surely they were on the right track! He remembered Elliott's description. "Isn't there supposed to be a map? Coordinates?"

"No map on file here, but there are always four corner posts in each claim to mark the boundary. We have the coordinates for six posts. But back then, working on foot and without the help of a GPS, those coordinates would have been approximate. And two of them are smudged so may be wrong. But here's my best guess for you." She read out six pairs of coordinates, and two alternatives. Green scribbled them down and read them back to her for verification.

Just as she was about to sign off, Kim gave a little chuckle. "This is a long shot, this claim. Someone was dreaming off the scale. Do you know what the Lasalles thought they'd found?"

"What?"

"The rarest gemstone in the whole world. Mainly found in the remote mountains of Burma. Rubies."

Green was still reeling from that surprise when he passed the coordinates to Jethro, who took them over to the map. Jethro outlined an area on the map in the Selwyn Mountains, exactly as Kim had described.

"Still a lot of ground," he said doubtfully. "At least fifty square miles."

"At least it's not the whole park," Green said. "Fifty square miles is a manageable search area."

"Pretty rugged up there. Could take all day to cover a square mile."

"Then the sooner we get started.... If possible, I'd like to fly up there today, to get an early start on the search tomorrow. Can you get us the gear and a guide that fast?"

Jethro looked at him. His face was inscrutable, but Green sensed a hint of affront. He forced himself to back off. "I'm sorry. It's a lot to ask on such short notice, and I'm grateful for whatever you can do."

The cousin moved toward the door. "I need half a day to assemble this gear. You get us a plane to carry four people and three canoes. A Cessna will do."

"What about a guide?"

"I have a guide."

"Should we bring firearms?" Sullivan asked.

"Have you got any?"

"My 308."

Green was startled. It had never occurred to him to bring his Glock, which was locked in his desk drawer in Ottawa where he preferred it. But Sullivan, country boy and avid deer hunter, had brought his hunting rifle.

"Good," Jethro said. "But keep it stored away in the park. The guide will have one too."

For such a quiet, calm man, Andy's cousin could move very fast when he wanted to. He jumped into his pickup and tore out of the drive, spraying gravel into the purple flowerbed that bordered Andy's house.

No soon had he gone than Green turned to Andy. "Can I borrow your truck again? Ian Elliott may still be here, and if we're lucky we can catch a flight up with him on his way back to Whitehorse."

He found Elliott at the park office, conferring with the superintendent. They both listened as Green briefed the superintendent on the new developments.

"What a bunch of young fools," Bugden said angrily. "Rubies in those mountains? Impossible. The geology is all wrong. Emeralds yes, sapphires quite possibly, diamonds by the truckload farther north, and lots of other less valuable gemstones. But rubies? That's what happens when you give some dumb trapper a prospecting kit with a bunch of mineral samples in it and send him out to find riches. He thinks he's found rubies."

A long-forgotten scrap of information fell into place in Green's mind. "But Scott is not a dumb trapper. He's a geology researcher and he has spent many summers in the mountains. I don't think he'd be chasing this mining claim if he thought it was worthless."

"If it's in the park, it's worthless anyway," Bugden countered.

"The coordinates may straddle the park boundaries," Green said stubbornly. "It could be just to the north."

"But that adjacent area is a possible future park too, depending on how much of the Nahanni headwaters the government chooses to protect. Right now it's under negotiation, and development is frozen."

"But maybe Scott and his friends don't know all that!" Green exclaimed in frustration. "Or maybe they just want to find out what happened to his grandfather, not stake a claim. Regardless, this is our best lead on where they've gone. Now we know they probably left the river to explore inland, and they have no phone to call for help. They may be in trouble miles from where anyone would see them. I'm going up there, and Ian, if you're flying out, maybe we can hitch a ride."

The superintendent looked appalled. "You'll need equipment."

"We're getting equipment."

"You'll need a guide. You don't know a damn thing about —"

"Andy's cousin is getting us a guide."

"Jethro?" The super's scowl cleared. He swivelled to his computer and clicked it open. "Okay, let's get your paperwork done. I'm not having more amateurs wandering around up there without giving me one damn bit of information on where they are. And who to contact when they get killed."

Elliott had said nothing throughout this exchange, but now he smiled at the superintendent's mood. "The cousin is outfitting for four, you said? Who's the fourth?"

"I don't know. It doesn't matter as long as he knows how to paddle a canoe. Because I don't."

Elliott chuckled. He kept the smile on his face as he thrust his chair back. "Yeah, I can take you up. I've got some business here in town so give me a shout when you're ready to go."

It was a busy afternoon of phone calls, last minute shopping, and packing the waterproof sacs Jethro had dropped off. Green was astonished at the amount of gear they were packing for one week. Had Hannah known about all of this? Or had she been caught out, without those extra pairs of wool socks and long johns?

Sharon's voice sounded thin and tired when he called her, but she tried gamely to disguise it. "Don't think of it as the wilderness, Mike. Think of it as Algonquin Park, only three hours' drive from the comforts of home."

Algonquin Park was already too remote for him, but he didn't say so. He was focused ahead, facing the unknown but determined to master it.

But Sharon, as always, knew his every heartbeat. She sensed his fear. "You'll find her, Mike. I know it. She's your daughter, smart and resourceful."

She's also Ashley's daughter, dumb and hysterical, was Green's instant thought, but he banished it. It was unworthy of her. Hannah was not the least like her mother.

He signed off, filled with gratitude that Sharon was not at all like Ashley either. Sharon would cope, and she would manage not just her own duties but his while he was away. Sullivan was having less luck with Mary, who was clearly tearing a strip off him on the other phone. Mary, however, had lived through her husband's near-fatal heart attack and she was like a mother bear where his health and safety were concerned. In her eyes, Green brought nothing but trouble. She resented the bond the two men shared and Green's power to influence him.

Finally they were ready to go. Andy piled their packs into her truck and drove them down to the float plane dock, where Elliott's plane bobbed in the water. Next to it was a larger Twin Otter with Eagle Air stamped on its side. To Green's surprise, Elliott and Hunter Kerry were loading a canoe into the belly of the Otter.

Jethro's pickup was parked at the edge of the dock. Green could just make out the silhouette of a dog sitting alertly in the cab. Elliott jumped down from the plane and came over to greet them, dressed now in sturdy khakis, a bush jacket, and hiking boots. A moment later, Andy's cousin emerged from the plane and walked over to his pickup to open the door. A shaggy black dog the size of a border collie shot out and raced around the lot, sniffing excitedly.

Jethro grinned as he hefted the detectives' bags from Andy's truck. "Hunt's dropping us off, so we'll have plenty of room in the Otter."

"Us?" Green asked.

"Yeah. We four. We're it. The search party."

Green gaped at Elliott. "You?"

Elliott shrugged. "I wrote the book on this river. And Jethro's qualified in civilian search and rescue. More importantly, he's a damn good tracker."

Jethro grinned as he called his dog to heel. "Tatso's an even better one."

CHAPTER TEN

For once, it was a slow afternoon at the Fort Simpson RCMP detachment. The sergeant was cloistered in his office, cursing over the weekly ordeal of file reviews. The other duty constable was out on a routine traffic call, so Chris Tymko was manning the desk. He had seen the inspector from Ottawa storm out of the station just as he was arriving, and he knew all had not gone well. But when the sergeant briefed him on the day's alerts and assignments, he made no mention of it.

"Still no new developments in the Lasalle case," was all Nihls said.

Chris nodded. "I saw the father just as I came in. He looked black as sin on Sunday."

"He's off on some new theory that the group was looking for a mine."

"What mine?" Chris kept his voice neutral.

"They had some worthless old claim number from the 1940s. Green's grasping at straws. I told him if he found out the location and any useful history about the claim, we might look at it again. But we don't have the time or resources to dig in the archives."

How hard can that be? Chris wondered as he sat at the front desk, waiting for the phone to ring. He should have been grateful for the slow time to get caught up on his computer, but he felt oddly troubled. He'd seen the Nahanni after that storm, and he'd seen the canoe tossed up like broken refuse onto the shore. He'd even seen Hunter Kerry's peculiar interest in the document. He had only Hunt's word that the group had left the pouch behind. Was it possible that Hunt had stolen it, sensing it might relate to something of value?

By 2:30, Chris could stand the uncertainty no longer. The sergeant had gone off to a meeting with the band chief, and Chris knew once he was in Jim Matou's clutches he'd be gone for the rest of the shift. Chris looked up the Mining Recorder's Office in Yellowknife and put in a call. It took less than five minutes to connect with a cheerful young woman who exclaimed in surprise when she heard his request.

"Oh, no! I hope I haven't done anything wrong."

Baffled, Chris assured her it had nothing to do with her.

She giggled. "Oh, I didn't mean that. It's just, someone was asking about this mining claim just this morning. I still have the file box right in front of me."

"Let me guess. Some guy called Green."

"He said he was a cop too. I thought it was weird, because he came from Ottawa, but Ian Elliott vouched —"

"He's a persuasive guy. What information did you give him?"

She read out the coordinates, assuring him Green already had the name and date.

"What about the map?"

"No map. It's possible it got destroyed. Some of them were pretty flimsy back then. Or maybe there never was one."

"Anyone else made inquiries about this claim recently?"

She paused. "Hmm. Not *recently* recently. But the name Lasalle rings a bell. It was in the winter, mid-February maybe? Someone came into the office and asked to look at the records from the time period during World War Two."

Chris grabbed his notebook. "Did you get a name?"

"You know, I think it was Lasalle too. I remember more what he looked like. Hot-looking guys don't walk into this office in the dead of winter very often."

Her playfulness was so infectious that he had to remind himself to be firm. "Can you give me a description?"

"Hot looking isn't specific enough?"

"There's no check box on my computer form for it."

She laughed. "He was white, over six feet, slim but in shape. Like an athlete, maybe a runner, you know? Brown hair, brown eyes. His eyes were …" She paused as if groping for a word. She gave another laugh. "Hot."

"Would dark cover it?"

"It's more of a woman thing. It felt like he was undressing you, but … you wanted to be undressed." She gave another laugh. "I imagine that's not on your form either."

"I'll pencil it in. Did you mention it to the man who called this morning?"

"Mr. Green? Oh no! I didn't mention this guy Lasalle at all. It's only when you asked that I remembered him. He was interested in all the Lasalle claims from that period."

"You mean there is more than one?"

"No, no. At least, not that I know of. He took the whole batch of records from 1940 to 1950 and spent two days in the back room going through them. I don't know what he found. They're not searchable, obviously, so you have to hunt through them line by line and page by page. Really boring. He did seem mad that he couldn't find a map. He wanted to know who else could have looked at the files and when."

"What did you tell him?"

"I've only been working here for a year. I asked my boss, but he didn't think anyone had been in those file boxes for decades. He said more than likely there was no map. Things got kind of loose during the war, because they were understaffed."

"Okay, thanks, Kim. Can you stand another question?"

"Are you kidding? This is making my day!"

He chuckled. "We always aim to please. Okay, question: was there any work registered on that claim after 1943?"

In the silence, Chris heard the sound of paper rustling. "It might take awhile to figure that out," she said finally. "It looks like they just did the one exploration when they filed that claim and took some samples."

"Wait a minute. They?"

"Yes, the original claim was filed by Gaetan and Guy Lasalle, both of Whitehorse."

"When?"

"June 1943. If there's anything more recent than that, it might be in another box. But I can look for you, when I get the time."

"You're a peach. Thanks. One last question: is there any record of that claim changing hands? Being sold or traded?"

"Not under this claim number. It's a very thin file, not much activity on it at all. Nothing after 1944 in here anyway. But of course, it was rubies, so they would have been laughed out of the bar in Yellowknife if they'd tried to sell it."

"What's so funny about rubies?"

"Rubies up there? In their dreams. More likely rose quartz, or red beryl if they were lucky. A bushman with a prospecting kit couldn't tell the difference, but any geologist would know there are no rubies up there."

Chris thanked her, checked his watch, and on a whim ran the name Lasalle through CPC, the national police database. There were dozens of Lasalles, although a quick scan revealed that most were from Quebec. Refining the search further, he found none with birth-dates in the first quarter of the twentieth century. Not that he was surprised. If he were still alive, Guy Lasalle would be committing crimes from his wheelchair by now.

There were, however, two hits on a Scott Lasalle from Vancouver. One was a conviction for driving while impaired, registered late last year, and the other a guilty plea for assault on February 23 of this year.

The first offence had taken place in Vancouver, but the recent assault had occurred in Whitehorse, around the time of his visit to the archives in Yellowknife. Was there a connection? Details were scarce on the database. Just the location of the incident, which was a bar in Whitehorse, the time, which was 12:30 a.m., and the name of the victim, another man who was probably just as guilty as Lasalle: Victor Whitehead.

Chris put in a call to the Whitehorse RCMP, hoping for more details. The duty sergeant didn't recall the incident until he heard the victim's name.

"Oh, right. I took that call myself. It was a typical bar fight. Two guys sitting at a table and they started to argue."

"About what?"

"The bartender said it was about someone cheating someone. A woman, if you ask me. This Lasalle guy'd had quite a bit to drink by then, and the other man stood up to go. The bartender remembers him warning 'Stay down south where you belong,' and Lasalle took a pitcher of beer to his head. Knocked the guy down, there was blood all over his fancy suit. Nothing serious once it was all checked out and he didn't want to press charges, but by then we'd caught the call and so we wrote it up."

"And Scott Lasalle pleaded guilty?"

"Yeah. He probably could have got off if he'd fought it, because Whitehead didn't want to pursue it, but I remember Lasalle was in a hurry to go back down south and he didn't want to be stuck in Whitehorse any longer than he had to. Plus once he'd sobered up, he felt bad. He obviously hadn't meant to hurt the guy, it was a spur of the moment thing. If you know Vic Whitehead, it's not hard to imagine. So he pleaded to assault. Judge gave him a conditional discharge so he wouldn't have a record if he kept his nose clean."

"So just two strangers, had a run-in in a bar?"

"Well, no, I wouldn't say they were strangers. I think the bartender said they were cousins?"

Chris was startled. Cousins? "This Victor Whitehead, is he from Whitehorse?"

"Lived here all his life. Native. He works for the territorial government, really big on northern development opportunities. You either love him or you hate him."

After thanking him, Chris hung up and scribbled in his notebook, trying to fit the pieces together. He had a feeling he was on the brink of something important. An old mining claim, a fight between cousins, one of whom was a big proponent of northern development. That was code for mining, oil and gas, or some other massive industrial project that promised jobs and prosperity at the expense of the land.

Rubies were a recipe for trouble.

Prince Edward Island, July 17

Sue Peters woke to the hushed tones of Bob's voice, but when she opened her eyes their little cabin was empty. Through the window, bathed in the morning sun, she could see his tall, lean frame folded into a wooden deck chair. His cellphone was glued to his ear and his notepad was propped on the arm of the chair.

It was a small deck, weathered grey and black from the sun and salt, just large enough for two sagging deck chairs and a small table of equal vintage. The owner of the string of seaside cottages had brightened them with pink and yellow cushions featuring crabs and starfish and added a matching umbrella, which Bob had not opened. He was wearing a fleece sweater and had abandoned his flip-flops in favour of sneakers. On this breezy seaside morning he needed all the warmth he could get.

It was the last week of their honeymoon before they both reported back to duty Monday morning. Sue squinted at her watch. Barely seven o'clock. She wrapped the duvet around her naked body and went out to join him, sinking into the second deck chair with a murmured "good morning."

He cast her a quick smile before returning to his conversation. Listening to his side of it, she deduced that he was talking to the inspector again, who was asking them to track down more background information on Scott Lasalle. She was surprised. Unless the inspector was back east, he was up and at it awfully early. Five a.m. Mountain Time.

She and Bob had already spent much of yesterday trying to trace Scott's extended family and friends, with little to show for it. Scott's family was the very definition of estranged. There were several branches of the Lasalle family, which had originated in New Brunswick. Some had remained there, but during the great depression of the 1930s the two youngest brothers in an impoverished family of fourteen had migrated west and north. Bob and Sue had tracked down an old uncle, still living in New Brunswick, who remembered the stories of two brothers who had packed up all their belongings into a bundle and jumped a freight train west. Family legend had it that they had heard of gold lying for the taking in the creeks of the Mackenzie Mountains. Having no other skills, they apparently scraped out a living trapping in the winter and fishing in the summer, but despite their early boasting, very few dollars ever made their way back to New Brunswick.

Up until the Second World War the family heard sporadic stories about the brutally cold winters in a land teeming with furs and fish. There was money to be made if one could survive the harsh conditions. All correspondence ceased at some point during the war, and the family assumed the young men had perished. The uncle was surprised and pleased to learn that at least one of the brothers had survived long enough to produce a son and grandson who were successful on the west coast.

Sue could see the intensity and excitement on Bob's face as he relayed all this to the inspector. To quell her curiosity, she went inside to dress and pour a coffee before returning just as he was hanging up. He swung on her with dancing eyes.

"It's a treasure hunt!" he exclaimed. "Not gold, but rubies." He told her about the inspector's inquiries and his flight up to the Nahanni headwaters the evening before.

She was incredulous. "The inspector is going to canoe the Nahanni?"

Bob chuckled. "I don't think he's slept a wink up there in that tent, listening for wolves and bears. That satellite call will cost him a fortune. I told him about the brothers, so he wants us to dig up what we can about the old RCMP investigation into their disappearance." He grimaced. "Nearly seventy years ago, way up there in the north? God knows where that case file is."

"I suppose we start with their headquarters in Yellowknife. When it opens." She smiled as she eased herself out of her chair. Circling behind him, she slipped her hands across his shoulders. "That gives us three hours, Gibbsie. Whatever will we do?"

He half turned to her. "He also wants us to track down other heirs, and whether there's been any recent interest in the mining claim. That depends exactly where the old claim is."

She slid her hand down his chest and under his belt. "Morning is so delicious."

"Because if it's inside the new park boundaries —"

She sank into his lap and silenced him with a kiss. It was a full hour before he picked up the thread of his sentence again. He was balancing on one foot, pulling on his jeans.

"If the claim is inside the new park boundary, it's worthless, but if it's outside, even one kilometre outside, then it could be worth billions. The inspector has given me the coordinates, so it should be easy to determine. Rubies. Imagine!"

"Mmm," she said languidly. She was still lying in bed, the sheets a sweaty tangle beneath her. "Nothing is sexier than rubies. Blood red. Fire red. The stone of passion and death."

Within hours Bob had the answer to the question, but it did not advance their knowledge much. The coordinates Green had given him traced through a rough rectangle of land in the Selwyn Mountains around the Little Nahanni River. The land was partly within the park boundary, partly beyond, in an area criss-crossed with old mining roads and defunct exploration camps.

It seemed lots of prospectors and geologists had dreamed of riches in the Selwyn mountain range but none had ever found a viable motherlode.

Leaving Bob to fight RCMP red tape in Yellowknife, Sue took on the task of hunting down the offspring of Guy Lasalle and his brother. In the year since she'd been back on light duties at the police force, she had spent most of her time parked behind a computer and had learned a secret or two about the machines. Bob had taught her the rest. She loved piecing together the jigsaw of people's lives from the tidbits on the Internet. What she couldn't find online, she uncovered by phone.

By the time she called it quits for the day, her patience exhausted and the ocean surf beckoning, Sue had determined that the two brothers had built a cabin in the remote Nahanni above Virginia Falls and traded furs and supplies at the trading post in Nahanni Butte, a tiny First Nations village at the mouth of the river. In June 1944 a young Dene woman in the village gave birth to a daughter, whom she named Isabelle Lasalle. As far as Sue could determine, the Dene woman died of tuberculosis at the age of thirty in 1952. Her orphan daughter, Isabelle, was taken in by the nuns and placed in a residential school in Yellowknife, where she remained until her graduation from high school in 1962.

Halfway through her reading of residential school names and statistics, Sue paused to lay her head down on her arms. Within those cold lists lay the story of Canada's greatest shame. Of children torn from their communities and from the culture that gave meaning to their lives. The

Canadian government's ill-conceived plan to educate and assimilate thousands of Aboriginal peoples into white, Western, "progressive" society had backfired horribly. No one had thought about the psychological scars of losing one's family and culture, the message of inferiority, the simple terror and bewilderment of little children far from home. No one had thought about the flawed purveyors of so-called enlightenment. The pedophiles, the sadists, the righteous adjudicators of the saved and the damned.

Had Isabelle Lasalle been one of those casualties?

Sue wondered if she had been one of the thousands of survivors who appeared to seek compensation and healing from the Truth and Reconciliation Commission. An odd title for a government commission designed to identify and compensate the victims. There should be no reconciliation, she thought, only apology and restitution.

When Isabelle's name cropped up as a youth worker and as a winner in her age class in a recent Yukon Challenge bicycle marathon, Sue felt an unreasonable relief. The woman had not sunk into depression, alcoholism, and early death. Maybe she may have been one of the lucky ones.

Sue couldn't find any online records of marriages, births, or death concerning Isabelle Lasalle, so she resorted to the phone. Since it was by then late afternoon in their idyllic Prince Edward Island honeymoon cabin, Whitehorse City Hall was sure to be open.

At first the clerk on the phone wouldn't provide any details. Confidentiality, privacy protection, all kinds of stone walls. Sue identified herself as a police officer, leaving vague the jurisdiction, and explained about her efforts to track down relatives of a young man missing in Nahanni Park.

The clerk sucked in her breath. "Not Victor!"

"Who's Victor?"

"Her son. I don't think Isabelle has any other relatives."

"I believe the missing man is probably her nephew."

"No nephews, I'm sure. Isabelle's alone in the world except for Vic. Her mother died years ago. Oh! Unless you mean the kids she fostered."

Sue chatted a few minutes about the foster children Isabelle had cared for. Eight in all, all Dene First Nations. This was how the woman at City Hall had come to know her, through her community work.

Sue expressed her admiration for Isabelle's warmth and determination, and then casually slipped in her next question. "Do you know anything about Isabelle's father? Did she ever talk about him?"

"Never mentioned him. She was … I don't suppose she would mind me mentioning it. She was a res school kid. Orphaned early on."

"What about her son's father?"

"Never married him. Good thing, too, he was no good for her."

"Still, I wonder if he knows the nephew who's missing. What's his name?"

"Whitehead. I don't know his first name. He used to work for one of those big game hunting outfits in Yellowknife."

"Do you know when and where her son was born?" Sue held her breath, expecting the clerk to balk and demand to know just how that was relevant. "Just so I can figure out if there is a connection or if I've got it all wrong."

There was a pause. The woman's voice was doubtful. "I … I guess I could look it up."

"Only if you …" Sue trailed off. She waited, doodling on the sheet on which she was tracing the family tree. She still had a question mark beside the name of Isabelle's father, but it had to be one of the Lasalle brothers. She wasn't sure how this ancient history could be relevant to the present search for Scott, but her job was to fill in all the blanks. Maybe someone somewhere had reconnected with Scott, or knew something about the mining claim.

Finally the woman came back on the line. "Victor Whitehead, born Watson Lake, Yukon Territory, December 3, 1973. Mother is Isabelle Lasalle — well, you know that. Father John Whitehead. Isabelle worked hard all her life, trained as a youth counsellor, and worked for Social Services, camp director, women's shelter, all kinds of victims' groups. She made sure her son stayed on the right path, went to university, and got a good profession."

"Good for him. What does he do?"

"I think he's an engineer, but he works for the territorial government here in Whitehorse. In northern development."

Sue wanted to ask more, but just then the woman sucked in her breath and dropped her voice. "I gotta go. But you got what you needed, right? And I hope you find this young man, whoever he is."

Sue hung up and glanced over at Bob, who was deep in conversation with some clerk in Victoria, B.C. He was scribbling in his notebook. Must be the will, she decided. Her stomach was grumbling, her head was spinning, and the best part of the day was slipping away. She Googled Victor Whitehead and received nearly ten thousand hits, many of them to do with the long-delayed gas pipeline running from the Arctic down the Mackenzie River valley to the United States. Local news releases, press clippings, transcripts of hearings, survey results, petitions. Victor Whitehead was a busy man. She groaned at the prospect of wading through the websites in search of relevance.

Perhaps it was easier to call Victor Whitehead directly and ask if he knew anything about his cousin Scott. She'd do that, after she'd had some food.

White Horse, February 18, 1944

My Dear Guy,
Our baby was born three days ago but this is the first moment I have had to write. It is a boy, 8 lbs. 8 oz. Blue eyes like mine but they say that might change. He has all his fingers and toes, and he is beautiful. I am naming him William, in honour of our Shakespeare. I will write with more news when I am rested. Mrs. Quinn has moved in to take care of us until I am on my feet. I hope I can survive that!

Your proud but weary wife, Lydia

CHAPTER ELEVEN

Nahanni, July 17

Ian Elliott sank back on his canoe seat, his normally sunny face grim with dismay. Green had just run the canoe up on yet another rock, scraping the plastic bottom with an awful growl. Sullivan was sitting in the stern, flailing his arms.

"Jesus, Mike! I said back ferry!"

"I did! I fucking did! But you said it too late."

Elliott paddled alongside in his solo canoe and pushed their canoe gently off the rock. They were at the headwaters of the Nahanni, in a shallow stream barely wider than their canoes, practising manoeuvres they would need for the serious rapids downstream.

"No point blaming each other." he said. "You're a team. You make a mistake, you solve it and move on. Remember, Brian, this morning Mike didn't even know what end of the canoe paddle to hold. Now we're expecting him to handle class III rapids by tomorrow."

"It can't be done," Sullivan said. "It's suicidal. We

should have started farther down the river, below the rock gardens."

Green held his tongue. In truth, he was terrified. He knew he was putting the other paddlers at risk as well as himself by insisting on starting at Moose Ponds, but there was no other place on the upper river wide enough to land the float plane. The coordinates of the mining claim put the search area near the confluence of the South Nahanni and Little Nahanni, which was just below the terrifying sixty-kilometre stretch of whitewater. To land farther downstream at the next accessible place would be pointless.

Elliott steadied the two canoes and eased them up on the rocky riverbank. He looked thoughtful. "We'll manage," he said. "I know every twist and boil in this river, and we have a number of options. We'll take each stretch slowly. Scout, discuss, plan the route ahead of time. On some of them we can make a canyon rig by lashing two canoes side by side. Other places Brian can solo and I will paddle with Mike. If we need to, we'll portage or pull the canoes on ropes. We'll get there."

They had been practising basic paddling and rescue techniques all day. First in the placid water of the Moose Ponds and now in the trickling current of the rocky stream. Jethro had paddled ahead to wait just below the first run of whitewater. Elliott claimed it was an easy class-I stretch, which would be good practice to assess Green's skills. They would set up camp at the end so as to start the serious paddling fresh and rested the next morning.

Green ached all over. Blackflies had feasted on his bare flesh. His shoulders and arms screamed from paddling, portaging, and hoisting packs, and his new hiking boots were strangling his feet. His knees felt permanently locked in the kneeling position. Even Sullivan showed the strain of a long day.

To make matters worse, Green had woken up at 4:00 a.m. to sunlight pouring in through the tent window and the sounds of birds, insects, and frogs singing all around him. Picking up his rented satellite phone, the bug spray, and the turquoise bear horn, he'd walked down to sit on a rock on the edge of the pond.

He wasn't sure what he'd been hoping to see. Some sign that his daughter had been there, perhaps. A lost sock in the outrageous striped pattern she favoured, a lock of orange-tipped hair, a delicate footprint in the sand.

But there had been nothing. No sign even that dozens of campers passed through every year. That's as it should be, Elliott had said earlier. We have no right to desecrate this place. In the morning light, Green had to admit the view was magical. Tendrils of silver mist rose off the water, unveiling a pair of elegant grey swans patrolling the shore. Across the way two moose stood ankle deep, nibbling the reeds. The ponds shone like jewels in the palm of the distant mountain range, at the centre of which a pyramidal, snow-capped peak rose up into the lavender dawn. Mount Wilson, Ian Elliott had said. Now called by its proper Aboriginal name that Green couldn't pronounce.

Within that extraordinary setting, Green had managed to feel a moment of peace before he remembered why he was there. Then he'd phoned Gibbs and, fighting a cranky satellite signal, he managed to give him a quick update and some follow-up tasks. When he hung up he felt a twinge of guilt. The diligent, eager-to-please young detective was on his honeymoon. It had been long in coming and hard fought, because Sue Peters had refused to get married until she could walk down the aisle unassisted.

Now, twelve hours later, as he savoured a brief respite on the riverbank, he wondered what the two of them had uncovered in the course of the day. He fingered the phone in his pocket, but with an effort he resisted the urge to call them for an update. It would be 8:00 p.m. in PEI and the young couple was probably in the middle of a romantic, seaside dinner. Lobster perhaps. He'd never seen the appeal of the hideous creatures, but others rhapsodized at each succulent, buttery, hard-won morsel.

As if by telepathy, a phone rang. It was coming from inside Elliott's day pack. Green glanced down the river, but Elliott was standing on a rock in the river, deep in conversation with Sullivan. He seemed to be explaining water patterns.

Green dumped the bag, snatched up the phone and pressed the button. Silence greeted him, followed by a tentative, gravelly voice. "Ian?"

The voice had a familiar ring but Green took a moment to place it. "Warden Fontaine? It's Mike Green. Have you got something?"

"Yeah. Maybe. A canoe party just came in to Virginia Falls today and they'd spotted a backpack floating in the water. They hauled it aboard and turned it over to me.

There's a name sewn into it: Daniel Rothman. That's one of your daughter's party, right?"

Green felt the news like a physical blow to the gut. For a moment he couldn't breathe. "Yes," he croaked. He fought back a wave of panic. "Where did they find it?"

"Around Hole-in-the-Wall Creek. A little more than a hundred kilometres west of Virginia Falls, just below Rabbitkettle."

The unfamiliar names washed over him. "How far from the canoe?"

"Oh, a good sixty klicks or so. But things can drift pretty far down the river and the pack was very buoyant. Have you got your map handy? I can tell you exactly where it was."

"Just a minute." Green stumbled along the riverbank, tripping and slipping on the loose stones. He waved the phone but his shouting was drowned out by the rush of the river. Finally he got Elliott's attention and the man leaped nimbly ashore across the rocks. After handing over the phone, Green watched as Elliott bent over his map and traced the location with his fingers. His face had grown grave. When he signed off, he looked up at Green.

"What do you want to do? That location is below Rabbitkettle. We could call Hunter Kerry back to take us down there. Save a few days."

"But the backpack would have drifted from farther up, right?"

"That's likely. But no telling from where."

Green shook his head. A fierce focus had descended over his mind, sweeping away the panic. "Get someone else to fly up and check out the vicinity. There's nothing more we can do there." He swallowed and nodded down the river. "We have to go on."

It took them less than fifteen minutes to load the gear into the canoes. After a final check of the spray skirts, Elliott pronounced them ready for their very first real whitewater run.

Green took his seat in the bow and stared at the river ahead. More like a boulder-strewn stream than a river. One last time Elliott talked them through the complicated path they would take. It looked impossible. Some of the passages were barely the width of the canoe. On one side was a truck-sized rock and on the other a deadly looking cowlick that would flip the canoe in an instant.

"But remember," Elliott said with a grin, "you're wearing a helmet, a wetsuit, and a life jacket. Going for a swim is part of the whitewater experience. Just keep your head up and your feet downstream so you can see where you're going, and enjoy the ride. Your canoe will be waiting for you at the bottom of the run, with any luck still right side up."

Sullivan laughed, but only Green's desperate determination to save Hannah forced him to set foot in the canoe. Then Sullivan nosed them into the current and all possibility for thought vanished in the headlong rush of the river. Green felt the current snatch them and suck them downstream with a roar that overpowered all other sound.

The canoe pitched and rolled through the endless chop. They hit one rock, rode one stretch sideways, and emerged from the run backward, but they survived. Sullivan gave a whoop of joy as he swung the bow around and paddled. Farther downstream around a bend, ready to catch any wayward canoes or gear, were Jethro and his dog. He had already pitched his tent and gathered a pile of driftwood for a fire.

He broke into a broad grin as he grabbed their bow. "Awesome, eh?"

Green clambered from the canoe, weak-kneed and quivering, but he managed a nod.

Encouraged, Jethro continued. "And this is nothing! Wait till we get to Initiation Rapids tomorrow."

Elliott's canoe cruised around the bend and slid smoothly up onto the beach as if he'd just been navigating a kid's backyard pool. He was smiling broadly at the thrill. As they set up camp he talked Sullivan through some of the mistakes he'd made on the run. With adrenaline still coursing through his veins and the evening sun still high, Green was impatient to continue. Elliott, however, stood firm. Fatigue was the cause of many an accident when precise timing and bursts of strength were needed.

Green reluctantly admitted he was right when he found he could barely stand up after dinner. He crawled to the tent he shared with Sullivan and fell into a deep sleep, not waking until Sullivan waved a cup of coffee under his nose.

They were just packing up and loading the canoes when Elliott's phone rang. Without thinking, Green snatched it up. This time Reggie Fontaine recognized his voice.

"I talked to a guy who flew up the river as far as Rabbitkettle Lake early this morning. Saw two other canoe parties but nothing unusual. Nothing else floating in the water, nothing along the shore. Just wanted to let you know."

Green was not reassured. Bodies were something he knew a thing or two about. "In this cold water, how many days would it take for a body to surface?"

There was silence, probably as the warden tried to frame a tactful answer. "Hard to say, because in a river current lots of things could pin a body underwater. Like a whirlpool, an underwater rock shelf, or a submerged tree. Especially if the body gets trapped in the branches. But in the absence of those things, as much as a week to ten days. But if he was wearing a life jacket, as he should have, he'll pop up right away unless he's pinned."

Green stared out into the water. He pictured the panicked young man struggling to free himself from a tangle of dense spruce branches. His voice sounded dead to his ears. "And if he's pinned, how long?"

"Maybe never. I've just put in a call to the RCMP, officially reporting a canoeing party missing. I don't know what the hell's happened to them, but I figure it's time to call in the cops."

CHAPTER TWELVE

Fort Simpson, July 18

Now that the search was official, Constable Christian Tymko no longer had to fabricate an excuse to get permission for an overnight trip to Whitehorse. In a search area as vast and remote as the Nahanni watershed, the RCMP, Parks Canada, and Dehcho First Nations would coordinate the effort using bush pilots, skilled local civilians, and SAR personnel flown in from Yellowknife, perhaps even from Winnipeg.

The problem was that no one knew where to look. Bush pilots and helicopters could fly over the mountains, and teams on the ground could travel down the river, but with only the turquoise canoe and the floating backpack to help pinpoint the location, that was still a lot of territory.

Pearce Bugden and Sergeant Nihls stood in front of the large map on the wall in Bugden's office and scratched their heads. The locations of the canoe and the backpack were marked with two pins, along with the estimated coordinates of the mining claim. They minutely dissected the bends, currents, and gravel bars upstream, trying to estimate where the party had capsized.

"My guess is somewhere in this twenty-five-k stretch between Elbow Rapids and Broken Skull River," Nihls said. "It would be tricky for an empty canoe to get around that bend at the rapids without washing up on shore."

Bugden shook his head. "But the river below there is very slow and winding. Not enough force to crack up the canoe as bad as it was. Besides, the mining claim is way up here."

"But that's almost a hundred kilometres upriver!" Sergeant Nihls said. "Some canoeing party would have spotted them on the shore."

"Green thinks they might be trying to get to the mine."

"Green's grasping at straws! Have we confirmed the kids even knew where the mining claim is? You said Green had to phone the Mining Recorder's Office."

Chris had been listening quietly, biding his time. Now he cleared his throat. "Well, sir ..." He hesitated. His head was about to go on the chopping block. "In fact, Scott Lasalle did too."

Nihls crossed his arms over his chest. "Care to tell me what the hell you're talking about, Constable?"

"I made some background inquiries, sir. On my own time." He filled them in on his call to Kim Swift, and watched Sergeant Nihls's expression grow thoughtful.

"Maybe not such an off-the-wall theory after all," he said.

"Bloody idiots!" Bugden muttered. "College boys from Vancouver who think they can just traipse around in this wilderness and find a supposed ruby mine? What do they expect? Signposts? You know how many legends there are about secret fortunes up there in the mountains? Ever since the Klondike there have been morons tramping about in hopes of finding that one motherlode. Getting lost and dying too." He stalked back to his chair and flung himself into it, nearly tipping it over. "And for nothing. There's no mining in the park. Even if they're lucky enough to find this claim, even if there's a ton of gemstone grade rubies in it, it's worthless."

Chris was studying the map. It was the first time he'd seen the coordinates marked on the topographical map. Just beyond the boundary of the park lay the Cantung Mine, where the rare metal tungsten had been mined on and off for decades. Also beyond the boundary was an old mining road that penetrated deep into the mountains. The coordinates of the claim lay mostly within the park but extended some distance south and west of it, possibly as much as fifteen kilometres depending on which coordinates were accurate. If rubies were found there, it might still be possible to get them out across the Little Nahanni River via the mining road.

"I think we need to know more about what Scott Lasalle was up to, sir," Chris said. "He had an altercation with a cousin in Whitehorse last winter. It's possible that man knows something."

"And how the hell do you know —?" Nihls checked himself. "All right, fine. We'll get the Whitehorse detachment to interview him."

"Since I know the background, sir — and this cousin may not wish to help us find Lasalle — it would be better if I talked to him myself."

"Out of the question. There's too much to do here."

"Well, at the same time I could talk to the outfitter who equipped Lasalle, and the bartender who witnessed the assault."

Nihls's eyebrows shot up. "I thought you said altercation."

"It got physical. That's why the victim may be less than co-operative."

"I don't want to lose you to the search effort, Constable. Your Cessna will be needed."

Bugden was back at the map, frowning. "This doesn't make sense. That whole area is serious mountain-climbing territory. They'd be fools to try to get in that way. Of course, we already know they're fools."

Chris pointed to the deep fissures, creek beds, and glacier lakes cradled in the middle. "Maybe they were trying for an easier access through one of these creek valleys." He turned to the sergeant. "I think it's worth a shot, sir. If we can find out where he intended to go, we'll be able to narrow down the search area considerably. Twenty-four hours, that's all I need. And if you want, I'll take a SAR team up the river and drop them off on my way."

Chris could tell from his tight lips and ramrod shoulders that the sergeant didn't like being outmanoeuvred, but he couldn't argue with the logic.

In the end the sergeant sent him off to Whitehorse later that morning, empty-handed, arguing there was no point wasting a SAR team on a speculative run without any clear idea where they should be looking.

"The sooner you gain the intelligence, the better, and meanwhile we'll start mobilizing down here. Besides,

Ian Elliott is already up the river. He may have two city greenhorns with him, but he also has one of the best trackers around."

Whitehorse, July 18

Carrying nothing on board but his overnight bag, Chris pushed the Cessna hard and splashed down into Schwatka Lake just south of downtown Whitehorse in a little over three hours. Mindful of protocol, he dropped into the RCMP building to introduce himself to the desk sergeant and to fill him in on his plans.

With nearly twenty-six thousand people, Whitehorse was the largest city in the Yukon and home to nearly half its population. The RCMP station was a fancy glass and brick building that took up half a block in the historic waterfront downtown. To Chris's eyes, it looked completely out of place in the north, but Whitehorse was a modern metropolis and the RCMP was a state-of-the-art police force, so both were trying to look the part.

Sergeant Doran too was a complete contrast to Nihls. Roly-poly and out of shape, he sweated from the effort of rising from his chair to shake Chris's hand. But his grip was warm and his grin infectious.

Until he heard Chris's request.

"Vic Whitehead, eh? Hmm. Want some company?"

"Do I need it?"

"Well, let's just say, if you're a cop it's best to have a witness to back up your version of the interview."

"I'm not accusing him of anything."

"I know, but you're asking him about that assault. That's probably enough to get his back up."

Chris wavered. In truth, he didn't want this interview to seem too official. He was hoping for a friendly chat, but this was Doran's turf, and his call. "Okay, can you spare someone for an hour?"

"I'd say me, but I don't think that would improve Whitehead's mood. So I'll get someone off patrol." He winked.

That someone turned out to be rookie Constable Jennifer O'Neill, who was younger than Chris thought possible and who filled out her uniform in all the right places. Crafty old bugger, Chris thought as he folded himself into the passenger seat of her cruiser.

In keeping with his low-key approach, Chris had phoned Whitehead's office and arranged to meet him in the coffee shop around the corner. He kept his reasons vague: "Hoping you can help us with an ongoing inquiry."

Victor Whitehead was fifteen minutes late, and strode into the coffee shop with the impatient scowl of a man far too busy to be inconvenienced by police inquiries. At the sight of Constable O'Neill, his frown faded and he even smiled as he squeezed into the chair opposite her. Knees almost touching.

Constable O'Neill kept the poker face that Chris suspected she'd had to perfect early on to deal with the frontier male of the north, often drunk and always on the make. Victor Whitehead was no prize worth going for in any case. He might have an engineering degree and a high-profile job, but as a man even Chris could see he was as ugly as the devil himself. Short, bow-legged, and top-heavy, with a face carved up by acne. His chest and shoulders rippled with steroid-enhanced muscle, like he spent every spare hour in the gym.

After undressing Constable O'Neill with his eyes, Whitehead turned a contemptuous stare on Chris. Despite himself, Chris felt his face flush. He rushed to take back control.

"Thank you for meeting me, Mr. Whitehead. I'm from Fort Simpson and we're trying to locate a canoe party that has gone missing in Nahanni Park. One of the party is your cousin, Scott Lasalle."

Surprise flickered in Whitehead's eyes, but he said nothing. As if he were waiting to see what else Chris would lay on the table.

"I understand you met with Mr. Lasalle a few months ago here in Whitehorse. Can you tell me what that was about?"

"Why?"

"Why what?"

"Why should I tell you?"

"We hope it will provide information that might lead to his whereabouts." For once Chris was glad of the rote line that had been drilled into him in training.

"I know absolutely nothing about this Lasalle fellow, or about any cousin for that matter. I assume you've been misinformed and I'm sorry you've wasted your time. And mine."

"Sir, you met with him in the Rocky Mountain Bar and Grill. February 23rd, to be exact."

"Says who?"

"There was a police report filed. You had an altercation in which Scott Lasalle struck you. You declined to press charges but the police laid them anyway, based on eyewitness accounts. I'm sure you wouldn't forget an incident like that."

Whitehead said nothing for a moment. His ugly face was expressionless. "I do remember some drunken idiot in a bar, but that's all. I didn't know he'd been charged. Who says he's my cousin?"

"It was in the police report. I'm assuming he did."

"Well, that's news to me. I had no idea who he was and I forgot his name — forgot the whole incident — until you reminded me."

"So what was the fight about?"

"What is a bar fight ever about? Who the fuck knows? I looked at him wrong, or he didn't like my face."

"The report says you were talking together."

Whitehead shrugged. "I don't honestly remember. It was a crowded bar, everyone is pretty friendly up here, and sometimes people get to talking. Most times they don't even remember in the morning."

"So you're saying he was a complete stranger who just happened to punch you out?"

Whitehead nodded. "It was kind of embarrassing. I don't usually get in those situations. That's why I didn't press charges. I just wanted to put it behind me."

Chris took a sip of coffee, stalling for time as he searched for a thread to unravel. "Do you remember talking to him about a mine?"

"A mine?" Whitehead barked a laugh. "Everyone talks to me about mines. Especially when they're three sheets to the wind. Always looking for special treatment or inside information, as if I'm a fucking oracle when it comes to mining."

Chris gritted his teeth. "Did Scott talk to you about a mine. Please try to remember, sir. It could be important."

Whitehead paused, but Chris had a feeling it was all for show. Then he shook his head. "He had liquor and women on his mind, as far as I remember. Nothing about a mine."

Chris declined Jennifer O'Neill's offer of a ride to his next destination. He didn't want to spend one more minute in humiliation. He was furious with himself for letting that smirking asshole wipe the floor with him and for letting her watch. He should have been better prepared, he should have known how to turn the tables, get under the man's skin, and box him in. But he was not an investigator. He had no special interview training, he was just a Prairie farm boy.

He stormed around the streets of Whitehorse for an hour, ignoring the warm evening sunshine and the bustle of tourists on the busy streets. Aware only of the black cloud inside his own head. What a loser he was. On his weeks off, instead of heading to the big city where he could meet new people and expand his horizons, he always went home to the farm. To his mother's perogies, his sisters' giggles, and his father's stiff, quiet pride in him. Neighbours he'd known all his life came by to visit in a steady stream. They asked him about his adventures in the faraway world he'd gone to, as if he was their link to bigger dreams.

When in reality he was just a two-bit constable in a six-man detachment in the back of beyond.

He didn't even dare report back to Sergeant Nihls. The man had clearly thought the whole trip a waste of time and resources, so he'd better have something positive to report by the time he got back.

Downtown Whitehorse was a whole lot bigger than Fort Simpson, but even its novelty had been exhausted in Chris's hour-long walk. He was still deep inside his black cloud when he passed — possibly for the second time — the Rocky Mountain Bar and Grill. He remembered the bartender. Surely a more co-operative witness. A shot at redemption.

A band that sounded awful even to Chris's Manitoba farm-boy ear was tuning up on the stage at the back. The bar was dimly lit and half full. Dishes clattered as patrons dug into platters of nachos, wings, and burgers. Reluctantly Chris's appetite crept back through his humiliation. He took a stool at the bar and ordered a buffalo burger with all the trimmings. The bartender pulled him a pint of Yukon Gold with a practised hand.

Chris waited until he was on his second pint and halfway through his burger before he introduced himself. He'd worn civilian clothes for his interview with Whitehead, but the bartender pegged him right away. Frank Flaherty had an east coast accent you could cut with a knife and he proved as talkative as Whitehead was tight-lipped. He was no fan of Whitehead.

"Look around ye," said the bartender, leaning on the edge of his bar as if he had not a customer in the place. A couple of waitresses rushed around, coping with huge trays of food. "I makes most of my money off tourists, and they don't come up here to see tailing ponds and ugly gashes in the mountainside, boy. They don't want to hear company jets flying overhead or eighteen-wheelers hauling ore down the river valleys. Vic Whitehead peddles a line of bull that he's just after bringing jobs and prosperity to the people of the Yukon, and God love 'em, they need it, but he would sell out our future to the highest bidder, which these days are the Chinese. All those jobs and riches will go to China, not us. Just you watch. We'll be like the girl at the end of the party, lying on the bed with her legs spread. Oil, natural gas, gold, diamonds, and all them rare earth metals everyone is hot for these days — all that will last just a few decades but the rape of the earth will last forever. You can never put it right again, once you've destroyed it."

Frank was obviously winding up for his favourite rant, but Chris didn't take the bait. "So Whitehead is a big supporter of mines?"

"Vic is the best thing that ever happened to them. He recommends in their favour every time."

"What can you tell me about the scuffle he got into back in the wintertime, with a man named Scott Lasalle?"

The bartender grinned. "That was a beaut. Nice to see Vic taken down a peg or two, even though I didn't think the young fella had it in him. Vic's built like the side of a mountain, and whatever time he doesn't spend chasing the ladies, he spends in the gym. Did college wrestling too, a few years back."

"I guess the other guy took him by surprise?"

"I don't know how much of a surprise it could be. Things been heating up pretty good between them for awhile there."

"Oh, they weren't just strangers passing by?"

"Oh no, boy. They were together a good hour or so, sat right at that table in the corner there." Frank pointed across the crowded room to a table by the window. "They had dinner together and went through two, three pitchers of Yukon Gold."

"Maybe the place was crowded and there was no other place for either of them to sit?"

"Oh no, no. The young fella was waiting here at the bar, and soon as Vic walked in he introduced himself, they shook hands, and Vic pointed to the table in the corner. The place was crowded, but not that crowded. Looked like they was after a private chat."

"Could you hear any of their conversation?"

"Not at first." Frank squinted through the noisy bar at the table, now occupied by five young men intent on getting drunk. He seemed to be trying to replay that night. "At first it was just talk, you know. What the young fella was studying, what places he'd visited in the Yukon, a bit about adventure trips. Then they got into it. The young fella —"

"Scott?"

"Scott, yeah. He had a backpack and took out a bunch of papers. Some of them were maps, I could see that, and a couple looked kinda legal. I remember Vic got pretty excited. Then the young man got mad about something. They started to argue. Scott showed him some more papers. Vic said it was all worthless anyhow, and how could he prove he was who he said he was." Frank chuckled. "Scott called him a cheater and Vic called him a fraud and that pretty much did it. Next thing I knows, the pitcher of beer went flying. Sliced Vic's head up good. Jumpin' Jaysus, there was a lot of blood!"

Frank seemed caught up in the bloody aftermath, but Chris was back in the thick of the conversation. Before the argument. "Do you have any idea what the papers might have been? A mining claim or a map of one, for example?"

"Mine?" Frank's expression cleared. "Now that would make sense. Nothing would get Vic's blood up like a mine. And come to that, I did hear something about rubies. Vic said, 'Rubies!' And he laughed. The kid said, 'Somebody thought so.' I didn't hear exactly, but something about his grandfather getting cheated, maybe even killed. Vic got mad then and that's when the young fella — what's his name again?"

"Scott Lasalle."

"Lasalle." Frank's eyes widened. "Lasalle, you said? Jumpin' Jaysus! That's what this is about!"

"What?"

Frank laughed. "I'll be the devil. I never made the connection!" He pulled two pints of beer and nodded his head toward the patio. "We'd best sit down for this one, boy. It's quite the tale. Angel, I'm going out for a smoke, can you take the bar for me? And watch those young fellas at table five."

Settling outside, Frank took a long swig of beer, lit a cigarette, and blew out a slow, lazy stream of smoke. "Lasalle. That's a legend up here with the old timers. More in Yellowknife and Fort Simpson than here in the Horse, but good stories travel far. There was two Lasalle brothers come up from New Brunswick during the Depression to make their fortune. Not a penny to rub together but there was good money to be made if you knew how to trap, and lots of shifty-eyed speculators willing to take advantage. They'd hire them to trap and prospect. Drop them in the bush for the winter and pick up the furs in the summer. Summertime, they set them to prospecting with nothing but a kit, a compass, and a lousy map. The Lasalles worked the Nahanni-Flat River area, panning for gold in the creeks and taking rock samples. One time, so the story goes, they failed to make their pickup point and then they showed up instead down at Nahanni Butte."

He sucked deeply on his cigarette and blew the smoke sideways. "This was back when the Butte was a trading post, before all the tourists started using it. They had a sack full of rocks they said were rough rubies. They went to record the claim and round up some backers. Next summer, they went back up for more samples and that's when things started to go to shit. The geological report on the new samples said they were worthless. No rubies, no red stones of any sort, so the story goes. The investors pulled their money, called them a fraud, said they must've salted the original claim. The whole venture collapsed and left them penniless. But they were tough buggers. They set up their own company called Northern Rubies, and one of them went to work the oil pipeline where there was big money to be made — this was during the war and the Americans wanted it built in a hurry. The other brother, Guy, stayed in the bush trapping. Good money in furs in those days."

"So they were going to develop the mine themselves?"

Frank nodded, pausing long enough to drain half his beer and take another long draw on his cigarette. The street was still busy and the patio was filling up with revellers enjoying the warmth of the northern summer night. Chris found himself holding his breath as he waited for the story to resume.

"Yeah. Word is Guy Lasalle got a touch of bush fever and started getting suspicious, thinking the other was in league with the backers, maybe trying to squeeze him out. So he stayed behind at the base camp all winter to guard the claim. All alone, all winter long in the dark with his suspicions. That's the last anyone ever saw of him."

"Was there a search?"

"Oh yeah, people looked. Locals and you fellas. It was like the wilderness swallowed him up." Frank shrugged dramatically. "Some say the wolves got him. Some say he went bush crazy after that long winter and killed himself rather than face the humiliation," Frank leaned forward and waggled his eyebrows, "and some say he was murdered."

Chris grinned. "And why would that be?"

"No shortage of motives where gemstones are concerned, boy. Maybe the local Indians objected to him trapping on their land, maybe the backers got greedy, maybe the other brother came back and finished him off. Who knows? But the point is, the story never died. Every now and then someone comes back from a hike with a tall tale about red stones lying for the taking in the till on the mountainsides. Or glittering from the bottom of creeks. And now it sounds like the Lasalle blood has risen up again to take up the cause."

"What do you think Scott's relationship is to Victor? Both grandsons of Guy Lasalle?"

"Could be. I can tell you there were some lively times out there in the bush back in those days. Lots of kids weren't sure who their daddies were."

Chris made a mental note to check birth records for the name Lasalle during the period around the 1940s, as well as Scott and Victor's birth records. The registry offices would be closed for the day, but he'd get an early start on the search in the morning. At least he now had some interesting information to report to Sergeant Nihls when he got back. He wasn't sure what relevance all this history had, and he suspected Nihls would say it had none, but Scott clearly had planned something bigger in the Nahanni than a summer wilderness trek.

A tall blond young woman was coming toward the bar, a look of intense concentration on her face. She was dressed in blue jeans, flip-flops, and a tight tank top, with a bright pink purse slung over her shoulder. With a jolt of pleasure and surprise, Chris recognized Olivia Manning.

He called her and jumped to his feet, knocking his chair over. She stopped. For an instant, confusion and alarm flitted across her face, but then her big, beautiful smile came back.

"Well, well, well. Flyboy! What are you doing here?"

It was too much to explain, especially in his tongue-tied state. "A case," was all he managed. "What about you? I thought you were doing a Nahanni tour."

Her gaze flicked to Frank, who was stubbing out his cigarette and scrambling to his feet.

"Only as far as Glacier Lake," she said once he'd gone back inside. "I had a meeting I couldn't miss here in Whitehorse." She wrinkled up her nose in distaste. "School stuff. But not till tomorrow. It looks as if I can buy you that drink I promised. And you can tell me all about your case."

He nodded. As she pulled up a chair and stretched out her long, lithe body, all words, and all thought of the case and his plans for tomorrow, fled from his brain.

CHAPTER THIRTEEN

Little Nahanni cabin, March 12, 1944,

Mon amour pour toujours!
I am so happy to receive your letter. An Indian trapper from the Butte brought it today, and I am so glad to have some news of our baby. I knew he must be born. William is a fine name. It is also English for Guillaume, my full name. How I wish to see him and hold you in my arms. It is so quiet up here. I have no company but the dogs, and at night the wolves. It seems colder than other years, and this time Gaetan is not here. At least now the days are longer.

Do you have news of Gaetan? I hope he got a good job on the pipeline. The furs are not so good as I hoped, even the Indians say so. I am obliged to extend my lines farther west.

I am reading *Romeo and Juliet* you gave me, but the English is hard and it makes me lonely for you. What a grand love they shared. I confess sometimes I read *Huckleberry Finn* in its place.

I live for your letters, and promise to come home to you and the baby soon!

Your ever devoted husband, Guy

Chris woke the next morning to the caress of unfamiliar sheets and the delicious scent of female skin, overlaid with musk and sweat. He hardly dared move. He could hear the soft rhythm of breathing next to him and the distant rumble of traffic though the closed window. He blinked at the white ceiling of the hotel room. Plain, cheap, anonymous, but transformed to a sensual paradise in the heat of last night.

He could barely believe his luck. They had shared two bottles of wine with dinner, walked the streets arm in arm, and finished up in the small bar of his hotel, ordering the only brandy on the menu before picking up their glasses, wavering down the hall to his room, and tearing off their clothes. In the end, no words, no awkward requests, no coy innuendos. Just a look exchanged between them.

He wondered if she'd regret it when she woke up. Did she do this often, or had she really shared the connection he'd felt all evening? Had she found him lacking, despite her three orgasms and his considerable staying power, at least for that third one? The wine and brandy had barely touched him, although he knew he'd talked too much. The isolation of months, the rigid control of the job, the pent-up need.... He'd unleashed it all last night in his eagerness to keep her with him. He'd talked about his farm, his homesickness, his dreams for advancement in the RCMP, his impatience with the promotion process, with the unspoken motto of the RCMP: "Don't screw up. Follow procedure. Cover your ass, cover your boss's ass, and above all, cover the force's ass." Too much turmoil and bad publicity, too many complaints and bad choices, had made cowards of them all.

It wasn't the noble vision he had dreamed of when he joined the force.

"Oh how the mighty have fallen," Olivia had said at one point, midway through the second bottle of wine. She'd commiserated, saying that university had been just as disillusioning. The world is a compromise and if you want to do even some small bit of good, you have to wade in the crap where the game is being played.

He told her about his attempts to investigate Scott Lasalle's disappearance, about the contortions he'd gone through just to convince his sergeant that this trip was important. That tracing Scott Lasalle's recent movements and checking out his relationship to Victor Whitehead was important.

He didn't mention what an idiot he'd made of himself during the interview, but she seemed to sense it.

"Whitehead is a creep," she'd said. "It's bad enough he wants to put roads and dams and pipelines all over the north, but he's the slimiest slug a woman ever had to pick off herself. You get him, flyboy."

Last night, fuelled by the wine and her obvious admiration, he'd wanted to march right over to Whitehead's house, grab him by the lapels, and demand to know why he'd lied about his meeting with Scott. This morning, however, he felt far less confident. Much as he wanted to squash the slug for the woman who slept like an angel next to him, he knew Whitehead would wipe the floor with him again. He hated to admit it, but he needed reinforcements.

As he slipped on his clothes and tiptoed around the room, hoping not to wake her, he stubbed his toe on the table. A curse escaped his lips. She stirred. Opened her eyes. Miraculously, she smiled.

"Mmm. That was a night."

He paused, shoes in hand, and came back to the edge of the bed. "Sorry. My feet aren't looking where they're going this morning."

"I wonder why." She yawned and stretched like a cat, long limbs arcing through the air. "What's on the agenda for today?"

"I want another crack at Victor Whitehead. But I have to figure out the connection between Whitehead and Lasalle first. They're related somehow. Cousins of some sort."

"No kidding."

He nodded. "And whatever it is, it seems to go back to Lasalle's grandfather. To that mining claim."

"But that's ancient history."

"Maybe. But maybe people have long memories. Frank Flaherty says the grandfather disappeared. That may be ancient history but if Frank's ears aren't deceiving him, Scott still thinks there's a score to be settled."

Prince Edward Island, July 19

Sue permitted herself a long, silent wail. It welled up from the core of her battered body, a cry of both anger and despair muffled by the months of self-discipline she had imposed. It wasn't often that she felt sorry for herself, but this morning, as she watched Bob put on his running outfit and jog off along the beach, she cursed her limitations. Every ounce of her cried out to join him, to feel the salt wind against her skin and the wet sand beneath her bare feet. To feel the strength of her muscles and the pounding of her heart.

To know that she was his equal, by his side in all things.

Instead she stood in the cabin doorway, cradling her morning coffee and searching for distraction. This was their last full day on the island. Tomorrow they had to pack up the car for the two-day trek back to Ottawa. Their new home and their old jobs waited for them there.

Inspector Green was never far from her thoughts but now he loomed up to fill her mind. He would not be in the office when they got back. He was still up in the north, searching for his daughter. Guilt distracted her from her frustration. Compared to his ordeal, what was a minor limitation on her part? To make matters worse, she had made almost no headway unravelling her part of the mystery in the past two days.

So far Bob had hit a wall of procedural red tape from the RCMP records department in Yellowknife, but he had managed to obtain faxes of both Scott's father and grandfather's wills and had tried to trace the inheritance of the mining claim. The grandfather's will had left everything to his wife, Lydia, rather than to Scott's father, William, who would have been only a baby at the time. Lydia had moved south to Vancouver when Guy died in 1945, and as far as Bob could uncover she had never remarried or had further children. It appeared that she had lived with her son in his Richmond house, possibly helping to raise Scott, until her death in 1984. Sue recalled the ex-wife's description of her: "A bitter old hag stuck in the past." Poor Scott.

"Not exactly one big happy family," Bob had observed. "Everyone seems to have existed on their own little islands. Lydia and Guy, William and Scott, and now Scott all by himself. No aunts and uncles, no cousins to help out in a pinch. What a sad, lonely way to live."

Sue, who had grown up on an Eastern Ontario farm with two dozen cousins living almost within shouting distance, could barely imagine such loneliness. She vowed that no matter how overwhelming and intrusive the family became, she would never again complain about the noise and crowds at holidays.

There was no mention in either will of the brother, Gaetan, and his share in the claim, nor of a Dene wife and child. Nor could Bob find any information about Gaetan's later life. Lasalle was too common a name to search the Internet without having a starting point. Nonetheless, Bob tried searching databases for the Yukon and Northwest Territories. Nothing. If Gaetan was still alive, he was leaving no digital trace. More likely he had died sometime in the pre-digital era, but a search of dusty census listings and city directories would have to wait for another time.

Yesterday Sue had started the search at the other end of the trail, with Victor Whitehead. She had placed two phone calls to him in an attempt to find out what he knew about Gaetan and Scott, but the man had not returned her calls. Now, tired of feeling sorry for herself and determined to be useful, she marched back into the cabin and put in a third call. Too late she checked her watch. Nine o'clock. That made it six a.m. in Whitehorse. A ridiculous hour to solicit co-operation.

Preparing herself to leave another message, she was surprised when the phone was snatched up before the second ring.

"Yeah?" a man barked.

"Mr. Whitehead?" Sensing he was about to slam the phone down, she rushed on. "I'm Sue Peters, Detective Peters of the Ottawa Police, and I apologize for calling so early."

Silence greeted her, but at least he was listening. "I miscalculated the time difference."

"How did you get this number?"

After the two unanswered calls she had coaxed his private cell number out of the clerk at City Hall, but Sue wasn't fool enough to tell him that. "This won't take long. I'm working on a case involving a young man missing up in the Nahanni —"

"Goddamn it, not that fucking Lasalle business again. I already told you guys I don't know anything! So quit hassling me or I'll lodge a complaint."

Sue was startled. "What are you talking about?"

"You know what I'm talking about! One of your guys was nosing around here yesterday, making all sorts of insinuations —"

"Who was?"

"Some two-bit Mountie from Fort Simpson. Are you guys so incompetent the one hand doesn't know what the other is doing?"

"What insinuations?"

"Well, I'll save you the trouble. I told him he was flat wrong. I never heard of this Scott Lasalle, I don't know where he is, and he sure as hell isn't my cousin!"

Sue scrambled to keep ahead of him. This was getting interesting! She tweaked the truth for effect. "Our information is that he is your cousin."

"Says him! I don't know what his game is, but I never saw him before that night in the bar."

Sue's mind raced. Clearly there were developments she and Bob knew nothing about. She sensed he was only one question away from hanging up on her, so she'd better make it a good one.

"What do you know about your grandfather Gaetan?"

The phone slammed in her ear. Okay, wrong question. But at least she had opened up several leads. First of all, Scott and Victor had connected before, and Scott knew he was a cousin. Secondly, for some reason the Fort Simpson RCMP had questioned him about it. Was it possible the RCMP was quietly investigating behind the scenes? For a force obsessed with protocol and red tape, that would be a surprise.

But the third lead was the most telling of all. The name Gaetan Lasalle had touched a nerve.

It was nearly two hours before she could reach the commander of the Fort Simpson detachment. The sergeant was clipped and professional but initially unwilling to discuss the details of an ongoing investigation. She had to drop not only Inspector Green's name but also the Ottawa Police Chief's, and was well on her way up the RCMP ladder before he capitulated.

"Constable Tymko is conducting some inquiries in Whitehorse, yes. But only regarding the missing man's recent activities."

When she asked for Tymko's contact information she met with further resistance, until she informed him she might have information that would assist him in his inquiries up there. Nihls requested that she give it to him to pass on, and it took several more exchanges to convince him that direct communication between herself and Tymko would speed up the process.

Just as she hung up with Constable Tymko's cellphone number in hand, she spotted Bob's lanky figure jogging toward her along the sand. He was red-faced and dripping with sweat, but his eyes sparkled.

"Man, I'm going to miss this!" he exclaimed after he'd downed half a litre of orange juice.

"Maybe Prince Edward Island could use a pair of crackerjack major crimes detectives."

He laughed. "Major crimes? Here? I bet the worst thing that happens on this island is someone robbing the collection plate on Sunday. Besides, we'd have to transfer to the RCMP."

She made a face. "How to ruin a good idea. Speaking of the RCMP …" She filled him in on her phone calls. "You'd be proud of me. I was very well behaved."

He leaned over to plant a sweaty kiss on her forehead. "I'm going to jump in the shower. See if you can work your magic on this Tymko guy."

Unfortunately Constable Tymko didn't answer his phone. As she listened through eight rings, she glanced at her watch. Almost eight o'clock Yukon time. Surely not too early for a cop on the job. When his voicemail kicked in, she left a detailed, professionally-worded message dropping not only Inspector Green's name but also Sergeant Nihls's. If he were acting true to RCMP form, he would no doubt check with his superior before returning her call.

Sure enough, he called back fifteen minutes later, just as Bob was emerging, naked, from the shower. She took the phone and herself out onto the deck. She needed all her wits for this call. As it turned out, Constable Tymko was a sweetheart. As informal and co-operative as Nihls was uptight. He waved aside the constable label in favour of Chris, and he sounded very excited to have someone other than himself investigating the mysterious connection between Scott Lasalle and Victor Whitehead.

"Wow!" he exclaimed when he'd heard her out. "So you think Victor Whitehead might be Gaetan Lasalle's grandson?"

"That seems most likely. Both brothers spent time in the bush in the Nahanni area where Victor's grandmother grew up. She got pregnant about the same time."

A rumbling roar drowned out his reply. "Hang on!" he shouted. "I'm on the street playing chicken with semis. I have to find some place to hide so I can write all this down."

She waited, listening to the sound of traffic and heavy breathing as he found a place to settle. "Safe," he said finally, "I'm all ears. Take me through this step by step."

She consulted her own draft of the family tree before starting at the beginning, with the two brothers heading west during the Depression and ending up in the Nahanni region. She explained about the Dene baby named Isabelle Lasalle.

"There's no father listed, but with that name, it's a strong possibility it was one of the brothers. Guy was by that time married to Scott's grandmother, Lydia, and from the wording of the will, he seems to have loved her very much."

"That doesn't mean much after months in the bush, I can tell you," Chris replied. "For a lot of those bush men, Native women were just ..." He hesitated.

Sue appreciated his discomfort. "Play things?"

He mumbled agreement.

"My money's still on Gaetan," she said. "Guy does seem like an honourable man. A loyal one too. He used to send money home to his mother in New Brunswick whenever he could. If he'd made some woman pregnant, I think he'd have done something for the child, at least in his will. Remember, when he wrote that will, he thought he'd struck it rich."

"But he disappeared himself about the same time. Maybe he never knew about the Dene baby. It's not like news travelled fast in those days, especially during the winter."

"What do you know about his disappearance?" Sue asked.

Chris filled her in on the story the bartender had told him, concluding with the mystery surrounding Guy's death. Sue bent over her chart. "All right, let's see what we have so far. We have two brothers who discover a possible ruby mine and stake a claim. They register the claim with the Mining Recorder's Office in 1943 and raise funds for exploration in the summer of 1944. But the samples prove to be worthless and the investors pull out. Lots of people lose their shirts, so they would have been angry with the brothers."

There was silence on the end of the line. Then Chris grunted. "Funny. The brothers don't give up on the claim. Guy spends that whole winter in his cabin, trapping to make money but mainly to guard the claim, so the legend goes. And Gaetan goes to work on the oil pipeline. They're still trying to raise money."

"And less than a year later they've both dropped out of sight. Guy is presumed dead, but Gaetan?" Sue stared at her family tree. At the links as yet unexplored. All women. Scott's grandmother, who must have known something about her husband's intentions and his continued belief in the mine. The Dene woman in Nahanni Butte, who had borne a child from one of the brothers. And that child herself.

Isabelle. Victor's mother, the only one still alive who might have heard stories about Guy and Gaetan. Who might know what had happened that summer in Nahanni Butte and up in the mountains where the rubies were. Sue had wanted to talk to the woman herself, woman to woman, victim to victim. A woman like herself who had fought adversity and, despite the crippling scars of residential school, had risen above it. But she knew this interview had to be conducted face to face, so as to read the silences, the nuances, the shared moments.

Chris seemed like a nice man. Maybe he could handle it. Much as she hated to, she had to hand it over.

"Can you find Isabelle?" she asked. "She lives in Whitehorse. We need to know what she knows."

CHAPTER FOURTEEN

Whitehorse, July 19

After he hung up, Chris remained sitting on a low retaining wall outside the Whitehorse RCMP detachment. He was oblivious to the morning traffic and to the sun already heating up the crisp northern air. Instead, through the faint throb of his lingering hangover, he contemplated the information that the Ottawa detective had presented. How could he break down Victor Whitehead's wall of denial? How could he find out his true connection to Scott Lasalle?

And more importantly, his reason for lying about it.

Chris could see no good reason why Victor would deny a connection unless he was up to something. Surely if he had simply been ignorant of Scott's possible relationship to him, he would have expressed curiosity, maybe even excitement given that he was an only child with very little family. Not flat-out rejection.

In Chris's opinion, Victor knew exactly who Scott was, but wanted at all cost to cover up the connection. Chris was dying to confront Victor with the bartender's statement and demand the truth from him, but now he hesitated. Victor could still weasel out of all the bartender's accusations. He could still say it was a chance encounter in a crowded bar and they had shared a table out of necessity. He could still say their hour-long conversation was nothing more than harmless drunken banter, their fight the result of the other man's inability to hold his liquor. He could even concede with astonishment that maybe Scott was his cousin after all but that it was complete news to him.

Chris had learned two basic tenets of police interrogation strategy: leverage and corroboration. Sometimes the second provided the first. He needed confirmation of the blood ties. That meant talking to Isabelle first.

With this new goal in mind, he headed to City Hall. Contact information for Isabelle Lasalle was not hard to find, including her date of birth: June 19, 1944. The time frame was perfect.

He'd expected Victor to warn his mother that the cops might come snooping, but when the woman opened the front door to her small wood-frame house she was smiling cheerfully. Her smile crinkled her eyes and accentuated the deep laugh lines carved into her face. Chris could tell at a glance that she had some white blood. Her skin was honey-coloured, her eyes brown, and her thick salt-and-pepper hair pulled back into a single braid. Her face, however, was narrow and angular, her nose aquiline, and her eyes too round to be pure Dene.

He introduced himself. He had dressed in uniform today for his confrontation with Victor, but the sight of the uniform did not seem to disturb her. Her smile faded and she looked concerned but not alarmed. She was probably used to police, but as a counsellor and community activist she was not afraid of them.

She drew her short, squat form to its full height and nodded for him to enter. Inside she settled him on a sofa that sagged in all the right places, and then offered him coffee. He accepted, welcoming the trappings of an informal chat. The yeasty sweetness of fresh bread filled the house, but he resisted the urge to follow her into the kitchen. Instead he looked around.

The house was quite old, possibly even from frontier days, and it still had its original plank floors, pitted and knotted but polished to a golden gleam. The living room was tiny but packed with mementoes, plaques, and odd bits of artwork that looked homemade; beadwork, wood carvings, woven mats, leather hangings. On the floor was a large braided rug in a Dene design. Above the fireplace hung a framed photograph of Virginia Falls shot through golden mist.

"One of the Creator's great wonders," she said, startling him as she came up behind him. She set down a tray with two cups of black coffee and a plate of buttered rolls. The butter had melted and oozed down the sides. He suddenly realized he was famished.

"How can I help you, Constable?" she asked once he had sipped his coffee. He suppressed a grimace, for it was strong enough to peel paint.

"I hope you can provide me with some background," he began, picking his words with caution. "I'm investigating the disappearance of a party of young canoeists up in the Nahanni. One of them is Scott Lasalle." He watched carefully. Surprise flickered across her face. "He may have been trying to find a ruby mine that his grandfather had staked out over sixty years ago, up in the Mackenzie Mountains."

Now she leaned forward, listening intently.

"There were two brothers involved in the claim. Gaetan and Guy Lasalle. Guy was Scott's grandfather. Does either name mean anything to you?"

She shook her head, but slowly as if wary. "But Lasalle is my last name, of course."

He hesitated. His heart was racing and he set his cup down to hide his trembling. "They would have been friends with your mother, in Nahanni Butte back in the mid-1940s."

Her face grew rigid. She didn't speak but she left the hint dangling in the tense air.

"This is ... awkward," he said. "The fact is, Scott Lasalle met with your son Victor a few months ago about this mine. He called Victor his cousin."

"Cousin."

"Yes."

"Tell me about this Scott Lasalle."

"He's a young geology student. He grew up in Vancouver but his father was born in Whitehorse, the only child of Lydia and Guy Lasalle."

"Are you implying Guy Lasalle is my father too?"

"No." He coloured. "Not necessarily. I mean ... well, I think one of the Lasalle brothers may have been your father."

She sipped her coffee and took a careful bite of her roll. "I never knew my father, barely remember my mother. She died when I was six. I was … sent away."

"And no one ever mentioned who your father was?"

"I didn't stay in Nahanni Butte. After I got out of residential school, I mean. I lost touch with the place."

"Did you ever try to track down your father?"

She shook her head. "Not seriously. I know he was white. My uncles told me he was a kind, gentle man who treated her well, not like a Native squaw. But he left her. Got her pregnant and disappeared, so I didn't believe them." She straightened her shoulders, as if she was trying to shrug off the resentment that was creeping in. "That must have been a surprise for Vic. Some white boy showing up claiming to be his cousin."

"They were meeting about the mining claim. Victor flatly denies they're cousins."

She nodded. "He would. I never told him anything about my mother except she came from Nahanni Butte. When he was young, I wanted him to look ahead, not back. Now I wish I'd given him more pride in the traditional ways."

She stared out the window into the quiet street and a puzzled frown crept across her face. "Even if this was true, how would this man Scott have found out about us? Did his grandfather tell him?"

Chris shook his head. "Guy died — or at least disappeared — in the 1940s. The mining claim was abandoned."

"And what about the other brother?"

"We don't know what happened to him. He seems to have disappeared too. I can find no record of him."

She sat back and looked at him. For the first time, she seemed excited. A young girl peeked through the wrinkles and pouches of middle age. “My father went away. I remember my uncles saying he promised to come back and marry her, and they’d be rich. She waited and waited while the village ridiculed her, until finally she believed them that she was nothing to him but an Indian squaw. But —”

Her eyes snapped wide. She set her cup down and hurried out of the room. He heard her thumping around overhead and a moment later she called for his help to drag a wooden crate down the rickety stairs from the attic. Both of them held their breath as she pried it open on the living-room floor.

Inside it was packed to the brim with a young woman’s memories. Beaded pouches, dried and curled with age, an old bearskin hat, caribou hide boots, skirts, jewellery, old books, baby clothes …

“When my mother got TB, her brothers packed up her things instead of burning them and sent them to the nuns who were taking care of me. I think my uncles wanted me to have some connection to her. But the nuns didn’t show them to me for years. They wanted me to forget, or maybe they were superstitious. Maybe I was too. I have hardly looked at this, but now I remember there was a book …”

She began to dig in the box, eventually pulling up a battered hand-stitched leather journal from the bottom. Inside, its yellowed pages were covered in large, awkward print. She ran her fingers over them. “My uncles said my mother was trying to educate herself, because she wanted to please him when he came back. She was afraid he’d be ashamed.”

She gave an odd little smile as she scanned the pages, peeling them back carefully. “She wrote about daily events, ordinary things. Her father shooting a bear, the ice breaking on the river, her dreams. She wrote about being pregnant and having to make new clothes, being sick, wishing my father was there. I didn’t read it all, but I seem to remember …” Her voice trailed off as she stopped to squint at some pages.

“Interesting. She’s keeping track of the CANOL pipeline project.” She frowned, focusing her thoughts inward. “That was a massive oil pipeline built during the Second World War from the Norman Wells oil fields to Alaska, to supply the American military with oil.”

Chris felt a surge of excitement. Was this a lead he could trace? “Right. It only lasted a couple of years, didn’t it?”

“The war ended. And it was an environmental and financial fiasco. Oils spills, forest fires, no permits or assessments. I wonder why she —?” She bent her head back to the book. “My mother even tracked the movement of the workers. She worried about the dangers to the crews from the cold or lack of food. Oh! Here she says, ‘Good news, the war is over. I can’t wait. How long?’ And here again ‘The pipeline is closed. How long now?’”

She raised her head, looking pale and moved. “By the end, she thought he had abandoned her. But what if something happened? What if everything she believed was wrong? What if my father died on the pipeline?”

“I can check. There should be records of that,” Chris said.

"Would you?" She smiled and took the leather book over to the sofa. Sitting back down, she laid it on the table beside her. "I will read this in more depth later. But I thank you for this. It's an odd feeling to have one's past defined."

He nodded. His eyes strayed back to the box and to the little pouch of jewellery inside. He picked it up and fingered through the trinkets, stopping when he came to a stone roughly the size of a cherry pit. It was rough and oddly shaped, out of place among the cheap glass and painted baubles around it. But held up to the light, he could see, glinting through the dark exterior, a deep, rich red.

He looked up, his heart racing. "Do you think Victor could have looked in this crate?"

"I don't see why." She snatched the stone back with alarm. "I doubt he even knows it's here. He has no interest in our past."

Chris could barely hold back his excitement as he left Isabelle's home. He'd been careful not to reveal his suspicion to her for fear she might tell Victor about his visit and their discovery of the journal. If he was to have any leverage against Victor, he needed the element of surprise.

Like all mothers, Isabelle wanted to believe the best of her son, but all Chris's instincts were screaming that Victor had not only snooped in his mother's attic but he'd figured out the significance of the journal and the rough red stone. Had he connected them to the Lasalle brothers and the old mining claim? Had he figured out that his own grandfather might well be one of the Lasalles? If so, then he knew Scott was a cousin, perhaps even before he'd met the young man in the bar.

By then it was noon and the streets of Whitehorse were awash in tourists. Every kind of language and accent chattered around him. Japanese, Germans, British, and Scandinavians were everywhere, all soaking up the last of the world's great wilderness. He barely noticed them as he worked away at the puzzle. There were way too many ifs in his theory, way too many gaps that needed to be filled in before he could present it to Nihls or the Ottawa detectives with any confidence.

This theory of Victor and the crate, for example. It provided some clue as to how Victor knew Scott's identity, but it hinged on Victor knowing something of his grandmother's life in Nahanni Butte and of the legend of the Lasalle brothers there.

There was one more lead he should follow before facing down the slippery weasel. He put in a phone call to Fort Simpson and got hold of the number for the band office in Nahanni Butte. It was a bustling, enterprising little village with close ties to Fort Simpson. Its business people were co-operative and always alert.

Chris had met the chief himself on several visits to the local school. The man had been part of the local council for over a quarter century and he knew everything. What he didn't know, he could find out.

Chris had one simple question for him, but with Jim Matou nothing was ever simple. After an exchange of greetings, news, and good wishes Chris eased into it sideways. "How's the busy metropolis, Jim?"

"It's July. Hopping."

"Have you had a visit recently from someone asking about the old days?"

"Lots of interest in the old days recently."

"I mean about mining and prospecting."

"People from all over come to our village in the summer. We teach them about the traditional ways."

"But anyone in the winter? From Whitehorse, say."

"Maybe." Chris could almost see Matou leaning back in his chair, enjoying the game. "There were questions about my family, the Konisentes, the other first families here — how did we get along with the white trappers and big game hunters. Especially the prospectors."

"Who was asking these questions?"

"A party came in March, not the usual time for visitors, wanted to talk to the elders about their treatment by the whites. Not the residential school stuff, they weren't interested in that, but the village. How much the whites mixed with us, and with our women. One of them was a student from the university, doing research. The elders said they got pretty personal, wanted to see documents like birth and marriage certificates."

Chris's excitement stirred. "Whose documents?"

Matou paused, then dropped the playful tone. "Is this about that Lasalle kid who disappeared?"

"Could be. What happened?"

"Yeah, these guys were asking about the Lasalle brothers. One of the great legends of the river, they said, trying to act all casual. Did anyone in Nahanni Butte ever meet them? Know anything about what happened to them? Of course we did. The Lasalle brothers spent lots of time in the community every spring and fall. Traded furs, picked up supplies. This was before the park and all the tourists. It wasn't really a town like today, more like a trading post and a few tents."

"Jim, whose documents did they look at?"

"They talked to my mother, who was a young woman at the time. She told me they were very curious if any of her girlfriends got cozy with the Lasalles."

"And?" Chris pressed. He sensed the minutes slipping away from him.

"She told me the same she told them. Her friend Nicolette got pregnant by one of the brothers and he promised to come back for her. Nicolette always believed he would, but she died waiting. Took the fight right out of her, waiting for that bastard to come back for her."

"Which brother?"

"Not the one disappeared in the bush. He was the shy one, my mother said. Always lonely for his wife, never mixed with the village girls. No, this was the one went to work on the CANOL pipeline. Guess the big money and all those city girls took his mind off her."

Chris thought fast. It was a small piece of the puzzle; someone was trying to confirm the existence of Gaetan's child. But the inquiry had occurred in March, after Scott's confrontation with Victor, not before.

Jim's voice broke into his thoughts. "I think they were interested in the mine. The research was just an excuse to talk to the elders, to find someone who was close to the Lasalles. They didn't know where the mine was, you see. I bet they were hoping we knew. They sure asked my mother enough questions about it."

"Who, Jim?"

"Some big mining guy from Whitehorse. I remember my mother thought it was funny. Whitehorse, Whitehead. She didn't like him much. Indian but not interested in our traditional ways at all."

"And the other guy? Was his name Lasalle?"

"Never got his name, just kept in the background taking notes. He was supposed to be researching the elders. Could have been the Lasalle kid, but Whitehead seemed more interested in the old family connections than he was."

This time Chris did not bother to play the nice guy. He didn't phone ahead for an appointment either. With Sergeant Doran in tow, he marched straight out to Victor Whitehead's workplace, waved his badge, and demanded to speak to him.

Victor wasn't there, the secretary informed him.

Chris checked his watch. One o'clock. He asked where Victor usually had lunch. The secretary hesitated but before she could answer, another co-worker bellowed over the top of a partition in the open office room. "He took the rest of the day off."

Frustrated, the two officers drove to his home, a large, rambling house in one of the expensive new developments nestled in the hills west of town.

"Huh. Looks like we don't pay our public servants enough," Chris said as they pulled into the drive, which was empty. The three-car garage door was closed.

Doran grunted. "He's pro-development, and those guys can be very grateful."

Chris shot him a sharp look. "Pay-offs?"

"Did I say that?" Doran laughed. "Nothing's been proven, but then no one is looking too closely either. Especially not with the economy in the shape it's in. Anything that brings jobs and money to the north is a good thing, right? Can't say I blame them."

The two cops walked up the expensive stone path and rang the bell. No answer. They rang again. Still no answer. Because they were there, they walked around the house to peer in windows. The blinds were drawn tight on most of them, but at the rear they found a stone patio with a built-in barbeque and a seating area of rattan sofas and chairs. The patio door had no covering. Chris shielded his eyes from the sun's glare and peered through the glass. Inside, he could make out a huge room with the latest in big-screen TV, leather furniture, and slate floors. The room had none of the scattered newspapers, clothes, or dishes he would have predicted from a bachelor's pad, but in the middle of the slate floor was a neat stack of sweaters, socks, and rain gear. A pair of knee-high rubber boots stood beside the stack and a hooded Gore-Tex jacket was slung over a chair. Was Victor packing to go somewhere?

Chris stepped back, puzzled.

"He's probably off running errands," Doran said. "We could wait. These look like mighty comfy chairs."

Chris wavered. The booze and lack of sleep were catching up with him. He knew if he sank into a chair he'd be snoring in an instant. But time was running out on his trip to Whitehorse. His tight-ass boss was expecting him back that evening. "We'll come back. I have another inquiry to make. If you lend me the cruiser, I'll drop you back at the office and swing by in a couple of hours."

Doran had Chris drop him off at McDonalds instead. Chris left him ordering a bacon double cheeseburger combo and headed back onto the road. It turned out that the outfitter Scott had used was in the heart of the historic downtown, right on the edge of the Yukon River and a mere half dozen blocks from the RCMP. Feeling conspicuously official in the RCMP cruiser, Chris left it in the police lot and walked down to the river, where he joined the throngs on the waterfront walkway. Kayaks and canoes were stacked at the water's edge and outside the outfitter's itself. Inside, the store was packed with adventure enthusiasts browsing the aisles for the latest gadgets and space-age clothing. At the desk, every clerk was occupied, but Chris spotted a glass-fronted office at the back of the store, where a couple of men were bent over a computer screen. There was no sign on the window but Chris assumed one of them would be the manager.

He headed toward them. When he was about ten feet from the door, one of the men looked up and pointed through the window at something in the store. Chris stopped in his tracks and ducked behind a rack of life jackets. The man nodded and returned to the conversation. Chris watched from his hiding place as the two of them — outfitter and customer — worked their way through an online order form.

What the hell was Victor Whitehead doing in a wilderness outfitter's store?

White Horse, April 14, 1944

Dear Guy,

Your letters take an eternity to arrive! Every day I wait for the post. Will this winter never end? Thirty below for days on end, without a ray of sunshine to lift the spirits! William has been sick with the grip for weeks, and I daren't take him outside. I sent Mrs. Quinn packing, which may have been a mistake since now I can't get out at all. But the wretched woman disagreed with every aspect of my childcare, from his feeding to his crying. He cried every night but she would not let me go to him. I admit that it was exhausting but I cannot think that such callous disregard for a crying infant is character-building.

I am counting the days until you are back home, but I am giving you fair warning. This is the last winter I spend alone in this dreary, frigid, small-minded town. Nothing but rations, secrets, drunken Americans, and horrible news of the war.

Impatient for your return, I remain,
Your loving wife, Lydia

CHAPTER FIFTEEN

Nahanni, July 19

Green had intended only to rest. It was their third day on the river and they had pulled ashore for lunch. While the others inspected the equipment and unpacked the food, he had crawled onto the shore, propped himself against a boulder, and shut his eyes. His hands and feet were blistered raw and every muscle in his upper body screamed, but he was so exhausted that he promptly fell asleep. The murmur of voices blended with the soft hiss of the current as he drifted into oblivion.

He awoke with a start and blinked in confusion. Clouds had blown over the sun, bringing a chill to the air. A plate of bannock, beef jerky, and dried fruit sat on the rock beside him, along with the bear horn. The canoes were repacked and lined up at the water's edge ready to go, but the beach was deserted. As far as he could see, there was nothing but brooding pewter skies, endless rows of jagged spruce, and the silty grey river. He was alone. An irrational fear shot through him.

He shouted, but his voice was dwarfed by the emptiness. Nothing but a faint shred of sound echoing down the valley. He gripped the bear horn and scanned the shore for grizzlies. The wolves would only come at night but the grizzlies were unpredictable. He tried to picture the lunch spot on the map. They had finally reached a lull in the rock gardens. Up ahead the river was wider and deeper, but they were still miles away from a cabin that might provide protection from either beast.

The last set of rapids had been a nightmare. He and Sullivan had hit a rock and flipped the canoe early on. Green had ridden a long, terrifying surf through the boiling foam, struggling to keep his head above water, his feet downstream, and his sights on the path ahead. He had no idea where Sullivan and the canoe were until he crashed into some rocks and scrambled to his feet in time to see his canoe sail past, miraculously upright again but sideways. Sullivan followed, hanging on to the tow rope.

Downstream, Jethro and Elliott were standing on the gravel shoreline ready to toss the rescue bags. Jethro had managed to snag the canoe and clip it before it and Sullivan disappeared around a bend. The river broadened where a small creek fed in, and the gravel bar was wide and flat.

"Well done!" Elliott had shouted, with a hint of disbelief in his laughter. "We're almost through. A bite to eat, and then we tackle the last two class IVs."

Now Green glanced up at the sky. The clouds were darkening to the west, skimming low over the mountaintops. Their gear had barely begun to dry out, and now it threatened to be soaked in an afternoon storm. Where were the others? They needed to get back on the river to face those rapids before the weather became impossible. Anxiously he scanned his surroundings for movement.

Just downriver, he spotted a motionless figure sitting on top of a bluff. At first he thought the man was catching a snooze until he realized he was looking through binoculars at the mountains ahead. Green gathered his lunch and picked a path down the creek bed and up the side of the bluff. As he came over the rise, he saw Sullivan and Jethro sitting on the ground with the topographical map spread out before them. Elliott sat on an adjacent rock.

Elliott put down his binoculars. "How are the blisters holding up?"

Green flexed his hands beneath the bandages and grimaced as pain shot through them.

"I'll dress them again before we leave. And you should put on some more bug spray after that swim." Elliott held out the spray can.

Green took the spray and eased his aching body down onto the rock beside them to apply it. "Here you go, you little buggers. Martini time."

Elliott laughed. "You could always try bear fat, like Jethro here. Jethro's been doing some thinking."

Green looked at the small, quiet guide, who hadn't joined in the laughter. "What?"

It was Elliott who spoke. "You know how there's been no sign of them farther down the river. No one has found any trace of their camp either. No tents, tarps, canoe. That's a lot of gear to lose. Even if the remaining canoe dumped and everything was lost —" He held up his hand to forestall Green's protest. "Someone should have spotted something. Not everything would sink to the bottom of the river."

Green turned to Jethro. The man's unreadable stillness irritated him. As if he had secrets he was unwilling to share. "So what have you been thinking?"

"They have left the river," Jethro replied quietly.

"What? And carried all that stuff inland? Over that?" Green nodded to the thick forest and steep mountains to their right.

Jethro bent his head and traced his finger over the map. "No. They set up a base camp on one of these creeks, out of sight of the main river."

"Why?"

Jethro and Elliott exchanged looks. The Native's face was still inscrutable, and once again he left the talking to Elliott. "Probably precisely so they wouldn't be spotted from the river." Elliott leaned over the map and pointed to a series of squiggly lines. "If they camped in one of these bigger creeks, they would have access to these mountains behind while at the same time being invisible to other parties passing by on the river. We're here." He pointed to a spot on the map. "And the coordinates of the mining claim are around here." He traced a large circle through the mountains inland. It seemed to encompass miles.

"But we don't even know if we have the right coordinates. What about those directions to Watson and Dawson?" Green squinted at the map. "That's a lot of territory to cover!"

"Not all the creeks are good for setting up camp," Jethro said. "We're almost through the serious whitewater now. I suggest we check out each creek as we go downriver."

Green eyed all the lines on the map with dismay. "But that will take hours."

"Not as bad as if we canoe on past without seeing them." Jethro folded the map and stood up. "This is our best shot. The official searchers will find them if they're on the Nahanni somewhere. But if they're hiding their base camp inland, the planes might not spot them."

Green turned to Elliott. "What do you think?"

"I think Jethro is right. There are probably dozens of creeks feeding into the river through these mountains. Most are not navigable, some even dry in summer. But they can make a good pathway, and we might miss them unless we check."

Green swivelled to Sullivan, who was seated cross-legged on the grass, stroking the dog's shaggy fur. She lay quietly with her eyes shut, as unreadable as her master. Sullivan gave Green a long stare before he nodded. "They're the experts, Mike."

Reluctantly Green capitulated. But silently, he cursed. Cursed his aching body, his clumsiness, his complete ignorance. This wilderness made him feel small and weak and incompetent. Feelings he'd not had to face in a long time.

They woke up the next morning to light rain and paddled in the chilly drizzle without much conversation. Short forays into shallow creek beds yielded no signs of a camp. The mist lay low over the spruce trees and the river was as damp and gloomy as Green's mood. It was wide and leisurely now, its slopes and bends seemed endless. Jethro and Elliott were mere specks up ahead, scouting the riverbanks for traces of camps. At each meander, Green lost sight of them altogether.

The river silt was a dull hiss below their hull, but gradually through the noise Green became aware of a louder roar. One he'd come to know.

He looked back at Sullivan nervously. "More rapids?"

Sullivan shook his head. "There aren't supposed to be any more along here."

They rounded the bend and saw the other two canoes pulled up on the gravel shoreline to river right. Beyond them Green could make out the white tips of churning water. His stomach clenched. Only once Sullivan had steered the canoe to shore did they see the other river pouring in from the right. A wide, flat river delta lay just beyond.

"This is the Little Nahanni," Elliott said as Green and Sullivan hauled their canoe up beside the others. "We'll camp just in there, grab some lunch, and then we'll explore up here on foot."

Green felt a surge of excitement. The Little Nahanni River was near the boundary of the mining claim. "You think they went up there?"

"It's one possible route they could have taken up into the mountains back there. There were all sorts of mining exploration up there in the past."

Green eyed the tumbling water dubiously. "But surely they couldn't canoe up that."

Elliott shrugged. "An expert could. You can paddle the easy parts and line your canoe up through the fast parts. But people canoe down it all the time. Helluva lot of fun, actually."

"Down, yes, but ..." Green struggled to slow down his impatience. These were the search experts, not him. As Sullivan kept reminding him.

As usual, Jethro had said nothing to that point but now he handed Green a thermos of hot soup. "Another thing. On the other side of those mountains there's an old mining road. Not much of it left anymore, but you can still get out that way on foot." He pointed into the snow-capped mountain range in the distance. It was the longest speech he had made all day.

"On foot?" Green sized up the mountains. "But it's got to be fifty miles!"

Jethro shrugged. "Locals used to walk that easily. Take a month to walk out from their traplines in the bush in the spring. But it's not fifty miles. Maybe only a few days' walk to the point where an ATV could manage it. There's an operating mine back up in there, and they've fixed up some of the road."

For the first time in days, Green felt a surge of hope. He turned to Elliott. "We should inform the SAR team. They should keep an eye on that road."

"Trust me, they're on top of it. If the kids come out through there, they'll know."

After lunch they began to hike up the Little Nahanni River. The light drizzle continued. Between the steep slopes and slippery rocks, progress was slow and frustrating. At times they had to hack a path through dense brush and other times they splashed through the shallow water's edge. Smaller, nimbler, and more experienced, Jethro went ahead with his dog to check out the trail for signs of other people. He had retreated back into his silence. The other three straggled along in single file, their mood like the mist hanging heavy around them. After an hour, Green's whole body was scratched by spiky spruce branches, his clothing was soaked, and his spirits sodden.

But he trudged on. If somewhere back in here was the mining claim and an exit road, he would walk through fire to find them.

Until they reached an impasse. Rounding a bend in the river, Green could see a canyon cutting through the mountain ahead of them. Nothing but sheer rock and rushing water. Then, high above them on top of a cliff, he saw Jethro searching the distant peak with binoculars. Elliott held up his hand and Green stopped. After a few minutes Jethro turned to go back into the bush. Still Elliott waited without speaking until Jethro emerged from the forest, barely ten feet in front of them. He walked slowly, peering at the branches and ground carefully.

"They didn't come this way," he said.

"How do you know?" Green asked.

Jethro merely looked at him before pushing past and heading back down the river.

"They would have had to set up their base camp here," Elliott explained. "If not earlier. And they would have taken that path on foot. If Jethro saw no tracks, there are none."

"But it's raining! And animals could have disturbed the trail."

No one replied. Green looked up at the tumbling river. "We've wasted the whole fucking day!"

"Mike, shut up," Sullivan muttered as he turned to follow Jethro. The others trudged back without a word.

That evening, while the rest pitched camp, Jethro stripped a willow branch and, without a word, headed along the riverbank with Tatso at his heels. A short time later he reappeared with three large trout. Elliott cheered and stored the dehydrated stew he'd been preparing back into its container.

A small grin sneaked across Jethro's face. He gutted and filleted the fish with a few swift knife strokes, and within minutes the aroma of frying fish and wood smoke filled the air. Green's stomach contracted. He realized he was famished. As he polished off two helpings of fish and bannock, he felt his tension slip away.

After the dishes had been washed and the food safely stored, they gathered around the fire, drooping with fatigue. It was past ten o'clock. The valley was still misty grey, but shafts of sunlight lit the clouds with gold. Elliott rummaged in his backpack and pulled out a bottle of single malt Scotch. Sullivan whistled. Elliott poured a generous measure into their plastic mugs.

As the Scotch burned down Green's throat, it brought tears to his eyes. He took a deep breath. "Sorry for being such a jerk today. This is tiring, discouraging work, but I know we all want the same thing. Jethro, you're the expert, and I'm so damn grateful you volunteered to help. Brian here will tell you I can be a real pain in the ass sometimes —"

"Sometimes?" Sullivan said. Smiles broke out.

"When I fix my mind on a goal, it's hard for me to set it aside or listen to others' points of view. But you two — Ian and Jethro — are lifesavers." He looked into his Scotch glass, mostly empty now. "Don't ever think I don't appreciate what you're doing."

Elliott leaned over to top up his glass. Green hesitated, tempted, before moving his glass out of reach. "It certainly takes the edge off all this crap, but I'd better stop. One more sip and I might say something dumb."

"Impossible," Sullivan said.

Elliott grinned. For a man of action, he seemed remarkably at ease with sentiment. "A lot happens around these campfires," he said. "What is said here stays here. I have two kids myself. Grown and married now, but you never stop worrying about them. If it was me in your shoes …"

Jethro glanced up. He was sitting by the edge of the camp, drinking his own tea rather than Scotch. He looked far less at ease with sentiment. "We will find them. Tomorrow we go on. There are other creeks. Other places to hide a camp."

Green awoke the next morning with a fresh optimism and a surprisingly clear head. As if in concert, the rain had stopped and the sun was breaking through the clouds in the east. They were back in the canoes by eight o'clock, with their damp rain gear spread over the packs to dry in the sun. The river was muddy with the silt from the Little Nahanni, but its flow was steady and deep. Occasional branches bobbed downstream beside them. Green and Sullivan drifted on the current and focused on watching the shores. Not just scanning the muddy gravel bars but peering into the dense forest as well. If Scott's party was trying to avoid detection, they would camp inland under cover of the trees.

In almost no time, the next inlet was upon them. Smaller and shallower than the Little Nahanni River, it rumbled through a narrow gap in the steep banks. Hugging to river right, Jethro paddled hard through the gap toward a far bend. Green and Sullivan drew their canoe alongside Elliott's.

"What's in there?" Green asked. "Looks pretty small."

"It is, at this point. But there's a —"

A shout up ahead stopped him. Jethro. At the second shout, this one sharp with excitement, the three of them dug in their paddles and fought the current through the gap. Green was panting hard by the time they rounded the bend and found themselves in an open area with a cliff on one side and a flat expanse of mud on the far side. Tangled in a mess of mud and debris was a jumble of brightly coloured gear. Jethro raced his canoe across and ran it up on the beach.

Green could barely speak. Joy and terror shot through him. Joy that maybe they had finally found the camp. That everything wasn't at the bottom of the river. That maybe he was one step closer to finding Hannah. Terror because the camp had been obliterated. Limbs, boulders, and whole trees were strewn across the gravel beach, their leaves still green even in death. A canoe had been picked up and tossed halfway into the willow thicket behind, and tarps and dry bags were scattered.

Everything was covered in mud. Backpacks had been ripped open, clothes and supplies hung in the trees.

Green's voice stuck in his throat. He felt a gentle squeeze as Sullivan placed his hand upon his arm. Sullivan found the words he couldn't.

"What the hell happened? A bear? Caribou stampede?"

Elliott shook his head. "Last week's storm. Caused a flash flood down this valley. Probably swept right across this beach, and everything that wasn't nailed down ..."

Green found his voice. "What does that mean?"

Elliott pointed to the snow-capped mountains that towered to the south. "All the rain that falls in those mountains flows down into these creeks. If it's a lot of rain in a short time, as it was last week, the water coming down this creek can triple in volume within hours. Less. It's got nowhere to go but down that canyon and across the flat bars like this."

"But ..." Green groped for hope, "there would be a warning, right? They'd see the water rising and they'd move to higher ground."

Jethro had been picking his way carefully toward the woods beyond the beach. He looked back and merely shook his head.

"Last week's storm was in the middle of the night," Elliott said. "If they were inside the tent, sleeping ..." His voice trailed off, leaving the worst unsaid. Somewhere beneath that pile of mud and debris, four young bodies might be buried in their beds.

* * *

Elliott clambered to the top of the canyon and phoned in a report to the SAR team, requesting assistance in the form of digging equipment, extra manpower, and paramedic support. Planes could not land in the area, but a helicopter could do a drop or pickup. Green listened as he argued with Bugden over jurisdiction, because the location was outside the current park boundaries and therefore under RCMP rather than Parks Canada control. Even out in this wilderness, the fucking red tape ruled, Green thought.

In the end, Bugden agreed to liaise with the RCMP, but indicated it would take at least twenty-four hours and a hefty chunk of local resources to organize a search. He hoped the missing party had insurance.

Green stared at the piles of debris, fuming. Every hour counted. What if Hannah was trapped under there? What if she could hear him but hadn't the strength to call out?

"We can't wait," he snapped once Elliott had reported on the call. "What if someone is alive under there?"

"That's unlikely," Elliott said softly. "It's been over a week. With the cold nights and with no food —"

"They could get water, and that's the most important thing. Earthquake victims survive for days!"

Jethro had walked to the far end of the mud flat with Tatso, where the two stood motionless. Green realized he was sniffing the wind. Green's skin crawled. He knew the smell Jethro was trying to detect. He forced himself to take a short, tentative sniff. Mud, musk, and the tang of spruce, but not a whiff of body decay. He allowed only a tingle of relief to sneak through his fear. Jethro probably had a much better nose. Certainly the dog did. He watched as both turned and walked back along the water's edge. Jethro seemed to be studying the flow of water and the pattern of debris on the shore.

"They would have drowned," he said. "To move these heavy trees and boulders this far up onto the shore, the water had to be very high. All this gravel flat would have been covered with water, probably for almost a day before it started to recede."

A chill of dread coursed through Green anew. He fought for a toehold of hope. "But it's still possible they found a shelter or an air bubble. You didn't smell their bodies, did you? We have to search!"

Jethro started to shake his head but Elliott intervened. "You're right. No point doing nothing while we're waiting. Let's start digging."

After rounding up sturdy branches, pots, utensils, the hatchet, and the camp saw to aid in the digging, they began to tackle the wreckage. For hours they searched. With a process to focus on, Green could distract himself from the horrific possibilities of the end result. He insisted that the whole operation be treated like a crime scene, with careful excavation, notes, and photos at each new step so that afterward they might be able to piece together what had happened. No one dissuaded him.

The boulders and the uprooted trees presented the greatest challenge. With no means to dislodge them, the team dug around and under them. It was slow, tedious work and often the surface debris was cleared away to reveal nothing underneath.

Out of the muddy, rocky mess, they unearthed tarps, packs, life jackets, and canoe paddles, as well as the contents of bags broken open and strewn around. But they did not find a single body part. Each new discovery was cleaned and laid out in the sun on the riverbank. By the end of the day the remaining canoe was the only thing that had not been checked out. It lay pinned upside down beneath a massive tree trunk. The cavity beneath it was large enough to conceal — and possibly protect — a person, but all their efforts to push, pull, and pry it away had been in vain. Elliott had even cut a hole in the hull and peered through, but could see nothing through the debris.

The others paused for rest and food. Elliott was doctoring blisters, but Green couldn't relax. "We need to get underneath that," he said to Sullivan.

Sullivan was sitting on a rock, propped against the canoe and looking tired and discouraged. "It won't budge."

"We can rig up a pulley by wrapping ropes around several trees so we can pull the tree off."

"There is no one underneath," Jethro said.

"I don't see how you —"

The guide gestured to his dog, who sat peacefully at his side. "She would tell us."

Words stuck in Green's throat. Furious, he grabbed a few lengths of rope and headed over to the fallen tree. The others watched for awhile as he fed the rope around the trunk and wound the other end around a nearby spruce. Soon the others set aside their food and joined the effort.

It took all their ropes and numerous configurations but the large tree finally began to shift. An inch or two at a time, until Green and Sullivan were able to pull the broken canoe out.

There was nothing underneath but sand.

Green sank back on the ground. He wanted to weep. "Where the fuck are they?"

"Swept down the river," Elliott said. "I think that's what happened to the turquoise canoe and the backpack we found. The canoe didn't dump, it was broken right here by the force of the flood. Probably dashed against the rocks and then swept out into the main river."

Green was shaking his head. "Okay, I buy that, but all four bodies? Why hasn't anyone found a single body floating on the river?"

"They wouldn't have been wearing life jackets," Elliott said. "They could still be on the bottom."

"One of them would have washed ashore. Surely! Along with more gear."

Jethro had left the group again and was walking through the debris they had salvaged and spread out in the sun. They had opened all the dry bags and sifted through the contents for identification.

"Their tents are missing," he said, so quietly that the others had to go closer. "And their sleeping bags and personal backpacks."

"You're right," Elliott said. "Half the camping equipment is missing."

Jethro nodded. "And none of it has shown up downstream."

"They weren't here!" Green cried. Long-abandoned hope slammed through him. "The night the storm hit, they weren't even here. That's it! They left their canoes and some of their heavy gear here, but they've gone."

Excitedly the four of them scanned the mountains, as if certain the four small figures would be visible perched on some distant slope.

Green grabbed Elliott's arm. "We've got to figure out exactly where that mine is."

Elliott was already pulling out his phone. "I'll call this in to SAR. They can do flyovers and start concentrating their search area."

Jethro called his dog to his side. "I'll see if we can pick up a trail from the perimeter. A lot will be washed away but maybe I can figure out what direction they headed."

Juggling his GPS, maps, and phone, Elliott had headed across the rocks to the canyon top where he could get a signal. Green could see him on the phone reporting in to Bugden and tracing routes on his map. Afterward he stayed where he was, his head bent over his map. Green watched with mounting excitement as Elliott trained his binoculars on a distant peak.

Sullivan had made himself useful brewing fresh, strong coffee, and he brought a cup over to Green. "We're closing in, Mike. We're going to find her."

Green fought a sudden tightness in his throat. "When I saw this mess here, I can tell you ..."

"Me too. But you're right, they're off somewhere. Completely oblivious to the fact we're all scared out of our wits and half the territory is looking for them. When we do find them, do I have your permission to personally strangle her?"

Green gripped his cup in two hands to steady himself. He sipped his coffee, which was strong enough to straighten hair. Shook his head. "You'll have to stand in line."

"How about Scott?"

"Absolutely. Although I suggest beheading. But Hannah ... I think I'm just going to hug her and maybe never let her go."

"Yeah. I hear you."

They watched in silence as Elliott began his descent toward them, jumping nimbly down the rocky slope. He was holding his map in one hand and binoculars in the other. As he drew nearer, Green could see the excitement on his face.

"I think I know where they went!" he cried when he was close enough. He flung himself down on the gravel beside them and spread his map out on the upturned canoe. "Those words that were handwritten on the will? That we thought were directions? I think it's a coordinate. I think Scott's grandfather, or whoever pencilled the notes in the margin, was trying to pinpoint a location but in a way that wasn't obvious. A clue to be deciphered."

He held out the paper on which they had written the claim number and the mysterious code:

> 60 to Dawson, 20 miles to Nahanni, 128 days 30 miles to Watson.

"If we use the numbers and the first letter of the words, we get sixty degrees, twenty minutes north, by one hundred twenty-eight degrees, thirty minutes west."

Green grabbed the map. As he traced the measurements, his hope faded. "But that's way off! The one hundred twenty-eight longitude is close, but sixty latitude is on northern Alberta."

"Exactly, but what if we read it as 'sixty-two' and 'twenty-two' instead? If I'm not mistaken, that coordinate is the top of that mountain right over there." He pointed to a tall, rounded mountain inland from the river. It loomed in the sunlight, smooth, barren, and serene.

"That's where they've gone."

CHAPTER SIXTEEN

Edmonton, July 13, 1944

Mon Cher Guillaume,
I'm sorry I have not written, but I have not had good news before this. The pipeline is completed now, so they don't have need of workers anymore. I have a plan for a new job, and if it works, I will make much more money.

I hope you are well, and the trapping was good this winter. Does all go well with Lydia and the baby? I long to see Nicolette and my new daughter, who is named Isabelle after Maman. I miss them more each day. I think I will settle in Nahanni Butte after the war. That feels more like my home than New Brunswick or Whitehorse ever did.

I promise to send money to Northern Rubies as soon as possible so we can build up the capital for a new exploration. Can you give some to Nicolette? I don't know when I can write to you again, but I will when I can.

Try to be patient. I am doing what I can for our future. Don't tell Maman about Nicolette.

As always, P'tit Gaetan.

Whitehorse, July 21

Despite a very late start to his day, Chris was having trouble mustering any sense of urgency. His body was singing and his mind a delightful, hazy mush. He'd been wakened early enough by the soft nuzzle of lips on his shoulder, moving down to the small of his back. He'd rolled over and she had not missed a beat. His navel, his thighs, his knees.... When she reached his toes, he'd wrapped his fingers in her long tumbling hair and drawn her to him.

They had not left the bed until almost eleven, when Olivia had glanced at her watch with a gasp. "I gotta go!"

"Where?"

"Another meeting. Boring academic stuff."

He pulled her back. "It's Saturday."

"I know, but my prof is in town on some consultant gig and he wants me along. Corporate brunch." She made a face. "I'm window dressing. Besides, don't you have cop stuff to do today?"

He sighed. She was right. He had managed to persuade Sergeant Nihls that he needed another day in Whitehorse in order to follow up on Victor Whitehead. The truth was, however, that he could have wrapped up that lead yesterday and been out of town before sundown. The promise of Olivia had kept him here.

He hadn't quite believed she would actually show up last night, so he'd had a thousand excuses stockpiled in his mind if she hadn't. She couldn't get the extra night off, her meeting ran late, her professor had other plans for her. That last one scared him the most. Admittedly, he didn't know much about postgraduate school or research consultants, but he could think of no plausible reason a professor would insist on flying his graduate student all the way to Whitehorse to hold his hand during meetings. Unless he wanted to do more than hold her hand.

If so, how could Chris hope to compete?

True to her promise, however, Olivia had bounced into the hotel bar only five minutes late. When she enveloped him in a kiss, he vowed to keep his childish insecurities to himself. Even if the professor had entertained other hopes for this business trip, she had obviously dashed them.

He fought back a renewed stab of jealousy now as he watched her pull on her jeans and zip them over her flat, sexy belly. He reminded himself she had chosen him last night over the professor, who was rich, powerful, and way smarter than he was. That morning, on a scale of one to ten, Olivia was a twelve. Everything else, including Sergeant Nihls's orders and Victor Whitehead's meeting with the outfitter, had plummeted below one.

"I do," he replied. "But I don't know when I'll see you again. Will you be still here tonight?" He had no idea how he'd swing that with Nihls, but he'd find a way.

Placing her finger to his lips, she shook her head. “But don’t worry, flyboy. Next time I’m in Fort Simpson, you won’t escape me.”

“Lunch at least?” He winced. He was whining.

She laughed. “Wasn’t that lunch? But maybe coffee later, if I can get away. What do you have planned today?”

“I have to touch base with Whitehead. I missed him yesterday.”

“Oh, right. About his relationship to Scott.”

“Yes. I talked to his mother yesterday, and it looks like he might have known about Scott all along. Looks like he might have known about the rubies too.”

Her eyes flew open. “How?”

“That’s what I have to check.” He grinned. “And if you meet me for coffee …”

She sat on the edge of the bed and slid her feet into her sandals, wiggling her toes. “You devil, you. Is that a bribe, officer?”

“Absolutely.”

“I’ll see what I can do.”

She was out the hotel room door in a flash, her musky scent lingering in the air with the memories. He showered and dressed in a daze, forcing himself to put one foot in front of the other to begin his day.

His first stop was Isabelle’s house. Sergeant Nihls had torn a strip off him for neglecting to take the red rock sample with him. “Of all the fool things, Constable!” he’d said. The phone line had practically snapped taut at the urgency of his voice. “We need to have the damn thing analyzed.”

“I don’t see how that’s relevant, sir.”

"It's relevant to Scott Lasalle's intentions, Constable! And, as such, to his possible disappearance. I've got half our SAR annual budget committed to this thing, an armed forces helicopter coming all the way from Winnipeg, and if this thing is going to blow up in my face, I damn well want to know so I can pull the plug!"

Put that way, Chris could see the sergeant's point. If Nihls dragged not only his own staff, but civilians, park staff, and even the goddamn Canadian army into this search, his ass would be in a sling if it proved a wild goose chase. Nihls might be stuck commanding remote northern detachments for the rest of his career.

So Chris put Victor Whitehead's follow-up on hold and headed back to Isabelle Lasalle's house. This time she didn't offer him tea or cookies. She barely invited him in.

"I really think, if you have more questions, you should talk to my son directly."

"And I will, Mrs. Lasalle," he replied, trying to keep his friendly smile in place. Why was she frowning? Why was she blocking the doorway? There was no car in the drive, no sign that Victor was there. "This is not about your son. This is about the contents of that crate. I wonder if the police might borrow it for a week or so."

"Why?"

"Well, I'm just a constable at a local detachment. Our experts would like to examine your mother's diary and her other personal effects. To see if there are any more clues about what's going on."

"About Scott Lasalle, you mean."

"Yes. About his disappearance."

She folded her arms. "You want to test the stone, don't you."

He didn't reply but his expression must have given him away. "No," she said.

"Pardon?"

"No. I won't allow you to analyze the stone."

"Why not?"

"Firstly, I don't like being misled. Secondly, I don't like being taken for a fool. And thirdly, I don't want to know if the damn thing is a ruby, and I don't want anyone else to know."

A slow flush crept up his neck. "I'm sorry. I didn't mean to mislead you."

"Yes, you did."

He bit his lip. There was no escaping, except through the truth. "My boss did. I'm just the poor guy delivering the request."

He was hoping she would laugh, but she grew red. Her eyes sparked. Stepping out onto the porch, she slammed the door shut behind her.

"Think for yourself, Constable! There are plenty of powerful people in the north, people who hire and fire cops, people who would love to see this part of the country opened up. They claim there's a fortune under the ground up here. Enough to make us all rich and maybe even save the bankrupt south too. They think the territories can be the new Alberta, pave the streets with gold and give every poor little Indian a job. I'm having no part of it."

He'd heard the arguments before, even broken up the fist fights in the bars in Fort Simpson. One side pointed to construction and service jobs for the locals, fat royalties to the First Nations who owned the land, and taxes to the governments. On the other side, the tree huggers, traditionalists, and conservationists argued about chemical leaks, global warming, soil erosion, contaminated watersheds, and the ruined balance of nature. Chris hadn't figured out where he stood on things himself; he only knew the world couldn't stand still.

"The analysis will be confidential," he said. "The results will be known only to you and to the police —"

"And to all the lab workers involved in the test. Don't underestimate the gossip chain up here, Constable. Before the report is even typed, someone will have told their cousin, who will tell their friend. The answer is still no. In fact, frankly I think your boss's rationale for wanting the test done is suspicious."

She was no longer red with outrage but she looked as resolute as ever. He knew he would not budge her. Not without a subpoena, which he had no wish to pursue. Her protest and her suspicions about Nihls's motives had struck a chord. If Nihls really wanted the ruby identified, let him take charge of it.

"Okay, I accept that. But I have to ask you, do you think your son had it analyzed? Do you think he knows whether it's a ruby or not?"

Her shoulders sagged, and the resolute snap vanished from her eyes. "I don't know. I honestly can't say, because I've paid no attention to that crate for years. I hope to hell he didn't, but there was less dust on it than you'd expect. But I want you to know, in case he hasn't got hold of it yet, that I've disposed of it. No one is going to be able to misuse it, ever again."

When Chris phoned in his report, Nihls wasn't as upset as Chris expected him to be. He made a half-hearted stab at reprimanding him.

"Did you ask her where she disposed of it?"

"Well, no, sir," Chris said, flustered. "I didn't think she'd tell me. But the stone is less than a cubic centimetre. You could hide it in plain sight in your river stone walkway and no one would ever find it."

Nihls grunted. "Not so important now anyway. We've located the mispers' camp. Technically, Elliott and the cops from Ottawa located it."

Chris let out a whoop. "That's great news, sir! Are they all right?"

"We have no information at this time, but the camp was extensively buried in a flood. We're sending a recovery team in there in the morning. I can tell you it doesn't look good."

Chris's euphoria died. He asked a few more questions but Nihls had no details. "Do you still want me to follow up with Whitehead, sir?"

"That was your initiative in the first place. But yes, until we have further confirmation on the mispers, carry on."

Chris trudged back down to the waterfront. Much of the glow of the morning had worn off. He had grown to admire Inspector Green's tenacious passion to find his daughter, so to have it end like this weighed heavily.

It being Saturday, the outfitter's store was more crowded than ever. Chris waded through the customers toward the office at the rear. Inside he spotted the man who'd been talking to Victor Whitehead the day before. Chris's uniform announced his presence and his authority even before he knocked on the window. He saw the man frown and close the ledger he was working on before he rose to open the door. Once they'd finished the introductions, he invited Chris to sit.

"Fort Simpson," said the man, who'd identified himself as the owner Quincy Burke. "You're a long way from your jurisdiction."

"Anything to get out of the office," Chris said with a grin. When the man didn't respond, he switched gears. "We're trying to trace the whereabouts of a young man who's gone missing in the Nahanni Park. We have receipts that indicate he purchased supplies at your store." Chris decided to ask about Scott first, hoping Burke would relax enough that he could broach the more sensitive subject of Victor Whitehead.

Burke showed no signs of that. Instead he folded his arms. "What's the man's name?"

"Scott Lasalle. He was here on June 18th."

"There have been a lot of customers in my store since then. Almost all of them purchase or rent equipment."

Chris showed him a photo he'd taken from Scott's Facebook page and described some of the items on the purchase receipt. "Sounds like he bought half your store."

Still the man continued to frown. "And this relates to his disappearance how?"

Chris had not expected resistance and his police antenna went up. "Maybe not at all. But he did not file a trip itinerary, so I'm hoping he discussed his destination and his needs with you. Maybe asked you for advice on what equipment to get."

Burke studied him without blinking for what felt like an eternity. Chris forced himself to hold his gaze. He was used to public suspicion, even antipathy, but sometimes it annoyed the hell out of him. I'm one of the good guys, he wanted to say. I've got no hidden agenda here. I'm helping someone in distress, not threatening to bring down the law on them.

He added a touch of humility. "We don't know where to look for him, and time may be running out."

Abruptly Burke went to his filing cabinet, flipped through it, and yanked out a file overflowing with papers. He searched these until he found the one he wanted, and read it without expression. He was an unusual man, Chris noted. He had curly, carrot red hair, a full beard, and pale blue eyes, yet he had none of the constant animation of the Irish. He was almost Native in his stillness.

"You called about this man last week," he said. "He and his friend rented two canoes for a party of four. I advised them to rent three, for safety reasons and because they had a lot of gear, but his friend said no."

"Anything unusual in that gear?"

"Not really."

Chris sensed a split-second hesitation. "Perhaps a little?"

Burke shook his head. "No. They just didn't seem to see eye to eye. I remember the friend wanted some pretty heavy-duty lighting, enough to light up the entire camp, and a bigger camp tarp than they needed, considering he was skimping on the canoes."

As Chris jotted down the information, his mind was already making connections. Lighting and tarp to protect and illuminate a substantial area. Was Scott planning to take rock samples and test them on the spot?

"Did they have any research equipment? Anything fragile?"

Burke shrugged. "Well, I wouldn't know that. They didn't volunteer much. Didn't talk much at all."

Chris pretended to study his notes. "I was in here yesterday," he began "But you were busy with Victor Whitehead. Someone else I want to talk to. Was he asking about this guy Scott?"

Surprise flitted across Burke's face. "No, why would he?"

"Well ..." Chris tried to keep his voice casual, "Scott is his cousin."

"You're kidding. Really?" Burke blinked a few times. "Then maybe that's what he's doing."

"What do you mean?"

Burke shrugged. He seemed to have abandoned his earlier suspicions. "He was planning a trip. Rented a canoe and a bunch of gear. I was surprised because he's more the city type and he didn't know much about tripping. But maybe he was going to search for Scott."

Chris was in a taxi on his way back to Victor Whitehead's house, determined to talk to the man even if he had to stake out the premises and wait for him, when he received a call from his boss.

"We're calling off the investigation," Nihls said. "You're to return to Fort Simpson ASAP."

"Has the party been found?"

"Negative."

"Have they reported in?"

"Negative."

In the back of the cab, Chris rolled his eyes. He pictured the sergeant in his office, ramrod straight behind his spit-and-polish desk, secretly enjoying this little power trip. "Then why are we calling it off?"

"We have obtained new information."

Silence again. Chris decided not to play anymore. "Sir, I have some new information of my own. Scott Lasalle's cousin Victor Whitehead has an interest in northern development initiatives and it would appear —"

"Yes, I know him. I heard him speak at a conference on the Mackenzie Valley pipeline."

"Well, he may have independently learned about the ruby mine, and he's just rented a bunch of wilderness gear for a river expedition."

"Nothing unusual about that, Constable. This is July, prime holiday time."

"Except he's not the wilderness type. Likes the inside of a smoky bar better."

There was a pause. "What are you thinking? That he's going to meet up with Lasalle on the Nahanni?"

"I don't know yet, sir, but since Scott tried to crack his head open in a bar fight. I don't think their interests are the same."

"Not a police concern, Constable. We have no evidence a crime is being committed."

"No, sir, but I'd like to question Whitehead one last time before I fly back. I know there's been no report of a crime but I think one or more of these parties may be up to no good in the Nahanni. We should know what they're up to, so we can be prepared —"

"It wouldn't matter if they were meeting ET, they're not breaking any laws. And Whitehead is not a guy you want to get on the wrong side of, Constable."

Chris bit back a protest. Nihls's last words held a warning. Whitehead had friends and influence in the upper reaches of power, perhaps even of the senior RCMP itself. So far Nihls had not outright forbidden Chris to question him. It would be wiser not to push his luck.

The taxi had pulled into the drive of Whitehead's expensive home. The drive was empty, the blinds were drawn, and Chris could see no signs of activity. He cursed and checked his watch. Olivia had said she would meet him for coffee between three and four if she could escape from her professor's clutches. If he waited here for Whitehead, possibly in vain, he might miss her.

"Very well, sir. I'll return to base. Are there any other leads I should follow up on before I leave?"

"Negative, Constable." Nihls paused. "The missing party appears to have gone inland in pursuit of this mining claim, so Bugden has called off the search."

"Why would he —?"

"We have no reason to believe they are in distress, and I needn't remind you of the cost of this wild goose chase."

Chris cut short his protest. He knew he was the one who had started the wild goose chase when he spotted the turquoise canoe. It was best not to argue. Once he'd signed off, however, he felt a surge of frustration. There were too many unanswered questions, too many hints of conflict and threat to simply abandon the entire investigation. The answers to many of the questions were tantalizingly within reach. But if he wanted any career in the RCMP, orders from the sergeant could not be ignored.

After double-checking that Whitehead wasn't home, he instructed the cab driver to take him back to the hotel to pick up his overnight bag and from there to the coffee shop. Light rain was falling, chasing all the patio patrons inside. The interior was dark, warm, and noisy with the hiss and clatter of the espresso machine. He pushed through the crowds eagerly, but there was no sign of Olivia. He picked up a coffee and chose an armchair by the window so he could keep a hopeful eye on the street.

Sipping his coffee, he opened his laptop and typed notes as he let his mind roam over the case. Over the past week he had chipped away at the mystery of where Scott and his party were and what they were up to. He'd uncovered a few facts, enough to hang a pretty good theory on. First Scott had come into possession of his grandfather's will, which mentioned a mining claim. After that he visited the Mining Recorder's Office in Yellowknife to discover further details regarding its location and operational history. He met Victor Whitehead in Whitehorse shortly afterward, apparently to discuss the claim, but the meeting had degenerated into a fight and an accusation of cheating. Then Scott had returned to Vancouver to plan an exploratory trip to the Nahanni to check out the claim.

At the same time — and here Chris was far less sure of his facts — Victor had gone through his grandmother's effects after Scott's visit and had come across both the ruby and the diary. He'd visited Nahanni Butte to find out more about his ancestry. It seemed likely he'd figured out he was Gaetan Lasalle's grandson and learned about the existence of the ruby mine claim. Since it seemed to be common barstool gossip, that would have been easy. He was strongly pro mining, a view his own mother did not share, and now he was packing up for a river trip of his own.

Studying his notes, Chris could see some striking gaps in the theory. Most important, how had Scott found out about Victor? There were no official birth records linking Victor to Gaetan Lasalle, let alone to Scott's own grandfather. Had Scott also visited Nahanni Butte? Or had there been mention of Gaetan's romance in his grandfather's other papers?

Equally puzzling, why had Scott set up the meeting? Had he hoped that Victor, with his inside connections, would work with him to explore and finance the mine's potential? Had Victor refused, precipitating the argument? Why had Victor denied the blood ties and why had he refused to work with him? Did he have his own plans to exploit the mine without sharing the success with Scott? Since neither cousin had any legal claim to the mine after all these years, whoever could slap a new mining claim down first would walk away with the prize.

Chris felt his heart spike with excitement. Was that the real reason for Victor's sudden trip to the Nahanni? To beat Scott to the claim? It was a theory with a lot of whys and ifs, but now at least the picture was slightly clearer. That only served to bring his own vague unease into starker relief. Scott seemed like a lamb among wolves here, eagerly contacting his cousin for help and then setting out on his own to find the claim. Victor's motives were murkier. Darker. Like a wolf circling its prey in the night.

The thought chilled him further, yet there was nothing he could do. He felt like a dog who'd caught a whiff of scent, only to be called back to its pen.

His cellphone rang, jerking him from his thoughts. He glanced at the display. Olivia. His hopes surged and he realized he'd been waiting over an hour.

"Hi, flyboy," she shouted above the rumbling in the background. A truck engine, possibly.

"I'm still here," he said. "On my third cup of coffee." Then he winced. Did that sound too eager?

"Oh, how I wish. But the meeting ran late." She lowered her voice until he could barely hear it above the noise. "I tried to sneak out but there was no way. And now I'm out of time."

"Where are you? I could come —"

"No. It would be too rushed and we'd have no time alone." He heard a man shouting her name in the background. "Let's hold on to our goodbye from this morning. That was delicious. And next time —"

"When will that be?"

"I'm on a trip for a couple of weeks, but don't worry, I'll be back." The man's voice was closer now and Chris could hear her reassuring him that she was just checking her messages. Then she returned on the line with a breathy whisper. "Gotta go, love. But hold me tight in your dreams."

Then she was gone, leaving him in a flush of arousal. The word *love* danced through his blood. Lifted him, buffeted him. For a moment he thought only of her and of her whispered promise. Before long, however, the man's voice broke through his euphoria. The man had sounded insistent and in charge. He'd clearly expected her to jump to his tune, and she had. She'd lied about talking to Chris. Why? What kind of hold did he have on her? Why would she need to hide her personal life from any man, especially one who was only her professor?

Chris didn't like the answer he came up with. He flipped open his laptop and began a Google search of Olivia and geology and Waterloo University. Very quickly he pinned down the name of her professor, Dr. Anil Elatar. A further search for his bio revealed that he was a mining engineer with an expertise in ground geochemical sampling, who served as advisor to governments and mining companies worldwide, including a company with the odd name of Northern Rubicom. Elatar's publications ran several pages long with technical titles Chris couldn't begin to understand.

His attention was distracted by the photo accompanying the bio, of a middle-aged man with a shiny bald head, a thin grey comb-over, thick eyebrows, and the beaked nose of a hawk. He looked at least fifty years old, maybe more. His skin hung in folds around his scrawny neck and Chris doubted the rest of him looked any better.

No way this man could give Olivia what she wanted. Not if the last two nights were any sign. Chris felt his pulse slow with relief. Maybe she was just trying to show the man how committed she was to their work and to her future career.

He closed his laptop, grabbed his overnight bag, and headed outside to find a taxi. Darkness was still several hours away but it was time to get back to Fort Simpson. Time to put this frustrating case on the back burner and return to regular duties. He felt a twinge of regret and disappointment at the thought.

The taxi drove down Miles Canyon Road alongside the broad, bustling Schwatka Lake. Float planes bobbed at docks all along the shoreline, and boats big and small were out on the lake despite the fine drizzle. Steep, dark cliffs rose up on the other side.

Chris was leaning forward to scan the docks for his own plane when an Otter with a familiar Eagle logo on its tail caught his eye. He was startled. Hunter Kerry usually operated out of Fort Simpson, or occasionally the smaller towns up the Mackenzie River. Rarely did he venture to Whitehorse. He noticed Hunt loading a canoe into the belly of the plane. More gear was piled on the dock. A moment later, Victor Whitehead emerged from the plane and began to pick up the gear to toss it inside. Another man was supervising from the dock. Curious to see who else Victor was travelling with, Chris signalled the taxi driver to pull over out of sight.

He watched as Victor loaded the rest of the packs and turned to speak to Hunt, who climbed into the cock-pit and started the engine. A few seconds later a fourth figure appeared in the doorway and hopped down onto the dock. The figure was dressed in jeans, hiking boots, and a hooded rain jacket, but as Chris watched she thrust back her hood and shook lose her ponytail.

Olivia.

He sat frozen, wordless, as Olivia turned to the mystery man, rose on tiptoe, and gave him a soft, playful kiss. He was still watching as Victor climbed into the plane, Olivia unhitched the ropes, pushed off, and leaped nimbly aboard. The mystery man remained as the plane taxied away toward the middle of the lake. He lifted his hand to wave as it gunned down the water and rose into the air, its wings dipping in the cross wind. Only then did he turn and walk back down the dock to shore.

By then Chris felt no surprise. Professor Elatar.

Fort Simpson, September 24, 1944

My Darling Lydia,

It broke my heart to say goodbye. I miss you and little William already, but the cabin in winter is not a place for a baby. Or you, ma cherie. In Whitehorse you will have company, help, all the comforts. I know it's difficult, but I don't want to give up on the mine yet. When the war is over, there will be lots of people looking for new investments. For now, we just need a little more money to bring more equipment to the site. I hope we hear from Gaetan soon, or at least receive the money he promised. I am very upset with him. It has been more than two months. Nicolette is in despair. He has not even written her to ask about his child.

Please be patient, my love. The war is almost over. The Germans are in retreat. Imagine the future. Imagine peace, no more rations, everyone driving cars, buying gas and jewellery for their girls. One more winter. Maybe less if the fur is plentiful.

Yours forever, Guy.

CHAPTER SEVENTEEN

Nahanni, July 22

Green paused in his climb and leaned against a boulder at the edge of the trail, gasping for breath. Sweat poured into his eyes. He dropped his pack to the ground so that he could peel off another layer of clothing. Up ahead, Sullivan was wearing only a T-shirt as he strode confidently upward.

They were following what Jethro called a game trail almost straight uphill toward the ridge. Must be a mountain goat trail, Green thought. It had rained lightly overnight, and the stones still glistened damp and slippery in the pale mist. Like Hannah and her group, they had left their canoes and heavy gear down by the creek and were carrying only the essentials for inland camping. The other three were shouldering most of the weight, leaving Green ashamed and cursing his desk-bound existence. Once again, in an effort to distract himself, he planned the fitness regime he would institute once he returned home. He even managed a private grin at Sharon's imagined reaction.

They were above the treeline now, scrambling up barren slopes of loose shale and rock and past clumps of lichen and wild grasses that nestled in the damp pockets of the hillside. To Green, the acres of rock and grass looked undisturbed, but Jethro pointed out the minute signs of intruders. Lichen nibbled by sheep, stones overturned by a passing foot. He even pointed out a tiny set of parallel ridges carved into wet sand.

"A hiking boot," he said. "We're on the right track."

After years of looking at crime scenes, Green thought his eye should be better attuned to the minuscule bits of trace evidence. As he pushed off the boulder to continue the climb, he focused on the ground and trained his eye. Soon the stones lost their grey uniformity and became multicoloured, shot through with rust, white, purple, and green. The grasses took different shapes and sometimes he even spotted tiny flowers nestled at the centre.

When he finally topped the crest, he found Jethro and Sullivan sitting on the ground, eating pita with peanut butter and dried apples. Jethro was slipping dried moose meat to his dog. Green unsnapped his pack and let it drop to the ground with relief. He flexed his shoulders and took a long swig of water as he looked out over the valley. The sun was beginning to burn through the mist, lighting the land with silver and gold. Below them lay the dark folding swaths of boreal forest and the winding silver ribbon of the river. In the distance, tumbling one behind the other in a timeless skyscape, the gauzy silhouettes of the Ragged Range. For a moment he was transported from the fatigue and fear he had carried up the mountain.

"God, it's beautiful," he muttered.

Sullivan arched his eyebrows in surprise. He held out a pita rolled with peanut butter and apples.

"Not exactly smoked meat on rye," he said. "No one is going to recognize you when you get back, Mike. Look at those biceps already!"

Green chuckled. "Yeah, and it will take me months to lose this tan. My reputation may never recover." He flopped down at Sullivan's side. "Where's Ian?"

Sullivan nodded to a small dip farther along the ridge. "He got a phone call and he went over there to take it. Better reception, or privacy. Not sure."

The distant drone of an airplane caught Green's ear and he shielded his eyes to search the sky. The sound grew louder, and a few seconds later a float plane appeared through the wispy cloud, flying low over the mountain range to the south. Green felt a surge of hope.

"Part of the SAR operation?" he asked.

Jethro trained his binoculars on the sky. Green watched as the plane dropped lower and circled back. "That's Hunt Kerry's plane," Jethro said. "Flying awfully low for those mountain peaks."

"I wonder if he's spotted something."

The plane was a mere pinpoint of white against the clouds as it banked in a wide circle before disappearing behind the mountain peaks. It looked to be several miles farther inland, away from the river where the search had been concentrated.

"Looks like he's going to land."

"Pretty tricky to land in there, even for Hunt," Jethro said. "No water big enough."

As if in answer, the plane reappeared a few minutes later, banked east, and climbed rapidly until it was swallowed in the distant clouds. At that moment, Elliott came into sight over the rise.

"Did you see Hunter Kerry's plane?" Green asked excitedly. "Looks like they're expanding the search farther from the river."

"Hunt's not part of the search," Elliott replied. His normally sunny expression was taut and his tone brusque. He stood over them a moment in silence, fingering his satellite phone. Green recognized that look. He'd used it often enough himself when he was trying to formulate bad news. His gut tightened.

"What is it?"

"The Mounties called off the search."

"*Why*?"

"They think the group is not missing or in jeopardy."

"But Hunt was clearly looking —"

"Then he's acting on his own initiative. The Mounties now think the group is on a hike inland, and no longer their concern." He imitated Nihls's prissy tone. "'Until we receive new information to the contrary, we will not be committing costly resources to the search.'"

Green was driven to his feet by outrage. "A thousand square kilometres of trees and ravines and wolves, and they're not going to help? Not even flyovers or infrared imaging?"

Elliott shook his head unhappily. "You have to admit things have changed. This is looking less like a crisis and more like an expedition."

Green swung on him. "Are you pulling out too?

"Mike, that's not fair."

Elliott held up his hand. "No, Brian, it's a fair question. I'm not pulling out. We'll find these kids. For one thing, I'm not convinced they have the expertise or the equipment to survive in the wild. They've already made some very stupid mistakes, including failing to register their itinerary with anyone. Not even their families, let alone the Mounties or the park. This is not some city park. People die up here."

Jethro shot him a swift glance and Elliott winced. "Sorry. I didn't mean to imply —"

"But it's true," Green said. "That's why we have to find them. And why the RCMP's decision is so infuriating."

"I know, but from the SAR perspective, a full-scale search is premature. Park staff and trippers will still be on the lookout, of course, and Nihls did ask me to keep him posted. At the first sign of danger, they will re-evaluate."

"These are professionals, Mike," Sullivan said. "We have to let them do their job."

As they were talking, Jethro had packed up his lunch and wordlessly left the group. He carried a short willow branch that he called his tracking stick. It was marked with O-rings that he moved up and down with precision. With his dog criss-crossing behind, he was exploring the ridge top.

"Just like him," Elliott added softly.

"I'm sorry. You're right." Green started to pack up his own lunch. Most of his pita was uneaten but he'd lost his appetite. "Should we be helping him?"

Elliott shook his head. "We need to stay out of his way until he picks up the trail. He'll let us know."

Just like an Ident officer, Green thought, taking out his phone. "Fine. Maybe I should phone Hunter Kerry and find out what he was looking for, and whether he saw anything."

"Hunter flies people up here all the time. Over to the Cantung Mine that's back in there, or up the Flat River for fishing." Elliot seemed to read Green's expression, because he smiled sympathetically. "He wouldn't call you back before next week anyway."

Green had to admit the truth of that. He sank back down on the ground and pulled his notebook from his pack. He had intended to keep a detailed log of their activities and observations for the future, but he found himself instead watching Jethro with fascination. The man was wandering in seemingly aimless loops across the ridge, backtracking, studying, retracing his steps. Now and then he'd bend down to study the soil. He'd lay out his tracking stick, mark, measure, and then examine another spot. His brow was furrowed in concentration, his movements precise.

Green knew that tracking, like crime scene searches, was meticulous. Down to grains of sand, sometimes. But after half an hour he felt his impatience mounting.

"Were they even up here?" he shouted finally.

Jethro looked over, his expression unruffled. "Oh, yes. But there are four of them, all going in different directions."

Green approached. "Can the dog help?"

Jethro glanced up in search of Tatso. He had sent her to the farthest perimeter of the ridge, where she was zigzagging methodically along with her nose to the ground. So far she showed no signs of being on the scent.

Jethro shook his head. "The scent's too old. Might be ten days since they passed through here. Probably before the flash flood. There are a couple of good tracks but very worn. But they are changing directions, sometimes taking big steps, sometimes small. Like they're looking for something. Or undecided." He straightened. "If we can figure out what they were looking for, we may be able to pick up a trail."

In his quiet way, Jethro seemed to read Green's pent-up impatience and helplessness, for he pointed to the edge of the ridge where the land dropped precipitously into a gully. The terrain was a series of folds, like a clumsily folded quilt that had been tossed open upon the land.

"I'm going to follow the edges of the ridge to see where they began their descent. You three can do a line search of the middle area here for any signs of them. Tent peg holes, flattened vegetation, burnt stones. It's open land so twenty feet apart should do."

Green had ordered enough line searches in his career to know what to do. Usually they were in dense shrubbery or woodland, where the smallest piece of evidence could be invisible one foot away. In comparison, this search was easy. The three of them soon developed a rhythm that covered half the top of the ridge in less than an hour. They had just finished their eighth pass across and were approaching a small, lichen-covered ledge when a flash of sunlight caught Green's eye. It seemed to be shining from a jumble of rocks beneath the ledge. Was there something reflecting the light?

He broke formation to get a closer look, expecting a shred of foil or plastic wrap. Instead, nestled amid the odd pile of rocks was a broken mason jar.

He stepped away and shouted for Jethro. The man was the closest thing he had to an Ident officer. If anyone could read the evidence to find out how it had been broken and how long ago, it would be Jethro.

Soon all of them were clustered in a circle as Jethro crouched on the ground. He balanced a shard of glass in his fingertips and studied the glass, the broken edge and the debris that had collected inside.

"This break is very new. Almost no wear from the weather and no dirt inside. Even the outside is clean. But the metal top ..." He looped the rusted metal ring around his finger. "Is very old." He sat back on his heels to study the scene.

"So what you're saying is that this jar has been here a long time. Years?"

"Yes, years."

"But it was broken very recently?"

Jethro nodded. "But I think it was inside a cairn — this pile of rocks has also been disturbed recently — so it was protected."

Green's heart began to hammer. "You mean someone deliberately hid this jar years ago, and just recently it was found and broken open?"

"To get what was inside," Elliott added.

"What would someone hide inside a jar like this?" Green asked.

Elliott shrugged. "Typically mementos, notes left for others to find, a token to mark their reaching the summit."

"But it could be something more," Green said. "Scott's grandfather left a cryptic clue in his will that pointed to this spot. Maybe up here, he left another clue. More coordinates, or directions, or a map."

Sullivan snorted, but Jethro didn't react. He reached to move some of the other pieces of glass. Belatedly the policeman in Green snapped to attention.

"Don't touch those! Brian, we need to photograph these, bag them, and tag them." He saw the bafflement on the others' faces. "A precaution. In case this ever turns into a crime scene."

Jethro and Tatso spent most of the afternoon searching far and wide along the periphery of the ridge, looking for tracks. The other three chafed under the forced inaction, but Jethro was adamant.

"Better to get this right than to spend days going in the wrong direction." He gestured out over the folding hills. "There is a lot of room for mistakes."

Knowing he was right, Green stifled his grumbling and walked over to the rise to phone Sharon. She sounded weak and far away, but he hoped that was just the weak signal.

"We're all fine down here," she insisted. "Much better now that I know Hannah's not in trouble on the river somewhere."

He looked out over the steep, rocky ravines and suppressed a twinge of worry. Sharon didn't need anything else to fret about.

"But Mike, will you please phone Ashley before I

get out the voodoo doll? She claims she has stuff you should know."

"About what?"

"About the other campers. She wouldn't tell me. You know Ashley — knowledge is power."

After Green hung up he immediately phoned Ashley. There was certainly no problem with the connection this time. Her shriek could be heard fifty feet away by Sullivan, who smiled in sympathy.

"I've been waiting for days, Mike! Days! Did you phone *her*? Pardon me for being catty, but I am the mother here."

"Sharon said you had information?"

"Oh, and I'm supposed to give it to you before you even tell me whether my daughter is dead or alive?"

"She's alive," he said, rubbing his temples. "I'm really sorry, Ashley. You're right, I should have called before this. But I'm sitting on top of a mountain in the middle of nowhere. Satellite phone connections are iffy and I had no news till now." He filled her in on the discovery of their base camp, omitting the flash flood and the broken glass jar. "We've found their tracks. We're going to follow them and find them, believe me."

"Oh." Ashley managed a sob. "The other families have been calling me demanding to know what's going on. It was driving me crazy."

"They're worried too, Ashley."

"Well, I didn't hang up on them, if that's what you think. Jesus, Mike."

"What information did they give you?"

"I don't think they're going after the mine. Pete's sister called me from some island somewhere. She'd been doing more checking on Pete. When I mentioned the mine, she said Pete was a real eco-nut. He'd never want a mine up there. He and his prof had a big fight over it."

Green fished his notebook from his day pack and flipped it open. Scott had also had an argument with that professor. "What exactly did she say about the fight?"

"I don't really get all this scientific stuff, Mike. You know that. It goes in one ear and out the other."

"Try."

Her sigh lasted a full five seconds. "It's something to do with temperature and how it freezes and thaws the ground, and how the ground is thawing more and more up north. This geology professor was studying what happens to the rocks near the surface. Pete and Scott have the same prof — Valencia. Anyway, Pete found out the prof owned shares in some mining company —"

"What's the name of it?"

Another sigh, this one short and impatient. "I don't know, Mike! Northern something. Anyway, Pete freaked out."

Green felt the frustration of being thousands of kilometres away. Ashley was the most unreliable of witnesses but he had no way of verifying her story. But if she was correct, it added a new twist to the tale.

"Give me the sister's number."

"Like I said, she's on an island somewhere, Mike, and doesn't seem in a hurry to get off it. Unlike Daniel Rothman's sister, I should tell you. Another one who's been driving me crazy. I don't know what's with these sisters. I wouldn't care less if my brother fell off the face of —"

"What about Daniel's sister?" Green was watching Jethro out of the corner of his eye. The tracker was squatting in the short grass at the far end of the ridge, poking it with his tracking stick. Green sensed a potential breakthrough.

"You finally call me and then you hardly give me —"

"Ashley! What?"

"She wants to come up to join you." Green thought he heard a hint of triumph in her voice. "She doesn't think you guys from Ottawa know what you're doing. She's a doctor and did some training up north. She thinks she can help, and she's the type who doesn't take no for an answer."

Green rolled his eyes. Just what they needed. "She's wasting her time. She won't be able to reach us."

"Don't count on it," Ashley said. "I bet she'd parachute in if she had to."

Green mouthed a silent curse. In the distance, Jethro rose and turned to them. "Listen, Ashley, I gotta go. I suppose a doctor might come in handy."

"She's a shrink. Good luck with that." With a triumphant laugh, she hung up.

Jethro was beckoning to them. As they gathered up their gear to follow him, Green filled in the others. "When we stop for the night, I'll try to reach Daniel Rothman's sister, to tell her not to come," he said. "But with this trail getting colder by the hour, we have no time to lose. If Jethro has found something, we're going on."

Jethro had found the most microscopic trace of human passage — a dried twig broken in two places about five inches apart. "About the width of a man's hiking boot," he said. "Look at the broken ends. Still quite clean, so it's a fresh break. They passed through here. If we assume they were following a map or a compass setting, it's likely they would head in a straight line that way." He pointed down a steep ravine. "But they would also follow the path of least difficulty, so we'll do the same. Me first. I'll track as we go along. It will be slow, so …" He raised his eyes to Green, "patience."

Shouldering their gear, they proceeded single file down the slope. Jethro picked a wavering route, avoiding steep drops, pockets of loose gravel, and boulders the size of trucks. Every now and then he would stop to study a stone or a low-lying bush. He'd point out the flattened leaves or the hole where a stone had been dislodged.

Sullivan seemed to hang on his every word. "How do we know it's not an animal?"

"There are plenty of animals who take this path. You can see from the scat and the torn bits of grass where they have grazed. But only a human boot flattens grass like that."

The sun was sinking below the mountain peaks by the time they reached the bottom of the ravine, deep in the woods. Mosquitoes closed in gleefully. By then every muscle in Green's back ached and his legs quivered with fatigue. Despite bandages and moleskin, he knew his feet were a mass of blisters.

Even Sullivan looked weary. He leaned against a tree trunk and swatted bugs away as he took a long swig of water. For a moment Green's pulse spiked with fear at his red face and laboured breathing. "We should stop for the night soon," he said.

Jethro nodded. "We're going to lose the light, no good for tracking. But I'd like to find their camp. They wouldn't camp in here. It's too dense and buggy, and they'd want to find water. Let's see what's ahead."

Arms raised in self-defence, they ploughed along an animal track though the dense bush. Branches scratched their legs and whipped their chests. Their eyes struggled to adjust to the deep shadows. From up ahead the sound of rushing water grew from a murmur to a roar. In the damp, shaded underworld, blackflies joined the mosquitoes in their quest for blood. The bugs filled their eyes, ears, and noses. They were swearing, sweating, and exhausted by the time they emerged from the woods onto the rocky shore of a small stream. Sunlight burst through a gap in the mountains and lit the distant tree tops.

They stood staring in disappointment at the damp, boulder-strewn terrain. It was impossible to set up camp here.

Elliott dropped his pack onto a large flat rock. "We need a rest and some food. We'll cook dinner, then scout upstream for a suitable camping spot. We still have some daylight left."

"I don't want to lose the trail," Jethro said.

"We won't. But they didn't camp here, obviously. They'll be looking for a good campsite just like us."

They were silent through dinner, Elliott's dehydrated stew this time. Their euphoria of the afternoon was replaced by exhaustion in every bone. Afterward Green just wanted to curl up on a rock and go to sleep, but he forced himself to follow the others up the creek bed. The sunlight had left the valley in twilight now, but the mountain peaks and clouds overhead still shone with gold.

After a few painstaking moments, the creek banks became steeper, and the trees grew gnarled and desperate as they clung to the rocks. Jethro paused to look up at a dip in a gentle slope high above.

"We have to go up there. I think that's where they would camp. There are some trees for shelter but it's high enough to see their surroundings. Away from the grizzlies and wolves that come to the stream for water."

He led them away from the creek, back through dense forests, and upward in a seemingly endless climb over rocks and scrub. Green fell twice, scraping his knees and palms. He struggled to keep one foot in front of another. One more step. One more step....

Until finally the path opened up onto an unexpected ledge high above the creek. Flat and spongy with lichen and sage. The perfect camping spot.

"They were here!" Jethro cried in a rare show of excitement. Even Green could see the flattened sage and the tent peg holes in the rocky soil. A few charred branches lay on the ground. Relief and joy crashed over him in waves. When he sank to his knees to kiss the ground, the others didn't even laugh.

They didn't bother with a fire. It was a warm night, and their exertion had made them hot. They erected their tents, unrolled their sleeping bags, and fell into bed.

In the morning, Elliott was up early. He had sausages and eggs frying on the griddle and a full pot of coffee sitting on the fire by the time Green crawled out of the tent. Jethro had already gone out to scout the area but Sullivan was still asleep. Elliott greeted Green with a hot cup of coffee and a big smile.

"Eggs and a hefty dose of cholesterol to stoke the body for the day. Brings me back to my guiding days. A quarter century ago. Never realized how much I missed it."

Green nodded. Every muscle screamed, but his mouth watered. "There is something to be said for this. Kill yourself during the day and the rewards seem even better at the end. Sleep, coffee …"

Elliott laughed as he shovelled eggs and sausages onto two plates. "We get awfully far away from it in the city, don't we."

"I was born in the city. Never saw a blade of grass till I was ten and went to a friend's who owned a real house."

"We get a lot of Europeans up here, looking for wilderness. There's not much of it left in the world. That's why we have to save it."

Green looked around at the ragged peaks that cradled the valley. "Is there a lot of mining potential in these mountains?"

"Everywhere there is geological upheaval and instability, everywhere there are mountains, there are rich mineral deposits. Silver, copper, and zinc, all through here. Emerald deposits just west of here in the Yukon, diamonds to the north in the Barrens. And rare earth metals, tons of them, the hot new metals that we use in everything from cellphone circuits to aerospace coatings. That's where the big money is today. Even now we're in a fight to protect the headwaters of the Nahanni from mining interests. There is going to be a new national park, extending to Moose Ponds and protecting the whole watershed, the animals, the ground water, and the unique wildlife habitats."

Green mopped up egg yolk with a chunk of sausage. "Oh, damn, this is good, Ian. Amazing what you can whip up with a bit of deadwood and an open fire."

"This is the only way I can cook. My wife complains whenever she wants me to cook dinner I have to set fire to half the backyard."

"I can relate to that. Only I don't do it on purpose. The barbeque and I are only just making friends." He waved his fork to encompass the mountains around him. "Do you think this area will be protected by the park?"

"Some of it. That's the big question mark. There have been consultations with the Dene Nation, resource developers, tour operators like me, environmental experts, and other interested parties. We're still waiting for the decision. The government has to decide how much of these mineral-rich mountains to leave open for mining, and how much to protect."

"Not a reassuring thought," Green replied, thinking of the government's track record and its emphasis on jobs and money compared to environmental concerns.

Elliott shot him a grim look. "I'm not against all development, but it has to be sustainable and responsible. So far the companies have not shown they can be trusted to put the greater good of the environment ahead of jobs and profit margins. This river's ecosystem is unique in the world, but it's hard to get the rest of the country to care about a few caribou and a remote river they've never seen when they are losing their own jobs. But it's nice to know these kids we're following may be on our side."

"Then what are they doing out here?" Green asked. "Following cryptic clues from a will and tracking down an old ruby mine."

"That, of course, is something we will ask them, once we get them safe and sound." Elliott pointed toward the edge of the plateau. "Jethro thinks they were here the night the storm hit. That means from now on, the trail will be easier to follow. Wet ground means more prints."

Cradling his coffee, Green headed over to take in the view from the far side of their camp. It was a glorious morning. A brisk breeze tugged at his hair and sunlight bathed his face. Once again he felt hope. A massive ridge rose up on one side, and down below on the other lay the creek bed. Deep, boulder-strewn troughs had been carved out of the mountainsides, as if a giant had raked his fingers through the land. Not a giant, Elliott had explained earlier, but glaciers scouring the mountains millions of years ago.

Overhead the sky was a blue he'd never seen in the city. Three large black birds floated in lazy, wide-winged circles above the valley, their plumes burnished almost purple in the sun. The legendary ravens, he wondered, or just some country cousins of the scavenging city crow? As he stood at the edge of the ledge looking out across the valley, a spot of colour at the base opposite caught his eye. Bright red against the greys and browns of rock. Hints of blue too. Quickly he took out his binoculars and focused them on the hillside. It was a steep, almost vertical drop from the ridge above. The sheer rock face glistened with moisture in the morning sun. He moved his binoculars toward the base, searching for the spot of colour. He caught a flash of red. He moved his glasses, twirled the lens, and gradually the shape came into focus. Half red, half blue, a small figure at the base of the cliff.

A human form.

CHAPTER EIGHTEEN

"What colour is your daughter's hair?" Elliott asked.

Green struggled to remember, but fear obliterated all thought. Blue? Orange? She'd gone through a Goth black-as-death phase and a blue Mohawk. But now? He shook his head in defeat. "I'm not sure. I haven't seen her in awhile."

They were all clustered at the edge of the plateau. When Green first spotted the body he'd tried desperately to find a way across to it, but a steep ravine separated him from the narrow ledge on the other side where the body lay. The descent was too treacherous. His shouts had brought the others running, and they had descended as close as they dared. Elliott had trained his powerful binoculars on the crumpled form.

"It's not moving," he said. "I can't tell much else."

Green took the binoculars. He was sure he'd be able to identify Hannah. What father wouldn't recognize his own daughter? However, once he focused on the shape, he couldn't distinguish a thing. The body was splayed face down, the neck twisted and the face turned away.

Hannah was petite but the victim's clothing was bulky, making it impossible to estimate size.

Several crows flapped around the body, squabbling as they tried to peck. Nausea swept over him, the sausage and eggs roiling inside. His hands shook as he moved the binoculars over the steep terrain, looking for a path. He sensed Sullivan behind him before the man put his hand on his shoulder.

"Any chance they're still alive?"

Lowering the binoculars, Green pointed to the crows. "Looks like quite a crowd is gathering."

Sullivan fell silent. It was answer enough to his question. Jethro stepped away from the group and shaded his eyes from the sun as he peered at the ledge.

"I wonder what they were doing down there?"

"I don't care how or why they got there," Green replied. Impotent anger billowed through him. "Our first priority is to get down there. We need to see what the hell happened to him." He clenched his jaw. "I'm assuming it's a him. Odds are three to one."

Elliott was already heading back toward the campsite. He turned. "Our first priority is to report this. This changes the whole game." Shading his eyes, he studied the peaks all around them. "Helicopter is the only way in here, but it will be tricky. Especially if the wind picks up any more."

"How long till they get here?"

"No idea. Let me try to call."

Green left the edge of the plateau and followed Elliott to the middle of the clearing, where he located a signal. Green listened without interruption as Elliott spoke to Nihls. After reporting the body and their GPS location, he argued about the urgency. "We don't know," he said. Followed by, "We don't know that either, Sergeant." Finally he held out the phone to Green. "He wants to talk to you."

Before Green had even raised the phone to his ear, Nihls started in. "Can you confirm this individual is dead, Inspector?"

"We haven't examined him, but it seems likely."

"How likely?"

"The crows are circling."

"Do you regard the death as suspicious?"

"We need to get at the body before we can determine that, Sergeant. How soon can you get a recovery team up here?"

"Tomorrow, first thing."

"Tomorrow!" Green nearly choked on his outrage. "The crows will be done by then."

"I'll expedite it as much as I can, but the wind is too strong today for that kind of operation. Besides we just sent the army helicopter back to Winnipeg and it will need turn-around time."

Argument proved futile in budging the sergeant's timeline. Elliott smiled sympathetically when Green signed off and handed the phone back to him. "Nihls is one of those managers whose default position is 'no,'" Green muttered. "We've got a whole day to twiddle our thumbs, so let's get started. Let's find a way down to that body."

They had to clear up the breakfast, bury the fire, and secure the food before Elliott gave the approval to leave the camp. Green fought back overwhelming worry by concentrating on the mundane. With Jethro in the lead, they retraced their route back down the stream and followed it up over steep bluffs and boulders. At times they splashed through water. Green was completely disoriented by the time they came to a small gap in the bank where a smaller stream tumbled in. The merest trickle over slippery rocks. Jethro turned to clamber up it.

They slogged through dense forest, swarmed by mosquitoes and ankle deep in muck. Gritting his teeth, Green prayed Jethro knew where he was going. After an apparent eternity, they emerged onto an open stretch of gravel bordering a steep slope. Green recognized the view and caught the dreaded smell of rotting flesh.

"The body's up there!" he shouted, pointing to a pile of boulders up the slope on the right. Leaving the others, he scrambled up over the debris, slipping and tearing his hands as he fought for purchase. The stench grew stronger. He pulled his shirt up over his nose and pressed on. Finally the crumpled red-and-blue figure came into view. He covered the last few yards in a blur of panic, scattering the crows in his path, and flung himself down beside the body.

It took a moment for the horror of the sight to strike. He reeled backward and vomited onto the rocks. He'd seen animal destruction before. He'd seen the crows at the body. He should have been prepared.

The figure before him was beyond recognition. The eyes were plucked out, the face and hands were gnawed off, and flies buzzed around. Maggots seethed in the exposed flesh.

"Jesus, Mary, and Joseph," Sullivan muttered as he knelt at his side. Green said nothing. He concentrated on trying to see the little things. The remains of an ear, unpierced. Strands of short, wavy black hair still clinging to the swollen head. He breathed. Once. Twice.

"It don't think it's her," he said through chattering teeth.

"No."

Jethro and Elliott loomed over them briefly before reeling away, pressing their hands over their noses. Both men struggled with their breathing before Elliott managed to speak.

"Can you tell who it is?"

In this rocky, treacherous, mosquito-ridden corner of hell, Green summoned his professional self. Taking shallow breaths, he looked back at the body and made calculations. "It's a male, dark, wavy hair, about five-eight. With the bloating it's difficult to estimate weight, but I'd say he's slight and small-boned." He scanned the body slowly, then forced himself to run his hands over it. It was flaccid in his grip, moving like limp pasta. He pressed and probed. Without a word, Sullivan took out his camera and began to video the scene — first from a distance before coming in for close-ups. Green dictated a running commentary.

"One leg and both ankles appear broken. It's difficult to tell what else is broken, but the skull —" Steeling himself, Green probed the underside. Broken bits of bone pricked his fingers. "— appears shattered above the orbital on the left side. A sharp, penetrating injury from —" He scanned the ground for a likely sharp rock but saw none. The ground was loose rock, covered with rusty dried blood that glistened amber in the sun. There had been a lot of blood. "At a guess, I'd say the blow to the head knocked him out, and bleeding did the rest."

Sullivan stepped forward for close-up stills of the body and the surrounding rocks. "We should cut his clothes off," he said.

Green grimaced. He knew Sullivan was right, but the thought of bloated flesh teeming with maggots and already turning glossy green felt beyond his steel control.

Jethro pulled out his sharp hunting knife. He was beginning to recover some colour as he knelt down, prepared to slice open the jacket. Grateful for the chance to escape, Green went to join Elliott, who was slumped against a boulder thirty yards away.

"Jesus. You guys do this all the time?"

Green shook his head. "Sometimes they're bad. Worse. But this.... With the animals having at him too."

"Who do you think it is?"

"I have photos and descriptions of them all. Scott is over six feet, Pete's blond. Daniel is the only one with dark curly hair. Of course, we have to wait for the autopsy to confirm it."

"Dental?"

Green nodded. "And DNA."

"Can you tell how long he's been dead?"

"Again, we'll need to wait for the autopsy. The pathologist will need temperature records for the last week here, because that affects decomposition. We'll collect maggots and other bugs." He paused. "I'll ask Nihls to send along some evidence sample kits. Never thought to pack any of those." His eyes narrowed as he forced himself through his mental checklist. "Based on the degree of decomposition and bloating, I'd say close to a week."

Elliott's eyebrows shot up in surprise. "That long? How did he get here? What was he doing here?"

Green studied the landscape. It was a narrow gully, with no easy way in or out. He looked up at the steep slope of loose rock and debris above them. Farther up it became a sheer cliff. Higher still, a ragged mountain ridge. "From his broken ankles and legs, I'd say he fell. Possibly from way up there."

Elliott looked up and blanched. "Holy shit. A hiker's worst nightmare. This rock is very unstable. One slip and the scree slides out from under you and down you go. Not usually over a cliff, though. Poor bugger."

"We need to get up there and see what happened." Green frowned. "This makes no sense. Why was he by himself? Where were the rest of them? Where *are* the rest of them?"

"And more importantly," Sullivan broke in, coming back to join them, "why didn't they sound the alarm? If he fell, why didn't they try to rescue him, or at least signal for help? Stand on the top of the mountain, light a bonfire, anything!"

Green felt his professional control waver. Fear bubbled up again. He didn't dare articulate the answer that came to him.

"We need to get up there. ASAP. We need to see if they're still there. To see if anything else happened."

* * *

The body looked forlorn, like a used handkerchief crumpled and tossed aside. It went against all Green's instincts and training to leave it there, but they could not afford to split up and they needed to find out what had happened on the ridge above.

The day had grown cooler as charcoal clouds shrouded the sun. When they climbed above the trees onto the open slope the wind picked up, sharp with the chill of glaciers. Digging his heavier jacket out of his backpack, Green reluctantly conceded that Sergeant Nihls was right. To bring a helicopter into these narrow gullies in this wind would be deadly, and even if the pilot succeeded, dropping a line down to extract the body would be deadlier still.

It was early afternoon by the time they crested the top of the mountain. As the vista opened up before him, Green held his breath in fear that they'd find a scene of carnage, with bodies torn limb from limb. But there were no ravens circling, no stink of rot on the wind, so he allowed himself a faint hope. Maybe they'd be there, bustling around brightly coloured tents and chatting over maps.

But the ridge was empty; nothing but grass, rock, and lichen. Beyond, white-capped mountains stretched in folds and peaks to the horizon. While Elliott studied his compass, Jethro strode across the rock-strewn grass to the edge, where the ridge seemed to fall away into nothingness. Green followed, inching toward the edge. His hands clammy and his heart in his throat, he peered cautiously over.

Not the vertical cliff he'd been expecting, but a steep gravel slope. With nowhere to grab a toehold, however, just as lethal. Below the slope, an abyss. The base of the mountain where Daniel's body lay could not be seen.

Jethro walked along the edge, his feet sinking into the loose gravel at times and sending it cascading down the slope in silver streams. Green forced himself to follow but at a safer distance from the edge. He could stare a killer in the eye, face the most deranged and volatile witness, but heights reduced him to jelly.

Abruptly Jethro came to a halt and peered at the ground ahead of him. He pointed. The ground was churned up and rounded indents were visible in the gravel leading to the edge. A thin, straight trough was carved down the slope to the abyss. Jethro looked out over the valley, his brow furrowed.

"This is where he went over," he said. "That long mark is his body sliding down. At the top, see all these footprints? Maybe a struggle. Or an attempt to scramble back to safety."

Green studied the impressions in the gravel. He was used to analyzing footprints, but these had no form. "Can you tell if it's one person or two?"

Jethro shook his head. "Can't even tell if it's human. There's no edging, no definition. It could even be someone trying to save him."

Green shuddered as he tried to imagine the terror of those last moments when Daniel realized that he couldn't stop his slide. That he was heading toward certain death. Had he clawed desperately at the loose ground, scrambled for a toehold? Or had he frozen in terror and abandoned himself to his fate?

Green could see no sign that Daniel had struggled. He felt sick as he backed away. A shout pulled him away from his dark place. Sullivan and Elliott were standing in the middle of the ridge, where the land dipped slightly to form a bowl and where the grass, sage, and moss formed a soft carpet. He walked gratefully away from the edge.

As he drew nearer he could see clear depressions in the grass. Big squares where tents had flattened it and smaller squares where presumably their packs and other gear had been stored.

"This is where they camped," Elliott said excitedly. "Two tents, a firepit, and Brian found a latrine over behind that rock."

Green followed his gesture to a rock some distance from the campsite, close to the point where Daniel had fallen. The wind was brutal across the top of the ridge but the shallow bowl at the centre offered protection as if cradling hands welcomed the feeble sunlight in.

"Jethro, can you tell how long ago they were here?"

Jethro looked deadpan. "Sure, I'll just get my crystal ball out of my bag."

It was the first moment of levity in the grim horrors of the day and they all welcomed the chance to laugh. Elliott felt the ashes in the firepit.

"Before today, for sure. Stone cold."

Jethro squatted to examine the holes left by the tent pegs. "A few days. It's rained and dried since then, and the edges are crumbling. See how they're smoothing out? And rain has washed soil into the holes. Nature reclaims its own."

Green thought back to the last rainfall, three days earlier, and his heart sank. The trail was days old. They were still far behind.

He tried to put himself in the group's shoes. They were excited, hot on the trail of a treasure, and following directions left decades earlier by Scott's grandfather. In a mason jar, of all things. It was beyond a fairytale.

But the fairytale had turned deadly when one of them had drifted too close to the edge and slid to his death. Had it been an accident? Was Daniel stumbling around in the dark, maybe drunk and looking for the privy? Or had it been a terrified run for his life, away from a bear or a pack of wolves?

He glanced at the surrounding ground, trying to read the land as Jethro did. He saw lots of flattened areas, piles of firewood, and some flat stones, but no obvious signs of violence, like churned up earth, bloodstains, or fragments of torn fabric.

"Jethro, can you tell if there was a struggle or an animal attack?"

"I'll just get that crystal ball again," he said. Then his eyes rested on Green thoughtfully. "I'm sorry. No, I don't see that. They were here awhile, or planned to be here awhile. They had collected firewood and flat stones to serve as tables. And when they left, it was not in a hurry. They put sand on the fire, covered over their latrine, and cleaned up after themselves."

Green frowned. "Then they were not under threat when they left?"

Jethro shrugged. "Not immediate. That doesn't mean they weren't scared."

Green looked around the pristine campsite. An inconsistency nagged at him, and the possible answers were even scarier than the questions. He signalled to Sullivan to come away from the group. He'd always done his best thinking with calm, practical Sullivan as his sounding board.

"I don't like this," he murmured. "Something doesn't add up. If one of us had just fallen off the cliff, what would be our natural reaction?"

"To go look for them. Which they don't appear to have done."

"Or if they did, they just left him there once they found out he was dead."

Sullivan didn't reply, merely waited, as he always did, while Green followed his train of thought. "The only reason they wouldn't go to look for him would be if they were running for their lives."

"Which also doesn't appear to be the case."

Green stared bleakly out over the mountains. "Why did they just pack up and leave? They even covered their shit hole, for God's sake. Why did they leave him there? Why didn't they call for help? Surely to God —" He swallowed. "Surely to God Daniel's death was more important than their damn treasure hunt!"

"There might be another explanation. They might have decided to abort their mission, gone back to their canoes to get help."

"We would have seen them when we came up. We were following their trail."

"I know, Mike. I don't have an explanation. I just think there probably is one. They panicked when Daniel died. They didn't know what to do, so they packed up and moved on." Sullivan pursed his lips and grew thoughtful. "You know, most animals are nocturnal. Maybe a bear or wolf attacked the campsite at night and drove Daniel to his death, but the rest of them fended it off. In the morning, the animal would be gone but they knew he'd be back the next night, so they packed up camp and left. Careful to leave no trace of their presence so it wouldn't attract the animal again."

As an argument, it hung by a thread. Green searched his face. He saw no hint of deception or disbelief, but he suspected Sullivan was just trying to reassure him. Sullivan, the pragmatist, the devil's advocate, had relinquished that usual role in favour of friendship.

Movement distracted him. He turned to see Elliott and Jethro setting up camp. He glanced at the sky. The wind was still sharp but the sun was struggling to shine through the clouds in the west.

"What are you doing?" he demanded. "We should be looking for their trail."

Elliott shook his head. "We're going to wait for the recovery team. This is an excellent place for a helicopter to land, and they'll need us to lead them to the body."

Green's face flamed red with shame. How quickly he had forgotten the poor man lying at the bottom of the cliff. Even now, his frustration battled his shame. The recovery team would be bringing Daniel's sister as well, at her own insistence. She would need, and deserve, answers and support. But all the while, Hannah was forging ahead through the wilderness, her whereabouts and safety unknown.

And all the while, the scariest question of all. He didn't know Scott. He didn't know Pete. But he thought he knew Hannah. How could she have simply packed up camp and moved on, leaving a fellow traveller dead or dying at the bottom of the cliff?

"I have to go after them," Green said.

Elliott was pounding a tent peg into the rocky soil and he paused in mid-swing. "The SAR team and helicopter will be here in the morning. That will be soon enough."

Green shook his head. "Something is wrong. My daughter wouldn't take off like this unless she was in trouble."

"Maybe she just went along with the others' decision."

"I know Hannah! She's stubborn as they come. She wouldn't let someone else call the shots. She's scared, or she's being forced."

Elliott scanned the endless hills, as if in search of them. Or answers. "We can't split up. Too dangerous."

"I'll take that risk." Green bent down to pick up his pack, summoning a semblance of calm. He knew Elliott would never let emotion be the guiding principle in a dangerous situation. Nor would he, if he were in charge of this operation. "We'll go two and two. Brian will stay with you. He's an investigator second to none and can give the Mounties all the advice and help they need. Jethro is a tracker. Let me take him and the dog with me."

Elliott started to shake his head.

“This is my daughter! I don’t have a choice. Do you want me sneaking off by myself into the wilderness? Because that’s your choice.”

Elliott flushed a dangerous red. “You’ll be dead in a day, you fool. What good will you do your daughter then?”

Green straightened up, slinging his pack onto his back. “Let’s put it to a vote.”

“A week ago you couldn’t even pitch a tent!”

“Desperation makes a fast learner,” Green retorted. Without giving Elliott more time to protest, Green turned his back to round up the others. Much the same arguments ensued.

“I have no problem surviving out there by myself,” Jethro said to Green finally. “But I don’t want you getting me killed. I’ll take you as long as you promise to do everything I say.”

Sullivan had said nothing but he’d been frowning. Now he grunted. “That’ll be the day.”

Green swung on him. “I don’t want either of us killed, Brian, so yes, Jethro will be in charge of protecting us against nature. But if it comes to danger by people, then I call the shots.” He turned to Jethro. “Deal?”

Jethro nodded but Sullivan still wasn’t done. “Mike, you’re not a SWAT team. And don’t forget, you have others relying on you too. A five-year-old son, a baby on the way. Don’t they rate?”

“Fuck off, Brian. This is not an either or. This is about Hannah, period.”

Fury quivered in the silence between them. Finally Elliott stepped into the brink. “I still want you to wait till tomorrow. Then we can send a properly equipped team.”

Green steadied himself with a deep breath. "Tomorrow you can send all the teams you want after us. We'll even mark the way for you. But we have to get started today." Fed up with the united front, Green turned on his heel to stride across the grass. With daylight waning, he knew they had little time to get started on the trail.

"You don't even know where the fuck they went!" Sullivan shouted.

"I do, in fact," Jethro said, calmly packing up his own bag. "I picked up their trail on the far side of that mound. They're heading south into that valley."

It took the four of them half an hour and more argument to divide up the supplies. Green chafed as he watched the precious daylight trickling between their fingers, but there were still a few good hours left when Jethro led off at a half trot. Green pushed himself to follow, determined not to be a hindrance to the mission.

The valley was deep in twilight by the time Jethro stopped at the base of yet another bluff. They had slogged through forests, up boulder-strewn creek beds, and across alpine meadows, all the time working their way farther and farther south. Away from the Nahanni and into the deepest, most untouched backcountry. Jethro had rarely broken the silence except to give instructions, but Green was grateful. He needed every breath for the journey.

Up ahead rose the grey flank of another formidable mountain. Jethro pointed toward it. "Looks like they're headed through there. Probably skirted around it or went through that pass. But it's getting dark and dangerous. We'll camp here and figure that out in the morning."

Green sank to his knees and pulled out his water canteen. He doubted he had the strength to pitch their tent, let alone prepare dinner, but Jethro wasted no time. Barely an hour later, warmed by a roaring fire and a bowl of rehydrated chili, Green was dead asleep.

CHAPTER NINETEEN

The next morning, half an hour after waking, they were tackling the mountainside, following a dry stream. Green's body protested every move, but he kept quiet. Luckily Jethro moved slowly as he picked the trail from the rocky ground. Just after lunch, he lost the trail. They were working their way across a broad slab of rock toward a gap in the mountain range ahead. He roamed in a wide arc, sent Tatso out to search, backtracked, juggled his map and compass, retraced the wide arc, and finally returned to Green. He spread out the map on the rock.

"No physical trail," he said. "Solid rock. So we use logic. Our party has been heading pretty steadily southwest. Even when they detour to go around a difficult point, they return to that direction, as if they're following a compass reading."

"So that means they're probably going to carry on southwest."

Jethro nodded. "I think they're going toward the Little Nahanni River. There used to be a lot of prospecting interest up in those mountains. But this ridge is in the way. They might go around it through this valley —" He traced a large arc on the map.

"But that might take days."

"Right. Or they might go through that pass up there."

To Green, the solution was obvious but he held his tongue. He'd made a deal; Jethro was in charge. "Which do we do?"

Jethro eyed the steep, barren slope up to the gap. The ground was unstable, the climb formidable. "We go around."

"But —" Green stopped himself. "How much time would we lose?"

Jethro shrugged. "As long as time is all we lose, we're ahead."

"If you were on your own, would you go over the pass?"

"We each know our own wilderness," he replied.

In the background a dull roar began to grow. It swelled until the thundering drumbeat of a helicopter echoed off the mountainside. Jethro lifted his binoculars and pointed. At first the helicopter was a distant speck against the leaden sky, but soon it took shape, circling and swooping downward out of sight like a huge yellow bird. With a nod of satisfaction, Jethro sheathed his binoculars.

"Good. We'll leave them a marker of the direction we've chosen."

They made better time now that they were walking across open ground. Jethro paused now and then to check for tracks, but he had his eye on the thick forest that marked the ravine at the foot of the mountain. By mid afternoon they had reached the trees and stopped to pull on bug shirts before working their way slowly through the dense brush. Jethro found an animal track and followed it, carefully examining the soft forest loam.

"Wolves, moose, grizzlies.... This is a busy highway. Can't tell if any humans used it yet."

Up ahead they heard the gurgle of water, first a soft whisper that soon grew to a sibilant rush. Both Jethro and Green quickened their pace. They needed to replenish their water supply and Green longed to plunge his burning feet into the ice-cold stream.

Jethro stopped so abruptly that Green crashed into him. "Look!" Jethro whispered.

Green peered ahead, but could see nothing but trees. Jethro inched forward. He was crouching, every sense alert. At his side, Tatso wagged her tail excitedly. Slowly the silhouette of a peaked roof emerged through the brush.

"It's a cabin," Jethro whispered.

"A cabin! Here?"

Jethro nodded. "There are old cabins scattered all through the mountains around here. Trappers built them, sometimes prospectors too. Mostly in the valleys and by creeks where the game is plentiful." He approached until the whole outline of the log structure was visible in what had once been a clearing but was now filled with wildflowers; pinks, purples, and vivid red. The cabin was little more than a shack with a filthy window, a splintered front door, and a roof that was collapsing on one side. The rough spruce logs were grey with age, the corners encased in blackened tin.

Green was about to rush forward when Jethro grabbed his arm. He pointed to the ground, where even Green could distinguish the faint outline of a tread.

"Someone's been here."

Jethro left Green on watch at the edge of the clearing as he circled the cabin and approached from the rear. Green waited impatiently as the man slowly worked his way around, inspecting the ground at each step. Finally he reached the splintered door, which had been patched with a chunk of rough lumber. After a cautious push, it creaked loudly open.

They both froze, listening. Nothing. Jethro sniffed and poked his head inside.

"Sometimes porcupines take up residence in this prime real estate," he said. "Or wolverines. Don't want to surprise one of those." After a quick peek, he motioned to Green and stepped through the crack. Green rushed forward.

The first thing to hit him was the stink. A powerful musky animal smell that choked his lungs.

"Is there an animal in here?"

Jethro shone his flashlight across the floor and into the corners. "Porcupines, but they've been evicted. Someone has swept this place out."

As Green's breathing and eyesight adjusted, he noticed the primitive but neat interior. The cabin was about twelve feet square. A rough bunk bed took up one corner and a makeshift oil-drum stove the other. A table and two wooden chairs, one with a broken back, sat in the middle. Cool, fresh mountain air blew through the broken window at the back.

"Oh, wow!" Jethro was looking around the room and for the first time since Green had known him, he looked excited. "This is it! There was an old rumour in the bush about a lost cabin up near the Little Nahanni. A trapping cabin built by a couple of prospectors near their claim."

"You mean the Lasalles? This is the Lasalle cabin?"

Jethro nodded. "No one's found it in years."

"Obviously ..." Green picked up the fresh spruce bough with its needles still green that was propped against the wall by the door. "Someone found it."

"And recently."

"My daughter's group?"

"Probably. That spruce is less than a week old and that patch on the door is new. Most of these cabins are fifty to a hundred years old, from the trapping and prospecting days, and most have fallen down. The land reclaims its own. But hikers and trippers do use them, and they're encouraged to repair them the best they can."

Green looked around. There was not a single trace, not even a food wrapper, to suggest anyone had been there. His wave of euphoria crumbled. "They're gone," he said. "Almost looks like they were trying to erase their tracks."

"That's common. 'Leave no footprint' is the park motto. And you don't want to leave anything that would attract animals." Jethro was inspecting the interior of the wood stove. "But there was a fire in here recently. Not today, but recently." He pried the cabin door open further, allowing daylight to flood the interior. Green began a systematic examination of the room, as if it were a crime scene. The table top was clean and free of dust. There were no mattresses on the bunk beds but the wooden slats were also free of dust. Swept into a crack between the floor planks, he found the foil wrappings of a pill. VIL was visible. Probably Advil, which was hardly a surprise. He'd consumed almost his whole bottle of the anti-inflammatory pain reliever himself on this trip.

The walls were rough logs with moss, lichen, and mud stuffed in the gaps to ward off the cold. Visitors had carved initials, dates, and simple messages into the wood. Most were quite old, with dates in the 1950s and 60s. Some of the messages were hard to read. Some were funny: "Beware the killer stove," "porcupine heaven." Some hinted at trouble: "Snowed in," "Love you, LL Scary mountain." The date of that one was 8/4/45, signed GL. Green's pulse spiked. Guy Lasalle? Was he referring to the mountain behind them?

"Bullet hole," Jethro said. He was standing on the front stoop, poking at the door.

Green spun around. "Don't touch it." He hurried over. In the middle of the door, about chest high, was a small round hole.

"Some nights when you're staying in these cabins you get a visit from a grizzly," Jethro said, "or a pack of wolves. Especially in the early spring when they're hungry and you've got food in here. You're not going to open the door to go after them, but you might shoot through it if you're desperate."

Green shone his flashlight at the hole and shook his head. "This bullet was shot from outside, into this room." He fished around in his pack for his camera and took a series of shots. Then he took out a long, thin steel tent peg, cleaned it off, and slid it carefully into the hole. The peg pointed straight across the room toward the broken window on the opposite wall. With his flashlight he inspected the window. Fragments of glass littered the ground outside, but there was no sign of the bullet or an indent outside.

Fear stirred in the pit of his stomach. "It looks as if the bullet broke this window and disappeared somewhere into the woods. Judging from the diameter of the hole in the door, it's a large calibre rifle, probably pretty powerful."

"Most rifles in these parts aren't toys. They're made to stop grizzlies or moose."

"A grizzly or moose wouldn't be inside here," Green said. "Someone fired a shot at something in here."

"Fired two shots." Jethro had moved to the other side of the window near the front corner, where another hole was barely discernible in the log. Like the other hole it was waist high and had a horizontal trajectory. This time, however, the shot was angled to the right and when Green searched the other side of the cabin, he found the exit hole buried in the corner.

Bile rose in his throat. Forcing himself to think, not like a father but like a police officer, he squatted to examine the floor. The plank floor was well swept but decades of debris had collected in the cracks. Water stains and black patches marred the old wood, but he couldn't see any traces of blood. Not even the smallest drop. Maybe both bullets had missed their mark and passed harmlessly by. How he wished for luminol!

He went outside to see where the bullets had come from. The wildflowers in front of the cabin were undisturbed, but he traced a line with his eye back to a copse of trees about twenty feet away. The gunman might have hidden there and fired at the cabin wall, but he would have little idea what he was shooting at, beyond a vague form visible through the front window. The two shots, aimed more than three feet apart, suggested he'd been guessing.

Green walked out to the copse of trees and studied the area. Propped against a tree was a very old axe with a rusty head but polished blade. On the ground sat an upended stump, which was covered with wood chips, as was the surrounding ground. Even Green, who bought all the wood for his fireplace precut, recognized this as a chopping block.

He picked up a wood chip and held it to the light. It had not yet turned grey. He sniffed it. Sweet resin tickled his nose.

Jethro had been watching him and now joined him with a smile. "You read the signs just like me. Just different signs. The cuttings are very recent."

Green was on his hands and knees, probing the soft ground. "No casings, but the shooter might have picked them up, if he was trying to cover up all evidence of the crime."

"Crime? There are lots of stories about shootings in the bush, half of them maybe even true. Freaked-out hikers mistaking a person for a bear, or getting bush fever and shooting anything that moved. Like a porcupine in the cabin."

Green pushed himself back to his feet and dusted off his hands. He shook his head. "Maybe, but I don't like the looks of it. The wood fibres in the hole don't look weathered. That means those bullet holes are recent. I don't know how recent, but certainly not from Guy Lasalle's time."

White Horse, October 20, 1944

Dear Guy,
The trip home was difficult. Endless delays and detours! Whitehorse had six inches of snow when we arrived, with more promised. There is nothing in the stores. Nothing! I am not spending another winter here. My mother insists we go to Vancouver. She says they have fresh milk, butter, and sometimes even eggs in the stores. I love you, and I worry about you in that wretched cabin all winter, but I have to think of our little boy now too. He's not going to remember his father by the spring.

There is no money in the bank, and still no letter here from Gaetan. No one in town has seen him. He is probably having a gay old time in Alaska somewhere and has forgotten all about the squaw and the child.

Forgive me, that sounds petty. I am not myself. William and I are both tired and hungry and cold. I promise to take care of us if you take good care of you, my love.

Your loving, ever-waiting wife, Lydia

Green had to clamber halfway up the hillside behind the cabin, to a point where the forest thinned abruptly, before he could get a signal on the sat phone. He checked in first with Sullivan, who reported that a single rescue helicopter with a long extraction line had flown in. Rothman's sister had bullied her way onto the crew manifest by virtue of being a medical doctor. A rookie constable from the Fort Simpson detachment had also accompanied the SAR team, but she had almost no clue how to evaluate the scene.

"I gave her a crash course in the basics," he said with a chuckle. "They're just setting up the extraction now, and once we get the post-mortem results we'll know whether a full Ident team needs to be deployed here. I had a lot of time yesterday to search the campsite and the body for evidence of foul play."

"And did you find any?"

"Not directly." Sullivan paused. Green could almost see him running his broad hand through his brush cut, as he always did when he was disturbed. "Just a minor inconsistency. As you recall, Daniel had a penetrating skull fracture like he'd hit a sharp stone, but I couldn't find any stone consistent with that in the vicinity. Nothing with blood, tissue, or hair on it."

"That could have been washed away."

"Agreed. Or he could have hit a rock halfway down. It's impossible to search that cliff face without rappelling equipment. It's just a small thing. Maybe I've been spending too long with violent death."

"How's the sister taking it?"

Sullivan's levity vanished. "Like a trooper, under the circumstances. She's mad as hell, but mostly at Daniel. She says he should have known better. He's been a wilderness nut and rock climber all his life, but he's never been reckless. Super safety conscious, in fact, especially since he started medical school and saw how vulnerable the human body is."

The fear coiled in Green's core began to grow. "Sounds like he was scared. Maybe running from something?"

"Possibly."

Green heard the hesitation in Sullivan's tone. He tensed. "What?"

"Well … I don't think it's relevant. I mean, don't read too much into it."

"Brian, *what*?"

"She said the only reason Daniel agreed to go on the trip was Hannah. Scott asked him to go, Pete was apparently against it."

"So what —"

"Daniel was sweet on Hannah. The sister put it bluntly: 'He would have followed her off a cliff.'"

Before Green could recover his voice, Sullivan exclaimed. "Oh crap, I didn't mean … I meant, I'm sure *she* meant that his objectivity was compromised. He might have taken risks to protect her that he wouldn't just for himself."

"You mean like fending off a bear attack?"

There was silence on the line. Green felt a wave of lightheadedness. Sullivan wasn't going to say it, but the answer was there in the silence. Daniel might have died so Hannah could live.

Jesus. Poor Hannah.

"So … so how does the sister know about Daniel's feelings? Are they close?"

"Since he started med school, yes. She's eight years older than him and was always the big sister who babysat him and took care of him. He'd go to her for advice rather than his parents. So she says, and I believe her. She's a dynamite woman."

"So he told her about Hannah?"

"He wasn't going to go on the trip. He didn't want to take the time off his studies. But then he met Hannah at a planning meeting and he was head over heels inside of an hour. Cancelled his whole summer program."

Green thought of Hannah's record with men. "Was there anything between them?"

"The sister didn't think so. Daniel was an awkward guy, never the guy to get the girl. Daniel himself figured he didn't stand a chance against Scott. But he went along just to be with her. And to …" Sullivan's voice faded.

"To what?"

"Well, he had some doubts about Scott's judgment. He even asked his sister's professional opinion. He thought Scott was a bit too high. Too obsessed, too reckless. He wasn't sure he had a good handle on the challenges of the trip or Hannah's skill level."

"Fuck," Green breathed.

"I'm sorry, Mike. But I thought you should know. It means Scott may have ignored danger signs and pushed them all too hard."

"And now …" Green squinted down the rocky slope toward the cabin. "They're running around in this goddamn wilderness without their voice of caution. Without their first aid specialist either."

"Look, one step at a time. Things are about wrapped up here. Elliott and I will start out first thing tomorrow morning to join you."

"That's good. The cabin's at the base of a steep mountain, you can't miss it, but we've left you markers too. But before you leave I want you to ask Hunter Kerry if the kids had a hunting rifle among their gear."

"There's no hunting in the park."

"I know, but …" Green explained about the bullet holes in the cabin. "They look recent but I can't tell how recent. And if one of these guys is carrying a firearm, I want to know …" His voice trailed off as an odd-looking orange object caught his eye through the trees down near the cabin. He pulled out his binoculars and trained them on the spot. Slowly a food barrel came into view, suspended about ten feet in the air between two trees. Hastily he wrapped up the conversation, gave Sullivan the cabin's coordinates, and hung up.

For a moment he remained where he was, crouched down behind a boulder. When they'd reached the cabin, they'd been so excited by the discovery that they had not done a search of the area. An amateur oversight. The cabin was cradled in a small valley, fronting on a creek and backed by a steep slope that rose to the tall peak behind. On either side, willow and spruce fringed the water's edge. Now he scanned the area through binoculars carefully for more packs and gear. If they had left some of their food behind in a cache, that suggested that they were coming back. Or perhaps that they weren't far away, despite the empty cabin.

He was about to return to the cabin to report his discovery when his binoculars caught a flash of light farther along the slope. He swung back, focusing as he tried to distinguish the faint, dark smudge hunkered down in the brush, partially hidden behind a tree.

It was a person, with their binoculars trained on him.

CHAPTER TWENTY

For an instant both men froze. Then the stranger dropped his binoculars and ducked back behind the tree.

"Hey!" Green took chase, tripping and slithering down the hillside as the figure disappeared through the trees. "Wait!" he shouted between gasps. "I won't hurt you!"

The stranger didn't even break his stride as he ploughed through the woods diagonally toward the creek. Green kept shouting, more to alert Jethro than to stop the man. Up ahead he only caught occasional glimpses of the man's grey camouflage jacket.

The man was younger and more agile than Green, and soon even those glimpses ceased. Green stopped, cursing his weakness as he dragged air into his lungs. Cursing his twenty years behind the desk, his love of smoked meat and cheese bagels, his aversion to all things fitness.

Finally he straightened up. All was not lost. Running full tilt through the woods, the man would have left a trail that probably even he could follow. He had just turned back toward the cabin in search of Jethro when a frenzied barking broke the silence of the forest. He froze.

The echo ricocheted around the hills, but the barking seemed to come from the direction the man had fled. Excited, Green turned and hurried through the dense brush. Roots twisted his ankles and sharp branches left welts on his hands, but he ignored them all.

Soon he burst through the dense willow onto the stony creek's edge, where he spotted Jethro kneeling in the icy mountain stream. Pinned beneath him and thrashing with fury was the man in the camouflage jacket. The man had easily four inches and fifty pounds over Jethro, but he was no match. When he spotted Green, he went limp and held up his hands in surrender. Jethro hauled him, dripping and shivering, to his feet.

Green scrutinized him in silence. He looked younger than Green had first thought, with a tangle of blond hair, a lean, muscular body, and the deep tan of an outdoorsman. He carried a small day pouch around his waist and binoculars around his neck, but no other gear. Sullen defiance blazed in his eyes.

"Who the hell are you?" Green demanded.

"Who the hell are you!"

"I'm Inspector Michael Green of the Ottawa Police, and this is —"

The defiance vanished. "Hannah's father. Thank God!"

Green's eyes narrowed. "Are you …?"

"Pete Carlyle." Pete splashed through the water toward him. "Am I glad to see you!"

Jethro grunted. "You sure didn't act like it. I caught him trying to escape up the creek."

"I didn't know who you were. I thought you were Scott!"

"What the hell are you talking about?" Green said. "Where are Scott and Hannah?"

"I don't know, I don't know. They …" Pete's teeth chattered and he swayed sideways.

Green grabbed his arm. "They what!"

Jethro took his other arm. "Let's get him inside. He needs to get out of these wet clothes. That water comes straight off the glaciers."

Pete stumbled as they led him toward the cabin. Green could feel the man's shivering but his own fear made him impatient. "Where are they?"

Seconds ticked by before Pete shook his head. "Gone."

Inside, Jethro built a fire with a few quick, expert moves, while Green helped Pete strip off his soggy boots.

"Where are your dry clothes?"

Pete shook his head. His fingers fumbled with his jacket zipper. "They took everything."

Jethro unrolled his sleeping bag and held it out. "Here, get everything off and wrap yourself in this. We'll get you warm. Mike, go get some water from the stream."

"But —"

"For tea. He needs to get warm."

Green studied Pete closely. It was true that he was shivering and his teeth were chattering, but Green wasn't convinced. Although chilly out, it was still summer. Pete's colouring was pink and healthy, and only a few minutes ago he had been running through the woods without difficulty. But he opted to go along with the pretense, if there was one. He needed the young man's co-operation, and accusing him of lying would not secure that. There was still an aura of stubborn defiance in his mood.

As he filled their pot with water down at the creek, he scanned the surrounding woods carefully. They were silent, undisturbed. Back up in the cabin, Jethro's fire was blazing and Green set the pot upon the stove. Prying open the food barrel, he rooted inside for tea. Pete was by now wrapped in the sleeping bag with only his head visible.

"I thought I was going to die. I've been here for days! No food, no shelter, no clothes. At night the wolves came so close." He shuddered. "I didn't know how to get back. Scott had all the maps, so I was trying to wait it out here until someone found me."

Green held off his questions until he'd made the tea. He poured a cup and held it out to Pete. One hand snaked out from the warmth of the sleeping bag to hold it. Green pulled a chair close to sit in front of him.

"Okay, now what happened? Are Scott and Hannah all right?"

"I don't know."

"What does that mean?"

"I mean … there's something wrong with Scott. He's lost it. A few days ago …" His voice faltered and his hand shook as he raised the cup to his lips. "Daniel was killed. I don't know how, I was asleep. I heard this awful screaming outside the tent, and when I got outside Daniel was gone. Scott said it was a grizzly attack, Daniel ran outside but it was dark and he didn't see the edge." Pete shut his eyes. A single sob broke from his lips.

Green was unmoved. A much greater panic was howling at the gates. "Why didn't you go for help?"

"I wanted to! Hannah too! But Scott was obsessed. He's been obsessed from the beginning with what happened to his grandfather. But after Daniel died, he just lost it. He said we couldn't help Daniel because it was too dangerous to go look for him, and his grandfather's cabin was safer because no one knew where it was. He said we could use it as our base."

"But why didn't you and Hannah go back for help?"

"Because … because Scott had all the maps, the compass, the emergency supplies. And he said people were after him."

"What people?"

"I don't know! That was part of his paranoia! He said years ago his grandfather was murdered, but the killer got away with it because there was no body. He was convinced the brother did it to get the whole claim. He said he had to find proof and stop bad people from getting it now." Pete shook his head in bewilderment. "I've known Scott for a few years now and he's always been kind of driven. Didn't let anything stand in his way if he wanted something. But this … this was crazy talk!"

Green forced himself to stay focused on the questions. "All right, so what happened when you got here?"

"He made us search the whole area for his grandfather's body and the old mining stakes. So we'd do these trips around the cabin and up the mountain, and when we didn't find anything, he got more and more paranoid. He said we were sabotaging him because we wanted the mine for ourselves. 'You're working for them,' he said to me. 'That's why you were so eager to come along on this trip.' Hannah was scared of him. She even thought … Oh fuck, it seems impossible!"

"What does?"

"She was afraid he'd killed Daniel himself."

"Why?"

"Because Daniel wanted to turn back. Hannah was having dizzy spells, she was falling down. It got scary on some of those clifftops. Daniel and Scott had a huge fight about her the night he died."

Green struggled to breathe. Focus. "Is she all right?"

"This is all my fault, but I didn't know what else to do. One night, I tried to sneak into his pack to get the maps and compass, we figured we'd make a run for it. He caught me and he just went ballistic. He grabbed this rifle — I don't even know where it came from, I'd never seen it! I tried to hide in the cabin but he shot right through the door! I dove out the back window and hid in the woods. Then he packed up all our gear — except one food cache that he forgot — and he and Hannah took off."

"Where?"

Pete shrugged. "Still looking for the mining claim, I guess."

Green fought the bile rising in his throat. "So Hannah is out there with the wolves and the grizzlies and a crazy man with a gun?"

Pete nodded. His lips trembled but he didn't speak. Didn't need to, Green thought. Imagination filled in the silence all too well.

* * *

"We've got to find them," Green said. He and Jethro were conferring outside the cabin. Pete had fallen into an exhausted sleep by the fire. Green had already reported in to Sullivan, who was still back at the scene of Daniel's death. He and Elliott had planned to make their way to the cabin the next morning, but with this new threat they had rethought those plans. Sullivan said he would contact the RCMP to initiate a more official search. Helicopters and surveillance aircraft would be deployed and more officers dropped in to provide backup.

"Good idea," Green had told him. "But then you and Elliott get down here. Bring any cops and SAR people who are already on the scene. I need all the help I can get, and I can't wait around for official search parties. He's got Hannah, Brian."

Sullivan had conferred with Elliot and they agreed to set off the next morning at first light, which was 4:00 a.m. Green had calculated quickly. Too late, damn it! It meant twelve more hours with Scott on the loose with Hannah. Doing God knows what.

"This guy Pete will be here at the cabin," he said. "He's pretty shaken up but he'll tell you where we've gone."

"Mike, wait!"

Green had hung up. He didn't have time to waste arguing with Sullivan. He expected enough trouble trying to convince Jethro.

But to his surprise, when he told him Jethro merely nodded and began packing up. It was Pete who panicked. He struggled to throw off the sleeping bag.

"But what about me? You're just going to leave me?"

"We'll leave you that sleeping bag and some more

food. You'll be safe until the others get here tomorrow. They should be here by late morning."

"Can I at least have a gun?"

Green eyed him sceptically. Jethro's rifle was their only firearm. "Do you know how to use a gun?"

"Yeah. Well, no. But if a grizzly comes at me, or Scott comes back, I'd rather have a chance!"

Green shook his head. Sullivan also had a hunting rifle, but Sullivan was a full day behind. Green needed Jethro's rifle for the pursuit.

"We'll leave you our bear banger and some flares," Jethro said. "If you run into trouble, go up to the open slope behind here and signal. Flares, smoke signals, everything you can think of. Before long, this area is going to be thick with planes. They'll see you."

Pete was clearly not convinced. He stood in the doorway scowling as Jethro and Green set off. Jethro had sent Tatso on a long, circular scouting expedition, and she had picked up a trail with little difficulty. It continued to trek southwest up the creek bed toward the valley of the Little Nahanni.

"The trail must be more recent," Jethro said as he scrutinized a patch of soft loam once they were out of Pete's sight. "She's picking up a scent without trouble." He pointed to a print that even Green could recognize. The checkered grooves of a hiking boot. "But they're moving fast. See how deep the depression is? The push off at the toe? They're running."

"Can you tell who?"

Jethro nodded. "The size of the boot, the weight it carried, I'd say a small woman."

Fort Simpson, July 24

Constable Christian Tymko had flown back to Fort Simpson from Whitehorse two days earlier. Instead of being assigned to the helicopter recovery team, however, he found himself behind the desk while Sergeant Nihls sent the rookie constable instead. His excuse was that it would be an excellent training exercise for her, but Chris suspected a more petty reason. Chris had been the one to sound the alarm first about the missing trippers, and now that he had been proved right Nihls wanted him as far from the action as possible.

News of the hiker's death in the Nahanni had been all over town that morning, and rumours of the Lasalle party and its search for the lost mine were rampant. Chris spent more time fielding calls and handling curiosity seekers than he did on his paperwork backlog. All the while he kept a sharp eye on the sky and an impatient ear for the roar of a Twin Otter coming in. Hunter Kerry had not returned to Fort Simpson since leaving Whitehorse. His flight logs revealed trips to Cantung Mine, Flat Lake, and Yellowknife, but made no mention of Victor or Olivia.

It was close to noon by the time Chris made it down through his inbox to a pile of faxed documents from Yellowknife RCMP headquarters. He glanced at the first page and his excitement shot up. It was dated September 13, 1945, and labelled SUMMARY REPORT, INVESTIGATION INTO MISSING PERSON GUY LASALLE.

He waved the papers under Nihls's nose. "When did this come in?"

Nihls's eyes strayed briefly from his computer to the papers. "Oh, they came in while you were in Whitehorse. More Ottawa cops sticking their oar in, requisitioning old files. HQ decided it should go through us, and since you're the one most familiar with this Lasalle file it's all yours. Not much there or I would have told you. The Ottawa officer's contact info is on the cover letter there, if you want to follow up."

Chris glanced at the name. Detective Bob Gibbs, not the woman he had dealt with. He returned to his desk and began to decipher the faded and uneven typing of the original report, made even more illegible by the fax. It appeared that the disappearance of Guy Lasalle had remained unsolved, and the case was still technically open. Two officers had flown up to the cabin in June when Lasalle's wife reported him missing and it became clear he had not shown up at the trading post as arranged. They had found the cabin empty. There was no sign of violence, animal or human, and no sign of Lasalle himself. However, the cabin had not been cleaned up, let alone closed up for the season. His food and furs were still in the cache. His coffee pot was on the stove top, his bedding was still on the bunk, all his clothing and gear were stored in the cabin, and even his breakfast dishes were unwashed, as if he had intended to return at any moment.

Letters to and from his wife sat in a neat pile on the little kitchen table along with other mail, sacks of rock samples were stacked outside the door, and his dogsled was propped against the cabin. The two officers noted that his parka and mukluks were missing, however, as were his axe, shovel, and rifle. The officers had searched his trapline and the area around the cabin, including the creek, to a radius of one kilometre, but without success. His two dogs were long gone, of course, but the remains of their gnawed harnesses were still attached to the tree outside.

The fur trader and various Indians in Nahanni Butte had been interviewed, but the last confirmed sighting of the missing man was in February, when an Indian trapper had come by the cabin. Lasalle was reportedly in good health at that time, but suffering from loneliness and anxiety about the poor haul of furs he had made so far. Lasalle had also asked numerous questions about the activities and whereabouts of his brother Gaetan.

For lack of evidence, the officers ruled out suicide, but left the results inconclusive. The officers speculated that perhaps Lasalle had gone hunting and had fallen prey to a surprise storm, an animal attack, or the treacherous ice on the creek. In either eventuality, his carcass could have been carried off by wolves. In the absence of clear leads the officers had concluded their investigation and packed up all Lasalle's effects from the cabin, including the letters and the sacks of rocks, to be sent off to his wife in Vancouver.

Chris reread the report twice. No wonder rumours had been rampant. The man had disappeared, apparently almost in the middle of breakfast, and had never been heard from again. The facts seemed to rule out death by misadventure during his return from the bush. Lasalle had simply walked out of his cabin one morning and never returned. No wonder the wife had cried foul. No wonder speculation about murder had run wild.

Chris was about to phone the Detective Gibbs listed on the cover page when he caught the faint drone of a small aircraft coming from the west. He looked up. Listened. It was a Twin Otter, possibly Hunter Kerry. Shoving aside the file, he grabbed his keys and utility belt and raced out of the station. Hunter Kerry was as slippery as an eel and he had no intention of letting him disappear.

He intercepted Hunt just as the man was unloading his overnight gear from the plane. Chris skidded the Jeep to a stop in a cloud of dust. Hunt raised his head, bemused and wary. He said nothing as he watched Chris approach.

"Welcome back, Hunt. Enjoy your trip around the world?"

Hunt scowled. "Just dropping off customers, picking up supplies. Busy."

"In Whitehorse? A little out of your territory, isn't it?"

Hunt tried to hide his surprise. "I offer services all across the Southwest. Didn't know there was a law against that."

"As long as you file all the proper flight plans and passenger manifests. Which you always do, right?"

Hunt's expression shuttered. He glared through narrowed eyes. "I'll get to it. What's it to you, anyway?"

"That missing Lasalle group you flew in early in the month? One of them has turned up dead."

The pilot's eyes widened briefly before he could hide his shock. "Sorry to hear that."

"So I need to know who you flew into the area. I've got all the tour groups covered, but it's the private parties that might get in our way." It was a ludicrous explanation but he hoped Hunt was too rattled to question it.

But Hunt merely shrugged. "They weren't going into the park, so it's not an issue."

"Then where were they going?"

"I don't see how —"

"Let me explain." Chris thought fast. He didn't want to mention Victor Whitehead and Olivia, in case Hunt tipped them off that Chris was on their trail. He took a guess. "You've got to know who your friends are, Hunt. Your clients, who asked you not to register the flight or their names? Or us, who watch out over your pilot's licence, your income tax, and your nice little, private, energy-guzzling bungalow in the country?"

Hunter Kerry blinked. Three times. As if his mind was having trouble weighing the odds. Finally he slumped. "I dropped them at Flat Lake. A celebrity honeymoon couple. They said they wanted the privacy and the whitewater challenge of canoeing the Little Nahanni."

Chris drove straight to the Parks Office, where he found Bugden in his office in animated conversation on the phone. With a free hand, he beckoned Chris to enter. Chris went immediately to study the map of the park and surroundings. The locations of the turquoise canoe, the flooded campsite, and Daniel Rothman's body were all marked with red pins. Daniel Rothman's body was inside the current park boundaries but near the southwest boundary.

Still on the phone, Bugden walked over to peer at the map and picked up another red pin. With his finger he traced coordinate lines and stuck the pin into the map just southwest outside the park boundary.

"Got it. Huh. What do you know, the mystery Lasalle cabin. Yeah, it's outside the park as it stands now, but who knows what the new boundaries will be, once the government is through twiddling its thumbs? Looks like your party is heading pretty well due southwest but they'll run into the Little Nahanni. Unless they have a boat, they'll be pinned down. I'll let the Mounties know. Tymko just walked in. And keep me posted on when you get the body out."

Bugden signed off and turned to Chris. "SAR's just relayed the latest report from Inspector Green. He and Jethro found a cabin in this region here. It's empty, the Lasalle party are gone, but the cabin shows signs of recent use."

Chris studied the location of the latest pin. It looked as if the Lasalle party was continuing its southwest trek, over rugged, rarely travelled backcountry. They were now outside the park boundary, but Chris was interested to note that since his last visit Bugden had pencilled in the three possible boundaries of the new section of park being planned by the Canadian government. That park would protect almost all the South Nahanni watershed from development, all the way up to Moose Ponds. The final boundary was in hot dispute. The mountains were rich in mineral resources and there were already a number of mining operations in various stages of development.

It was also home to possibly the most stunning, varied, and fragile ecosystem on the planet. Chris knew the arguments well. On the one side, invasive roads, acidic waste rock dumps, chemical spills, tailing ponds, and waste water contaminating all the creeks and rivers downstream. On the other, prosperity and growth in a largely uninhabited land. With all the environmental protection measures in place and the royalties and jobs flowing to the local First Nations, mining was not always the exploitive and destructive force it once was. Whatever the government's decision, the final boundary would be a compromise. For now, it was still caught up in consultation and red tape, although Chris suspected the conservationists would not be pleased. In recent years the government had shown a decided bias in favour of industry and jobs over environmental protection.

As a Parks Canada employee, Bugden had to stay neutral but his decision to pencil in all three boundary possibilities was telling. Chris studied the map, the pins, and then Bugden's face, which was deadpan.

"Hmm," Chris said, "if the ruby mine is near the cabin, which makes sense, and the government goes with the most protective boundary for the new park, it looks like this ruby mine will be inside the park."

Bugden said nothing.

"But if the government chooses the more limited boundary, which leaves lots of land for further mining development, this mine might actually be viable."

"Yes."

"Assuming it even has rubies."

"It doesn't. But there are other valuable red stones, there's gold, copper, silver, and zinc. Not to mention the hot new rare earth metals. No end of riches are possible. And if they rebuild this old mining road up from Cantung, it will be easy to get them out."

Chris followed the man's finger and his pulse quickened. The little red pin marking the cabin was maybe six kilometres away from the old road, although over very rough terrain. But more importantly it was even closer to the Little Nahanni River, which at this very moment Victor Whitehead and Olivia Manning were preparing to descend. In less than two days they would pass within a few kilometres of Green, Jethro, and the mythical ruby mine.

Little Nahanni, January 8, 1945

Dear Lydia,
This is a difficult winter. I have not seen a human being since November, when Albert visited on his way to a new trapline. I don't know when this letter will get to you, and I despair with no letters from you. I will walk down to Albert's when it warms up. I think it will never stop snowing. It is now as high as the window ledge, and new snow falls every day. Every day I dig the traps out and start again. Many days I have no meat for myself or the dogs. Even the wolves have trouble finding food, and I hear them at night around the cabin. I sleep on the top bunk, with the rifle and the axe nearby. I am reading

Twelfth Night, a silly play that takes my mind off things. Your *Macbeth* is too hard.

I am happy you are in Vancouver with your family. I know Whitehorse is difficult in winter, but don't forget it's our home. Don't forget the rivers and the mountains purple with fireweed in summer. I hope you will be back in our home when I come out in the spring. Who is watching out for the house, and the bank? There is still no news from Gaetan. I don't think he's putting money in the bank.

Embrace my son for me, and don't let him forget me.

Your Guy

In less than ten minutes Chris was back at the station, making preparations to fly up to the Little Nahanni. He had a bad feeling about this. One group of people hiking in overland, another coming down by river. The motives of both were unclear, but he was pretty sure Scott and Victor were not on the same side. And with potentially millions of dollars in play, the stakes and the danger were high. Caught up in the middle of this, with her own motives the most unclear of all, was the woman he'd spent two perfect nights with.

It didn't bear thinking about.

It was a seven hundred kilometre round trip from Fort Simpson to the headwaters of the Little Nahanni. In case he had to get down on the river, he needed a boat and camping supplies for at least one night. It would be a reconnaissance mission to see where they were and what they might be up to. If he spotted the Lasalle or Green party as well, all the better.

Neither Bugden nor Nihls were happy about his solo venture, but they couldn't argue with his reasons. Even Nihls admitted the advantage of having more eyes in the sky over the search area.

At first light he was airborne, watching the town drop away as the Cessna's nose lifted into the pale pink clouds. He flew high, hoping to make maximum speed. By seven o'clock he was flying over the ragged, snow-capped peak of Mount Nirvana poking through the mantle of cloud. He dropped back down as he approached the Flat Lakes and was startled when jagged scars of waste rock, roads, and buildings emerged out of the wilderness. Cantung Mine.

From this height, he could see nothing but trucks and loaders beetling back and forth, and smoke belching from the flat concrete buildings at the edge of the mine. He circled to give it another pass, but could see nothing unusual. Men glanced up, shielded their eyes, and waved at him before carrying on.

He flew on, following the path of the river up toward Flat Lake, where Victor and Olivia would have started their journey. There was no sign of them. High above sea level in the cradle of snow-capped mountains, the vegetation was sparse and the land desolate. Beyond the perimeter of the mine lay nothing but wilderness. He could just make out a thin, faint scar running alongside the water, all that was left of the mining road that had once brought prospectors and speculators deep into the core of the Mackenzie Mountains. Nowadays only backpackers and adventurers, along with the occasional mountain biker, used it.

Chris planned to follow the Little Nahanni River but didn't want to fly directly overhead because Olivia would recognize his plane. The very thought of her brought a surge of very unprofessional anger. He didn't want to tip her off that he was searching. She and Victor would hear the plane, of course, but might think it was mining personnel or even a commercial pilot bringing in a party of canoeists. The presence of his plane would mean only one thing to them; that he — and perhaps the RCMP — was suspicious of their activities.

He edged the plane left to fly over the gravel road, keeping one eye on the river and another on the ragged terrain below. He had covered less than ten kilometres before a flash of metal on the road below caught his eye. Had he imagined it? A mere wink of water through the trees? Or something else, something manmade where there should be nothing at all?

Curious, he banked and flew back over for a second look. This time he caught a glimpse of a shape before the canopy of trees shielded it from view. It was shiny, solid, and black, larger than a bicycle but too wide for a canoe.

It was impossible to know how long the object had been there, but its shiny exterior suggested that it might be recent. It could mean nothing. It could be an old piece of mining equipment junked long ago. Or it could be a sign that someone was in trouble. Chris had worked in the wilderness too long to ignore even the smallest irregularity.

He headed back toward the mine, landed in the lake closest to it, and taxied up to the dock. By the time he had secured his plane a truck was pulling up. A man climbed out and introduced himself as the site supervisor. He was wearing a hard hat with mosquito netting and a heavy jacket. Chris was in civilian clothes and immediately regretted his bare arms and head. The air was cold but still the mosquitoes descended.

"Have you got a vehicle stranded up on the track about thirty K north of your mine?" he asked once he'd identified himself.

The site supervisor looked astonished. "What kind of vehicle?"

"Can't tell, but big enough to be a truck."

"That road's not passable, at least not yet. There are beaver dams, washed out culverts, and trees down all along it. We get adventurers on ATVs and dirt bikes sometimes, but anything bigger … Maybe a modified Land Rover, if you don't mind taking the bottom out of her."

"Have you seen any vehicles or other visitors in the vicinity in recent weeks?"

The supervisor frowned. He was a large, beefy man and his jacket buttons strained against his gut. "This is a private facility with a valuable product, so we keep a close eye. I'll check with security but I don't think so. Of course, we've heard about that man dead in the Nahanni. That why you're here?"

Chris nodded, letting the explanation ride. The supervisor gestured him toward his pickup and Chris climbed in, grateful to escape the mosquitoes. Back at the mine, a check with the chief of security revealed no unusual sightings.

Chris consulted the large topographical map on the wall and tried to pinpoint the location of the mystery vehicle. "Do you guys have a couple of ATVs that can handle that road?"

The two men nodded simultaneously. "We both have one. Other guys too."

"How long would it take to get up there?"

The supervisor grimaced. "Thirty K on that road? At least three hours, maybe more. And that's if the bridges aren't washed out or the road swamped. We had a hell of a rainstorm a couple of weeks ago."

Chris hesitated. The trip there and back would take the rest of the day. On the one hand he wanted to pursue his original goal of checking up on Olivia and Victor. On the other, the presence of that vehicle was very odd indeed, especially if the road was nearly impassable. Cantung Mine itself was at least a hundred kilometres from the nearest civilization, and this road was more remote still. No one drove up that road by accident, or just to take in the scenery. If the truck had broken down, they would be in serious trouble.

"How soon can we get started?" he asked.

Half an hour later, three ATVs drove out the gates of the mine and headed up Nahanni Range Road. The security chief and site supervisor had both chosen to come along and the ATVs were loaded up with winch, pulleys, ropes, and chains as well as emergency and medical supplies. Chris said nothing when the men secured a couple of big-game rifles on top.

Initially the going was smooth, but once they left the mine entrance the ruts and boulders grew bigger. Soon the road became nothing but an overgrown track, bone-jarring and mosquito-infested. Chris was glad he'd put on his helmet with mosquito netting. The three men didn't talk as they slogged up the road, powering through ditches, over broken culverts and massive stones.

Faint tire tracks carved ruts into the marshy sections, but when Chris dismounted for a closer look he could see they were not fresh. They were nearly obliterated by weeks of weather and rain.

They were nearing the three-hour mark when Chris drove around a curve and came upon a big, black, late-model Yukon SUV pulled to the edge of the track under partial cover of overhanging pine boughs. He skidded to a stop. The Yukon was mud-splattered and speckled with debris but a quick visual inspection revealed no obvious damage. No flat tires or broken axles. The windows were tinted, making it difficult to see inside. Chris signalled the others to stay back while he scanned the ground around it. Rain and erosion had wiped out all prints to his inexperienced eye. He circled the vehicle and cupped his hands to peer inside. There was no one inside, but he spotted some waterproof containers, blankets, and small packs, along with chains, axe, and shovel. This vehicle was well equipped for trouble. He wiped the mud from the plates. Yukon plates. He pulled out his notebook and jotted down the number.

In full investigative mode, he used his glove and tested the door handles, careful not to smudge any prints. All the doors were locked. He attempted to phone the plate in, but his sat phone registered no signal. The group was halfway back to the mine, driving through open scrub, before his phone finally came to life.

He called the detachment, relieved to hear a cheerful young voice instead of Nihls. He waited while the constable ran the plate.

"It's registered to Enterprise Rent-A-Car in Whitehorse."

Chris grinned. Enterprise would be thrilled to see the condition and location of their expensive new vehicle now. He asked the constable to find out who had rented it, when, and for how long. The constable called back in less than ten minutes. He sounded excited.

"It was rented on June 15 by a company, Northern Rubicom, on a long-term rental due back August 15."

Chris's pulse spiked. Northern Rubicom was the company to which Olivia's professor consulted.

The constable was rushing on. "It was charged to the corporate account, but get this! Guess who the designated driver is?"

Chris could think of a few possibilities. Scott Lasalle himself had been in Whitehorse in the middle of June, buying his trip equipment. "Scott Lasalle?"

"No, but close. His travelling buddy, Peter Carlyle."

CHAPTER TWENTY-ONE

Chris and the mine employees had just arrived back at the mine when the call came in from Sergeant Nihls. After six bone-jarring hours on the ATV, Chris was exhausted, sore, and starving. The mine supervisor had offered beer, a hot meal, and a soft bed for the night. With that temptation, Chris had already decided to wait until morning to check out Victor and Olivia. It was nearly 7:00 p.m., and although there were several hours of daylight left Chris suspected the two would have set up camp for the night.

The sergeant's call changed all that. He brought Chris up-to-date on Green's encounter with Pete and the likely route taken by Scott and Hannah. "They're on the run. If they hold that direction, they're going to intersect the Little Nahanni, probably just south of Crooked Canyon. Your location is ideal so we need you to conduct aerial searches up that way." Nihls's parting shot was almost an afterthought. "Surveillance only, Constable. The male subject is armed, mentally unstable, and should be considered extremely dangerous. Report any sightings but do not, under any circumstances, engage either subject, is that clear?"

Chris couldn't see how he could possibly engage the subjects from a hundred metres up in the sky, but he dutifully agreed. The sun was a ball of flame suspended over the western mountaintops by the time he'd fuelled up and become airborne again. His flight path took him almost directly into its glare, and his visibility was further hampered by the deep purple shadows in the valley below.

He flew over the lakes quickly before edging over to the west side of the river valley and dropping altitude as much as he dared. The surface of the meandering Little Nahanni became ruffled as the river gradually picked up speed, and the shoreline of willows and reeds gave way to rocky twists. He was still at least fifty miles south of Crooked Canyon when he started to search in earnest for a single canoe and a couple of tents tucked onto shore. He spotted the camp on a broad, flat gravel bar just below a particularly scary stretch of whitewater. Two figures were sitting on a tarp by the fire. He peeled away, but not before he saw one of them glance up and shield his eyes. Chris knew his plane would be almost invisible against the sun. The two would know they'd been spotted, but not by whom.

He continued downriver until he saw the steep canyon walls and foaming water of the Crooked Canyon. From this height, it looked unnavigable, and many paddlers did portage around it, but the true thrill-seekers went right down the middle on the tongue of rushing water.

The canyon was deep in shadow at this time of the evening. Chris dropped his plane lower and his eyes strained to penetrate the gloom. The canyon and the cliffside looked untouched. He banked the plane inland toward the east, flying low over the ridges and up the creeks that rushed between them. The forests huddled black and impenetrable in the valleys, the alpine slopes gleamed almost blood red in the sunset. He suspected this assignment was a waste of time. If Scott and Hannah were really on the run, they would not be standing out in the open waiting to be spotted. They would be hunkered down under the dense, dark canopy of trees. At most, he might glimpse a pinpoint of light from their fire.

After circling the area in ever-widening spirals three times without success, he called in his report and headed back to the mine. As he flew back over Victor and Olivia's camp, he saw no lights or signs of activity. The busy pair had gone to bed.

The next morning, after a hearty breakfast with the mining staff, he checked in with Sergeant Nihls again. Continue your aerial sorties, he was told. He raised the question of Peter Carlyle and Northern Rubicom.

"We need to check out the company, sir, and find out who set it up. Who else is a director."

"Not now, Constable. We have our hands full."

"But it could be Scott Lasalle, sir. If so, he's got some pretty heavy-duty consulting and lobbying help all lined up. Victor Whitehead and Professor Anil Elatar, who is on half a dozen mining companies' boards."

"Let's concentrate on apprehending Mr. Lasalle without loss of life, Constable. All the rest can wait."

Chris could hear the edge to Nihls's voice, picture the tight line of his lips. He changed tactics. "Agreed, but what about the abandoned Yukon SUV, sir? It appears functional. It could provide an escape route for him. We need to keep it under surveillance."

"Negative, Constable. No manpower. Can it be towed to the mine?"

"Negative, sir" was on the tip of Chris's tongue but he stopped himself. "The terrain is too rough, sir."

"Then disable it," Nihls snapped before hanging up.

Chris considered asking the mine personnel to puncture the Yukon's tires but it was a long trek not without risk. Instead, he asked them to block the exit road with boulders.

Fog had rolled in overnight, blanketing the ground in a damp, chilly mist. It was nearly nine o'clock by the time the shroud had lifted enough for him to get into the sky again. He stayed low as he flew along the abandoned road, spotting the SUV at exactly the same spot he had the previous day. It was still too early for Scott and Hannah to have reached it, assuming that was their goal. The slog up the creeks, through the mountain pass and across the Little Nahanni itself, would likely take several days.

He returned his attention to the Little Nahanni River valley, flying across the broad flatlands and down over the first rapids. The cloud cover was thick and low, blocking the glare of the sun and washing the landscape in a pale, moody glow. He banked away from the gravel bar where Victor and Olivia had camped, hoping to avoid detection this time. The shore was empty. He flew on downriver, expecting to spot them in the wide gentle valley. Nothing but stands of silent spruce and a couple of startled moose.

After half an hour he saw the Crooked Canyon up ahead, where the placid river churned white as it hurtled through the narrow funnel. He banked, flew across it, circled downriver, and flew back. Wind and mist buffeted the plane as his eyes combed the landscape below.

Nothing.

He flew further downstream, puzzled. How could Victor and Olivia have travelled this far downstream in a few short hours, unless they'd left camp at four in the morning? He flew on until he was convinced they were not further downstream, before he circled back up to the canyon. Maybe they'd taken the portage. Olivia was a daredevil who loved every boil and wave, but Victor was a city boy. Perhaps she had played it safe for him.

If they had been hidden by the trees on the portage during his first pass, they would have emerged by now. But the river flowed beneath him, empty. No sign even of a capsized boat or a figure stranded on the shore.

Fear began to crawl its way into his belly. Olivia was an experienced guide, but this was dangerous territory. Besides the lethal class IV rapids on the river itself, there were grizzlies and wolves, used to prowling the land unchallenged.

And there was Victor Whitehead.

The liar, the schemer, the unknown factor in this expedition. Olivia's words from the week before came back to him. "Sometimes if you want to do some small bit of good, you have to wade into the crap where the game is being played."

What if Victor was using her? Using her knowledge and contacts as a mining engineer and as a wilderness guide for his own ends? What if she was not his willing partner but his dupe? She was alone with the man, hundreds of kilometres from safety.

At that thought, he gave up all attempts to go undetected. Fighting back fear, he dropped still lower over the wide valley above the canyon. His eyes raked the treeline, looking for any sign of them.

Finally he spotted a small scrap of green tucked deep in the trees. It blended so well into the landscape that it was barely visible through the canopy. If Chris hadn't known their canoe was green, he would never have noticed it. He circled and flew lower, skimming the river as he tried to make out details. It was a canoe all right, stashed out of sight.

The rest of the gear, and the two paddlers, were nowhere in sight.

At the last second, he spotted the cliff ahead. He pulled up sharply just before the canyon walls, clipping the tops of the spruce trees on the clifftop. Heart pounding, he climbed high into the sky to catch his breath. Questions crowded in. Had they gone inland? Had they arranged a rendezvous? Cresting the mountain peak, he headed north over the inland creeks. He scanned the ground below for signs of them. Nothing but wilderness. Endless wilderness. He felt as if he'd been staring at wilderness for days. Steadying the plane, he radioed Nihls to report his findings.

"Sir," he added, "I think we need to send a team in by boat down the Little Nahanni. ASAP, sir."

He listened to the man mutter as if he were studying the map. Finally he grunted. "Duly noted, Constable.

For now, let's hold off. We'll have helicopters in the air and men on the ground out there soon. Once I have the search commander's report —"

"Sir, all that takes time. If you fly the equipment and personnel up here to the mine, I can have us on the water this afternoon."

More silence. "As I said, Constable, duly noted. Meanwhile, you work from the air and coordinate your search sectors with the field CO."

Chris checked his frustration. He peered one last time out his side window at the tangle of creek beds below. "There is one thing to note, sir. If Whitehead and Manning are going straight inland, as I assume, and Scott Lasalle continues his route southwest, the two groups are going to intersect."

Nihls muttered. "How soon?"

"Depends on their speed and terrain. It's pretty rough out there, and unless they know the terrain —"

"We assume they don't."

Chris didn't argue. He had given up assuming anything. He didn't know what anyone was planning, nor what they were capable of. It seemed safe only to assume the worst.

"Tomorrow some time is my guess," he said. "Time is ticking."

Nahanni, July 26

Green hunched over the fire and cradled his coffee cup, trying to draw every bit of warmth from it. Everything was wet. Their tents, the ground, the firewood, the tarp under which all their gear was stored. Moisture dripped from the overhanging spruce boughs. The morning dew had been heavy and now fog suspended them in nothingness.

Jethro had already been out scouting the area and had returned with two fish caught in a nearby stream. Fried up over the fire with bannock, fish had never tasted so good.

"I don't know how you do it," Green said, "but thanks for this."

"The fish gave themselves to me," Jethro replied, deadpan. "They knew we needed them."

Green eyed him across the smouldering flames. "Do you believe that?"

Jethro grinned. "I don't disbelieve it. I walk two worlds. I didn't used to, when I was at res school and university. But there is a lot of wisdom in the traditions of my ancestors. The Dene belong to the land. We take care of the land and it takes cares of us. We have survived for millennia because we listen to the land and respect the spirit of all things. I know about science, but I also know these waters, these trees, and these mountains have a lot to tell us. You have to feel their spirit."

"Right now I feel only myself," Green replied. "My aching feet. My fear. Can the trees speak to me? Tell my where my daughter is? Tell me she is safe?"

"Well, we can ask them. Whether they'll talk to you is another story. They probably know you don't much like them."

Green glanced across at Jethro's solemn face. Irrepressibly, he laughed. His sodden spirits lifted. They had made slow progress the day before, inching their way across marshes and over rocky bluffs. But instead of heading straight southwest, the trail was erratic, as if Scott were lost and overwhelmed. Or crazy. By the time the light grew too dim, there was still no sign of them.

But this was a new day. A fresh day. And suddenly Green felt anxious to get on with it. Anywhere, it didn't matter. He tossed the dregs of his coffee on the ground and stood up.

"You won't stumble upon her walking around out there without a plan," Jethro said. "This isn't the city. This is a thousand times bigger than any city. You need to watch for the signs the land gives us."

While Jethro brewed a second pot of strong, hot coffee to fill their thermoses, Green began walking around the area, practising his newly acquired tracking skills. But he could see nothing but rock and spruce and emptiness. A moment later Jethro appeared, striding confidently with Tatso at his heels.

"Tatso found the trail," Jethro said calmly. "It is not the smartest trail, not the fastest, easiest route to take."

They followed the dog as she led the way back and forth across a narrow creek bed toward a distant slope shrouded in mist. Clumps of pink and blue wildflowers dotted the path.

"Monkshood," said Jethro with a chuckle. "Very poisonous if you don't know what you're doing."

"Crime scene investigation would sure be different out here," Green replied. They were almost up the creek and he was breathless from the climb. Tatso was ranging ahead, her tail waving and her nose to the ground. She searched in a tight, zigzag pattern, and each time they crossed the stream, Jethro sent her out again. After the third such crossing, Tatso began to roam back and forth, following trails that seemed to disappear and loop over each other. Her tongue was lolling and her tail whipping with frustration.

Green's experience with dogs was limited to Modo, his hundred-pound rescued mutt that admittedly was not a typical example of the species. But he thought Tatso looked excited and confused.

"She is," Jethro agreed as they stopped for a coffee break to watch the dog track. "Something strange is going on. She follows any human scent, but she's acting like there are several, going in different directions."

"You mean Hannah and Scott are going in different directions?" Green pictured his daughter in a panic, running to escape the madman her lover had become.

Jethro shrugged. "Maybe they're just collecting firewood."

After the coffee break, Jethro set off again to try to pick up the trail amid the maze of conflicting clues. Tatso had disappeared through the trees toward the slope, and as Green stood on the creek bank he was struck by the solitude. The silence was absolute, save for the trickle of water over the stones. No planes, no cars, no hum of human life. Even the songbirds were quiet, and only a single red squirrel chattered at him from a high branch.

The fog had lifted but the grey clouds hung close and heavy over the land. Green shut his eyes. Tried to feel the spirit that Jethro described. He just felt trapped. Closed in by the land, unable to see the sky or the distant glacial peaks that soared above.

Tatso barked, once, twice, followed by silence. Jethro emerged from the trees and beckoned to him. "She's found something," he said once Green reached him. He gestured to the dog, wagging her tail some distance away, alert and intent. They both followed her to a soft marshy dip in the land. Here she stopped, her nose to the ground. To Green's astonishment, she began to dig.

"Something is buried there," said Jethro, heading over to join her. Her digging was determined, focused, even a little frantic. Loose clumps of grass flew back from her paws. Jethro extracted a small, folding shovel from his backpack and began to dislodge large rocks from the soil. Green joined him, tearing at the rocks with his bare hands.

Five minutes later, Jethro gave a little cry. He fell to his knees and began to paw the dirt. Green stared. His mind refused to analyze. Even when the first fingers were uncovered, he refused to acknowledge the possibility.

One careful shovelful at a time, they unearthed the body. Jethro had tied Tatso to a tree to prevent her from interfering. Belatedly the police officer in Green's screaming brain snapped into gear and he fetched his camera. Only by an extreme effort at detachment was he able to photograph the remains as they emerged. Fingers, hand, arm, shoulder. Jethro brushed the debris away carefully. The fingers were almost perfectly formed. Brown, curled, unmarred by decay or insects.

A recent burial, Green realized. He'd been concentrating on the camera, but now he stared at the hand. Lean fingers, short blunt nails, broad palm. Not Hannah's, his mind looped over and over. Not Hannah's hand at all.

Together they uncovered the hip and left leg. The body was lying on its side with the head thrown back and out of sight. Slowly they began to dig around it, freeing up the neck, the ear, the jaw, the strings of short, dark hair. No piercings, no blue tips, no pointed pixie jaw. Green fought a lump in his throat as he dared to hope.

When the head was entirely excavated, both Jethro and Green squatted beside it staring. The hair was short and dark, the eyes wide and filled with sandy grit. Despite the opaque, milky film, they looked blue.

Like Green's, Hannah's eyes were hazel.

He studied the full length of the body. Even dressed in jacket, jeans and hiking boots, it looked tall and lean. He tried to conjure up the photos he'd seen on the Internet, of Pete Carlyle, Daniel Rothman, and Scott Lasalle. One was lying dead at the bottom of a cliff, another cowering in fear in the cabin they had left. The third was here.

"It's Scott Lasalle," he breathed when he dared put his thoughts into words. "Scott Lasalle is dead. That means my daughter ..." His brief surge of euphoria died. "My God, she's wandering around out here all by herself!"

Jethro was very still. His steady brown eyes rested on Green. "He didn't bury himself."

Green's thoughts floundered. "Maybe ... Maybe she buried the body so the wolves wouldn't get at it." He leaned forward for a closer look at the body and gently brushed some dirt from the man's chest. Revealed the jacket, ragged and stained, with a hole ripped through the centre of it and a familiar red stain blooming out over the fabric.

Green fell back on his heels, fighting for breath. Suicide? Please let it be suicide. He forced himself to poke through the hole to feel the path of the bullet. Straight in, angled slightly down. It could have hit half a dozen vital spots — arteries, stomach, heart, spleen — causing massive internal bleeding that would have killed the man in minutes. There were no powder burns on the jacket. No suicide would have created such a wound.

He forced words through his dry, numb lips. "We need to excavate the rest of him. Search for the weapon. We need to photograph —"

"We need to notify the RCMP," Jethro countered quietly.

Up on a rock, out of earshot and in satellite range, Green called Sullivan. He relayed the news along with their estimated coordinates, and asked him to inform the RCMP. "I don't know where Hannah is. For all I know, she's underneath ..." His voice cracked. He dragged air into his lungs. "She doesn't know how to fire a gun. She hates guns. She couldn't have done this."

"Mike —"

"We have to ask that bastard Pete —"

"Mike!"

"What?"

"We're here at the cabin. Pete's not here."

* * *

Sullivan phoned back an hour later. By that time Green and Jethro had methodically excavated a deep circular trench and laid bare the young man's entire body. Besides the bullet hole in his chest, he had scratches on his hands and face that were still fresh and bleeding at the time of his death. Green photographed each carefully. The pathologist would be the one to determine whether they were inflicted by tree branches or human nails.

Careful digging had turned up no sign of another body underneath. The ground under Scott was rocky and difficult to penetrate, as if it had been undisturbed for a long time. There was no knapsack, no rifle or gear of any kind. Green had sent Jethro off with Tatso to scout the area. He had told him to look for human tracks, but they both knew the main reason. If there was another body or burial site, Tatso would find it.

"Any news?" Sullivan's voice was very faint.

"Nothing so far." Green stood up, unable to say more. As he walked up to higher ground, he fought for composure. "No sign of her."

"I'd say that's good news, Mike. We've got a search team coming in to help you. Just have to get the helicopter in place. The fog is holding things up a bit. And the RCMP is going to drop in a crime scene team from Yellowknife too."

"I've dug him up."

"They won't be pleased."

"I don't give a fuck. I had to see if she was there with him."

"I get it, Mike. Ian Elliott and I are on our way —"

"No, wait. I need you to search the vicinity of the cabin."

"We've done that. He's not here."

"For her. For … a burial site."

Silence. "She's alive, Mike."

"I know. But …"

"Okay, but we'll get to you as soon as we can."

Green had just hung up when he spotted Jethro coming across the slope toward him. His face was tense with excitement.

Green's hopes leaped. "You found her?"

"No, but I found something you should see."

He led the way farther up the hill with long, loping strides. The meadow thinned to loose, stony soil dotted with boulders left eons ago by glaciers. The whole area looked undisturbed, but hidden in the shadow of one boulder was a large canvas bag. It was open, and a dozen wooden stakes were strewn on the ground. They were numbered, and Green saw that one had a shiny metal plaque on its side. On the plaque was a number, a name, and a partial date: NORTHERN RUBICOM, a blank space, and 2012.

He straightened. "This is very recent. Not an old stake!"

Jethro nodded. "My guess is Scott was getting ready to stake the claim when he was killed."

"And what the fuck is Northern Rubicom? His company?"

"Probably. There should be at least three other stakes in the bag, one for each corner of the claim. Unless he got them in the ground before he was killed."

A quick search of the bag revealed only one other corner stake. Jethro was scrutinizing the bag. He lifted it to peer underneath. Even Green could see the gouges in the ground around it.

"I think this bag was dropped from a height." Jethro searched the surroundings. There were no hills or cliffs. "Maybe even from a plane."

They exchanged looks. Read each other's minds. "Hunter Kerry," Green said. "That's what he was doing when he flew over here. The bastard. He's in on it." He shoved himself to his feet. "You keep looking for Hannah. I'll call this in."

Green watched Jethro set off with Tatso before phoning Sullivan back to relay the latest discoveries. "Get the RCMP to find out about this company and to question Hunter Kerry about his involvement. Find out what the bastard knows. And keep an eye open for other stakes between the cabin and here."

"None around the cabin, Mike. We've just finished another search and there's no sign the ground has been disturbed. Or ..."

It was a small relief, but Green seized it like a drowning man. "How long till backup gets there?"

"Probably not till the morning. The fog's still a problem farther east."

"Fuck!"

"But we're on our way. Hang in there."

Green's respite from panic was brief as he contemplated the impossible task ahead. One lone little girl, probably blind with fear and grief, was stumbling around in this vast, unforgiving land. He walked back down the slope toward Scott's body. It needed to be guarded against animals and covered with a tarp to protect it from the elements. Whatever Hannah's fate, this murdered young man might hold the answers to what had transpired between the foursome on this tragic trip.

He was anchoring the tarp with boulders when he heard a shout from farther upstream. It was Jethro calling. Green abandoned the tarp and rushed over the uneven shore, slipping and stumbling over the wet rocks. Some distance up, he found Jethro waiting for him on the shore. He gestured to a narrow animal trail barely visible through the willows, leading away from the stream.

"I think I've found something," he said as he followed the trail. "Watch your step, it's muddy. Moose, bear, wolf, they all use this path to get to the water, but up here …" He stopped and stepped off the trail. Squatting, he pointed to the trampled ground. "This is a human boot print. Not as recent as the wolf tracks, but still visible. In the last couple of days, I'd say."

Green leaned over. The print was small and made a shallow indent in the ground. He held his breath.

"If we go further," Jethro was saying, stepping over the print to carry on up the trail, "we see more of them. Here and here …"

The next print was overlaid with a paw print, too large to be Tatso. A wolf. With an effort, Green pulled his attention back to Jethro, who was squatted over another print. He laid his tracking stick on the ground and moved it back and forth across the rutted soil.

"She's running now," he said. "The strides are far apart, the impact heavier. And she's digging in with her toe."

"She?"

Jethro smiled. "Yes, she. She's getting away."

Green had to put his hand down to steady himself. Emotion closed his throat. He pictured her scrambling up the trail, terrified, lost, stones tripping her and branches tearing her limbs. Breath ragged, not daring even to scream.

CHAPTER TWENTY-TWO

"We can't wait for them," Green said. "We have to go after her."

The fact that a man was lying dead with a bullet in his chest and his daughter was running away didn't bear thinking about. There would be an explanation — an accident, a struggle, self-defence. Pete had said Scott had gone crazy. Perhaps he had turned on her and she'd reacted the only way she could. Hannah hated guns, but she was a fighter. Enraged or cornered, she could be a firestorm.

He couldn't think about that now. He had to take it one step at a time, follow her tracks, find her, make her safe. And only then would he worry about the explanation.

Jethro stood on the path behind him and folded his arms over his chest, expressionless. "We wait. They'll make good time with the GPS, and it's much safer to travel together."

"But every hour we wait, we lose precious daylight."

Jethro smiled. "There are eighteen hours of daylight. For now, we wait. And we eat."

Green knew he was right, but that was no comfort. His stomach was in knots. Leaving Jethro to unpack the food, he climbed to the top of a nearby rise and looked out. The fog still hovered over the mountain peaks but slivers of sunlight shot through. Touched the valley floor. A small lake glistened in the distance, nestled between rolling hills.

On a distant slope he caught movement and a flash of white, but when he trained his binoculars it was two Dall's sheep bounding across the alpine grass. He swept the binoculars slowly across the landscape. Nothing.

He cupped his hands. "Hannah!"

Her name echoed over the endless folds of land, inconsequential, like a pebble dropped into the ocean.

"Haan-nahhh!"

He listened to the ripples of sound until they faded away. No answer came back to him.

He circled the rise, calling in all directions, before acknowledging it was futile. When one is running, one hears only the pounding of footfalls on the ground, the crunch of gravel, and the ragged gasps of one's own breath. He walked back down the hill. Jethro handed him a hot cup of tea and the two ate in silence. By the end of lunch, there was still no sign of the other two men. Green paced. He cursed. And finally he climbed the rise again and called the Fort Simpson RCMP.

Sergeant Nihls sounded brusque and harried, but he took the time to outline his plans to fly in additional SAR and crime-scene personnel first thing in the morning. These latest developments have brought the original death of Daniel Rothman into question as well, he said.

"Any intel yet on this company Northern Rubicom?"

"Not been much time to work on that, Inspector. But I did ask Yellowknife HQ to look into it. So far they have just the obvious information. It's a new company, registered in March of this year. Two partners, each in for a hundred thousand."

"What are their names?"

"Not our subjects. Two professors. Dr. Valencia of Vancouver and Dr. Anil Elatar of Waterloo, Ontario. One's a geologist, the other a mining engineer. A sensible combination for the start-up phase, I might add."

Green sucked in his breath. Valencia was the thesis advisor both Scott and Pete had fallen out with. "Any business activity in this company yet? Any mining claims or other assets?"

"Yellowknife HQ is looking into that. So far there are no claims registered at the Recorder's Office."

"What about Hunter Kerry? What does he know?"

"Mr. Kerry is being uncooperative. So far. But we'll work on that. For my money, he's just an errand boy. No one would trust him with any serious responsibility."

Green revised his earlier opinion of the man. In a pinch, Nihls was proving a capable leader. Green thanked him and rang off, now more puzzled than ever. He tried to link the information together to see where it led. Both Scott and Pete were reportedly against mining development, and yet Scott had devised this whole adventure trip as a pretext for tracking down his grandfather's old ruby claim. Scott claimed to feel so strongly about mining that he had thrown his geology career out the window and walked out on the geology advisor who only a month later founded a mining company with the suggestive name of Northern Rubicom. Now someone working on behalf of that company — Scott, Pete, or someone else? — had planned to stake a claim to that very ruby mine Scott had been seeking.

Nihls thought Hunter Kerry was peripheral, yet he had been the one to fly the party in the first place, and the will and the initial clues about the mining claim had "accidentally" been left in his plane. Quite the coincidence.

It felt like a Chinese puzzle, with the solution just one twist away. But the more he worked one twist free, another twist emerged. He knew his mind was only firing on one cylinder, and the more frustrated he became the more scrambled his thoughts. He was grateful when Tatso's loud barking announced the arrival of Sullivan and Elliott.

After a quick exchange of updates, Sullivan drew Green aside. His broad, freckled face looked pinched. "How you holding up?"

Green shrugged. He didn't dare open the door to his feelings. "I just want to find her."

Sullivan nodded. "Where's the body?"

Green led him back down the stream to the tarp. Sullivan squatted down, peeled back the tarp, and studied the body quietly. He poked the toes, the hands, and the head. Then he gazed at the horizon, his eyes narrowed. "Rigour's dissipating but still present in the legs. Buried like this, with the cold nights, hard to say. What do you think?"

"Thirty-six to forty-eight hours?"

Sullivan nodded. "So she's been out there, on her own for almost two days." He prodded the stony ground thoughtfully. "How big is Hannah?"

Green stared at him. Sullivan knew perfectly well how big she was. Barely five feet. "What does that mean?"

"I know people can summon incredible strength when they're desperate, but burying him like this would have taken hours. More like deliberate intent than desperate impulse. The question is, why bother digging such a deep hole in this hard soil?"

Green shrugged. He'd not lingered on that puzzle, merely assumed she wanted to cover up the killing. But now, as he walked through the scenario in her shoes, he could see the flaw in that logic. Why would Hannah, panicked and overwhelmed, have taken the time and effort to bury him?

Another possible scenario came to mind. Perhaps the killing had been a desperate act of self-defence or accident, but in her grief and guilt afterward she had resolved to give him a loving burial. That way his body wouldn't be ravaged or carried off in bits by wolves and crows. Hannah had the steel determination to carry out such an act, but did she have the strength?

"I don't know, Brian. Let's hope we get a chance to ask her." He drew the tarp back over the body and began to pile the heavy stones on top. "We can't do any more for him. Let's get the hell away from here."

They found the other two on the rocky slope farther upstream. Elliott was squatting on the ground beside the mining stakes. His topographical map was spread out on the ground and he was shaking his head.

"Interesting. Presumably the other two corner stakes are already in the ground somewhere."

"Is it still legal with only two?" Sullivan asked.

Elliott shook his head and consulted his map. "I doubt this claim is legal anyway. It's outside the present park, yes, but remember, the government is in negotiations about a new park up here. The boundaries aren't decided yet, but all resource development on the land has been frozen until a decision is made. Mining interests are fighting hard to keep this area outside the boundaries because there is so much mineral potential in these mountains. There is already a mine quite close to here in Lened Creek and another being considered for just the other side of the Little Nahanni River."

Green and Sullivan clustered around the map as Elliott traced his finger down the river. Green was studying the map for clues to where Hannah might go, but Sullivan was listening intently. "When will this boundary be decided?"

"Who knows?" Elliott grinned. "This is the Canadian government we're talking about. No matter which way they go, they know there will be howls of protest. But right now Canada needs all the economic stimulus it can get, and the present government has few qualms about the environment, so I'm guessing the mining interests will win out."

"So this claim could be okay?"

"In the future, but not while the freeze is on. That's why the date is not filled in yet. I'm guessing either they're just hoping to get the jump on it —"

"Or they know something the public doesn't." Sullivan's eyes were grim with suspicion.

Green broke in impatiently. "How close are we to the Little Nahanni River?"

Elliott measured with his fingernail. "Only a couple of kilometres."

"How wide is it?"

"At this point? A good size. And fast moving." He glanced at Green. "She couldn't get across without a raft or boat."

"So she's going to be trapped."

"Assuming she goes that way," Jethro said. "We don't have any idea where she's going, or even whether she has a map. We found no gear with the body, so she may have it all."

"I'm assuming only one thing," Green said grimly. "That she's trying to find a way out. So let's get tracking."

Because both Sullivan and Green had developed some skill in reading the ground by this time, Jethro took the lead with his tracking stick but spread the other three out in a horizontal line behind him to search for signs. Slowly but surely they worked their way across the slope, saying little as they concentrated all their attention on the ground. At one point Jethro squatted and measured, then nodded.

"She's stopped running. Maybe she's not as scared."

Or she's exhausted, Green thought, but he said nothing. A few moments later the land dipped sharply toward a ravine below and Jethro stopped. He carefully moved some loose stones ahead.

"She fell here. Probably slipped." He moved a few yards farther and pointed. "Blood."

A single drop glistened on a rock, so tiny that Green was astonished he'd seen it.

"Not a serious injury," Sullivan said. Too quickly, Green thought. Thanks for trying, my friend, but I know all too well the danger she's in. Would the bleeding attract the wolves? Or bears? When he asked, Elliott pursed his lips.

"Any scent attracts animals," he said. "Even hand soap. But wolves are shy. If there is plentiful game, they won't bother her."

They picked their way down the ravine into the softer grass below. Here, a ribbon of flattened grass was clearly visible. "She's limping," Jethro said.

"How close are we?" Green asked.

"She was here, maybe yesterday?"

His heart sank. Still so far behind. Each time Jethro paused to study the ground, he chafed. They were moving more slowly than she was. Losing ground every moment. How were they ever going to catch up? By late afternoon, as he scanned the surrounding hills for the hundredth time, he spotted a familiar bluff.

"We're going in circles!"

Jethro nodded gravely. "She is disoriented. Sometimes she moves fast, sometimes slowly. This is the pattern of someone without a plan. Panicking. I think she has no map or compass. After a while, these hills and trees all look the same."

"She may have nothing," Green said. "Not even food or water."

"Water is easy. As for food, there are berries."

"She won't eat berries!" Green said. "She's a city girl. Berries come in a plastic box from the supermarket."

Jethro picked up a willow branch that draped over the trail. Its end was cut cleanly through. "She's eating these, and she's got a sharp knife. Trust your daughter, Mike. I've seen this before. People have an instinct to survive. Her actions tell me she's exhausted. She will find a stream and she will make a bed for the night. In the morning, she will make a plan." He smiled. "Even a city girl knows the sun rises in the east."

At 10:00 p.m. that evening, just as the shadows were deepening across the valley floor, they came across a pile of flattened willow and spruce branches at the edge of the creek. "This is where she bedded down for the night," Jethro said. He was optimistic, even smiling as he pointed out that she still had the presence of mind to prepare a primitive shelter rather than collapsing without care. No fire, but possibly she had no matches.

The foursome pitched their tents hastily, cooked dinner, and curled up for the night. "We've almost got her," were Jethro's last words. "Tomorrow, at 5:00 a.m., we go on."

That night, while the others snored, Green drifted in and out of sleep, his ears sifting the night sounds — the gurgle of the stream, the howling of the wolves — for the scream of a terrified girl. There were two wolves close by, possibly watching from the hillside above the campsite. They were just curious, Elliot had assured him. But Green pictured them circling slowly, heads lowered, eyes gleaming. Hunting for prey. Looking for weakness. He shivered and wrapped his sleeping bag more tightly around him. Forced his thoughts away from Hannah, huddling in some makeshift bed of willow boughs, listening too.

When the first shafts of sunlight struck the mountain peaks to the west, he crawled out of bed. He took his binoculars, satellite phone, and bear horn, and climbed up the rocky hillside. When he reached the summit, the distant ridges were ablaze in amber light. He searched. Cupped his hands and called. Nothing.

Why didn't she answer? If she was only a couple of kilometres away, as Jethro believed, why didn't she hear him?

He felt an overwhelming need to reach out. Hunkering down, he phoned Sharon, who would be awake with Tony by now. He imagined them in the kitchen, Sharon propped awake over coffee, Modo hovering underfoot for scraps, and Tony chattering away about his latest fascination. Was it still airplanes, or had he moved on?

Sharon answered on the fourth ring, sounding foggy with fatigue.

"Oh, honey, did I wake you?"

"No." She gave her wry chuckle. "Our children have already accomplished that. Any news?"

"We're very close. We should find her tomorrow." He skimmed over Scott's death, Hannah's frightened flight, and the wide open wilderness in which she was lost. "I just wanted to touch base. See how you are."

"I'm fine, Mike. I will be fine, no matter what."

"What do you mean, no matter what?"

"Nothing."

"Sharon, is something wrong?"

"No, honey. Aviva just seems to be in a bit of a hurry, that's all."

"You mean ...?" What the hell *did* she mean?

"Nothing. She seems impatient, that's all. Of course, what else? She's your daughter. She's not going to make things easy."

"But are you all right? Is *she* all right?"

"We're fine. I'm resting. I'm keeping my feet up. And whatever will be, I'll manage."

"She's not due for two months!"

"And we'll try to hold her to that, but you may be in for a bit of a surprise when you come home."

He gripped the phone. "I don't want to miss the birth."

Sharon laughed. "She may not give you any say."

He stared out over eternity, unseeing. Oh my God, please, God, no more. How much was Sharon holding back, to spare him the added worry? She was laughing now, the fatigue gone from her voice as she talked about the daily trivia of family. She spoke no more of premature birth, stubborn babies, or surprises. Before she hung up, she promised to phone him if there were any developments, but he didn't believe her. Like Hannah, Sharon would tell him only what she thought he needed to hear.

He rested his head in his hands, breathed deeply, and offered a mute prayer for the lives of all the women he loved. To whom, he didn't know. Perhaps just to Jethro's spirits that controlled this vast, open, sunlit land. If there was any way to reach those spirits, or his own austere, unattainable God, it was here.

When he raised his head again the first fingers of dawn were touching the hillside, glistening off the dew and burnishing the grey rocks with gold. It felt almost like an omen, a ray of hope in the bleak days he had endured. Further up the slope a huge boulder clung precariously to the edge of the slope, a perfect vantage point from which to watch the sun spread across the valley. As he climbed closer, he could see unusual scoring on its face, set into relief by the slanting light. Closer still, he froze.

It was a message, scratched into the surface of the rock by a ragged, uneven hand.

> *To Dad, Mum, Sharon, EB, and sister-to-be, I hope someone finds this and lets you know. Luv you, sorry Dad …*

The final words blurred in the searing pain that filled his eyes. He sank to the ground, his head in his hands. For a moment all thought, all strength, deserted him. Is this your omen, God? Is this your answer? Then he raised his head and ran his trembling fingertips over the stone. Touched where she had touched.

"We're going to find you, my little girl. No fucking way this land is claiming you."

Back down at the campsite, Elliott was brewing coffee. His eyes rested on Green's thoughtfully for a moment, but he said nothing. Waving off the coffee, Green began to pack up his things. As he packed, he told them about her etching.

"We're going. We'll eat on the trail. She's near the end of her rope."

Wisely, no one protested. He led them to the rock, where Tatso eagerly picked up the trail down the slope. As they hurried to keep up with her, Elliott fell into step beside Green.

"Who's EB?"

"Energizer bunny. My son."

"Your wife's pregnant?"

Green nodded. “It’s a girl. Aviva. Hannah’s been so excited.” It was one of the means by which he had hoped to lure her home. Hannah had grown up alone most of her life. She’d only had her brother in her life for three years, since she’d reconnected with Green, and she was thrilled at the prospect of a sister. She’d threatened to teach her everything she knew about being a girl. Green had shuddered in mock horror at the thought.

Now he’d give anything for that.

As they walked they took turns calling, to no avail. But the silence slowly filled with a sibilant murmur, which grew louder when they crested yet another hill. Below them, in the distance through the trees, shone the sparkle of water. High over the water a bald eagle surfed the wind in search of fish.

With fresh excitement they rushed forward until the wide flood plain of the river became visible through the trees. A broad, flat stretch of willows and marsh, followed by acres of river stone beach before the river itself. Broad, meandering, and deceptively peaceful in the misty sun.

“That’s the Little Nahanni,” said Elliott. Smiling, he took out his binoculars. “I’ve never approached it from here. Beautiful.”

“But she can’t get across it?” Green asked.

When Elliott shook his head, Green’s hopes surged. “Then we’ll find her.”

Elliott didn’t answer. He stiffened suddenly and adjusted his binoculars. “I see movement.”

Green and Sullivan both pulled out their binoculars. “Where?”

"On the shore. Wait." Elliott continued to stare. "See that big boulder on the other side of the river? Look across to this side and to the right a bit, maybe twenty feet. Through that gap in the trees."

Green could see nothing but a blur of green and blue. The water shimmered, the branches swayed in the gentle river breeze. Nothing. Nothing!

"Is it a person?" he asked in frustration.

"Yes. Wearing a red jacket." Elliott pointed. "Look, they're running."

Sullivan's binoculars were riveted to the spot. "Looks like they're trying to get across."

"Suicide," Elliott muttered. "It may look placid but the current's too strong."

"Hannah!" Green shouted, plunging headlong down the hill. They were still hundreds of yard away, but he had to try. "Hannah! Stop!"

He could hear the others pounding through the bush behind him, but he had only one thought. To save her. They reached the treeline and were swallowed in the dense willow brush. Holding his arms out to break a path, he stumbled on. Dodged around trunks, tripped over roots, ignored the long, thin branches whipping his face. He couldn't see the river any more, but above the snapping of branches and the rasp of their breathing, he could hear its hiss.

Finally a glimpse of water through the brush, much closer now. Shrubs and marsh. Mud sucked at his boots. He floundered and fell. Scrambling to his feet, he unsnapped his backpack and threw it to the ground. Saw the figure at last. A small red shape splashing along the edge of the gravel bar. Still too far! Miles of muddy marsh stretched between him and the river.

He clambered out of the mud onto a small knoll. Panting, his heart bursting his chest. “Hannah! It’s Dad!” He waved his arms above his head.

The figure turned back. Saw him, then wheeled and began to run.

“No!” he screamed. What the hell? Was it Hannah? Or someone else? Who?

As he shouted, the others came up behind him. They watched the figure disappear around the bend.

“She ran away,” Green cried. “Damnit! Why?”

“If it is her,” Sullivan added.

Jethro looked worried. “She’s not rational. She’s operating in full flight mode.”

“And if she tries to cross the river …” said Elliott.

“Don’t even think it!” Green snapped. “How do we get across this swamp? How do we reach her?”

As they searched the riverbank downstream, new movement flashed through the trees. Weaving in and out. Grey blending with rock. Another figure, running in the same direction as the first.

CHAPTER TWENTY-THREE

"No time!" Green shouted as Sullivan swung his pack from his back and fished his phone out. Stubbornly Sullivan shook his head, muttering something about backup. Green turned away. The figures had vanished from sight, but he plunged diagonally through the alder bushes in the direction they had headed.

He slipped, tripped, flailed, and cursed as his hiking boots squelched in the mud and his lungs burst for air. For each hard-fought yard of advancement, the shoreline seemed to recede by two. The copse of trees where the figures had disappeared seemed as far away as ever, the river bobbing and hissing as it swept toward the bend.

On the horizon far upriver, three tiny dots appeared. Bucking down the ribbon of water with the buzz of a hornet, leaving a widening ripple of white in their wakes. Green halted in surprise. Behind him, he heard Sullivan swearing at the phone as he tried in vain to raise a signal. On the river, the three objects drew closer and the buzzing louder, until Green realized what they were.

Zodiacs! Ploughing through the current under the power of a small outboard motor. One figure steered in the stern while the other leaned out over the bow with binoculars.

"Hey!" He rushed forward, sucked down by willows and reeds and mud. "Hey!"

The lead boat slowed. The driver paused, hand on the throttle, glanced in Green's direction, and waved. The boats were drawing directly opposite now, but still too far away to make out any features.

"Wait!" Green flailed his arms and quickened his pace. The lead driver signalled ahead down the river and turned the throttle back up. Cursing, Green glanced back at the others. Sullivan had given up on the phone and both he and Elliott had their binoculars trained on the river. Green could barely make out a logo on the side of the boats.

"They're from the mine up the river," Elliott shouted over the noise. "That's their company logo on the boats."

Sullivan was shaking his head. "I think they're cops."

Green couldn't see how anything could be gleaned from the figures, who were concealed from head to toe in helmets and bulky orange life jackets. The first two boats had disappeared around the bend and the last was fast approaching it. Soon nothing was left but the ribbons of wake on the grey water and the hum of distant engines in the air.

Green fumed as he waited for the others to catch up. "They saw us! They fucking saw us and blew us off! We could have been in trouble or —"

"They were in a hurry," Sullivan said. "Whatever they're up to, it's a higher priority than us."

Green took a deep breath to rein in his temper. He was tired and frightened, but he needed to think like a cop. He turned to Sullivan. "What makes you think they're police?"

"Instinct?" Sullivan said. "They were searching for something, but very methodical. Moving fast but efficiently like a trained team. One guy steering, the other scouting." As if he read the doubt on Green's face, he shrugged. "Pretty professional for a bunch of miners."

"Mining companies often hire ex-military and ex-cops to run security," Elliott said.

Green felt himself go cold. The lure of a mine had drawn them all into this wilderness, cost two young men their lives, and now put his frightened daughter at risk. "We've got to get moving!" was all he said as he surged toward the river. Once they had reached the gravel flat he broke into a run. Sounds filled his ears — the crunch of boots on stone, the ragged hiss of his own breath — but nothing else. No shouts, no screams for help.

No gunshots.

He faltered midway to the bend, his lungs on fire. Jethro passed him with ease, his head down, his soft boots floating over the stony ground. He too had shed his heavy pack, but in his hand was his rife. At his heel, tongue lolling and tail straight out, ran Tatso.

"Wait!" Green gasped. "Don't try anything —"

Elliott placed his hand on Green's shoulder. "Let him go ahead. He'll scout it out but he won't tip anyone off."

Grateful, Green lowered his head, channelled his breathing, and concentrated on a long even stride. The ground rushed beneath him. Reeds on one side, river on the other, driftwood, boulders, wildflowers, all unfurled beneath his stride.

Before he knew it, the bend was upon them. Ahead, the river ran through a wide valley of beach and trees before narrowing between high canyon walls at the end. The cliff above the canyon walls was the perfect spot to lie in ambush.

They all skidded to a halt, panting. There was no sign of Jethro, nor of the two figures they had been chasing earlier. Nothing but the empty beach and the dense, dark forest. However, at the far end, just before the canyon bluff, three inflatable Zodiacs were pulled up on shore. Nearby, one of the boaters stood under cover of the cliff face. He was looking up, searching the clifftop.

Green was about to call to him when he turned slightly, revealing the distinctive silhouette of an assault rifle cradled in his arms.

Seizing Sullivan's arm, Green dove into the cover of the woods. Huddled behind the shelter of a large pine, he tried to estimate distances. The forest was only about a hundred metres wide before the land rose in a sharp slope and the trees thinned. The valley looked about half a kilometre long before pinching into the canyon.

Not a large area to search, but with only three of them, a challenge. He dredged up his long-rusty knowledge of search tactics and beckoned to the other two to come close.

"We'll do a line search straight down the valley floor," he whispered. "As far apart as we can manage while still keeping each other in sight. Probably thirty feet in these woods. Hand signals only, except in an emergency." He paused. He'd always hated his firearm and passed his requalification test every year by the skin of his teeth, but now he fervently wished for its cold, alien weight in his hands. For its power to overcome, even to kill.

He picked up a hefty length of driftwood and told Sullivan to get his rifle out. Elliott and Green would walk the perimeter while Sullivan provided cover to both from the middle. They edged carefully through the underbrush toward their positions. At each snapping twig and rustling leaf, Green winced. They stood in position a long time while he searched the silence for sound. Footsteps, whispers, breaths. He heard nothing but the hiss of the river. How could eight people be moving through this forest without a single telltale crack?

There was still no sign of Jethro when Green gave the signal to advance. They inched forward across the spongy forest floor, gently easing branches aside and placing each foot with care. Ears and eyes sifted the stillness. Green felt a surreal calm, as he imagined soldiers felt when they went up over the trench wall into the guns of the enemy vastly superior in numbers, weaponry, and tactical knowledge. He had one goal: Hannah. Find her, shield her, and bring her to safety.

They had advanced less than a hundred yards down the valley when Sullivan signalled and pointed ahead to something bright green lying on the forest floor. A few steps farther on, peering through the overhanging boughs and tree trunks, Green recognized an overturned canoe. Tucked under it, a backpack.

Green signalled to Sullivan to ready his rifle and advance. Elliott slipped through the trees to his side. "Probably stashed there by some hikers," he whispered. "It could have been here for years."

"It looks new," Green said, taking in the shiny hull. Sullivan was just approaching when Jethro materialized at his elbow. Green had not heard a sound, and he nearly swore aloud in shock.

Jethro drew them deeper into the bush. "There was a tent and a campfire here yesterday. "Whoever it is, looks like they went inland. Up that slope toward the pass."

"How many?"

Jethro shrugged. "A canoe that size? Could take three, or two with lots of gear."

What the hell did this mean? Green wondered. Were they just a pair of random hikers who'd chosen this time and place for their adventure? Or were they connected to Scott's group? Rivals? Co-conspirators?

And more important, were they friend or foe?

"Did you see anyone else?"

Jethro nodded. "Looks like the guys from the boat are searching too. They're doing a sweep this way, like you guys, only they've got 308s and assault rifles."

"Did they look like cops?"

"They looked professional to me, but I wasn't getting close enough to those assault rifles to find out."

Too many dangers, too many unknowns, Green thought. "Stay out of sight," he whispered. "All we want is Hannah. Don't do anything to jeopardize that."

They had barely resumed their positions when a rifle shot cracked the silence. All four of them dove to the ground just as an answering volley of shots burst from the woods up ahead. Green signalled to Jethro and Elliott to stay down. Then he rose to a crouch and scurried over to grab Jethro's rifle. He'd never fired a rifle, but what the hell.

"You and Ian crawl back the way we came, out of harm's way. I don't know what the hell this is, but Brian and I are cops —"

Another rifle shot. Green spun around to search for the source of the sound. It had come from up on the open slope. As he watched, a figure raced from one boulder to another in a blur of grey. From down below came an explosion of return fire.

"Stop!" The cry came from another cluster of rocks, a few yards beyond the sniper. It was a howl of panic. Piercing, female …

A chill of horror raced through Green. He didn't dare call out, didn't dare put her in more danger. Waving Elliott and Jethro away with a frantic hand, he scrambled on hands and knees to join Sullivan.

The sniper on the slope fired again. This time the bullet slammed into the tree near Green's head, spitting wood chips into the air. The gunman had spotted him. A responding rifle burst from down below spewed rock and gravel at the boulder. The sniper fired back.

"RCMP!" came a shout from the woods. "Hold your fire, Whitehead!"

A head popped up behind the rocks above the sniper. "That's not me —"

"Hands where I can see them, Whitehead!"

The man ducked for cover instead. "Holy fuck!" Green whispered. "What the *fuck*?"

"Chris?" A blond figure jumped up beside Whitehead. Screaming Chris's name, she started to scramble down the slope. Rifle shots burst in both directions. The woman cartwheeled, arms flailing, blond hair swirling, and pitched face down in the gravel. Her body slithered to a stop.

Shouting erupted from the woods below. Automatic rifle bursts tore up the hillside as one of the Mounties raced toward the woman. Green started forward, but Sullivan grabbed him in a powerful vice.

"It's not her, Mike! The hair's blond."

"I don't know what colour her hair is, Brian!"

Sullivan tightened his grip. In the delay, the Mountie reached the woman and dragged her to safety. The sniper fired once as he raced from his spot up to the rocks where Whitehead was hiding. A moment later he rose from behind the rock, his body shielded and his rifle pressed to Whitehead's back. Green recognized the blond hair and the grey camouflage jacket.

"That's Pete Carlyle!" he exclaimed. The pieces of the puzzle realigned. Fucking Pete Carlyle had been the traitor all along. Green shoved Sullivan's hand away and scrambled to his feet. "The Mounties don't know who they're dealing with here. He's killed two people, he's got nothing to lose!"

Seeing Sullivan about to protest, Green spun away and began to run forward through the trees. Seconds later he heard Sullivan running behind him. "We've got no fucking radio and no fucking ID, Mike. We're going to get shot!"

Green spotted the cluster of Mounties hunkered down in the trees. They were dressed in black. Two had taken positions behind trees and had trained their weapons on the hillside. Another was crouched on the ground, shouting vainly into a phone. The last two were bent over the fallen woman, doing CPR. One of them had pulled off his helmet, and his young face was contorted with anguish.

"Chris!" Green shouted. "Constable Tymko!"

Two guns swivelled to face him. He held up his hands, one of them still holding Jethro's rifle. Hastily he introduced himself. The other cops looked to Chris for confirmation, but he was frantic.

"Call for the fucking helicopter!" Chris yelled at the man with the phone. "We have to get her to Yellowknife!"

"No signal, sir!"

The officer doing CPR sat back on his heels. "Chris, she's gone."

"You don't know that! We can save her. We have to save her!"

Green approached to look at the woman on the ground. Long limbed, tanned, and blonde. Not Hannah. "Who is it?" He hoped his voice was calm, unlike the cartwheels of relief in his head.

"A girl who —" Chris's voice snagged. "Who should never have got involved with that snake!"

Green glanced up through the trees to the slope, where Pete Carlyle stood, defiant with the rifle to his hostage's head. In that instant, old training kicked in. "Who's in charge here, Constable?"

Chris looked up from the injured woman finally. Took in the gunman, the hostage, and his waiting colleagues. He blinked. "Me."

"What's your plan?"

"I don't … I don't …" Chris took a deep breath. He signalled to his colleague to resume CPR and he hauled himself to his feet.

Green joined him and lowered his voice. "I suggest you radio the guy waiting by the boat. Send him and another officer around the side and up the slope behind Carlyle —"

"Carlyle? It's not Lasalle?"

Quickly Green explained about Scott and Pete. "Pete had his own agenda to stake the ruby mine. When he met with resistance from the others, he killed them. I don't know what these two had to do with it —"

"Victor Whitehead, total sleaze. He was meeting up with that bastard from the other side. I don't give a fuck if he shoots Whitehead!"

"Yes you do," Green murmured, drawing close. "So send your two men up around the back of him. Let him know there's no escape."

Chris nodded. He was deadly pale, but he retrieved his radio and relayed the order. Pete and his hostage were still on the hillside, but Pete was beginning to edge diagonally down the slope, careful to keep Whitehead as a shield.

"I want one of your Zodiacs," he shouted, "and a full tank of gas. And if I see anyone following me, today or any day, this slimy bastard will get a bullet in the head."

"Hey!" Whitehead cried. "We're supposed to be —"

"Plans have changed, partner."

"The Zodiacs can't handle the canyon, Pete," Chris replied. "You've only got one way to go — back up toward Cantung Mine."

"None of your business where I'm going!" Pete yelled. Green saw a flash of movement on the bluff behind him. Chris's men were about halfway into position.

"You won't get past the mine," Chris shouted. "It's crawling with Mounties."

Pete and Whitehead reached the edge of the slope against the bluff. Behind them, the two Mounties stepped out into the open with their rifles trained. They spoke too softly for Green to hear their words, but Pete reacted by tightening his grip on Victor and screaming.

"Get them the fuck away from me!"

Chris had knelt back down at the injured woman's side, but now he tore himself away and stormed to the bottom of the slope.

"It's over, Carlyle! You're done! There's no escape." He sucked in a deep, steadying breath and resumed, calmer. "We found the Yukon you stashed up on the old road and we immobilized it."

"Then you'll get us another one. I haven't made it all this way for nothing!"

To Green's astonishment, Elliott emerged from the woods, unarmed and hatless, and stepped in front of Chris. "I'm sorry to disappoint you, Mr. Carlyle, but that's precisely what you've done. The mining claim, even if it's full of rubies, is worthless. The government has finally chosen its boundaries for the new park, and the claim lies within it."

Pete's jaw dropped. "You're lying!" He jerked Whitehead's shoulder. "You told me it would —"

Whitehead looked about to faint. "He's bluffing," he stammered. "There's no decision yet, Pete."

"I haven't got where I am without having some friends on the inside," Elliott said. Chris shot him a surprised look, and very subtly Elliott waved his hand to silence him.

“Then you’re worthless, Whitehead!” Pete raged, jabbing his rifle into Whitehead’s back.

“No!” Whitehead slammed against him, throwing him off balance. Pete stumbled and tripped over a rock. The rifle fired. Whitehead flung himself to the ground. Simultaneously the two officers leaped forward, one to shield Whitehead and the other to pin Pete to the ground.

Seconds later, Pete was in handcuffs.

Pete’s bellows of rage were still echoing down the valley when Green detached himself from the crowd. He wasn’t needed here any longer, but Hannah was still at risk. Elliott, ever calm and focused despite the extraordinary gamble he’d just taken, had taken over CPR and Sullivan was helping with Victor Whitehead. Green could hear Chris up on the bluff, screaming over the phone to his superior, demanding a medical helicopter and backup immediately. Green didn’t think it would save the woman’s life, and from the frantic edge to Chris’s voice he suspected the young constable knew it.

Olivia Manning had been shot through the chest and back, and all around her the gravel was slick with her blood. Green knew that a thorough analysis of the bullet wounds, trajectories, and crime scene would be needed to determine who shot her. He hoped, for the Mounties’ sake, that it was Pete, but in the fog of war anything was possible. The Mounties had probably been trying to provide cover fire for her, but one of their bullets might have gone wrong.

He searched the woods as quickly and methodically as he could, but without making a sound. His senses were alert to unexpected danger. Jethro had said the canoe could hold three people, which meant that an unidentified potential enemy was still out there.

That was the first question Chris had demanded when Victor Whitehead stumbled down the hillside. As a precaution, the officer had cuffed him, but Green suspected he had no fight left in him. He was pale to the point of collapse and tears poured down his cheeks.

"I had nothing to do with this," he'd sputtered in response. "None of this was supposed to happen. I'm just an advisor."

"You weren't here to take Pete out the back door, once he'd killed the others?"

"No. No! Are you crazy? Olivia and I were just supposed to look for a feasible land route to the mine, linking to the old mine road on the other side of the river!"

"Bullshit, Whitehead!" Chris snapped. "This was obviously the rendezvous point."

"No! We were all supposed to meet at the claim site to collect samples. Pete knew we were coming in from the Little Nahanni. He must have decided to escape this way."

"In all this wilderness, he just happened to find you?"

"This is the only route in!" Spots of colour had returned to Whitehead's cheeks. "For fuck's sake, the bastard had a gun to my head! You think we were friends?"

Chris's reply was lost in the roar of the river as Green walked away. He'd heard it all so often before. One weasel turning on another when the plan went sour.

He stopped by the campsite in the middle of the forest, wondering where to look. Had Hannah escaped over the canyon bluff? Was she hiding in the dense brush, still too terrified to realize she was safe? Green wasn't even sure it was Hannah they had seen fleeing along the beach. It could have been Olivia or Whitehead running from Pete. But if she wasn't here, where was she?

Sullivan joined him. "Anything?"

Green shook his head. "I don't even know where to start. Where she might have gone."

"Dad?"

Green whirled. Stared at the trees, at the low lying bush.

The overturned canoe.

"Hannah?"

The canoe shifted. "Dad?" Quavering. Up an octave.

Green dropped on all fours beside the canoe and peered underneath. There, deep in the sheltered gloom of the hull, two huge, incredulous eyes stared back at him.

CHAPTER TWENTY-FOUR

Little Nahanni cabin, April 26, 1945

My darling, darling love of my life,
I pray you are well. No letters have come from you, and I fear someone is keeping them from me. Strange things are happening. I think someone was in the cabin while I was out on the line. They didn't take anything, but they were looking for something. Why didn't they wait for me? Why were they sneaking around? I think they were after the rubies. The samples or some kind of proof. Maybe Gaetan put them up to it. I don't know where he is. I don't even know if he found new work. The Indians at the Butte say he was not working up on the pipeline, and Nicolette and his daughter haven't heard from him either. Maybe all that talk about the good-paying job was a lie.

I think he's up to something. I think he and the geologists are lying to me. I have tracked the creeks and I think I know where the stones are coming from. I want to take some samples on the mountain just above the cabin. I will make very little money from the pelts this year. Without Gaetan paying his share, there will be no money for core sampling this summer. If I don't do it myself, no one will.

It is warm now and soon the snow will be melting on the mountain. It will soon be time to come out. But before I leave, I will take some samples myself up on the mountain. And I will get them tested in Vancouver. I do not trust Edmonton. I know there are rubies!

Your humble, devoted husband, Guy

p.s. I have hidden the map, but if anything happens to me, check the will. But don't tell anyone, especially not Gaetan.

Mesmerized, Green watched her sleep. He listened for every small catch in her breathing, watched for every small quiver in her face. She looked incredibly tiny, a pale wraith against the crisp whiteness of the hospital sheets. Her hair, not orange or blue but fine brown like his, spilled onto the pillow in sweaty disarray from the nightmares and the tossing.

Two days. At first, during the evacuation, she'd done nothing but cling to him and shake, barely letting the paramedics near her to do their job. Then later at the hospital in Yellowknife, during the tedious round of doctors, CT scans, and blood tests, she couldn't stop talking. Two weeks of terror, trauma, rage, and grief came tumbling out. Rage at Scott for telling her nothing of his plans, for tricking her into coming on a mission that had nothing to do with a river adventure. "Fucker lied to me," she kept ranting over and over, as if each time it was a new discovery.

Rage at Scott for ignoring her health too; for putting his obsession, however noble, above their very survival. "Daniel knew I had a concussion," she said. "He told Scott a hundred times, but the bastard didn't give a damn about me. Or Daniel."

Whenever her thoughts lighted on Daniel, they ricocheted off again into hurt and confusion. "What the hell happened to him?" she wailed. When she went to bed he was asleep in the tent he shared with Pete, and the next morning he was gone. Vanished without a trace, without a word of goodbye.

"He's dead?" she cried in horror when Green finally told her. "Oh my God, we left him there? Pete told us he'd just left. Said this wasn't the trip he'd signed on for, Scott was a domineering prick, and he'd had enough. He was going back down to the Nahanni to hitch a ride with another group."

When she learned the truth she wept for a long time for the gentle young doctor who'd tried to care for her. Her reaction to Pete's trickery was more muted. She had already endured his worst. She'd watched him turn his rifle on Scott and her, chillingly deaf to their pleas for mercy and Scott's last-ditch effort to bargain for her life. She'd watched him aim and fire from ten feet away, seen her lover's chest explode in red, seen the rifle turn on her. And after that, her scrambling, tearing, stumbling, breath-searing flight for her life.

The terror of that would never leave her. Even now, when she'd finally fallen into an exhausted sleep, the panic welled up within her. She was running and running from wolves, but when she rounded a bend, there was Pete. Face hard and eyes dead, as they had been when he pulled the trigger on Scott.

From that memory, finally, came her grief. Overwhelming, regretful grief for the young man whose longing for the truth and determination to protect his grandfather's land had cost him his life. Grief that he'd been betrayed by one of his rare friends, duped into leading the enemy straight to the prize.

Green never asked her to explain or to connect the scattershot of her memories. He was not the cop here, he didn't have to build a case. He simply held her, and waited.

By the third day, when she was recuperating in the Yellowknife hospital, the RCMP were clamouring to talk to her. She held the key to two deaths. Pete was in custody, spinning a ludicrous story about self-defence in which it was Scott and not he who had started it all. The RCMP investigative team from Yellowknife headquarters were late on the scene. They had interviewed everyone else involved, including Sullivan and Green, but the one witness who might know the whole story was out of their reach. Green, backed up by her doctors, refused to allow them access to her until she was stronger.

He got unexpected help on that front from the young RCMP constable from Fort Simpson. Chris Tymko had flown the prisoner to Yellowknife and had requested to stay on, hovering around the fringes to assist in the investigation. On Hannah's third morning in hospital he had come to check up on her. He looked pale and sad, and readily accepted Green's invitation for coffee down in the cafeteria.

"How's Olivia?" Green ventured once they were both seated at one end of a long table.

Chris stirred his coffee, his gaze fixed on the swirls of milk. Green could sense him drawing up his courage. Finally he shook his head. "Her parents are flying in this afternoon. They're going to talk about pulling the plug."

"I'm sorry."

Chris shrugged. "Once they do the autopsy, we'll know who actually shot her. It doesn't really matter. Pete Carlyle meant to kill her, and we meant to save her, but in the moment ..."

"These things happen," Green said. Knowing his words were hopelessly inadequate.

"She ... I know she wasn't innocent in this. She shouldn't have stepped into the middle of a firefight. She shouldn't have been there in the first place, working with that weasel Whitehead to help the mining company. She was in bed with crooks and liars and murderers, and she —"

"Was she?" Green interrupted softly.

"According to Hunter Kerry, absolutely. Hunt's usually not a big talker, but a whole day down at Yellowknife headquarters had him covering his ass big time. He says he would never have gotten into this if it wasn't for Olivia. She approached him last month, said she knew he was flying Scott and the others up the Nahanni, and asked him to find out where they were going. Eavesdrop, steal, she left it up to him, but there would be big money in it for him. So it was Hunt who hid the day pack under the seat. He started to have second thoughts about her when the group disappeared, so he brought the pack to me. If she hadn't done that … Maybe she wouldn't have died."

"But did she know what Pete was up to? That he was going to double-cross Scott?"

Chris deflated. His flush of emotion faded. "Probably not. At least not the whole story. Victor Whitehead is singing like a canary too. After his brush with death, he says he's a reformed man. Deception and betrayal have no part in honest resource development, he says. None of them knew Pete was capable of murder. He was just working for the company. They didn't know exactly where this mine was, you see, because the original map from the claims office was missing. So Pete arranged to go along with Scott, who was the only one with any clue. Victor and the rest of the company had no idea to what lengths he would go."

Green grunted. "Of course not. Snakes never recognize each other."

"Well, his story is consistent with the two company directors'. RCMP officers interviewed the two professors down in Vancouver and Waterloo, and they both hung Pete out to dry. They claimed to be a legitimate company exploring a potential mineral development in the north. Pete had been sent up to locate and stake a promising deposit, based on information from an expired mining claim, and they both thought Scott was onside as well. Whitehead had contacted them this spring, wanting in on the mining company, and they figured he might be useful because of his connections and influence in the north. So they signed him on, mostly for lobbying work, but they also contracted him to scout out possible land and bridge access routes. Olivia … she was the student of one of the professors, very interested in getting a piece of the action, her professor said. He had absolutely no knowledge of her offering Hunt Kerry a bribe —"

"Absolutely not," Green said drily.

"They said they hired her because of her mining expertise, but I'm guessing that her knowledge of the Nahanni backcountry and her skill as a wilderness guide were even more useful. I don't think they'd have been interested in her at all except for that. She was just a kid from a small town with big stars in her eyes. Her father said she believed in responsible mining and got into this thinking she could keep the company accountable. She got in over her head. Way over her head." Chris pursed his lips together. He swallowed. "Kind of … like me."

Green felt sorry for him. Chris's own losses — of innocence and of love — were etched on his pallid face. But that very pain was heartening. How many years would it take before he was as detached and hardbitten as the detectives assigned to this case? Or as he and Sullivan, for that matter.

"Chris," he said, "don't shortchange yourself. Without you, who knows… And now I have one last favour to ask. We have to get it past the investigating team, but I think I can persuade them."

* * *

An hour later, Chris was seated at Hannah's bedside. No notebook, no backup, no intimidating formality. Just a young, soft-spoken RCMP constable in shirt-sleeves, preparing to guide her through her story. Green sat by the window, listening and trying not to interfere. The RCMP detectives hadn't objected nearly as loudly as he'd expected. Perhaps they were intimidated by his rank and experience. Perhaps his bull-headed insistence that it was this way or no way had won them over.

Or perhaps they had more common sense that he'd thought.

Hannah was sitting up in bed, looking wan and fragile amid a mountain of pillows. But as she sized the young officer up, Green detected a hint of that familiar challenge in her eyes. His heart swelled. Hannah was coming back.

Maybe Chris too had noticed the challenge, for he seemed to be having trouble figuring out how to begin. He looked around at the dozens of flower bouquets that graced every surface, half of them from Green. He produced a bright smile that trembled at the edges.

"Any roses left in Yellowknife, do you think?"

Hannah didn't even blink. Flustered, he cleared his throat and changed tactics. "That was a terrible ordeal for you. Are you okay? To talk about it, I mean."

She shrugged. Didn't help him at all.

"We've interviewed a lot of the others involved, including your father here, and we've pieced a lot of things together. But you were there, at the heart of it all from the beginning."

Still she said nothing. She lowered her eyes and picked at the IV bandage on her hand. Took a shaky breath. Green felt her slipping under again. He bit his lip to keep from intervening. Chris must not be coached.

Finally the young man seemed to find his stride. "Why don't you start at the beginning? When you four were planning this trip."

"That's not the beginning."

"Okay, your beginning then. Please."

She sighed. "It started in January. After his father died, Scott began clearing out his papers from the basement, and he started to go weird. Not right away, but he had a fight with his professor and quit the program. Over his grandfather's letters. No, I mean the mine." She stopped and pressed her fingers to her temple. "Well, I didn't know that then. Sorry, can't go too fast. It hurts to think."

Chris held out her juice glass and she took a sip. Smiled at him, that lovely pixie smile.

"What did he tell you?" he asked.

"At first nothing. At least not to Daniel and me. We thought it was just an adventure trip. But Pete was in on it. Pete and Scott were friends — well, so he thought. Scott showed him the letters and the rock samples."

"What rock samples?"

"The ones he found in his dad's basement. I didn't know anything about it. Like I said, he confided in Pete, not me. I'm not a geologist but I'm not dumb! When he found that map in the Mason jar, I started to wonder. He said he wanted to follow it. Just a fun adventure. When we found the cabin, he admitted it was his grandfather's. He said his father had talked about it just before his death, about how his own father had died up there, trying to make a life for his family but betrayed by the person he trusted most."

She paused. Her chin trembled. "I never met Scott's father, but Scott seemed to think that explained a lot about him. He'd missed his own father his whole life, so the only thing that mattered to him was Scott, like he was going to be the father he never had. Scott thought it was very sad. At the end, his father said his big regret was that he never went up north to find out what really happened to him. 'Maybe someday you'll get the chance,' he said."

Chris was frowning. "So for him the trip was about finding out what happened. Not finding the mine."

"Yes. No. It was all jumbled together. Scott didn't want the mine. He wanted to stop their professor from developing it." Hannah's breath quickened. She started to quiver. "One day Scott and I were exploring near the cabin and we came across this open bag on the ground. It was full of wooden poles. Mining stakes." She opened her eyes wide. "Scott freaked out! Stormed back to the cabin and had a screaming match with Pete. He called Pete a traitor. Next thing I know Pete pulls this gun out of his pack. He said it didn't have to be this way, we could work together. 'Never,' Scott says. We ran inside the cabin but he fucking shot through the door!"

She broke off, shaking. Caught back in the memories. The whites of her eyes wild. Green was about to rush to her when Chris leaned forward. "Take your time, Hannah."

She waited. Breathed. This time Green let her fight. The clock ticked by. Finally she folded her hands, wet her lips, and resumed. "I didn't see what Pete did to Daniel, but I did see him shoot Scott and I'll stand up in court to describe every step of it. Scott only told me half this stuff afterward, while we were running for our lives. Back in the winter, Pete persuaded Scott to take the sample to their professor. He said if it was rubies it would be amazing, because rubies are very rare and this would contradict everything they knew. Turned out it wasn't rubies, but there was some really important rare metal that the whole world wants now. Behind Scott's back, the professor formed a company so he could stake it and explore it. When Scott found out he went ballistic. He's seriously against ripping up the north just to feed our hunger for oil and gadgets and pretty jewels. He thought Pete agreed with him. They'd both quit the program to try to figure out how to stop the professor from staking the claim."

"How?"

"A bunch of dumb ideas. First Scott was hoping he still owned the claim, but that was wrong. Then he figured he'd guard it somehow, maybe get the conservationists involved, try to get it included in the park."

"But Pete was really working for the professor?"

She nodded, and promptly clutched her head in pain. "Scott was so freaked out. Thought it was all his fault because he led Pete straight to it. I never liked Pete. Even the first time I met him. He didn't have any real friends. If he thought you could be useful to him, he was all over you. But everybody else, he just ignored. Scott didn't see that about him. Scott was all about his research and science. He didn't read people well. He thought Pete was interested in the same things as him. That was all that mattered."

Very perceptive of my little girl, Green thought. Pete was a user. He pretended to be Scott's friend as long as he needed him to find the mine. And he was on Victor Whitehead's side too, until Victor became more useful as a human shield.

A true snake in the grass.

Even now, in jail in Yellowknife awaiting charges, Pete was blaming everyone but himself for the carnage in the Nahanni. Daniel had come at him with an axe, they'd struggled, and he got too close to the edge. Scott had wanted that claim just as much as he did and had grown greedy. He would have killed both Pete and Hannah if Pete hadn't stopped him.

Hannah was tiring now. She leaned her head back amid the pillows and shut her eyes. Her features twisted with pain. "What a curse, that mining claim. Scott's father was convinced his father was betrayed by his brother over the mine. And now, seventy years later, Scott's betrayed by his friend."

She fell silent, her eyes still shut. Green eased himself out of his chair. "I think that's it for now."

Chris glanced up at him. Green could see his excitement on his face, his frustration at the interruption. "Oh, but I just need to know —"

"I think she's had enough for today."

"Dad, I can speak for myself." She opened one eye and fixed it on Chris. "What?"

"What did Scott tell you about his meeting with Victor Whitehead in Whitehorse in February?"

She shook her head, moving cautiously this time. "Not much. More betrayal, I think. I know he went up there hoping to track down his cousin. After his father died, Scott didn't have any family, and he was really excited when he learned about this guy." She paused. A frown flickered across her brow. "When he came back, he wouldn't talk about it, but that's when he got really determined to make a trip back to his roots."

"Do you know how he found out Whitehead was his cousin?"

"From the letters. They mention ..." Hannah drifted off. Her eyes were closed again, and this time Green sensed she'd really fallen asleep.

"You can get the Vancouver cops to check those letters," he said to Chris before remembering that he wasn't in charge of the investigation. "They're all stored in a box in my ex-wife's basement."

Dimly through the closed door of Hannah's room, Green heard a growing commotion in the hall. A woman's voice raised in shrill demand. Just as he recognized it, the door banged open and Ashley stood on the threshold with two large suitcases in tow.

"There you are!" she hissed at him. "You could have checked your messages. I had to get a cab from the air —" Her eyes lit on Hannah and her outrage evaporated. With a shriek she rushed over to the bed, where Hannah was now wide awake again. Ashley swept her up in a suffocating hug. For a moment she did nothing but weep, but then the questions began. Was she all right? What did the doctors say? Do they know what they're doing up here?

When Hannah didn't reply, she swung her sights on Green. Same questions, but with an accusatory tone.

Hannah looked at him imploringly. He laid a soothing hand on Ashley's arm and drew her out into the hall, easing the door shut.

"Ashley, she's going to be fine, but what she needs right now is rest." Ignoring the daggers in Ashley's eyes, he forced himself to speak gently. "Have a short visit with her now. Constable Tymko and I will wait for you down in the cafeteria and I'll update you on everything."

"Fine. But take these things with you. I'm not lugging them another inch." She yanked the smaller suitcase toward her and unzipped it. A faint odour of mildew wafted up. Inside was a shoebox and piles of papers separated into batches and tied with red ribbons. They were curled and yellow at the edges.

"These are all papers from Scott's grandparents that were in our basement," she said. "You asked me to check if there was anything useful to the investigation." She waved a dismissive hand. "Be my guest."

Five minutes later, waiting in the cafeteria for Chris Tymko to finish his report, Green picked up a packet of pale blue letters from the suitcase. He flipped through them, noting the faded, almost illegible handwriting. The personal letters that Scott had found, to be read another time. Another packet appeared to be official papers related to the mine and to geological results. The shoebox was tied shut with twine that had grown old and brittle with time. OLD BILLS was scrawled on the top. Green wrestled the twine off and opened the box. Inside was a pile of letters addressed to or rerouted to Mr. Guy Lasalle c/o Nahanni Butte. Most of them appeared to be bills and invoices from companies and the federal government, dating from the spring and summer of 1945 and unopened, Green assumed, because by then Guy Lasalle had disappeared. And his grieving wife had not had the heart.

At the bottom, however, was a sealed letter from the Government of Canada Radiotelegraph Service in Dawson City. Green slid his finger under the flap.

OTTAWA, ONT 1945 FEB 20 AM 10 42
MR. GUILLAUME LESSARD,
14 FOURTH AVENUE,
WHITEHORSE, Y.T.

DEEPLY REGRET TO INFORM YOU THAT YOUR BROTHER INFANTRY PRIVATE GAETAN LESSARD L NINE SIX ZERO THREE FIVE WAS KILLED IN ACTIVE SERVICE OVERSEAS FEBRUARY 18 STOP PLEASE ACCEPT MY PROFOUND SYMPATHY STOP LETTER FOLLOWS

CANADIAN ARMY CASUALTY OFFICER

Hannah ran her hand across the satin duvet, smiling as her fingers sank into its feather down. Amid the rich reds and creams of the hotel decor, she already looked less ghostly and frail than she had in the hospital.

Upon arrival in Yellowknife three days earlier, Green had booked himself and Sullivan into the most modern, luxurious hotel in the city. When Hannah's doctors had categorically refused to let her travel for forty-eight hours after discharge, Green had transferred to their biggest two-room executive suite, which had a king-sized bed and pullout sofa. The marble bathroom alone was twice the size of his tent. Seeing Hannah's delight, he was glad he'd persuaded her doctors that she would recuperate faster there than in a hospital room.

The most ordinary things seemed to enchant her: the crystal water glass, the tiny wrapped toiletries, the chocolates on the pillow. She flounced down on the bed, turned on the massive wall TV, and lost herself in a kid's cartoon.

Green picked up the room-service menu. Hannah had eaten almost nothing since her rescue and was in danger of blowing away. "Let's order up. Your wish is my command. Chocolate pâté? Crème brulée?"

She flicked her gaze at him before returning to the cartoon. "I'm not hungry yet."

He laid the menu on the bed beside her. "Okay. I'm going to give Sharon a call in the living room. When the mood strikes, have a peek at that."

"How long do we have before Mom descends?"

He grinned. "Probably only fifteen minutes. She's just down the hall freshening up."

She pulled a face and returned to the TV. Green slipped out. To his surprise, his mother-in-law answered the phone. Sharon's parents lived in Mississauga, west of Toronto, and even Sharon was glad of the five hundred kilometres between them. They loved her and Tony to pieces and over the years had grudgingly come to tolerate their cop son-in-law. He wasn't the doctor they'd hoped for and he didn't bend to their will in the least, but he did good work. And most of the time, he was good to their daughter.

"What's wrong?" he asked immediately.

"What should be wrong?" Pearl countered.

"Is Sharon all right?"

"As all right as any forty-one year-old woman in her seventh month of pregnancy with an active young son to chase around, a dog to walk, blood pressure up and down like a yoyo, and no husband within two thousand miles."

Against his better judgment, Green laughed. After a bristly moment of silence, she laughed too. "How's Hannah?"

"Better every day. We're at the hotel till this weekend. Once I see her and her mother off, I'll be on the next plane."

Silence.

"Promise."

The silence stretched on. Finally "You want to speak to Sharon?"

Sharon's voice sounded strong and cheerful, as if she had been laughing. Relief flooded through him. "Okay, now the truth, honey," he said. "How bad is it?"

"I'm fine. Really. Tony's been a trooper, takes his big brother responsibility very seriously. But I couldn't fend her off any longer. At least this way the house will be vacuumed and the sheets clean when you get home. Which is tomorrow, I hope?"

He filled her on the doctors' orders, Hannah's progress, and Ashley's arrival. He chuckled. "Ashley thought she was coming to the North Pole, so it was a shock to discover eiderdown duvets, wireless high speed, and a stunning waterfront view that stretches for an eternity. She's already booked a spa morning."

Sharon laughed. "Glad to hear the old Ashley is back in full form." She paused. "Is Hannah flying back to Vancouver with her?"

"I assume so. Ashley certainly assumes so. Hannah's enrolled at UBC for the fall."

"I wish I could see her," Sharon said. "If it weren't for her baby sister here, I'd be out there in a flash, making sure she's okay. As it is ..."

Hannah appeared in the doorway. She looked sombre, a girl with a heavy weight on her mind. Green cut short his phone call, sent kisses over the phone line, and hung up. Hannah came to sit on the sofa beside him. She held the room service menu in her lap. Fingered it.

"Dad, I don't want to go back to Vancouver."

She didn't meet his gaze. He waited.

"Would it be okay ...?" Her voice quavered. She shook her head as if angry at herself. "Can I stay with you?"

He wanted to crush her in his arms. Cover her in kisses. Instead he took her hand gravely. "I would love that. We would all love that."

Her fingers twined in his. Her eyes filled. "I just can't face ... Vancouver, Scott, the memories."

He folded her against him. "After what you've been through, honey ..."

"I want to be with you, and *Zaydie*, and the Energizer bunny, and Sharon. I want to see my little sister being born. After all this, I just want to go home."

"Me too."

"Can you explain it to Mom?"

"Ah."

Snuggled against him with her head buried in his chest, she giggled. “Sorry to dump the worst on you.”

“Yeah. But after facing wolves, grizzlies, and class IV rapids, how hard can your mother be?”

“You don’t want me to answer that.” She paused, tilted her head up. “I punched a wolf on the nose with my bare fist, you know. When it stuck its nose through the branches I’d rigged up for a tent.”

He tightened his grip. “My girl,” he managed.

She allowed him to cradle her a moment longer, then she picked up the room service menu. “We’ve been through a lot, haven’t we?”

“We have.”

“Done things we never imagined we’d do.”

He nodded.

“And survived.”

He nodded again. “And survived.”

“I’d like the 8-ounce tenderloin, rare, with Yukon Gold buttermilk potatoes.”

“But you’re vegetarian.”

She met his gaze. Arched her brow.

He reached for the phone. “Two tenderloins it is.”

“And Dad, what would you say if I decided to become a cop?”

EPILOGUE

Nahanni, August 24

Chris Tymko wiped the GPS and peered at its foggy screen one more time. He could see Jethro waiting impatiently for him down by the stream ahead. They were both tired, hungry, and wet. It had been a difficult trek from their fly-in at the little lake nearby. A violent summer thunderstorm had raced through the mountains the previous evening, drenching their campsite, washing out creek beds, and turning the ground slick with water. Despite their rain gear they were both soaked from the fine mist that hung over the mountains and dripped from the branches overhead.

"I know exactly where I'm going," Jethro snapped.

"Maybe, but give a Prairie boy a break. All these mountains and trees make me claustrophobic. I feel like I can't see a thing. But according to this, the cabin should be just over the next bluff."

"Uh-huh. Then you might want to use your eyes instead."

Chris squinted through the trees, where the vague contours of a cabin could now be seen. He flushed and put his GPS away. Together they approached the cabin nestled on a narrow strip of shore between the creek and the steep mountainside.

Chris had seen numerous old bush camps during his time in the north, most like this one, built in the heyday of trapping and prospecting and now overtaken by wolverines, porcupines, or the forest itself. This one was in surprisingly good shape, maybe because Guy and Gaetan had built it to last and serve as the original base camp for their mining explorations.

Perhaps someday it would again, Chris thought grimly. Two days earlier he had stood with Sergeant Nihls and the entire Parks Canada staff in Bugden's office, listening to the prime minister announce the final boundaries of the new park. The mining interests had won. The river itself would be protected but huge swaths of the surrounding mountains, including here, would be open for business.

"Do you think Victor Whitehead knew?" Chris had asked.

Nihls had started to equivocate, but Bugden cut him dead. "Absolutely. Why do you think they hired him?"

So we've come full circle, Chris thought. Back to the days when greed and paranoia ruled the day.

Jethro was walking around the perimeter, studying the ground and the cabin walls carefully. "Looks the same as when Mike and I were here," he said. "Here are the bullet holes."

Chris approached the door for a closer look. It wasn't that he disbelieved or distrusted the forensic expertise of Inspector Green, but he was hoping for some small detail the man might have overlooked in his haste. This expedition to the cabin was on his own initiative, and his reputation hinged on finding some answers. Sergeant Nihls was not interested in solving the seventy-year-old mystery of Guy Lasalle's disappearance. He argued that since the original RCMP investigation had failed to turn up an answer, he doubted there was one.

For Chris, it wasn't only a matter of justice, although dispelling the cloud of suspicion that had hung over Gaetan Lasalle for decades had been a form of justice. It was a matter of putting to rest the spirit of Guy Lasalle himself. It was clear now that Gaetan had not murdered him, but was himself dead at least two months before Guy disappeared. But Guy had obviously believed someone was out to get him. It was difficult to tell from the letters whether this was merely a delusion of a bush-crazed mind, but the fact was, he *had* disappeared under odd circumstances.

If his brother hadn't killed him, who had? Another trapper? The Indians of the Mackenzie Mountains, who had resented his intrusion into their land? Although most of the witnesses and possible suspects were likely all dead by now, the question still deserved an answer.

He took out his magnifying glass to study the bullet holes. As Green had reported, they were about chest high and clearly fired into the cabin. He examined the exterior wood of the cabin. It was faded and mottled from years of mould and moisture, but the interior surfaces of the holes were clean. He felt a twinge of disappointment. Green was right; the shots had been fired recently, rather than seventy years ago, and they backed up Hannah's version of Pete's assault on them.

He stood in the doorway surveying the small meadow. According to the RCMP report, Guy Lasalle had left his cabin as if for a normal morning outing. His tin coffee pot was still on the stove, his bedding lay rumpled on the bunk, and his food supplies and furs were still up in the cache in the nearby woods. His mukluks, parka, and fur hat, however, were missing. Had he wandered off in a snow storm? Been attacked by hungry bears just waking from hibernation? If so, no one in the intervening seventy years had ever found a trace of him.

At that moment, Jethro appeared around the edge of the cabin from the rear. "I don't know what I was hoping," Chris said. "That we would read something in the scene that none of the other investigators did."

Jethro gave him a strange look. "Maybe we can. I've found something you should see."

He led Chris to the back of the cabin and pointed to the earth that was pressed up against the bottom logs. Moss and rot had largely eaten the logs away.

"No bush man worth his salt would bury the logs like that. There was a landslide down this mountain after the cabin was built."

Chris looked up the hillside. Now he could see the difference in the trees that ran down the middle. They were younger and smaller, the boulders less overgrown.

"There's more." Jethro started up the hillside, passing from the woods to the steep, rocky slope. He stood on the gravel midway up and pointed toward a sheer cliff face above. "I'm not a geologist but I'd say the mountain face sheared off and came crashing down this slope."

"What caused it?"

"Happens all the time up here. Earthquakes, erosion, moisture seeps into the mountainside and cracks the rock. Could be a winter avalanche that brought the hillside down with it, could be spring run-off softened the slope. Or it could be — didn't Guy's last letter say he was going farther up the slope to take some samples? If he was digging through the snow and trying to melt the frozen ground …"

"You mean he could have brought the whole thing down on himself?"

Jethro was gazing up at the sheared cliff. "The mountain took its revenge."

A lesson for the politicos, Chris thought. He poked the unyielding, stone-covered ground. "In that case, no wonder no one ever found his body. Never will."

A faint smile played across Jethro's lips. "Not unless the mountain itself decides to give him up."

ACKNOWLEDGEMENTS

The Whisper of Legends has taken me, along with Inspector Green, on a geographical and cultural adventure into unfamiliar territory. I am indebted to the many books and articles on the Nahanni, Dene history and culture, policing, mining and gemstones, and wilderness search and survival that served as my guides. I am also extremely grateful to the experts who answered all my questions, in particular Drs. Steve Cumbaa and Scott Ercit of the Canadian Museum of Nature, Neil Hartling of Nahanni River Adventures, Susan McLeod of Parks Canada, and Mark Cartwright of the Ottawa Police. Any inaccuracies, whether accidental or deliberate in the interests of the story, are mine alone.

In addition, I'd like to thank all the people who undertook to read the first draft with understanding and good humour, and whose comments and corrections all enriched the final story: Steve and Penny Cumbaa, Neil Hartling, Mark Cartwright, and, of course, my invaluable critiquing group, Sue Pike, Joan Boswell, Linda Wiken, and Mary Jane Maffini. Finally, a big thank you to Sylvia McConnell and Allister Thompson for their long-standing belief in me, to Kirk Howard and Dundurn for their support of Canadian mysteries, and to my editor Cheryl Hawley and the rest of the team for shepherding this book to its release.

Despite the popular image, a writer does not subsist alone in a garret, but is nurtured and inspired by friends and family. I'd like to thank all my fellow writers for sharing this odd profession with me, and my family, particularly my sister Pamela Currie, for their patience, support, and continued good humour through the long writing process.

FROM THE SAME SERIES

Beautiful Lie the Dead
An Inspector Green Mystery
Barbara Fradkin
978-1-926607085
$16.95

Inspector Green explores a web of betrayal and deceit. In the dead of night, the phone rings in the missing persons unit of the Ottawa Police. A brutal blizzard is howling, and a wealthy social activist has not heard from his fiancée in over twenty-four hours. Friends, family, and police are mobilized to search the snowbound city. He comes to believe that his partner is fleeing for her life, possibly from his own family. When a frozen body is found in the snow, just blocks from the man's home, Green knows that someone is conspiring to keep the truth hidden.

Do or Die

An Inspector Green Mystery

Barbara Fradkin

978-0-929141787

$12.95

Ottawa Homicide Inspector Michael Green is absolutely obsessed with his job, a condition that has almost ruined his marriage several times. When the biggest case of his career comes up, his position, his relationships, and several lives are put into grave danger.

A young graduate student and scion of a rich family is found expertly stabbed in the stacks of a university library, but no one seems to have the slightest idea why. But as Green probes into the circumstances of the young man's life, a tangled web of jealousy and intrigue is revealed. Green finds himself in the middle of a rivalry in the delicate arena of university politics, where gigantic egos regularly collide. Was it the diligent but socially inept researcher, or the macho ladies' man, golden boy of the laboratory? Or was it a crime of passion involving the over-protective family of his beautiful new girlfriend? When the murderer strikes again, Green realizes that he must waste no time in solving the case, no matter what the consequences may be.

99%
FSC
www.fsc.org

MIX
Paper from
responsible sources
FSC® C004071

ANCIENT FOREST ™
FRIENDLY

new girlfriend? When the murderer strikes again, Green realizes that he must waste no time in solving the case, no matter what the consequences may be.